DOWN BROKEN LANE

AMBER HART

Copyright © 2024 Amber Hart

Editors: Jenn Sommersby, Jess Rousseau, My Brother's Editor
Interior Formatting: Sarah Barton, Book Obsessed Formatting
Cover designer: Emily Wittig

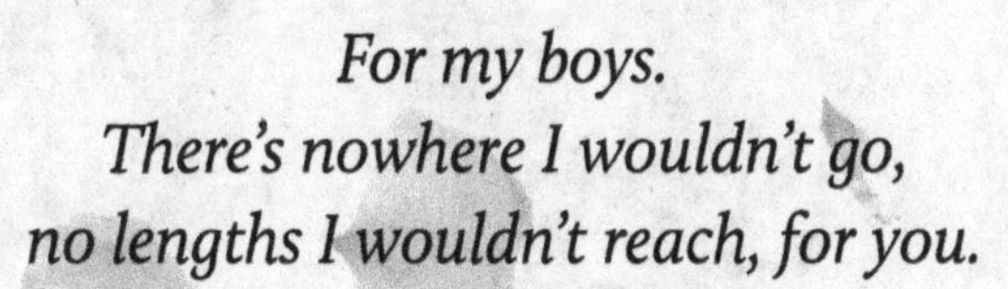

For my boys.
There's nowhere I wouldn't go,
no lengths I wouldn't reach, for you.

ONE

Camille

The wind slaps me awake. *Damn cold and its icicle fingers.* I'm not going to miss work on account of an early dusting of snow. Brushing the white powder from my tires, I climb into the old truck and blast the heat. Autumn has decided to be unforgiving this year—both beautiful with bursts of colors and mean with frosty temperatures. With only one month until winter, the cold creeps ever closer. Hanging from my rearview mirror on a thin leather rope is a gauge, reading twenty-one degrees. It laughs at me with untimely numbers.

Gloved hands on the steering wheel, groggy from sleep, I drive past snow-covered fields, occasionally seeing splotches of green too defiant to be deadened by the weather. Before me, the Smoky Mountains rise up like teeth biting at the sky, and on either side of the road, the cow pastures are empty, a ghostly mist hovering above the ground like winter's breath. Frigid and lonely as it is, it's the perfect place to live detached from it all.

Occasionally, a deer or squirrel or other animal will dart out in front of my truck—I always break for them—but this morning, there is nothing beyond the frosty windshield. Even the air is still. Aside from the rattling of the engine, no sound carries. Truth be told, I like the deadening silence.

I ease my truck into an empty parking space in front of Hill's General Store, the only store for twenty miles. As soon as I wrench open the truck door, pocket my keys, and hurry through the chill, he's there to greet me.

"Hell of a mornin'," Mr. Hill says, nodding to the wintry clouds, his breath shaped like a silver ball hanging in midair. "Reckon we'll get more, or is this the last of it?"

I don't have cable at home, and the truck radio isn't functioning, so I can't properly answer my boss's question. The store has cable, though. I open the door and sigh when heat cocoons me.

"Maybe more." I pull off my scarf, jacket, and thin gloves. Standing in blue jeans and a fitted red shirt, I feel the warmth of the store defrost my skin, giving me a welcome reprieve. I rub my hands together, fending off the needle-like pains as color seeps back in, turning my knuckles pink instead of bone-white.

"Didn't think you'd show." Mr. Hill follows me inside, his stride just a tad slower than my own.

"Of course, I'd show. It's not snowing *that* hard."

Give it a few hours, a day at most, and I would be willing to bet it'd disappear. That's the thing about the mountains, weather changes snap-your-fingers fast. It isn't a reliable thing. Plus, I don't want to mention that I desperately need the money.

I punch keys on the computer, clocking in, and get to work turning on the oven, giving myself a minute to hover my palms over the heat radiating from it so the cold will no longer hold my hand in its unfamiliar embrace. For these few moments, the shop is empty. I glance around, smiling a little to myself at the tranquility of it all, though I've already memorized it by heart.

The store is simply laid out with gas and propane outside, and everything else inside. Through the door to the right on the farthest wall are tools and ammo. The interior is mostly canned goods, drinks, and limited grocerics. To the left is a small room filled with candies and odd gifts—painted wood plaques, embroidered children's dresses, women's purses, men's knives, and mugs with different sayings on them. Separating the two distinctly different sides of the store is an L-shaped counter, holding ice cream and the cash register with an oven behind it—used for baking pizzas, breakfast sandwiches, chicken nuggets, and occasionally Mr. Hill's bagels from home that he prefers to toast and eat at the general store. Nearly ninety and widowed, Mr. Hill favors the store and the company of people, even if he does spend most of the day snoozing in the back office.

A small diner sits to the side of the general store, attached by a hallway and two bathrooms. A round lady named Rose runs it like she does her own kitchen, making whatever she pleases and posting a sign with the day's choices on the door. Southern cooking by a born and bred with mason jars filled to the brim with ice, topped almost always with sweet tea or Pepsi. Regulars like it that way. Practically no one leaves without a piece of cake. Rose is proud of her cuisine staple, as she should be.

Though the morning mist gives a deceptively calm appearance with its obscuring fog, three hours into the day, the snow begins to melt and the store bustles with customers. Mr. Hill is asleep in his plush office chair, door closed, leaving me to deal with the crowd alone. I glance at the clock, 10:00 am, the diner is now open. The store's always the busiest with the kitchen awake.

"Three-thirty-four," I tell the customer in front of me, smiling sweet-like and handing over his change.

Mr. Hill says I have a honey-smile. He claims I bring him more customers, though I doubt there's truth to his words. Timing, more than anything, had to do with me being hired eleven months ago, since the previous day shift employee had just quit. There weren't many other takers in this tiny town. The slim pickings were between locals who already had jobs and locals who were too lazy to work, mostly the latter. He needed someone dependable, which is where I came in.

"Thanks." The customer smiles back through a thick beard

the color of a mud wasp's nest. "See you tomorrow, Camille."

Everyone in the miniscule town of Darlington, North Carolina, knows each other by name, something I eventually got used to.

"Hey, Bonnie," I say to the woman who approaches—the head server at Rose's Diner. "How's your morning so far?"

She smiles, something she does often and with ease. I wonder what that's like.

"Not too bad. Yours?"

I shrug. It's nice to have someone the same age around. Occasionally, we chat about books or town happenings or small, insignificant matters. The way, I suspect, we both prefer it.

"Well, I better get back to work," she chirps.

"See you," I reply.

Bonnie leaves. The next customer approaches, ball cap low on his forehead, wiping the slush off his boots and onto the rug at the door.

"Forty on pump five." Taut muscles work under the long, white sleeves of his shirt as he slaps two twenties on the counter.

I don't recognize him, but no matter. That's normal this time of year, thanks to the tourist town thirty miles to the west. Its lake and famous landmarks fill the mountains with visitors. Usually, the ones looking for a cheap cabin to rent, not wanting to empty their wallet on the town's inn that charges an arm and a leg, come out to this neck of the woods. Once the leaves have fallen and winter rolls over the hills, visitors will empty like a sieve—only the locals remaining.

"Regular or premium?" I peer out of the window at his forest green truck. It matches the woods sheltering our town. The driver and passenger seats are empty.

"Regular," he answers, his voice rumbling like a brewing storm. "How much for a pizza?"

I attempt to smooth down my frizzy, corkscrew blonde hair—which falls to the middle of my back—but it's useless. My curls listen to no one.

I tell him a price.

"I'll take one of those, too." He slaps money on the counter and digs through his pocket for change.

"I've got the penny." I pluck one from the extra pile.

"Thanks," he murmurs, his eyes shaded.

"No problem. Give me fifteen minutes on the pizza."

The man looks around once and nods, leaving me to make his food. Another customer approaches, a constant trickle of business. I try not to watch the man in the ball cap, his nighttime black hair poking through the sides as he pumps his gas. He's hard not to look at.

"You have the prettiest hazel eyes," the new customer compliments.

I smile and ring up his items. "Thank you."

The guy in the cap finishes filling his tank and lingers at the information board just outside the store, which is pinned through with tacks and strips of paper advertising phone numbers of people needing work, like carpenters, painters, and handymen, and a business claiming to be the best, honest lawn company around. There are puppies free to a good home, gold buyers, collectors interested in civil war coins, and finally, a listing of places for sale and rent by owner. Mr. Ball Cap seems particularly interested in those.

"And how did you get so many freckles? Surely you didn't get them in this weather!" The customer laughs, reminding me I haven't given him his change.

"Sure didn't." I give no other explanation. "You have a good day and be careful out there." I nod to the scattering of snow, dropping a dollar ten into his outstretched hand. He leaves.

A regular walks in. A neighbor of mine.

"Hello, Will," I greet him.

Dark skin and a face that's been kind to him make him appear to be in his early, instead of late, forties. He sets several cans of soup on the counter, and I ring him up. He pauses only a moment right before he leaves.

"Have a good one." Will's southern accent is as thick as syrup.

This is our way, an easy air with very few words. He accepts my mostly elusive nature, and I accept his. He exits as quickly as he came.

The next person to walk in is the only person who knows a true thing about me.

"Hi, Luke," I murmur.

On autopilot, I grab a breakfast sandwich and a medium coffee—his usual. He stops in once a week. To the outside world, he appears to be as normal as sweet tea, another country boy, a staple here. He's a man with short blond hair, a slight wave to it, in his mid-thirties, with strong muscles he attributes to plowing fields on all the acres he owns, which is true. To an extent. To Mr. Hill and anyone watching, I know him as well as I know any of the others.

First name basis.

Friendly smile.

We don't talk about how we're connected by the lives we left behind before moving here. Him five years ago, and me one. We both prefer it that way, in a place where neither of us particularly cares for being known as anyone but the newer image we've created.

"Until next time," Luke calls, giving me a slight nod of his head before he's back in his truck and driving away.

I glance at the ball cap guy again, but he's gone.

"Got a phone?"

I startle and turn around, hand to my heart. He's at the side counter.

"Back of the room." I point in the direction, watching him go.

The pay phone is just barely visible from where I stand. It's a miracle we even have one with all the advances in technology. Most places have removed the old relics in favor of smartphones and modern conveniences. But not Darlington. That's part of the charm.

He reaches for it and dials, and a soft clicking noise sounds with each number pressed. Then comes his voice, grumbling something intangible into the receiver hanging up. I watch the way his hands hold it tightly, how his muscles move over the planes of his back. He tries another number. I take a moment to stare at his pillow lips. A strange tingle makes its way up my legs. To distract myself, I prod at his pizza in the oven. There's one bubble in the dough that I pop with the metal wheel cutter, and then smooth the cheese over it so that it looks as good as new. It's practically done, so I pull it out and slice it up, boxing it the way I've done a hundred times.

I try—honestly, I do—not to hear him as he says something that sounds like, "Too much money." If being in Darlington has taught me anything, it's that people like their privacy. I shouldn't be snooping.

I glance at him. He calls another number.

The phone at my hip rings. His head tilts toward me as he looks up at the sound. Or at least I think he does. I still can't see his eyes. I point to his cooked pizza. He holds up a finger as if to say he'll be over in a moment. My phone continues to ring, so I pull off my sanitary gloves and reach into my pocket.

"Hello?"

His voice is in my ear, deliciously deep and warm. "You're the one with the camper for rent?" He doesn't wait for a response. He hangs up and prowls toward me like a lion, his gait sure and strong. "How much?"

I don't know what to say. Not because he took a strip from my flyer—the one with pictures of the camper for rent...I thought he might have when he stopped at it—but because I hadn't decided on an exact price yet. I only just posted it a day ago. Things don't get rented that quickly around here. I thought

I'd have time to think about it. Figured I'd interview people, feel them out first.

"I'm not sure," I hedge. "When would you need it by?"

I concentrate on his jaw, the slant of it, the muscles moving as he speaks. I wonder what his eyes look like under that cap of his. If only he'd lift it an inch more.

"Immediately."

That shouldn't be a problem, considering the camper is ready to rent at a moment's notice, if only I can nail down a price.

"What are you looking to pay?" I ask.

He pauses for a moment, thinking, before offering me a number. It's slightly lower than I had anticipated. "Would that work?" he asks.

I'm tempted to say yes on the spot, money is incredibly tight, but I settle on, "I get off at five. You can come by at five thirty for an interview and to check the place out if you'd like."

It'll be dark by then, the mountains swallowing all remaining bleeding light, but with the porch light on, he'll see the camper well enough if he can navigate the winding, unlit roads to get there. The very same roads that are like black asphalt ribbons tossed into the night, hard to locate. For some reason, maybe it's the lack of accent and the way he carries himself, he reminds me of a city boy who may not know the narrow streets by heart.

I grab a paper from the counter and scribble the address with directions starting from the general store, since I'm not sure where he'll be coming from. I fold the paper over once and stick it in the side of the pizza box. A tucked and creased piece of myself.

He grabs it and the pizza. "See you then."

Only once he's gone do I realize I forgot to ask his name.

TWO

Dawson

The cold is not something I'm used to, nor something I want to get used to. I press my balled fists deep into my jacket pockets. *Jesus, Dawson, get it together. It's only snow,* I scold myself. The unbearable air crawls up my sleeves and over my skin. I peer at the barren woods as I make my way up the front drive of the place for rent. A shiver tiptoes down my spine as a gust lashes out at me, whipping stray hairs that jut out past my baseball cap, stinging my face. The temperature gauge at the door reads fifteen degrees. I curse and knock.

The woman from the general store opens the door with a

smile on her cherry red lips.

"Hi," she says.

Fuck me, she has dimples. Sexy dimples. I quickly glance back at the truck, at how dark and deep the woods travel beyond it. As far as I can tell, there's no one around but the two of us.

"So, the camper." I get right to the point. "Will you be handling the rent?"

There doesn't seem to be property management here. I've never lived in the country, so I don't have a clue how anything works. Not the one-lane bridges that I hadn't crossed before today. Not the accents that are so thick I resorted to asking a guy to repeat himself three times before giving up on using his directions to get to the gas station. Even the gas pumps are odd. In place of an electronic sign, prices are fine printed on the old-fashioned pumps.

She steps outside and shuts her front door. "I'll take care of everything, yes."

"Do you need me to sign a lease?"

She pauses, her eyes assessing me. When her head tilts to the side, I wonder what she sees. Then she shifts, and I get a whiff of her perfume. An urge to lean my face into her neck, right where her flesh meets her collarbone, hits me. *Shit.*

I stand taller and look away.

"I'd like to interview you, if you don't mind."

"Is that absolutely necessary?"

Interviews require questions I'm not altogether ready to answer. But I've practiced, just in case.

She looks skeptical. "Is there some reason I shouldn't? Do you have a criminal background? Tell me now, if so."

She doesn't know the half of it, and I don't need her thinking badly of me. All I need is a place to stay for a while, and I can't imagine a better spot than her property. So, I flash a smile.

"Sorry, I'm being rude. It's just so damn cold here."

Wearily, she says, "I'm Camille. Camille Ray."

"Dawson McGill," I respond.

"You're not from around here, I take it?"

Maybe my ineptitude to handle the weather gave me away. If there's something I hate, it's the damn cold. And liars. Now, here I am, a freezing cold liar.

"No."

"Where'd you move from?"

"Arizona."

A bold-faced lie. I've never even visited.

"Definitely warmer there."

My eyes are drawn to her dimples again. She moves a couple steps down the porch, peering at the camper.

"So," she begins, biting the bullet, "why'd you move here? What's your story?"

That, I will not answer with the truth.

"Recently lost my family—parents and brother—in a house fire and needed a change of scenery. Drove until I found a place that looked nothing like my memories."

It's true, the part about North Carolina. It resembles no memory of mine.

Her expression changes to complete shock, then sympathy. "I'm so sorry."

I'm counting on the fact that people generally don't ask personal questions about unfortunate accidents. Even if the accident never happened.

"Tell me about the camper," I request.

"Right. Well, it's one bedroom, pretty small, but it has all the necessities."

"Sounds good enough."

"So, Dawson from Arizona, how old are you? Have a license?"

"I have an ID," I say. "I'm thirty. Just out of the army. Looking for a place and yours seems as good as any."

Her face lightens when I mention the army. At least that's not a lie.

"I won't charge you an application fee," she says. "No one in this small town does anyway. All I'll need is a background check and the first month's rent up front. I hadn't decided on an exact price, but I think I'll need a little more than what you offered."

"I don't have more than that."

Not when I factor in groceries and other living expenses. The money I brought needs to last a while. I can't spend too much of it on rent and risk running out of cash.

"What if I..." I pause and try to think of something. I remember driving up and seeing the unkempt grass, my headlights hitting scattered walls of shrubbery and overgrown trees with fading brown leaves. "I could trim the dead branches and cut the grass and work around here if you'd like."

I'm grasping at straws, but she seems to consider it.

Then I actually do something genuine, imploring, "Please. I really need a place."

Her features soften. "Okay. But only if you'll do monthly work around the property to compensate for the difference. I could use the help."

I sigh, relieved. "Is it all right if I pay cash? Haven't set up a bank here yet."

And there doesn't seem to be a bank nearby, in any case.

"Spends the same."

"What about a lease?"

Something strange passes over her expression, but then, just as quickly, it's gone.

"How about you pay me monthly and give me a thirty-day notice if you plan to leave?"

"Sounds good." Almost too good to be true.

"Let me show you the place."

She leads the way across the property. She must have acres, and the only neighbor I noticed on the way was easily a quarter mile out. No peering eyes. That's a good thing.

The camper is tied down with straps, making it appear stable and more permanent than mobile. It's a stone's throw from the house, but still private with trees surrounding it. A canopy of branches reaches over the top, and I imagine how it must look in summer when it's full of leaves.

Camille climbs a few steps and opens the door.

The camper is nothing special. The kitchen boasts a two-burner stove, a fridge, and a microwave atop a speckled countertop. The floors are vinyl and designed to mimic sand-colored wood. My eyes land on the simple gray couch.

"It pulls out into a bed," Camille informs me, noticing my stare. "And there's a room in the back."

The room fits a queen-sized mattress that leaves little in the way of space, but the cabinets surrounding the headboard will surely be enough for what I've brought. There's a bathroom off to the side with a shower, sink, and toilet. Though it's small, everything I'd hoped to find is here. It's clean, but most importantly, it's cheap.

"It all works. You don't have to worry about dumping the black or gray water. It's connected to a private septic tank underground. You have heat and air. You'll need the heat this winter, for sure." She looks around the place once more. "As long as your background check comes in clean, it's yours, if you want it."

There's no need to think twice.

"I'll take it."

THREE

Camille

The smell of roasting coffee beans permeates the air, mixing with the scent of wood burning in the fireplace, making the air feel thick and textured. I pour a generous helping of cream into a mug and top it with freshly brewed caffeine, watching it swirl and settle like smoke. The world outside is ghost gray as the sun slowly wakes, not yet showing its face. I feel a shiver when peering out at the camper beyond, knowing I've handed over the keys, and now have a renter—a stranger on my property. It's clear in the composition of the land that this is meant to be a place to withdraw to. From the many skeletal trees that disappear into the fractured sky, to the thick brambles that choke much of the ground, the property is a haven cut straight out of the Smoky Mountains.

There's an old, country feel to my cabin that I love. The sofa looks as though it's seen its fair share of people, and a single bathroom sits in the back with a white, nicely folded towel hanging on a rack. The kitchen smells of cinnamon from the candle burning low on the counter. There's a door on each side of the hall, leading to bedrooms. It's small enough that I can see most of it from the living room.

It's six in the morning, no one should be up so early, but the birds won't quit singing and I can't seem to convince my internal alarm clock to sleep in on the first day off I've had in forever. Mr. Hill insisted I take it. He happened to mention yesterday I'll probably have a little more income now that someone has rented the camper. Somehow, he knows I work as hard as I do because I can't afford not to, kind as he's been to skirt the issue.

I take a scalding sip and sigh against the rim of my mug. The fire crackles and snaps, licking up the chimney. Its heat touches my skin and warms my lungs. I consider staying in my pajamas for the entire day, just sitting snugly, drinking coffee, and enjoying the nothingness.

That's one of the reasons I relocated.

For the entrancing quiet.

You'd think growing up around constant noise, having lived in Miami, the busiest of cities, would have made me used to it by now, but I'm not. A memory hits, the one that eventually led me here, my mind skipping backward in time.

Light blinks like stars in the night sky, my vision swimming. A sea of nothingness promises my safekeeping. I'm about to go willingly, anything to escape the last tendrils of a memory, of what landed me in the hospital in the first place.

"They always find me," I whisper into the nothingness.

A nurse emerges from the corner of the room. An IV twists like a tie beside my head. Something cold flows into my veins. A machine beeps, attached to me. The parts of the room I can see through my blurry gaze are covered in ethereal sweeps of gray, looking like shadows on the snow after the sun has set. I'm strapped to a gurney, unable to move, not that I could, anyway, under the heaviness of the drugs.

A doctor speaks in a hushed voice just outside the door. "Dr. Martinez. Yes, I'm in charge of the patient. She's claims threatening people are looking for her."

I take a deep breath and wince at the ache in my side. Someone intentionally caused me pain.

The nurse adjusts buttons on a machine.

"...begging to leave before she's found," he continues.

I do need to leave, but how? The sheets tangle around me and I can't move enough to escape the restraints.

"...doesn't remember the accident."

Accident? That's not right. I search my mind, attempting to swat away the lingering grogginess. Exactly how long have I been out of it? How long have I been here?

"...combative."

A memory comes. Agonizing pain. Being rushed into the emergency room. Medical technicians surrounding me, cutting my clothes open to determine the extent of my injuries. They wheeled me into surgery. What happened next?

"...delusions," the doctor suggests.

No. They're wrong. I didn't imagine anything. I was attacked. There were men. Screams. Too much blood. I need to get out of the hospital before they find me again.

I can never...

I won't ever...

Go back there.

There's no time to form a plan. The nurse plunges a needle into the tube attached to my vein. My eyelids grow heavy, dragged down by an invisible weight. I can no longer make out the doctor's words. It feels like biting snow is falling on me. I'm cold, frigid, unable to breathe under the solidity of it.

Help, I try to say.

No words escape.

Movement outside the window catches my attention and snaps me out of the terrifying flashback. A deer meanders close, just under the large magnolia tree that sits front and center in the yard. Its blossoms are now gone, not due to bloom again until spring, but when they do, they are my favorite. The deer approaches the house and begins eating berries and the few remaining leaves of a bush right beneath the sill. Sensing me, it stills and peers inside. I've been known to leave apple treats for the family of deer that beds on the south end of the property, just under the cover of a fallen tree whose roots and branches catch the leaves and moss that drift down.

Yes, in many ways this is much better than Miami.

Suddenly, the deer is frightened off, and a black cat wanders up the driveway with nothing more than a crunch of loose gravel, stopping at the front door and meowing loudly. I give it a once over, hoping it will move along. This particular feline is different than the strays that occasionally pass through. It seems to be waiting for the door to open. I decide to ignore it and take the last sips of my coffee before peeling myself away from the fire for a refill.

The cat scratches the door, and I take a second look. It's too skinny, with bones protruding from its hips.

"Okay, fine." I grab a leftover chicken thigh from the fridge.

Maybe breakfast will convince the cat to leave. Hopefully it won't return for more food later. It's best to not feed the animals, but I can't seem to help the soft spot I have for them. I can't leave the cat starving in the cold.

"Here." I open the door and set the chicken on the ground. "Now go. Shoo."

The cat ignores the chicken and darts inside, beelining straight for the fire. It curls up next to the flames, attempting to lick off what I now see is frost melted into its wet fur. I stand unsure at the open door, battling myself.

"Oh, all right." I shut it so as to not let out any more heat.

"But only until you warm up. Then, you're out."

It doesn't have a tag or a collar. Maybe I'll use Mr. Hill's printer to make fliers. I can tack them to the bulletin board at the general store. Around town, too. Someone must be missing the feline. It seems too domesticated, too used to a home, to be feral. Though, I'm not sure how happy I am about how little they feed it, judging by the bones showing under its fur. Or maybe the cat used to have a home but hasn't for a while now.

Behind the feline, smoke swirls like a twist tie up the chimney. I add another log from the pile I keep stacked on the floor next to the hearth, trying to move slowly so as not to upset it, but the cat doesn't even startle. It pauses once to glance at me, its yellow eyes like egg yolks, before going back to grooming itself.

I adjust the firewood I cut myself—hours spent dismembering the many branches from a tree I downed on the property. Whatever branches can't be used are set next to the deer bedding, while the usable wood is piled in the woodshed, which is built against the side of the house, a few steps away and easily accessible. It's almost always full. It, like most things around here, is old and could use a sanding and a new coat of paint, but for now, until I have enough for renovations, it'll have to do.

The cat looks at me again, blinks slowly, and meows, still not startled in the least by my presence, as though it's lived here all its life. A boy, I see as he turns around. He brushes against my hand, and I pet him tentatively, keeping in mind how easy it is for me to become attached. I plan to never be attached to anything, *or anyone*, again.

"You can't stay," I warn the cat, and maybe myself.

A knock at the door startles the breath out of me, fists closing around my lungs. I'm not used to unannounced visitors. Time blurs again.

The sun tucks itself away for the night, not to be seen again until morning. Twilight marches in, ready to take over, and I follow its moonlit trail up the sandy beach into the house that waits. It's a gorgeous thing, the home, mighty in its splendor, like one of the castles of long ago, though it isn't all that old. The house doesn't belong to me, but I dream that one day it will.

The back door is unlocked, awaiting my arrival. I step in and feel residual grains of sand between my toes. Relics that tail me most days. Over the calm soundlessness of the downstairs floor comes a scratchy noise. Then a louder one. I take the flight of stairs to the second level, pass several bedrooms, more than necessary for the occupant of the home, and stop outside of the farthest and grandest one. My hand is on the knob, ready to enter, knowing I don't need an invitation, but when I realize a phone call is in progress, I pause.

"You know the rules."

Then.

"This is confidential."

It's not the words that bother me so much as the tone of the voice that belongs to the man on the other side of the wooden door. It's cracked open a smidge, enough to fit the pointed tip of a shoe, and sound carries.

The voice is borderline angry. "You do not want to cross me."

His words are a threat. I wonder what will happen if the person does choose to cross him. Why would they want to in the first place?

There's a thump, and then something shatters. I throw open the door.

"Are you okay?" I ask.

But I see right away that it's only a broken vase, which toppled from the bedside table. No one is hurt. Nothing else is out of place. I know this bedroom well.

"I have to go," he snaps, and disconnects.

I didn't mean to barge in on his call. I only wanted to check that he was unharmed. He sets the phone down and comes to me.

"I'm fine, love," he soothes.

There's a grin playing across his beautiful features, as though nothing at all just happened. The phone call could have been my imagination for all the clues he gives me.

"Are you sure? You seemed—" I pause, weighing my words, trying to choose the right ones. "Angry about something. Did someone upset you?"

"Listening, were you?"

I blush. "I didn't mean to. I finished swimming and the beach grew dark, so I came back. I hope that's all right. We were going to have dinner, weren't we?"

He places a kiss on my mouth. It's deep and warm and everything I've grown to love. He pulls back just a fraction to whisper in my ear.

"Of course, I want to have you for dinner."

My heart knocks against my ribcage with excitement as flashes of me in his embrace come to mind.

"My chef will arrive in ten minutes. He'll prepare whatever you want."

He seems relaxed but, where my hand lands, I feel his pulse in his wrist, and I wonder if it's galloping because of my nearness or the charged manner of the call.

"I heard you talking about—" I hesitate, but only for a moment. "Someone crossing you."

I bite my lip, wondering if I've said too much. We've only been dating six months. I don't want to overstep my bounds.

"It's just business. People want money. I want to make money, too. Sometimes you have to play hardball with them. If I showed any favoritism or weakness, they'd eat me alive. You understand?"

I really don't.

"And what business is this?"

As far as I know, he owns a pricey club downtown. Not exactly the type of business where people double-cross one another. Though, I admittedly don't know much about that, so I suppose it could happen.

"The club." His eyes bore into mine. "Now, really, there must be something more interesting than my phone call. Tell me about your swim. How was the water?"

I get lost in the thought of it. "It was heavenly."

I begin telling him about the warm, salty breeze, and how I beat my last time by a second. I'm getting better and better, training for another triathlon, but the ocean is my favorite part, and when my head sinks beneath the waves, my blood comes alive.

Somewhere along the line, with his arms around me and thoughts of the sea, I forget all about his call.

I didn't realize then that'd been his objective all along.

Another knock sounds. I inhale deeply, shaking off the fog of the memory. I press a hand to my pounding heart while creeping to the side of the window to peek out the blinds.

It's the new renter, Dawson.

I unlock the deadbolt and greet him with a shaky voice. "Hi."

My gaze goes to his eyes, which I can finally see clearly in the early morning light. They are the palest, glass-bottle green. The most beautiful color.

"Morning," he replies, voice deep and scruffy.

His hair is mussed as though he just rolled out of bed. Suddenly, I have an image of him actually rolling out of bed. I wonder what he wears, if anything, under the sheets—my sheets on the camper mattress. My cheeks bloom with red like rose petals. It helps me completely forget the memory, which now fades from my mind.

"Do you realize you have a piece of chicken on your porch?" he asks.

I resist the urge to explain. I owe no one a justification of my life.

"Yes."

He holds my stare, sure and strong. "Okay, then. I was wondering if you could tell me the best place to get a cup of coffee?"

Dawson looks tired, dusty purple shadowing beneath his eyes. I can only imagine how far he must have traveled yesterday to get here. A thermal shirt clings to his sculpted arms. I wonder how many times he lifted heavy artillery. How many months, years, in battle it must have taken to get into the kind of shape he's in.

I mean to tell him that the general store is the closest place, not to mention that their coffee is delicious, but somehow, it comes out as, "I have half a pot left."

I freeze up instantly. I've just invited him inside by accident.

He looks longingly at the pot, which is visible on the counter through the open door. Steam rises from its surface like fog on a lake.

"Or you can take a cup to go if you want," I amend. That's what I should have said the first time.

Dawson pins me in place with his gaze. His stare drops south of my chin. My robe has slipped open, exposing my cream pants and button up shirt. The first two buttons are undone, not showing much, but I retie my robe, nonetheless.

His eyes snap back to my face. "I'll take it to go if you don't mind. I need to run to the store. Any chance you can tell me where that is?"

I'm glad he doesn't come in.

"The general store where I work is the closest, but if you're looking for a grocery, that's thirty miles outside of town. Take NC 9 straight up. It'll eventually get you there."

The cat meows by the fire, and I'm reminded that I now seem to have two new inhabitants on the property.

He nods. "I'll get started on those dead branches today when I get back. You can show me where you want me to begin, and tell me what exactly you need done around here."

"Sounds good." I busy myself with stepping back inside and pulling a thermos out of the cabinet. I fill it with coffee. "Cream or sugar?"

"Neither, thanks," he says from outside the door. His gaze slips again to where my robe opened a minute ago.

I hand him the coffee. Then do myself the favor of saying, "have a good day" before shutting the door between us. I take a deep breath, my hands shaking.

It's only a couple of glances that we volleyed back and forth, and some would argue harmless human nature, but I know better. I refuse to play any more dangerous games. I did that once. And I paid dearly for it.

FOUR

Dawson

Manual labor causes drops of sweat to bead across my forehead. I swipe the sleeve of my shirt over them and continue to hack at the branches. There's a stark contrast in temperatures between this morning, when I found the grocery store and stocked up on food, and now. It's no longer cold. But one thing that hasn't changed is the regret I feel for not accepting Camille's coffee invite. I would have if I didn't desperately need to fill the cupboards.

"Sorry I didn't have extra fuel for the chainsaw," Camille says, her spiraled hair bouncing like springs as she approaches with a glass of what looks like tea.

I'm happy to see it's iced. I grab it from her and down it quickly. It has just the right amount of sweetness, and I'd guess it's recently brewed. I already want a refill. She takes the glass back and watches me work.

"What did you do in the army?"

Harmless enough question, but thoughts flood my mind at the mention.

"I was a medic," I answer.

Piles of bodies lie on the floor because the beds are taken. I can't save some of them—hell, I can't even save half of them—but I'm by the side of the ones who have a chance. The doctor shouts at me to grab more bandages, start an IV, and apply pressure to a wound to stop the bleeding. There's too much to do, and not enough space or time or hands or resources to treat them all.

One of our best soldiers, Sanders, rushes in, covered in blood. He's a legend—many kills and even more saves. I finish what I'm doing and hurry to him. It's what our commander would want from me. We certainly can't lose Sanders. I shudder to think how many more of our guys we'll lose if he's not out there to assist them.

"What happened?" I question. "Bullet? Bomb?"

It wouldn't be the first time he's taken a hit.

His face is contorted into an expression I've never seen on him—fear.

"Help her," he beseeches desperately.

That's when I notice the bloody rags in his arms are not to stop his own bleeding, they're hiding something underneath.

There's a girl, maybe five-years-old, a tiny thing, with red pouring from her stomach. He places her in my arms. I set her on a counter—she's small enough—to check her wounds. She's unconscious due to the bullet lodged in her abdomen. Sanders yells for me to hurry. She resembles the girl in the picture he carries around. His daughter. Of course, his daughter is safe at home in America, miles and seas away, but I wonder if, in his mind, he's seeing the little girl he loves.

He tells me the target he was assigned to eliminate shot the child who simply happened to be in the wrong place at the wrong time.

"Did you get him?" I ask. "The target?"

Sanders nods, his eyes on the child. "Of course, but not in time."

I rarely see grown men cry in this wasteland of a desert, and today won't be an exception, but what I do see is how his throat works up and down as he swallows his emotions.

"She'll be okay." I know wounds and I wouldn't lie. "Go, help the others."

Because there are always others.

I did save the girl. Yet she still haunts me. Occasionally, images like hers follow me in my wakeful moments and even in dreams.

"Did you serve long?" Camille inquires.

"Eight years." Eight very long years.

"Do you regret it?" She places one hand on the rusted ladder, looking up at me with bright eyes.

"What would make you say that?"

I hack away at another branch, opposite Camille, that refuses to fall. The labor suits me. It's something to do, creating a blank space in my mind as I focus on tedious work, which I appreciate. There's no denying that after living through such a hectic career, the quiet draws me in, but still, I seek *something* to do, however small.

"Your expression," she explains. "You're frowning."

Am I? Not surprising.

"Certain moments are hard to remember," I admit. "But never for one second do I regret helping those men and women. It's the most fulfilling thing I've ever done, and I'd do it all over again."

The limb finally falls to the ground with a *thunk*. Overhead, the sun shines through mostly bare branches. A hawk perches nearby, watching my movements. Camille watches my movements, too. It seems like she enjoys the view, and I'm just worked up enough to indulge her. I never thought I'd leave my home or my job. Yet here I am, with a beautiful woman who doesn't mask the combination of skittishness and interest very well.

"What are you doing tonight?" I ask.

I glance her way, trying to read her expression, her reaction to my question. Her eyes trail over my body in a quick procession, but when she gets to my face, she winces, knowing I've seen her. I wonder if she has a hard time not looking at me the same way I have a hard time not looking at her.

"Nothing, why?" she replies tentatively.

Keeping my guard up is imperative. Friendly conversation with the woman who owns the property and is gracious enough to rent it to me for less than it's worth is fine, especially since I want to be a good tenant, but my living situation can't be compromised. I can't get carried away and let my walls down. I have to be careful how I approach her. I think about her wince just a second ago.

"Was wondering if you wanted to have dinner. Just casual. Maybe at the camper or your place? I'd love to learn more about the town."

Being close to Camille could invite all sorts of inquiries on her part, not to mention that being in close proximity to her ignites my blood in a way I don't need to be distracted with, but I can't seem to resist. I'm hoping she actually will tell me about the town. I don't know how long I'll be staying, but I saw an advertisement for an opening at the general store. I'm not sure whom to ask about it. Getting settled is easy enough, but meeting other people is different. This isn't the city. There are no people milling about. There aren't subdivisions or neighbors to shout, "Hello!" The trip to the grocery store taught me that even the office buildings are a good forty minutes outside of town. Unless you count the local vet, gas station, and hardware store.

"I'll probably stay in tonight." Her tone holds an edge, one that says she's hoping to ward off any further conversation.

I resume sawing. "Okay, well, thanks for the tea."

Maybe I should apologize. I obviously came on too strong. She's kind. She's allowing me to rent the camper—no contracts or strings attached. I shouldn't jeopardize that.

"I'll see you later." Her voice finally drifts up to me after a minute of silence.

She takes the tea glass with her without a single backwards glance my way. Finally, her cabin door shuts. It's obvious she's wary of letting people close. I saw the way she was with customers, neither answering their questions directly, nor accepting their compliments wholeheartedly. She keeps a low profile. Like me. I can appreciate that.

Another branch falls. After I finish, I'll need to cut them into smaller pieces. Perhaps leave them by that deer bed Camille spoke of.

I glance to the northernmost corner of the property, as far as I can see from this high up. There's nothing but nearly skeletal trees. Aside from the cold, I already love it here. It's the perfect place to settle into.

And hopefully, vanish.

FIVE

Camille

I t shouldn't have been hard to decline dinner with Dawson yesterday, and there's no reason for me to still be thinking about it the next morning. His muscles flexed and bunched as he cut branches, his beautiful features deep in thought as the words left his lips—an invite to dinner. It only took a moment for my self-preservation to kick in, a well-built wall sliding into place. The lie rolled off my tongue. I hadn't wanted to stay in, though that's not what I told him.

There's a small cinema in town, which plays old movies on Wednesday nights. I haven't been in a while. Originally, I planned on going yesterday, thanks to an invite from Bonnie, my diner friend. Too bad I couldn't follow through.

The thought of telling Dawson about the movie and him potentially wanting to join was more than I could handle. Mostly because "cinema" is quite a stretch. The room is really nothing but a small area with several couches and high-backed chairs stacked together like matches in a box, and an old-fashioned popcorn machine that cooks the buttery kernels during the film, always earning a complaint from someone who can't hear the movie over it—usually Mr. Hill, but no one ever gives him trouble. Dawson would be cramped in with other locals who would surely be watching him more than whatever movie they picked for the month. Nosy bunch of people.

I don't need anyone in my business.

And I especially don't need Dawson squished up next to me on one of the couches or chairs, for that matter.

So, of course, I lied and said I planned to stay inside. What other choice did I have? I suppose I could have had dinner with him and those piercing green eyes that remind me of the glass bottles people purposely drop into the sea, the type that contain concealed secrets. How much would he have seen, though? How much would my traitor lips have shared? It's better that I declined his invitation to dinner.

I sigh and adjust the rearview mirror. I can almost no longer see my property. As it is, the trees have already swallowed my house and the camper from view. One last quick glance and it's gone completely. My truck bumps along, over potholes and broken pieces of gravel, on the way to Mrs. JoAnne's house, my closest neighbor. Her driveway is laid with daffodil yellow pavers that smooth the ascent to her place. I park my vehicle, head up the walkway, and open the screen door, stepping onto the sparsely decorated front porch. My eyes take in the barely standing side table and two aged rocking chairs, the seats padded by floral cushions. The entire porch is surrounded by neatly kept soil in which she grows, in the warmer months, the most beautiful garden. She calls it a side project of hers, but I know it's her passion. Well, that and baking.

"Hi, dear," Mrs. JoAnne greets, opening the main door that has a wreath with a gaudy, silver bow attached.

The scent of freshly baked pie pours out of her home like the best smelling air freshener in the world. I inhale deeply and smile. It brings about an instant sense of warmth and comfort—two things I hardly ever felt before moving to the mountains. I don't trust easily, but for her I make a slight exception.

Mrs. JoAnne is an older woman who gladly lives in the kitchen. She refuses to voice her age, and due to common manners, I've never asked. But I'd guess late seventies, maybe early eighties, by the wrinkles etched into her skin and the shock of white hair crowning her head.

"I brought you something." I hold out a basket.

The vegetable garden I've grown from scratch is a source of pride. It's the only thing aside from the camper and house that I take extra good care of. Though, maybe after Dawson concludes his work around the property, I'll have more to be proud of. It's a good piece of land, after all. Rundown, but usable.

The garden is mostly gourds this time of year, not yet plowed for rows of corn. For now, a few remaining vegetables shoot through.

"Oh, you didn't have to do that." She takes the basket of squash, pumpkins, and eggplants, and sets it on the kitchen counter. I follow her inside.

She'll likely bake them, just as she did last year when I delivered a wagon full of pumpkins, from which she gifted me two pies.

"I sure do appreciate it," she says, pulling me in for a hug. She holds me like one would embrace something precious, long and with love. "Care for tea?"

I've already drunk a pot of coffee, but I won't decline her offer.

"I'd love some."

She drops three sugar cubes into the cup she gives me, and then pours boiling tea on top. A coo-coo clock against the wall spits out a bird, chiming noon. I sink into a couch that feels like a cozy sweater, pulling a throw blanket over my legs. Not for the first time, I wonder if this is what it's like to have a sweet grandma.

"So, you gonna tell me why there's been a truck parked at your house?" She brings a teacup up to her lips. "Did you purchase one?"

But seeing as though she's hiding a smile, I don't think she suspects me of buying a used vehicle at all. I suppose what she really wants to know is who's the new neighbor. People here in the mountains have a funny way of asking things. They don't always come right out with it. Sometimes, they make it look like another question in order to get the answer they want. I can't be upset with her for butting into my business, though. She's too sweet. Most days.

I'm the third to last property on our dead-end road. Me, Mrs. JoAnne, and finally, Will. Both of them have to pass my house to get anywhere they plan on going, so I suppose they would be the ones to notice a new truck in the drive. Though I have to follow the winding road to get to both neighbors, there is still one other path to Will's property, since it borders mine. Cross the creek by foot, down the way about a mile, and come to his place. The rest of my property line that doesn't touch Will's, borders cow pastures.

"I got a renter for the camper," I reply. "It's his truck."

"You don't say." She chuckles, as though knowing I'd say exactly that. "Well, what's he like?"

"He's nice enough."

I don't mention how Dawson seems closed off and cautious with the words he chooses. Maybe, like most people in Darlington, he likes his privacy.

"He's not from around here, I see," she remarks. "He has Arizona plates."

Leave it to her to go snooping.

Outside the window, a golden field winks in the sunlight. Grass sways and dances in the slight breeze, and I wonder at the possibility of my land looking like Mrs. JoAnne's one day if

I tend to it right. There's calmness in the back and forth of the long spears of grass. Cows are sectioned off by a fence, their heads bowed and mouths chewing on the bales of hay that speckle their part of the land like autumn-colored polka dots. Maybe I'll even purchase cows one day. Organic milk anytime I want. Or better yet, chickens. Fresh eggs would be a welcome breakfast each morning.

"What do you know about the newcomer?" She picks up a newspaper from the recliner to free a spot for herself.

"He's ex-military. Had a family tragedy. House burned down and took his mom, dad, and brother with it."

"Poor thing," she coos, genuine concern in her tone.

I sip my tea and relish the warmth. A hint of sweetness leaves the perfect aftertaste.

"Anyway, he's here to stay for a while, from what I gather."

Mrs. JoAnne grins conspiratorially, casually drinking from her flower-patterned cup.

"What?" I ask.

She takes her time answering, as she sometimes does.

"Would you mind if he did?" She schools her face into a mask of indifference. "Stayed, I mean?"

I wonder what she's getting at. "For the time being, no."

Now that she has her answer, her perceptive grin returns. "What's this ex-military man look like?"

"That doesn't matter, and you know it." I now clearly see the path her thoughts trot along. As I suspected.

My eyes narrow and I give her what I hope is a look that says

I know just what she's up to.

"For all the men that throw themselves at you at that store of yours—and don't shake your head at me, I've seen them— you haven't once smiled the way you do when talking about this new renter."

Was I smiling? I hadn't noticed.

"Men don't throw themselves at me," I argue.

"Do, too."

A timer goes off. She shuffles to the kitchen to remove a pie from the oven. The smell announces it as apple. After a moment of absence, she returns, pulls oven mitts from her hands, and sits beside me again where the recliner meets the couch, letting the pie cool on the counter.

"I've seen it happen from time to time. Men do approach you." She sips her tea calmly. "Surely you notice the looks and advances."

"I notice them, yes," I concede, "but I don't pay them any mind, and I wouldn't say they 'throw themselves' at me."

Most customers seem talkative, occasionally a bit flirty.

"I see other things, too, you know." She props her feet on the ottoman and leans back. "For example, you've been visiting for a year now without mention of your life before, which I told you I'll respect. Still doesn't mean I don't know you. You cringe at the sight of a spider. You prefer apple pie to pecan. You light up when Thanksgiving and Christmas decorations go up in town. You take pride in the things you do. You skirt most company, though it's more than obvious that you crave it. If I notice small things, other people can, too."

An uncomfortable feeling slides under my skin. I've shown too much of myself to her. I wonder if I've revealed too much to others as well.

"So, men have noticed me. It doesn't mean anything," I counter.

"I beg to differ. Many gentlemen would jump at an opportunity to take you out. You ought to give one of the locals a chance. Unless you have someone else in mind."

I imagine Dawson's strong jaw and bottle-green eyes, and heat surges in my veins.

"I don't have someone in mind," I lie.

"Well then, by all means, do yourself a favor and go out with one of the other men. It might be fun. Unless you feel like you need space. Maybe you've been burned before? Or maybe you just prefer your own company, which is fine. But if there's a chance you're missing companionship of that variety, then take a shot."

I don't want her to know anything about me being burned before, though she's right, so I say, "I'll think about it."

I check the clock on the wall. Half past noon. My shift starts in thirty minutes.

"I've got to get going."

"Come tomorrow for a pie," she tells me. "Tell the new gentleman hello for me."

"His name is—" I stop myself before mentioning more about Dawson, whom I have no business thinking about. "You know what? Doesn't matter. I'll tell him hi from the lady he doesn't know, sure thing."

She laughs. "You do that now."

She doesn't let up, even as I place my teacup in the sink.

"Bet you've noticed all sorts of things about him," she muses. "I know I did with my military husband. May he rest in peace."

She bows her head. For a moment, it looks as though she's saying a silent prayer, but then I spot her smirk.

"Those strong bodies are quite nice," she comments. "Those sharp wits."

Another lie rolls off my tongue. "I haven't noticed a thing."

I let myself out with a wave goodbye.

"One second." She holds up a hand.

I pause with the driver's side door half open, ready to head to work. She leans against the porch railing.

"What do you think of his blue eyes?"

"They're green," I reply, and then curse. I forgot to not notice anything about him.

Lord above, I sure do know how to get myself caught in lies.

SIX

Dawson

The television blares as I cut a swatch of fabric from the camper couch to hide the gun I've brought for protection. It's a necessity, and I'm grateful to have it. Hopefully, I won't need to use it. I don't know how Camille would feel about me leaving it in plain view, so I decide not to take any chances. I doubt she'll bother the camper with me renting it, but better to be safe than sorry. Hopefully she'll never notice the cut in the couch. Maybe I could sew it up before I leave? Being a medic gave me deft fingers when it comes to working with a needle and thread.

As a draft of iciness kicks up, I tuck the fabric back into place and take a seat on the couch, piling on a comforter for warmth. The heater works, like Camille claimed, but it's a small thing and takes a while to get going, though when it does, it's perfect. I imagine it'll even be enough for winter.

It's especially chilly tonight, just thirteen degrees. The only time I ventured out, a couple minutes before deciding the cold was too thick, the night air stole my breath and showed it to me in a silver mist. I wonder if people ever truly get acclimated to the bone-deep cold weather, or if they finally give up fighting and succumb to the inevitable frostiness. Dusk descends with the weight of a thousand sooty feather clouds, all sinking lower and lower until I finally fully understand why they call them the Smoky Mountains. The peaks are frosted over with misty icing, the bottoms so cloaked in shadows that I hardly see them anymore. Fog creeps over the grass, clinging to its surface.

My mind, on repeat like the commercials between shows I watch, won't stop thinking about the *real* place I come from. Hot weather year-round. Unlike North Carolina. I barely sleep here. I don't know how to with the stress of being on the run and hardly having any communication with the people I left behind. They settle into the sheets with me at night like another body, nearly suffocating me. Memories come at me fast and unannounced. I am torn between missing a life I knew, and needing to keep myself as far away from there as possible. I still remember with clarity my last phone call.

"I'm taking off," I say into the receiver, the phone pressed flat to my face, clenched tightly in my palm, nearly to the point of pain.

"What do you mean you're leaving?" the man asks. "To go where?"

Three beats of silence. He seems to understand the question won't be answered.

"How long?" the man asks.

The line crackles. I stand under a narrow, concrete bridge near a collection of littered garbage, likely left there by the occasional passersby. It's been naturally swept off to the side by the wind and elements. The area offers low cell service. A few yards away, my truck sits on the edge of the deserted road. The sun threatens to set soon, leaving me in unfamiliar territory at dusk.

"However long it takes," I reply.

The man chuckles, but there isn't any humor in the sound. "You're not telling me much here."

This time, I laugh. The sound is grating, even to my own ears. I never wanted to leave in the first place.

"I need to go."

I watch the last rays of light slide down the sky like oil, the heat and humidity suctioning my shirt to me like a second skin. I mop a bit of it off my forehead and adjust my hat.

"You can't tell anyone about this," I warn.

The man sighs. "I figured."

Crickets chirp loudly, an alarm alerting me that my time is up.

"Don't try to find me."

I glance toward the road once more, but I haven't seen another *car in hours, and now is no exception.*

"When will you call again?"

Uncertainty pinches my gut.

"I need to go," I repeat, giving a non-answer.

Then before the man has a chance to say anything else, I hit the end button. The line goes dead. I already did what I needed to— made the call, wiped the cell's memory, disabled the Bluetooth and any other location service, and made sure it can't be traced.

I pull my baseball cap off momentarily and run a hand through my hair in frustration. I peer once more at my phone before ridding myself of the last thing that belongs to me besides my truck, a duffle bag of clothing, and the hat I replace on my head. I toss the cell as far as I can, down an embankment and into a small pond, where it sinks to the bottom. With any luck, it'll never be found again.

Hopefully, if all goes according to plan, I won't be found either.

Maybe I should make another phone call soon. I'll need to be careful about it. I only have my gut to guide me now. One wrong move...one slipup...and it could be the end of everything for me.

Something flickers across the television, a reflection from the window at my back. I turn around to peer through a bent blind. Camille stands in the dark at a grill. The flames eat at a sky smattered with stars. I've never seen so many, a smear across an expanse of black. It's peaceful, I realize.

My eyes rake back to Camille. I can't help but watch her. It's the way she moves fluidly, as though an ocean tide carries her everywhere. It's the look she gives me every time we're close enough to touch, but never do. Her wide set hazel eyes—with a marbling of amber through them—create a gaze that seems to seep into the bone and marrow.

She grabs a pair of tongs from the side of the grill, and unwraps foil from a plate. I can see it all clearly in the light of the blaze. Is this what she normally does? Cooks dinner at night by herself in the dark?

There's a basket by her feet. She pulls vegetables from it—a raw, green pepper and an eggplant. I wonder what's wrong with her inside stove. Or maybe, like me, she enjoys the taste of wood-cooked meals.

What I would give for a wood-cooked meal.

She turns around, her gaze like a beacon homing in on the camper. For a second, I think she's caught me staring, but then she goes back to cooking. She, too, seems to be drawn to the stars. Between each flip of meat on the grill, she glances at the sky.

I take in her outfit—a thick jacket, a scarf wrapped around her neck several times, jeans, and boots with a rim of fur around the top, stopping at her knees.

While the food cooks, and Camille watches the stars, her hands move back and forth, warming over the flames. I'd love a fire to warm my hands, or maybe even just to warm my hands on her, but there's not a chance I'd risk joining her. Not alone. Not at night. Not when her hair is so thick and beautiful, I want to tangle my fingers in it. Or maybe that's exactly the right idea.

I war with myself. I could go to her. But she didn't exactly jump at the opportunity to have dinner with me. I sigh and rub the tension from my forehead. Maybe I should give her space. It's probably a lot to take in, having a new person on the property, sharing the land she's used to being on alone.

I turn back around to watch mindless television. The antenna I bought earlier today at a junkyard down the road connects to the outside of the camper, making it possible to get nine channels. I don't have cable or streaming services. I'm learning that Darlington is the type of place where people run businesses out of their own yards—apple orchards, scrapyards, pottery, and more—which is how I found the antenna in the first place, and thankfully I did, because I can't imagine sitting in the camper with nothing to do. The antenna only cost a few dollars. Things are certainly cheaper here, and unlike the city, prices are almost always up for barter. As the gentleman from the junkyard explained, many of the properties have been around for generations, handed down through families, and most are paid off. It's how so many can get by with making and selling straight from their homes, growing gardens and trading goods with neighbors. It's nothing like what I'm accustomed to, where almost all items are store bought, and definitely not at bargain prices. At least there's comfort in knowing I won't need much to get by here. As it is, the camper is a steal. It has everything I need, and now television, too. But no matter how hard I attempt to lose myself in the faces on the screen, I can't. Temptation demands that I turn around to peer back out of the window again.

Camille is finished cooking. She towers food on a plate, puts out the flame, and walks back into her house. Just as well. Now maybe I can concentrate on something else, like getting a job around here.

A few moments later, there's a soft knock at the door.

"It's me," Camille calls.

I attempt to untangle myself from the blanket. I must be taking too long, though, because her voice comes again.

"I know you're awake."

How the hell would she know that? Unless...

I unlatch the lock. The door swings outward, and I'm met with plate of food being thrust at me—vegetables and steak drizzled with a mushroom sauce.

Camille grins. "Oh, come on. Take it. If you're going to stare at me the whole time, you might as well not act surprised that I have food. You watched me cook it, after all."

I shock myself by laughing. So, she won't have dinner with me, but she'll bring it to my door. It's a small step, one that also tells me she caught me staring. For some reason, that doesn't bother me, because the only way she'd know I was looking was if she was looking, too.

SEVEN

Camille

"Would you mind if I used your printer?" I ask into the lazy blue day.

The sky reminds me of the salty turquoise water I used to swim in, the faint, briny aroma on my skin, minnows in the shallows occasionally brushing my shins, and my toes tangling in seaweed. I'd go deeper and dip my head beneath the surface with goggles on, opening my eyes to an underwater landscape. The sun's rays dancing through the ripples. Fish in underwater homes. A sandy ground with hills made of silt.

Here, fresh mountain air rolls down in cool waves without much of a bite. There is no open water to be seen. Even part of the sky is blocked by numerous peaks that stand tall, like giants. I sweep the front sidewalk while Mr. Hill sways in one of the three rocking chairs outside of the general store.

"I never mind if you want to use anything of mine. Like I told you when you needed the printer for the camper advertisement, you're welcome to everything in the store."

I sigh in relief. "Thanks. I need more fliers."

Mr. Hill blinks up at me. "Why? I thought that renter of yours was working out. You need another tenant? Is he leaving?"

I laugh. "No, not that."

He waits patiently for me to explain.

"I found a cat. Well, it found me, really. I'm thinking it must have a home somewhere. It doesn't seem to want to go back outside. I need to put up fliers around town."

"Come on, then." Mr. Hill beckons me to the office.

I'm surprised by how familiar he is with the old computer, pulling up a document to create a flier.

"What's the cat look like?"

This is just another thing I love about Mr. Hill. He doesn't scold me for being on the clock and tending to a personal matter. He helps me.

"Completely black. Older. Boy." As I give him the basics, he types them in and prints out a single paper, making sure to save the document and power down the desktop.

"Go ahead and tack this to the board out front. I listed the general store's number as the contact. If he belongs to someone, they'll call here."

Another generosity.

"I gave him a temporary name until his owner comes forward," I say. "I suppose I'll feed him and keep him until then."

Mr. Hill holds the door open for me as I step outside and pin the flier to the corkboard.

"How about this," he begins, as I come back around the corner. "You take him to the vet down the road, check if he's microchipped, and if he's not, we'll print more fliers to put around town."

"Microchipped. I hadn't thought of that."

The door closes behind us, the bell jangling as we reenter the store.

"The vet in town does it complementary with the first checkup. That's how I got one for Buster. They like knowing animals have a better chance of making it home if they're ever lost," he explains.

Buster is his overactive French Bulldog. Pale peach in color, and full of personality to go with his loud snoring and excessive drool, he keeps Mr. Hill company when he's home. The poor thing was found trotting along NC 9 one day. No collar and no owner. I suspect Mr. Hill had a soft spot for the orphaned puppy, which has now grown into an eight-year-old dog that sleeps at every opportunity between playing with his numerous toys.

"If the cat is microchipped, it'll show, and you can return him."

I make a mental note to call the vet.

"Hey, by the way, I need someone to clean out the storage sheds," he tells me.

Once back behind the counter, he begins opening the tops of the ice cream flavors to entice people with the display, even though it's only sixty degrees outside. Fluffy bubble gum, cotton candy swirl, chunky chocolate, ripe strawberry, smooth banana, and more. The drastic increase in temperature is sure to call people out, and some might actually buy a scoop. If I close my eyes to block the view of the nearly bare trees, and mostly melted patches of snow freckling the ground from last night, I can imagine it's spring, not the tail end of autumn.

"I also need someone to rebuild the broken, rotten shed pieces and organize everything. The store roof requires replacing, too. Got Kenny contracted for that, but he's asking for extra hands. That new tenant of yours lookin' for a job? Don't feel like wasting my money hiring lazy locals. Your tenant looks like he's worked in his life. He's in shape. Sharp eyes and practiced movements, as though he's aware of everything around him all at once. Reminds me of boys in my day. We paid attention. We worked for what we wanted. My momma woulda beat me blue had I ever pulled what half the lazy local boys do nowadays."

"I didn't realize you saw so much of Dawson," I comment.

In the week he's been in town, Dawson's only visited the store the first time and once afterwards, that I know of.

"I see all kinds of things," Mr. Hill replies vaguely. "Let your neighbor know that if he needs a paying job, hell, even if he doesn't need it but wants to pass the time, I'll be here. Have him talk to me."

Since Dawson says he doesn't have much to pay rent, and he's working off part of his stay by helping around the property, I'd say that Dawson, like me, very much needs the money.

There was a time when I didn't need money.

"I'll mention it."

"Good, because here he comes. I'm going to do paperwork."

Mr. Hill disappears to the back office and shuts the door. The main store door opens and in walks Dawson, a sureness and confidence to his gait.

"Hey." He stops and leans his elbows on the counter. Every millimeter of his body is fraught with power.

His face rests inches from my own. There's something in his eyes, almost a challenge. He grins and my stomach jumps. Lightning rips through my veins. Thunder booms in my muscles.

"Hey," I reply. "What can I get for you?"

"Coffee."

I notice the strips of paper in his hand, torn from the board outside. I catch scrawled words that advertise a part-time lawn worker needed and a construction laborer job opening.

Neither of us mentions last night, or the fact that I brought him dinner.

"My boss is looking for someone to clean his old sheds in the back. They're half falling apart. He'll want the rotting and broken wood torn out and replaced, and everything organized inside. He needs a roof man, too. It started leaking with the heavy rains and snow. You interested?"

"I'm listening," Dawson drawls.

I swear he leans in closer.

"That's all I know," I say, "but my boss is in his office if you want me to get him."

The office door opens, and Mr. Hill rests against it.

"Don't bother, already heard you. Come in and talk to me, boy, if you're interested. Need someone to start tomorrow. Can you start tomorrow?"

"I'm available," Dawson answers cautiously, still not having heard all the details. He follows Mr. Hill into the office, leaving the door cracked.

"Like Camille said, I need a good worker, 7:00 am sharp. Five days a week. You should finish in a month or so. But by then something else might need fixin' and I'm too old to do it myself. Not too old to fire lazy people who expect too much pay for the little work they're willin' to do, though. Damn kids around here. Think they know it all, and they don't want to work for anything. Hopefully you're not like them. Have a feeling you aren't. You interested or not?" Mr. Hill mentions a start pay. "It's the regular rate round these parts. You could make more in that city you came from, but you're here so take it or leave it."

"I never said I came from a city."

I watch them through the cracked door.

"Didn't have to. I smell it on you."

Dawson stiffens. "Maybe you're wrong."

Mr. Hill's voice carries to where I busy myself making a fresh pot of coffee.

"Maybe you spent a long time in a branch of the military—army, if I had to guess by the way you carry yourself—but you were born and raised in a city, that much is plain."

Dawson, possibly because he wants to change the subject, or possibly because Mr. Hill is wrong and he simply doesn't want to argue with the old man, gets back to the point.

"All right, here's the deal. I do need a job, so I'll agree to your pay rate," he says, "but only for the first week. If you don't like my work by the end of the week, fine. I'll go somewhere else. But if you do like my work ethic, I want three more dollars an hour. Your offer is too low, and you know it." Dawson's timbre drops an octave, deep and rumbly, causing my stomach to summersault like a tumbleweed caught in the wind. Then, he hand delivers Mr. Hill his own words. "Take it or leave it."

Mr. Hill laughs. Most people, aside from Mrs. Rose and me, don't even get smiles out of him—me because he's taken to me for some reason, and Mrs. Rose because she feeds him home-cooked meals.

"I like you, boy. I really do. How about I just give you the pay you want anyway, and if you don't do well after the first week, you're fired."

I nearly burn myself while pouring coffee. An employee once walked out because Mr. Hill refused to give him a raise and he'd been working for him for months. Yet Mr. Hill agreed to a raise before ever having seen Dawson's work.

Dawson opens the door and sticks out his hand. Mr. Hill

shakes it.

"I'm having a small issue with the roof, too. Hired a guy named Kenny for the job. He wants an extra hand. Might stick you up there as well."

"Fine by me," Dawson replies.

I try to act as though I haven't been eavesdropping when Dawson approaches for his coffee.

I push the sugar and cream container toward him.

"Hey, and here's the man I was just mentionin'," Mr. Hill calls as Kenny, a guy who recently took over his dad's long-standing roofing company, enters the store.

Hanner's Roofing is one of only two roofing businesses anywhere near town, and usually the cheapest with better overall work, therefore the busier of the pair.

"This is Kenny Hanner," Mr. Hill says, introducing him to Dawson. "He's the one you'll be working with for a few days."

Kenny, a man with a headful of coppery waves, sticks out his hand. "Nice to meet you. Happy to have you on board."

I've known Kenny for a year now in the same sense I know anyone here. He's a likable local who always has a smile on his face and a friendly word in his mouth.

Dawson shakes his hand, his expression passive. "Likewise."

"Damn, good grip," Kenny praises, releasing their clasp. "Strong is a plus in my line of work."

He smiles. He's paid Dawson a compliment, but Dawson doesn't react. It doesn't bother Kenny, though, nothing does really, from what I've figured out.

"When do you start?" he inquires.

Dawson glances at me once before answering, "Tomorrow."

"Perfect!" Kenny begins walking backward toward the water cooler. "Guess I'll see you then."

Dawson's attention is mine again. He reaches to take the Styrofoam cup with strong hands, turning down the sugar and cream I offer. That's twice now. It seems he likes his coffee black. He allows his fingers to linger against mine a moment longer than necessary before pulling his baseball cap lower, shielding his eyes.

"See you tonight." He leaves money on the counter for the coffee.

I watch him go with a sense of longing burning through my veins. He's bad news. It's written in the way he makes me feel more alive than I have in a very long time. It's nearly impossible to fight the pull I feel toward him, hard as I've tried. Case in point, I declined dinner with him, but ended up bringing a meal to his door not too long after. Also, there's a perfectly likable man—Kenny—in the store, and Mr. Hill is here, too, but I can't see anyone but Dawson. It's not that I want to stay away, it's that I *need* to. Guys who evoke a small response from me are safe. Guys who make me feel the way Dawson does, aren't.

I made three rules when I left everything behind to move to Darlington.

One, never let them find you.

Two, cover all tracks.

Three, don't ache for another man again.

A simple attraction is fine. Serves its purpose, casual vacancies to fill a need, but nothing else. As I watch Dawson walk away, pants snug in all the right places, ball cap low, and a slight hitch to his lips suggesting he's fighting a grin, I realize I've done it.

I've already broken one rule.

That evening, I do as Mr. Hill suggested and call the vet. They fit me in, which is how I end up in a cold metal chair at closing time, talking to Dr. Boyd.

"I'm sorry, Camille," he says. "It's an unfortunate situation. Most owners welcome their lost animals home."

I scowl. "I have a feeling he's not really *lost*."

The vet's look tells me he's thinking the same thing.

"How could the man let him go and not care?" I stroke the cat's fur, whom I've given the name Wizard.

One scan of his microchip confirmed that he's a ten-year-old short hair, adopted two years ago by a man who hadn't considered that the cat's claws might present a problem for his inside furniture. So, he let Wizard—who used to go by the name Felix—outside and stopped feeding him.

Wizard has been surviving on his own for a year and a half, and nothing is known of his life before the last adoption.

"He really doesn't want him back?"

Dr. Boyd closes Wizard's file. He's healthy and seemingly

happy. A bit on the thin side, nothing a better diet won't fix.

Also, he's homeless.

"No, I'm sorry," he replies. "We can catch him up on vaccinations and try to adopt him out."

Wizard's tail brushes against my cheek as he snuggles into my sweater.

"Unless you'd like to keep him."

Wizard meows.

"I don't want him to go to a bad home." The last thing he needs is to go hungry in winter. "Can you assure me he'll be adopted into a happy home?"

"You know I can't," he murmurs gently. "We try, really, we do, vetting homes, but there is no guarantee."

I figured he'd say that.

"Before you go, I'll give him these." He holds up vials of vaccinations. "You're welcome to foster him while we figure things out."

He administers the shots. Wizard doesn't seem to mind.

"I'll keep him for now."

Dr. Boyd chuckles, tossing the empty vials into a biohazard container. "For now, or forever?"

Purse on one arm, Wizard in the other, I pause.

"I could write your name on his file and be done with it. We'll give you a call when he's due back for an annual visit if you'd like."

I sigh and accept the inevitable. My stare trained on the pen next to the folder, I nod and confirm what he and I already saw coming. I don't need to be adopting animals. I never planned to. I moved to Darlington to be alone. No strings attached.

"Damn it," I mumble, earning a belly laugh from the doctor.

As much as I've tried to tread lightly, it seems I've already left footprints.

EIGHT

Before

The blue, overhead lights flicker throughout the club like they suffer from faulty wiring, winking at the man in the tailored suit. Impeccably dressed, he draws eyes, as his table often does. Women want to catch his attention—it's no secret he owns the club—perhaps hoping for a chance to garner one of the coveted spots in his employment. If not that, then they want in his bed, or to cozy up to his more legendary clientele—professional athletes, actors and actresses, musicians—whatever gets them closer to Miami's lifestyle of the rich and famous. His club is the hotspot for them all. He realizes many of the potential prospects *hole up in tiny, shitty apartments with one, two, sometimes three or four roommates, dreaming of sprawling mansions and beachfront properties. Envisaging city condos bedecked in elegance, and people to cater to their every need. The women want to walk into the club dripping in jewels gifted by him, as he's been known to do. He smiles at the thought. The leeches. He sees them for what they are, not that he minds a little fun here and there. They truly believe they have a shot, and therefore they'll give him anything.*

"Hey, sugar," a thirty-something purrs, winking at him. "Heard you're free tonight."

The other men at the table don't pay the woman any mind. One is his cousin, dressed more laid back than him in jeans and a button-down, and one is his hit man, or what others refer to as a "bodyguard," dressed in all black and wearing a stoic expression.

"Care for company?" she asks.

The VIP area is for his guests only, and for nights like tonight when he sends his scouts to search the club for his type. She made the cut.

"Perhaps," he says, reaching for his glass.

Scotch, neat. Nothing else. Always the same, and always from the trusted bartender who works solely on drinks for him and whoever he allows in his section. He doesn't trust any of the others. He pays the bartender—a redheaded woman who has no interest in drawing his attention—well enough to work long, late shift hours on the five nights he visits the club. She knows her schedule and never takes time off, sick or not, emergency or not, she shows up. He likes that about her.

His cousin smiles. The woman in front of him, who has now blocked his view of the club by bending low enough toward him that he can see straight down her slinky top, which he knows she's done on purpose, offers his cousin a look that promises second place should the man turn her down.

From the other side of the VIP, a petite brunette eyes him. He glances at the dark pocket of the room, waiting for the flickering light to hit her just right again. When it does, he takes interest in her toned legs and tiny black cocktail dress. Even though her siren red stilettos are inches high, she can't be more than five foot four.

"Another night," he tells her, waving the thirty-something on. She doesn't lose steam, deciding instead to drop into the lap of his cousin who, at four years younger than his thirty-two, is about a decade younger than the woman. Matters none. She'll spend the same between the sheets.

He stands and makes his way over to the brunette, whom he now sees is talking to a friend.

"Hi," he drawls, flashing a smile that's part friendly, part feral.

"Hi," she replies.

Her friend whispers something in her ear, and then leaves them alone.

"Enjoying yourself?" he questions, drink in hand.

Unless he's at his usual table, he never sets his glass down. There's far too great a chance someone could slip something into it, and he prides himself on not being caught off guard.

The brunette glances around the club, taking in a view he's seen thousands of times—painted gold walls with a bar stretching across one of them, filled with liquor bottles and wine glasses. Tap beer is available, but most choose the hard stuff. The metal counters gleam, the edge of which meets a waterfall encased in glass that drops off down the front of the bar. Tiled, smoke gray floors are topped with wraparound couches, plush chairs, and round tables with an ice bucket centerpiece, a bottle of wine in each. Down below, on the bottom floor, people dance and party.

"Yes," she answers.

Her hair curls at the tips and just barely brushes her breasts. He leans into her.

"Good. You should see the back. Would you like a tour?" he asks.

Her eyes wander over to the door that leads to the infamous quarters only a select few experience. He waves to the bartender to get the woman another drink. She's on it, mixing liquid in a short glass, topping it with four ice cubes, and sliding it down the bar. He grabs it and hands it to the woman, exchanging it for her now empty one.

"I'd love a tour."

She takes a long pull from the iced liquor and maintains eye contact.

"What's your name?" he inquires.

"Sarah."

Her tone has a roughened, honey texture, the type that draws men in enough to want to hear that voice in the bedroom, calling out their name.

"Follow me, Sarah."

His timbre is warm butterscotch and makes her squirm. Her

jade eyes peer up at him as he guides her through a door and into the back. It's more spectacular than the front. Chandeliers hang from the ceiling, jewels hitting the recessed lighting just right, refracting like bits of diamonds cascading down the walls. The short walk is narrow, and soon they come to a closed black door.

He motions forward and she opens it. The room within contains floors covered in marble and woven rugs from countries around the world. Royal purple is interspersed throughout the decor—a basket with flowers floating in water, a painting over the mantelpiece, and pillows against the lavish leather couch. It's an apartment where he likes to take women. One bedroom sits off to the back, dominated by a single, California king-sized bed.

Sarah's eyes go to the kitchen, where there's a fresh tray of cheese and crackers, and another of vegetables.

"Are you hungry?" he queries.

Her eyes flicker over his body. Yes, she's hungry all right.

"I'm okay, thanks."

He smiles. "Let me show you the view."

When he presses a button on the wall, the shade is gone. In its place stands a sweeping outlook of Miami, its lit-up buildings like multicolored flashlights pointed toward the sky. Her intake of breath is immediate. Her muscles relax.

"Wow," she murmurs.

"No one can see in," he whispers. "That's part of the beauty. It's mirrored to the outside world."

He pushes her hair over one shoulder, pressing himself against her. She's all soft curves. He's hard muscle.

He finally sets his drink down on a side table, finished, and lets his hands rest on her hips.

"You know who I am," he says.

He's known since the moment he asked her name. She didn't ask his.

She looks back at him and bites her lower lip. "Yes."

"What is it you want?"

If it's commitment, he's done. He'll be happy to show her to the door. But most already know that.

"Money is tight," she tells him. "I was wondering if you have a job opening."

He appreciates the way she holds her head high and looks him directly in the eyes. In fact, he appreciates it so much he actually laughs.

"You're willing to do whatever it takes for a job?"

"I happen to be single," she reasons. "I thought tonight could be fun. If you had any openings, that would be great, too. But if not, I'll walk away after having a night of free drinks, seeing a view of Miami that only few have, and hopefully feeling sated."

He likes the woman.

"Do you have club experience?" The corners of his lips tip upward. "Please tell me you at least know what you're doing."

"Ten years' worth," she answers. "I've worked in clubs since my sixteenth birthday, thanks to a fake ID. I need more, a place like this, where money flows in rivers. The clientele here doesn't compare to my other job where it's hard to make a decent living off tips."

Her presentation is crisp and to the point, businesslike. This is an approach he appreciates.

"I have a downstairs bartending position open for Wednesday nights only. It's yours if you want it. Come in during the day and ask for Raciel. He'll show you everything. You'll train for a month. I don't accept anything less than the best, no excuses, no exceptions. Can't keep up, you're out. Look at and speak to men the way you are with me, and they'll hand their money over for whatever expensive drinks you suggest. Can you handle that?"

She sighs gratefully. "I have a sister with extensive medical debt, a nephew who requires speech therapy, and so many bills to pay that I can hardly stop from drowning in them. I am more than grateful. You've handed me a lifeline."

Indeed, he has. "Even at only one day a week, you'll make thousands a month in tips alone. Just be sure to keep up."

"I will. Thank you," she murmurs.

He releases her. "You're free to go, if you wish."

But it's clear she doesn't want to leave. The look she gives him says she'd prefer to enjoy the relief coursing through her veins, and that she's sure he will know just how to help her finish the evening.

Instead, she turns and clasps the side zipper of her skintight dress. With one movement, it pools at her feet, leaving her in only heels and a matching black lace bra and underwear.

He shrugs off his jacket and tie. His shirt, shoes, and pants follow.

"Come back tomorrow for the job. Don't disappoint."

Her hands wander to his briefs, slowly tracing the outline of him.

"No problem. Can I at least know your first name, Mr. Cruz?"

They all feel a need to ask. His answer is still the same.

"No, you may not. In all cases, you are to address me like you just did, understand?"

She nods.

"One last thing," he demands. "Speak of this night to no one."

"I wouldn't dare," she replies.

He believes her.

NINE

Dawson

My breath puffs into the air and dissolves like mist, leaving a stinging cold bite in the back of my throat. As my knuckles rap on the wooden door to Camille's place, I notice her through the window, her nose in a novel, feet propped against the brick ledge of the fireplace that's heavy with logs and a thick flame. A cat is curled beside it. I don't remember seeing it before now.

She sets the book down and spots me, her eyes settling on mine.

"Hi." She opens the door.

"Hey, can I come in?"

She debates it for a minute, eyes squinting, a skittish look to her, making me think she doesn't like the idea of me in her place, but finally she sweeps a hand toward the quaint living room.

"Thanks." I smile and am rewarded with a loosening of her features.

I step inside. She seems to relax when I look around in wonder.

"This is amazing," I say.

Everything is quaint and old, but charming.

Camille grins at my compliment, and I try not to focus on her dimples. In another place, another time, I would reach for her and kiss each dimple, and then lose myself in the feel of her skin. She doesn't make it easy. Not with the delicate perfume she wears. Not with the way she quickly licks her lips. Not even with the placement of freckles just over one collarbone. I wonder what it'd be like to trace them.

"I wanted to thank you for getting me a job," I say.

Hopefully, I can keep the job. As far as I know, my fake ID should pass any background check, if the old man even plans to do one. It definitely passed Camille's check, because I'm still here. Something tells me the old man may not even do one, though, seeing as how he simply wrote down my ID info and handed it back to me. There was an application, of course, but that was easy enough. One page. Under work history, I put military. He hasn't followed up more than that.

I learned that Kenny is an awesome guy. He likes to

encourage his employees and never has anything negative to say. He's the type of friend I'd want if I decided to make any here in Darlington. I owe Camille for it all.

"You're welcome." She takes a seat in the chair by the fire.

I can't help but notice the way her eyes drink me in. I sit on the couch opposite her. The angle allows me a glimpse of what I assume is her room. Every wall, except for a single spot for a window, is lined with bookshelves and endless paperback spines.

"You read a lot," I observe.

"I do." She follows my stare. "There's a great used bookstore not too far. Matter of fact, they have an entire wall of books for one dollar. For every eight you buy, you get one free."

She seems strangely proud of her collection, and there's a note of fondness in her tone.

"I don't have cable. I have only two neighbors. There is no library here. As you'll soon realize, if you stay in Darlington, there's not much to do. Reading passes the time."

"But you have a television. Don't you want cable?" I glance at the device all her furniture faces.

"No. The place came with the television. The previous owners left it along with a couple chairs and a table. I suppose I could have gotten rid of it. I guess keeping it in the room is an old habit," she whispers, a faraway look coming over her features as though she can gaze straight into the past if she tries hard enough.

She fidgets, her hands running along the arms of the chair, and changes the subject.

"Anyhow, congrats on the job. Word of advice, though, Mr. Hill disappoints easily. If you're lazy, entitled, or slow, don't be. He expects the best."

I have never been lazy, entitled, or slow in my entire life, but instead of explaining this to Camille, I nod. The old man will just have to see some things for himself.

"Are you liking Darlington?" she inquires. "Do you think you'll stick around?"

"I like it, yes. Maybe enough to stay."

For now.

"At least until I finish your landscaping," I add. "Speaking of, I think I should remove some of the fallen logs. I was exploring the property the other day and found several piles."

"Could you drop the useable firewood by the side of the house? I'll chop it later. You know the difference between usable and not, right?"

"Yes." Only because I was a boy scout once upon a time. I haven't been to a forested area in a while, and to be quite honest, I'm rusty with my wilderness techniques, but I have a feeling it's a skill that boomerangs back easily.

"Good. You can have some, too, of course, for bonfires if you like that sort of thing."

I marvel over the fact that Camille chops her own wood. The amount of firewood she uses would have her chopping almost daily. Unless she prefers large quantities, which means she'd have to chop for long hours a couple times a week. Either way, it's quite the workout.

"What about after the branches?" I ask.

"There are a few bushes I want pulled up. I'd like to try to plant a small patch of corn next year and I need the plot cleared."

She plants her own vegetables, lives simply, and chops firewood. Everything about this small town—and her—is foreign to me. I lean forward. Her place is quaint enough that this puts me only a couple of feet from her.

"Camille," I murmur.

She looks up. "Yes?"

"Tell me something about yourself."

What I know so far is that she enjoys the seclusion of her property, she seems to like working for the old man, she's sometimes friendly with one of the servers, a woman named Bonnie from the diner who occasionally comes over to Camille's side of the store to chat on her short breaks from the busy restaurant, and she's sociable with her neighbors, but not many other people.

I wait, wondering if she'll humor me. When she does, it's not what I expected.

"I'm sort of discovering myself as I go," she tells me. "I didn't have the best upbringing. A lot of people form who they are from a young age, but not me. I'm doing it now."

I nod. Her answer makes perfect sense. "And what have you discovered?"

She grins. "That I like reading, farming, and apparently feeding wild animals. I prefer small places to big ones. Loneliness is in the heart, not the place. I thought moving here would be lonely, but it's not. It's freeing."

She doesn't seem to be finished with her list of discoveries, which is fine because I'm happy to listen to her divulge more.

"I hate dog-eared pages. I prefer hardcover to paperback. I'm not good at baking pies, but I make a mean veggie casserole. I love Mr. Hill like I would a father, if I ever had one."

Her eyes widen.

"I can't believe I said that," she whispers.

She shakes her head in surprise.

"And I guess I've now adopted a cat," she adds, moving on, glancing at the black feline curled up on the mantle. "I swear I don't know how this happened."

I bite back a grin. She has a soft spot for the cat, but she's not at all happy about it.

"Your turn," she declares. "Tell me something about you."

I don't mind that she redirected the topic. It's only fair, after all. I can keep the main things hidden, giving her only little pieces. Not enough to draw interest.

"I prefer old to new. I'm good with automobiles. I have one of the longest, successful target shots in the army. I'm loyal, competitive, and I hold on to the things that matter. I can't stand bananas, for some reason, and my favorite fruit is kiwi. Is that enough for you?"

I like what my answer has done to Camille. Her features melt into a softer form. Wood chips pop and crumble in the fire. The warmth, combined with the densely dark background sky peeking through her window and the small space between

Camille and me, makes the silent moment feel intimate.

As though thinking the same thing, Camille clears her throat.

"So," she starts with an air of finality. "Thanks for stopping by. Good luck with the new job."

She moves to the door. I stand slowly. The heat of the fire makes me sluggish, and for the first time in a while, I'm truly tired enough that I may get a good night's rest. My thoughts, surprisingly, are quiet. I take one more look around her place and commit everything I see to memory. Even the cracks in the floorboards and the framed landscape photos on the wall.

I squeeze past Camille on my way out of the door, but instead of walking outside, I take one step toward her. Our bodies touch and she inhales sharply, as though the now falling snow itself has pressed against her soft curves instead of my hard-earned muscles. This is the gray area I wasn't sure I was willing to cross, but I can't seem to stay away.

"Goodnight," she whispers, making the decision for me.

I fight the pull of attraction.

"Goodnight." I peel myself back.

It's no easy task. Actually, it's downright painful.

TEN

Camille

I don't care for the attraction I feel for Dawson. But it's just that—deep attraction. A feeling. Not an action. I must be very careful to never make it an action. I wake up with these thoughts on my mind.

The phone on my bedside table rings. I see Mr. Hill's number across the screen. He doesn't ordinarily call on my days off. I wipe sleep from my eyes and answer, surprised to see that I've actually slept in until nine. A miracle.

"Hello?"

Mr. Hill forgoes a greeting altogether. "The news station is coming today. Forcing me to do that interview about the damn town fall festival. Wants to get a local's take on the festivities this year. I tell you, I don't much care about the festival, but this time every year that anchorwoman comes round, interviews me for five minutes, and features our store name and location. Business triples for the entire month thanks to her, and you know how the end of fall and all of winter slows down some, so I suppose I ought to give her five minutes, don't you?" He hardly takes a breath between sentences. "Although, I think you're much more of a people person than I am. Is there any way I can get you to fill in for me and go on local television?"

Not if I want to live to tell the tale.

"No," I state firmly.

Mr. Hill sighs and it sounds like he mumbles, "Didn't think so," before his voice comes back on the line. "All right. Well, could you maybe come in and watch the bait shop, then?"

The bait shop is nothing more than a room off the back of the store where Mr. Hill sells night crawlers and crickets and small baitfish to the locals who want to fish the ponds.

"You think you'll have bait customers in the little time the news station is there?" I question. Otherwise, it seems pointless for me to come in. Matter of fact, maybe he can just close the shop for an hour. People would understand.

"I already have someone comin'. You remember Dennis down the road? Has a big pond and charges people a flat rate to fish from it all day. Well, he called and said someone booked his pond and he was sending him or her our way for bait. They'll be here soon, and I'll be in the interview. Dawson's here. Mighty fine worker, that one. Don't tell him I told you, though. That boy is worth way more than what I pay him and if you tell him, he might get it in his mind to ask for more. Thought 'bout requesting he watch the bait shop, but I'm not sure I want him handlin' the money. Don't know him well enough yet."

"What about one of the servers from the diner?" I suggest. "Bonnie is trustworthy."

Mr. Hill grunts. "Yeah, but the diner is slammed. I can't take one of Rose's employees in the middle of a rush. I'll never hear the end of it. Can you do it? Thirty minutes, that's all."

I suppose helping would be safe since I'd be in the back, nowhere near the cameras. Not that anyone but locals would watch the show anyhow, but I still like to be careful.

"Okay," I concede. "But it's going to cost you a bushel of apples."

Fruit trees are something I don't have on the property, and something Mr. Hill has many of on his.

"Deal." He hangs up without another word.

Adrenaline courses through my veins, the worry of avoiding the news station fresh on my mind.

ELEVEN

Dawson

Each time I swing the hammer, the sound pings off of the tree bark like a song.

I've ripped down more than half of the shed. I didn't realize so much of it would be rotten. Several pieces are infested with holes where wasps laid their larva and woodpeckers drilled away, ruining the structure.

I don't see why the old man doesn't just replace the whole thing. Only, actually, I think maybe I do understand. Perhaps he prefers not to pay for something new when there's enough spare wood to patch it up, though it takes longer. The planks aren't the same color, but by the time I finish painting, they will be.

I need a glass of water. I swallow the last drops from the cup of sweet tea the old man left for me from Rose's Diner, still parched. Sweat drips down my bare chest and stomach. My shirt lies forgotten on the ground. Manual labor makes my muscles ache, but I enjoy the burn. Sixty-two degrees feels good on my skin, especially with the wind occasionally making an appearance.

I've already helped replace the store's roof and removed all of the contents from the shed. Now that I see them outside, they somehow look bigger than they did in the cramped quarters, and I wonder how they all fit. I've swept cobwebs, killed a handful of spiders, and removed three live nests of wasps and one yellow jacket, and only managed to get stung once.

I've ripped down rotten pieces of wood and chucked them into the trash pile I've started. Even some of the shed roof has come down. It's heavy work, but the old man agreed to pay me decent, so there's that.

Kenny's still working like a mule on the roof, but the guy whose place I took for a few days is back from vacation. He doesn't need me there. The old man has shifted my focus to the sheds. In the time it took on the roof, I learned that Kenny likes to visit the bar most evenings, where he spends half his day's pay. But I suppose being twenty-seven with no wife and kids and nothing much else to do, he really only has the options to go fishing, go home, or go drink. Drinking's his first choice, but he does talk about apple picking and stopping at the town square, too. So, I suppose he's like most guys around here. Living simply.

Speaking of, Kenny comes into view. His orange hair is as bright as a copper penny, and his frame is solidly built from slaving so often on rooftops. He's a short guy, but he makes up for it with his boisterous personality.

"Dawson!" he calls. "The old man's got you working out here, huh?"

He wipes his dirty hands on his white shirt, which has begun to look grayer than anything.

"Yep." I swing the hammer again.

"Wanna grab a drink later?"

This is the third time he's asked. Maybe it wouldn't be such a bad idea.

"Sure."

Kenny pauses, startled, before recovering. "'Bout time."

His face splits into a grin. He's been asking throughout the week, ever since I started working at the general store.

I gaze at the line of sheds behind the store. The old man wasn't kidding when he mentioned needing help. There are seven others, all larger than the one I'm currently working on. I expect by the end of the day, I'll be finished installing the new wood and maybe the roof. I'll throw a tarp over the pile of junk I've left outside in case it rains or snows, though the weather isn't calling for either for at least a few days.

"I don't get off until six, though," I tell him. "How about I meet you in town at eight?"

That'll give me a couple of hours to get to the camper, and grab a shower and a bite to eat.

He points at me. "I'll see you there. It's called Water's Edge. Big, lit up green sign. You'll know the place when you see it. And fair warning, a couple of the guys from work will probably be there, too. Like Billy. Don't try to kill him this time."

I almost laugh. Billy is a grungy kid, just barely twenty-one, who got on my very last nerve, talking about this woman and that woman and how great he is at the work he does and just about anything else to annoy the shit out of me the entire time I helped replace leaky shingles, so I "accidentally" bumped into him on my last day. I knew it wasn't hard enough to hurt him—there's no way he would have actually fallen— but it was enough to make him topple a couple feet down the slope of the roof and scare the guy into silence. Kenny saw right through my "accident."

"Eight o'clock. Don't think about canceling. I'll drive to that cute girl's house and make you join us."

He knows I live on Camille's property. Everyone pretty much does. But I didn't realize he's attracted to her, too. Damn it.

"I'll be there," I assure him. Last thing I want to do is have people over. I like my space.

Kenny hops in his shiny Ford and drives off with a wave. I get back to work, hoping that going out for a few drinks might actually be fun. I'm still thinking about it when I hear her voice.

"Hey, stranger."

I pause, a shiver licking through me.

"Hi, Camille," I reply, my back turned to her.

I'd recognize her voice anywhere. It does a number on me when I'm only half dressed.

Hammer in one hand, in less clothes than is safe around her, I turn. Her eyes are glued to my stomach. She doesn't seem to want to get them unstuck.

"What are you doing here?"

Far as I know, she's off. Another guy is working the cash register. I've seen him take over shifts when Camille clocks out. I'd place him in his mid-twenties. He's definitely popular with the ladies that come through the store, with his quick smile and compliments. From small bits of conversation I've overheard when grabbing a drink or a snack, he seems to know the appeal he has with them.

Camille attempts to tuck a flyaway curl behind her ear, but it rebels and bounces back into her face.

"Mr. Hill asked me to watch the bait shop," she answers.

My eyes skip over her dress, my gaze stopping at her knees where the hem does, noting the pair of leggings underneath and boots. A long necklace dangles at the perfect spot between her breasts, with a pendant that looks like miniature cow horns resting just so.

I've learned that the old man also owns a café in a town just outside of Darlington, which he hardly ever visits because someone else runs it for him, but I've never heard of the bait shop.

"Where's the bait shop?" I ask.

She points to a square structure jutting from the back of the building a few yards from the shed, explaining away my curiosity regarding the door I'd wondered about earlier.

"He's expecting a bait customer soon and he'll be busy. So, I'm here." She glances at the truck that's pulling up, a smile forming on her face.

Her dimples sink into her cheeks, making me ache.

"Hey, Luke. Fancy seeing you here," she greets, addressing the man who steps from the driver's side.

He grins at her, and I don't miss the appreciation in his eyes, quickly there and then gone.

"Booked Dennis's pond for fishing."

Camille laughs. "Don't know how you stand the bait smell, personally."

"You just don't like worms, is all. They smell just fine."

As I watch the banter between Camille and the man, I realize I've stopped working. It's not my business whom she talks to, so I get back to it. When I begin hammering, Camille motions for Luke to follow her into the bait room.

She unlocks the door, and it groans open on arthritic hinges, allowing their entrance. They don't emerge until a few minutes later, Camille with a hand to her eyes to block the sun, and Luke with a bucket of what I assume is baitfish and a container of worms.

"See you next time," Luke calls, tipping his hat to her before climbing into his truck and driving away.

Camille watches him go.

"Boyfriend?" I inquire, and then mentally kick myself. I continue to hammer nails into the planks, hoping it'll relieve the tension that seems to be winding itself around my spine.

"No. Just a local."

"Really? Seems like you know him personally."

It's in the way she looked at him and in the way he walked right up to her side, sure of his movements and proximity to her.

Camille stiffens. "Nope. Like I said, just a local."

She's lying.

Why would she lie to me?

I stop hammering and peer at her. "Are you sure he doesn't want to be more than a local?"

Perhaps I read their closeness wrong. I'm usually pretty good at assessing people. Maybe they're secretly good friends. Why not make that known, though? He isn't just some local she doesn't really know.

"He's a customer, that's all. I see him around sometimes." Camille's voice is light. "Anyway, I'm heading back to the house."

Just as she turns to go, a van pulls up with antennas jutting from the roof. The doors open, and a man in regular clothes and a woman in a skirt, silky blouse, and pearls with a microphone in hand step from the vehicle. Camille glances around wildly, as though she's looking for somewhere to hide. The shed is see-through, thanks to so many missing boards. She rushes to the bait shop and slips quickly inside. I just barely make it in behind her as she pulls the door closed.

"Why are there cameras and a news station van out

front?" I ask.

"They came to film Mr. Hill for the annual town festival hype." She peers at me under the dim lights, her breath shaky. "I don't understand why they'd film the back of the store."

Voices near the door answer the question on both of our minds.

"Get a sweep of the grounds," directs the female. "Don't forget to record a shot of the front as well, including the sign, before we do the interview. That should be enough for the location piece."

Camille reaches for the lock on the door and flips it into place. She doesn't seem to want them nearby.

"Mind telling me what this is about?" I question. "Why did you hide?"

Camille bites her lip nervously. "It's a long story that I don't want to rehash. I can't announce my location to the world, or however far this news station audience reaches."

A bit of truth from her.

"Okay, fair enough." I take a second to look around. "Doesn't anyone clean this place?"

There's a stain on a wooden worktable that looks suspiciously like old, dried fish guts. Lures hang on the wall in no particular order, some of them dusty, as though no one has handled them in ages. One circular apparatus, reminiscent of a tall bathtub, holds hundreds of small fish, swimming back and forth in the murky water. The filter gurgles noisily. I'd be willing to bet it needs replacing. Across from it, a wooden crate with a mesh wire frame contains tons of buzzing crickets, the source of the sour smell. Camille had mentioned worms, and I know exactly where they're kept because I can hear them moving inside containers just by my head, stacked several to a shelf.

She glances at the mess. "Mr. Hill really ought to add this to your list. There is definitely no shortage of work to be done around here."

I wonder if she knows how sexy she looks with the hazy light bouncing off her curls, and a pinch between her brows.

She gives it another silent minute before unlocking the door and peeking out. She checks both ways and waits a few breaths for good measure before determining that the parking lot is clear of news people, though the van remains. They must be inside, conducting the interview Camille had mentioned.

"I have to run," she says.

I nod, watching her slip out quietly. She leaves me alone. I glance to where the van still sits, hoping that the reporter's time spent inside the store is brief. To be safe, I lock the door. Until she and the cameraman are gone, I vow to stay inside the bait shop. I don't want to take the chance of running into the reporter. I can't be on television either. Camille isn't the only one trying to hide her location.

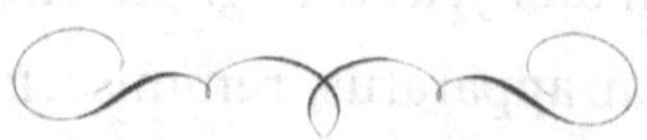

Water's Edge is a narrow tavern with a stage at one end, big enough for a stool and the guy atop, strumming a guitar and playing solo acoustic. A long bar stretches against the wall with endless, glittering bottles of alcohol behind it. Everywhere else is seating. They've somehow managed to fit a single pool table in the mix, people crowding it.

"So, this is the place," I remark.

Kenny looks as though he's already been drinking a while, his eyes glassy, his smile just a little wider than normal. At least he's a happy drunk, it seems.

"Yep! Best bar in town," he replies.

Kegs line the floor behind the counter, and there's a wide selection on tap above with spouts pouring frothy liquid into chilled mugs. I know from driving in that it's one of three bars on a tiny swath of road, each competing against the other. Two looked pretty grimy—the one I'm standing in included—and one seemed more upscale, with modern décor that actually has a design to it, clearly visible through its sweeping windows, unlike Water's Edge, which is a mash-up of old stuff.

My eyes fall upon the reason this must be dubbed the "best bar in town." A bartender rushes out from the back, hooking up a new keg line, and another pops out from below the counter, hauling up fresh glasses. I almost laugh at the way Kenny's eyes take on an exaggerated roundness.

"So," I begin, "do those bartenders have anything to do with this being the 'best place?'"

Kenny chuckles. "Might have something to do with it."

We approach the table where Billy and Dwayne wait, two of Kenny's workers I met while helping replace shingles. I try to ignore Billy the best I can, but Dwayne seems decent enough. I relax into one of four seats.

There aren't any servers. This is, apparently, the type of establishment where patrons approach the bar if they want a drink, and where they snag a table and keep it all night. It's not hard to feel the place out upon first impression.

"Which one are you seeing?" I ask, nodding toward the employees.

It must be one of the well-endowed bartenders, both of whom are wearing very little clothing and happily showing off their killer bodies.

Dwayne, a guy with dark skin, built as big as a linebacker, laughs loudly. "He's already got you figured, Kenny. Told you it was obvious."

For the first time, I see Kenny frown. "We're not together anymore as of a few months ago. But we were a couple for years."

From his tone, I'd bet he wishes they still were.

"Yet you can't help coming to see her practically every day," Billy comments, taking a gulp of his beer. "You should date her friend over there in the meantime."

"The other bartender?" I question. Of course, Billy would say something like that. Doesn't he realize Kenny will never have a shot at the girl if he dates her friend? The friend probably wouldn't go for it either.

"Yep," Billy replies. "That's the one. Cheyenne and Angel. Practically sisters. Angel, the one Kenny likes, grew up on the farm across from his property."

Kenny finishes his beer. "She used to ride horses. I begged my parents for extra chores on the farm just to spend more time watching her fly like the wind. She's good at it. She's even won competitions."

He's smiling again, which is encouraging, but then he goes to set his empty mug on the table and misses. I'm surprised it doesn't shatter when it hits the floor.

"Did you drive here, Kenny?" I inquire.

"Nope. Dwayne's in charge tonight."

I glance at Dwayne, trying to assess if he's in any condition to drive, because Kenny definitely isn't, and it's only a little after eight.

"My first and likely only one," Dwayne offers, lifting his mug, nursing the dark stout.

"Well," I say to Kenny, "I'm going to grab a beer."

I nod to the bar and Kenny is all too happy to oblige me. My hand dips into my back pocket and emerges with my wallet as we approach the selection. I decide on something light, because I do need to drive home in a couple of hours. The other girl—Cheyenne, I think Billy called her—turns around with a beer in hand, giving it to a patron and accepting his tip. Her eyes home in on me, a smile playing on her lips.

"You're new," she says by way of greeting.

"This is my friend, Dawson," Kenny informs her.

Cheyenne leans over the bar. Her black hair falls in cascading waves to her waist, and her eyes are the lightest shade of brown. I can see why she attracts customers.

"Nice to meet you, Dawson. I'm Cheyenne." She smiles coyly. "Rule of the bar: if it's your first time, drink's on us."

"I don't remember that being the rule," Kenny interjects.

Either it is the rule and Kenny has been a regular so long that he's forgotten, or the bartender wants to buy me a drink. Both work for me. I pull a couple of dollars from my wallet before replacing it in my pocket. I leave the tip on the counter.

"I'll have a Corona Light," I request.

"Lime?" she asks.

My eyes zero in on her red lips. Damn, I'm a sucker for red lips. But instead of it being a nice distraction, I'm reminded of Camille. Her perfect mouth. I take a small step back. Cheyenne's eyes go to my left hand. I wonder if she's searching for a wedding band. She won't find one. But that's not the reason I'm hesitant. No, that goes to Camille, even though there's probably no chance of anything happening between us.

"Lime's good," I reply, glancing away.

I don't want to give her the wrong impression. And, hell, maybe this is how she always is, flirting with customers for tips, licking her lips the way she just did to draw my gaze.

"Coming right up."

Out of the corner of my eye, I watch her turn away, grab a mug, and pour.

"Bud Light, Kenny?" she questions over her shoulder. "Or you want Angel to pour it for you?"

Kenny turns beet red.

The other woman, Angel, approaches. She looks like her

namesake. Exaggerated cherub blue eyes, straight blonde hair, and pale skin. "I've got it, Chy."

She pours Kenny's beer and slides it across the bar to him. Their eyes meet. Something unspoken passes between them. It's none of my business what happened to their relationship, but I'd bet a hundred bucks they're not over yet, despite whatever differences they seem to be having at the moment.

Kenny reaches for it and trails a finger across her hand. I look away and accept my beer. As I begin to walk back to the table, Cheyenne catches my gaze.

"Married?" she asks, straight to the point.

"No," I reply honestly.

"Divorced? Separated?"

"No and no."

"Taken?" She arches an eyebrow.

"Nope."

She smiles. "Maybe I'll see you around again, then? I work six nights a week. Off Sundays."

I nod and head back to my seat. I wish it was that simple for me.

"So, Cheyenne dug her claws in you?" Dwayne drawls with a grin.

He must have been watching.

"Something like that," I reply.

"She's cool, in case you were considering it. She doesn't do relationships, though, so if you're looking for one, you won't find it with her."

I'm not looking for a relationship.

"So, Dwayne, how long have you been married?" I inquire, changing the subject, noticing the gold band on his finger.

He smiles wide. "Five years. I have a little girl. She's two. Best thing that's ever happened to me. She's asleep by seven each night, which is why I sometimes join these fools and give them rides home."

But I can tell by his demeanor that he likes having time with his friends, too.

"I swear," he continues. "One day, seven years ago" —I mentally do the math, thinking that must have put him at about twenty-three or so— "I walked into the DMV needing to get a tag for my truck and there she was. The most beautiful woman I'd ever seen. A supervising manager. I fell in love that instant. There was never anyone else for me."

He gets a dreamy look that tells me he means every word.

"Damn it, Dwayne," Billy complains. "What did I tell you about being sappy? No one wants to hear that."

"You'll fall in love some day and, then—" Dwayne cuts himself off, and this time he, Kenny, and I laugh. The thought of Billy being in love, and anyone having the patience to deal with him, is absurd. "Never mind. That probably won't happen."

Billy mumbles something about us being assholes, but he's smiling about it.

I let my eyes roam the bar again. I can't help it. It's part of my training, of what I've known my whole life. Constantly assess your surroundings. Be vigilant. The more I observe, the more I realize the establishment does have charm, but it seems to be in the antiquity. Nothing is new. I imagine you could have walked in thirty years ago and come back today, feeling like a single aspect hasn't changed, aside from the employees. Maybe that's the way people like it.

The place seems to get busier by the minute, with patrons practically standing over our table, but I don't mind. Because here, no one knows the real me. For once in my life, I can relax.

TWELVE

Camille

"Hey, Will."

My voice rings across the creek that separates the two properties. Will swings from a hammock in the trees, banjo in hand, wearing denim overalls with a faded shirt beneath. A foot below him, resting on the ground, is a jug of iced tea and a pack of smokes. He doesn't care much that his life could be cut short by the tobacco he consumes.

"Brought you something," I tell him, as I maneuver from rock to rock, crossing the water without getting wet, careful to watch my step. The air holds the scent of wet stone and dank soil.

I look forward to our monthly exchange. Feels like Christmas twelve times a year. Seeing as how there aren't many people around these parts, I enjoy the occasional company.

I remove the backpack from my shoulders and drop it to the ground. It's the only way I'm able to haul the medium-sized, heavy pumpkin and a couple of onions just pulled from the dirt this morning, still smelling of freshly turned earth.

The release of weight causes me to sigh. I rub my shoulders, easing the ache.

"And for you." He withdraws a sack from beside him and flicks the ashes of his cigarette into the leaves. His offering is considerably smaller than mine, but that's because his crop is harder to come by.

I open it and find close to a hundred huckleberries.

"Thank you," I murmur, taking a seat amongst twigs.

Will nods and presses out his smoke before lifting the banjo and plucking a few strings. When he begins singing, I get lost in the twang of his voice, the soft earthy tones with a grassroots feel.

I first came across Will easily enough when exploring my newly bought property. He had been picking strawberries and offered me the bushel. I knew instantly he had a kind soul. One that, for whatever reason, craved solitude. He lives alone by preference. He also comes to see me on the fifteenth of every month at 10:00 am. That's the time he told me to meet him once, and it's been the same ever since. When I don't have gourds, I offer him herbs and spices, green beans, or whatever peppers I happen to be growing on the windowsill.

Will finishes the song on a high note in his southern drawl before plopping the banjo down.

I clap and earn a smile from him.

"So, who's the new fella I saw the other day?" he asks. "Seems to be hacking up a good portion of your woods there. Any particular reason for that?"

I try to squelch the nervous bubble forming in my stomach. I'm still not altogether used to answering questions truthfully. I never want to complicate the false story I told when I first moved here. The one where I claimed that I relocated from New York, explaining away my lack of a southern accent.

"He's renting the camper," I reply. "I asked him to help out. He's been trimming trees, and most recently, pulling up bushes so I can plant corn. I'll bring you some if the harvest is successful next year."

"I sure appreciate that," he drawls. "Thought for a while there that you'd never rent. End up a loner like me. Somethin' peaceful 'bout living by your own rules. I think it's the quiet, mostly."

"I think you're right."

I brush away a bull ant that's taken to climbing up my shirtsleeve. The ground is cool beneath me, a sure sign that winter is around the corner. Soon, the creatures will be gone, replaced by cold and ice and the occasional snow. The ground won't produce crops, but Will saves enough from his beehives to offer me raw honey, comb included, for trade.

"I'm still pretty alone, though," I comment. "The new tenant rents the camper and I keep to the house. The quiet hasn't changed much."

Will places a blade of dying grass between his teeth and nods.

"That's a good thing. So many folks gettin' lost in the noise. You're young. I expected you to be like them, but you're different."

I used to be like them. The ceaseless noise and city lights.

"I only just understood five years ago that my mam had it right, settlin' this land and calling it home. I took off soon as I turned eighteen, never lookin' back, thinkin' I wanted outta this tiny town. Should've listened to her sooner. Should've come back before she passed away. Could have enjoyed these trees and bees and sounds of insects with her. Maybe then, I'd have stayed out of trouble."

I perk up at the mention of trouble. Will rarely shares anything about his life prior to moving here. My interest piques.

"Oh, don't look so happy." He chuckles. "Raring to hear info, huh? Well, I'll tell you, if you really want to know. I got mixed up with the wrong people in my earlier years. Fast crowd. Dishonest life. I was dead dumb livin' the way I'd been. I returned for her funeral. Never left again. She willed the house and land to me. Hate that she can't be here, but I've been happy ever since."

He sways slightly in the hammock, a small smile on his lips. I don't know much about him, but I do know he's forty-seven, still plenty young. Still many years to enjoy his property.

"I have fifty acres, Camille. Chickens and plots of veggies galore. I don't need to go to town for much. I don't need to ever see trouble, or my past, again. You seem like the nonjudgmental type. Knew it the minute I met you. Little gift of mine, you could say, readin' people. I know you won't gossip. That's why I feel comfortable tellin' you snippets of my life. Some of it was nothing to be proud of, but it is what it is, so there you have it."

"Everyone has a past," I murmur.

He nods, eyeing me in a way that makes me wonder what he notices.

"I suspect you know that better than most," he remarks.

There's no harm done in silence, so I opt for it. A knowing grin disappears into Will's cheeks. I sense our time coming to a close, brief as it always is, so I stand and brush leaf litter from my clothes.

"Hope you enjoy the goodies," I tell him.

"You know I will." He swings his legs over the hammock's edge. "See you around."

He whistles a melody and walks away with the backpack slung over one shoulder, bulging from the pumpkin, our meetup done.

"See you," I call to his retreating form.

The next day, Dawson is shirtless again.

I try, hard as I might, not to let on how much he affects me.

A tingling spreads straight from my scalp to my toes. I swallow and seem to lose my ability to speak. In the middle of nowhere USA, he is quite the treat. His jeans hug his backside perfectly. It doesn't seem to matter that I attempt to avert my eyes and my growing attraction.

He washes clothes by hand in the basin I left outside the camper. It's a hard job, one that causes his muscles to tighten and move just right. His body ripples with strength.

I'm not sure if it's appropriate for me to offer my washer and dryer to him. I'm not sure I want the scent of Dawson's clothes in my home. It's hard enough to get him off my mind.

He rises to his full height, wiping his hands on his jeans, leaving a water mark.

"Do you have the morning off?" I ask.

Dawson lowers his piercing eyes to meet my stare and I swear I almost see the smallest of grins.

"Why? Did you need more done around the property today?"

"No, I'm actually on my way to work." I check my watch. It's thirty minutes until my shift.

"Earlier this morning, before I started washing clothes, I noticed you have a skunk hole on the property. Did you know that?" he questions.

"I'm not surprised," I reply. "You'll probably find even more creatures if you continue to explore."

I think about the huckleberries Will gave me—now washed and sitting in a bowl in my fridge. I guarantee the critter would appreciate those, but there's no way I'd give them up. They're too precious a trade. And besides, I don't care for going near skunk holes. Never can tell when they might spray.

He steps closer, hovering within inches of my face. I think he does it on purpose some days, trying to get a response out of me. The old me would have cowered, but Dawson has only shown an interest, never pushing. Never putting his hands on me, good or otherwise.

I back away, keeping my focus on him as though I'm not nervous, like I don't have a care in the world. Like my past doesn't threaten to crumble me daily.

I open my truck door just as Dawson calls out that he'll see me at work soon. It appears that, like it or not, I'll be seeing a lot of Dawson. I'm not altogether sure if that's a good thing or not.

THIRTEEN

Dawson

Sunshine stabs painfully at my eyes as I reach for the burner phone sitting in the passenger seat of my truck. I've waited until my day off to do this. I park in a Quickie Mart in Tennessee. Though I've been driving for hours to get here, it only takes a minute for nerves to skate up my spine. Not many people drop everything to hightail it to another state. Nor do they buy a burner phone and search it for location devices.

I checked the phone. Double, triple checked. It seems safe. But then again, some people have ways of finding things out, which is why I've made sure not to be in North Carolina. If on some rare off chance the phone is tracked, or I'm spotted on any security cameras, they'll find the phone in the grocery store parking lot dumpster. I'll be long gone.

I roll down the window and let cool air cascade across my arms, my long sleeves rolled up to the elbow. It's a few degrees colder in Tennessee, putting the temperature at forty-five. I close my eyes for a minute and let past memories flash through my mind. Nine years old, hanging out with my buddies next to the corner gas station, jumping our bikes over speed humps and concrete blockers in the parking spaces. Hitting my teen years and still visiting the corner gas station, the yellow exterior aging, too, chipping in places like peeling skin. Being in the same parking lot of the store I grew up near when I signed the papers to join the army, my knees knocking together because I was nervous to make such a big decision.

You never know what a shitty parking lot can mean to a person. Maybe the one I'm in now holds memories for someone else. It's quieter than the one I grew up near, only a couple of passing cars making a sound. A horn honks, followed by a woman's shout for someone to hurry up. The smell is different, too—fresh mountain air, much cleaner than exhaust filled grime. But that's the thing, I prefer the dense smog to the freshness. Or at least, I used to. Honestly, sitting here makes me think I might actually like this. A moment of peace and quiet with a clean breeze and no interruptions. I've survived in chaos for so long that I don't think I gave any other lifestyle a second thought.

I crack open my eyes to find a man approaching me. I never meant to be spotted at all. That's the sole reason I picked this store. It's far enough back in the mountains, half a day's worth of driving from Camille's place, that I don't have to worry about anyone knowing my real location. Unless I want them to know.

There are no cameras pointed anywhere here. No proof I ever stopped. But a witness can place a person at the scene. I wasn't supposed to be spotted. I was too caught in my memories and knowing I needed to make a call to be on high alert. I usually hear people coming before they get within twenty feet. I could gun it out of the lot. I purposely backed into the spot in case I needed to do just that. I could peel away, and no one would be the wiser, but I don't know how much farther I'd have to drive to find a perfect place like this for the call.

I make a split-second decision to pull my tattered baseball cap lower on my forehead. That way the man who stops a foot from my truck won't see my eyes. They are a dead giveaway. Always have been. A pale green not often seen on others. The eyes my mother gifted me. The ones I saw close permanently on her two years ago. Fucking heart attack. Though with all the shit I pulled throughout the years, it was no wonder she didn't have one sooner.

"Hey, buddy," the man drawls in his thick country accent. "Got a light?"

I nod once. If there's a way for me to remain quiet, for him to *not* have a chance to recognize my voice should he ever be questioned about it later, I'm taking it.

I press the car lighter in, waiting a moment for it to heat up. The man is middle-aged, with a belly like an overinflated balloon hanging over his belt. Maybe he approached me simply because he saw an old vehicle and figured it'd have a built-in lighter. If so, he's right.

I pull the lighter out and hold it to the tip of his cigarette, singeing tobacco and paper. He takes a deep drag, tilts his head toward the cloudless sky, and exhales a plume.

"Thanks." He turns and strolls the opposite direction, around the side of the store, leaving me alone again.

I sigh and roll up the window, not needing anyone to hear my call.

A few quick numbers punched in, and the phone is ringing.

He answers with a, "Yep?"

"Hey." My voice fills the line.

A pause, and then, "It's been weeks."

Right. I've left everything for weeks now. I've been settled in the camper, such a calm contrast to the city on the other end of the line. I'm due to pay another month's rent, and I plan to soon.

"I need longer."

He grumbles something I can't make out. I wait, knowing it's best not to say anything I don't have to.

"How much longer?"

I double-check my surroundings. Coast is still clear.

"As long as it takes. Maybe months?" I reply.

I need this break from the norm, a chance to get away.

"Months?" he yells into the receiver. "Dawson, you better fucking not take months!"

And I hear it then, the thinly veiled threat in his tone.

"Have I ever let you down?"

Silence as thick as cotton settles between us. He weighs my words, already knowing the answer. I have never disappointed.

Finally, he answers with, "I swear to God, if you're not back here in six weeks, I'll come find you myself. You have responsibilities. Don't fuck up."

The line goes dead. I lean back against the headrest with a "shit" slipping through my lips.

I take only a few seconds to gather myself before pulling out of the spot and around the back where the dumpster waits. In no time, I park, lift the trash lid, wipe the cell down so it can't be traced with prints, and toss it. The burner hits a pile of garbage with barely a sound at all. Less than five minutes later, I'm already back on the highway, heading to the seclusion of the camper where no one bothers me.

But still, a timeframe hangs in my mind as I replay his gravelly words. *I swear to God, if you're not back here in six weeks, I'll come find you myself.*

Honestly, the call went better than I thought it would.

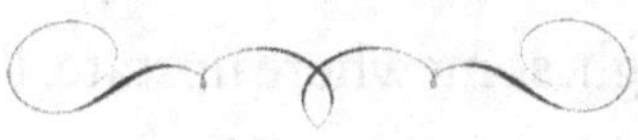

The other general store employee, whose name I learned is Miles, arrives just as I'm stepping inside for a cold Gatorade.

The old man promised me free drinks as long as I kept working hard, which is probably his way of making up for paying me less than I'd garner somewhere else.

I open the cooler and leave the door ajar for a moment, relishing the frostiness on my sweaty face. My self-imposed break is only ten minutes long, that way I can get back to organizing the shed, hopefully even finish it sometime this century.

"Hey, man. I don't think we officially met," Miles says, as he reaches into the same cooler for a drink of his own, a wide smile on his face. "I'm Miles."

He's pretty chipper for ten in the morning.

"Dawson." I extend my hand to shake his. My expression solemn, as it generally is.

I glance toward the front counter. Camille watches us intently from under long lashes, her curls in her face. Maybe she thinks that will hide her gaze, but it doesn't. I see her.

I let go and shut the cooler door. Miles notices Camille's stare and smiles wider.

"Man, she's a tough one to crack," he comments, low enough for her not to hear. "You know she's been living in Darlington for a year, and all I know about her is that she likes apple tarts and sweet tea, and that she used to live in New York? Not the busy city part, though, somewhere upstate. I'm not familiar with New York, I've lived here all my life, and no matter how many questions I ask, Camille won't tell me about it either. Kinda strange. She keeps to herself mostly. She sometimes has lunch at the diner with a friend of hers named Luke. I see her with her other friend Bonnie occasionally, too. That's it. A closed book."

His deep, country accent announces that he's definitely grown up in the South, but I don't really care about that. I'll keep listening to him if it means I might gain information on Camille. Also, for some reason, it bothers the shit out of me that I didn't know she likes apple tarts.

"Has she said much to you?" Miles asks.

"Nope."

He sighs and pops open his soda, the crisp sound of fizz filling the air. "Well, that figures, doesn't it? She's closed off, but just you wait, one day I'll get her to go out with me."

My eyes, which were focused on Camille, snap to him.

He smiles. "Yeah, I know, presumptuous of me, right? I mean, I guess it's wishful thinking. She'll probably say 'no' like she does to all the guys who come through and have the nerve to ask, but" —he shrugs— "I've got nothing to lose by trying, right?"

I grit my teeth. Guys come through trying to take Camille out? I wonder how often that happens.

"She has this certain charm," he continues. "She's a mystery, you know? But I think she might be different than the girls I date."

How would he know? He just admitted to knowing next to nothing about her.

"And there's the fact that she's older than me." He grins. "But only by three years. I saw her application when she first applied. She's twenty-seven."

The guy sure is a talker, and so far, it seems like he hasn't said too much of worth.

"Gotta get back to work," I grumble.

"Oh, right!" He chuckles. "Sorry to keep you, but good to meet you."

"You, too."

He approaches the counter as I toss the empty bottle into the garbage and grab another from the cooler.

"Hey, Miles," Camille says as he sets his soda next to the register.

"Camille," he replies.

I don't miss the way Camille spares me a fleeting glance. I make work of removing the bottle cap and taking big gulps, trying not to notice Camille's curls that I still fantasize about losing my hands in, or her snug jeans that fit just right, or the red lipstick she's chosen today to match her shirt. But I can't seem to stop myself.

Miles leans in closer and I have to look away, staring through the glass in the front doors at sparse fliers taped here and there, then toward the peacock blue sky. The temperature is pushing sixty, even hotter under direct sunlight. Despite the nice day, I'm not fooled. It'll be winter shortly. Even though the weather is unreliable, I expect the cold and snow to soon set in for good.

"Let me take you out."

"I don't know," Camille hedges, drawing my attention back to her.

She flashes a grin. Miles is asking her out. There's a genuine, honest lilt to his tone and I hate that my voice seldom carries that anymore. Not since leaving what I once knew as home, creating a thousand lies on the journey.

"One date. That's not too much to ask," he cajoles, a broad smile flashing across his face.

"Maybe another time," she tells him.

"I don't give up easily."

Camille catches my stare. I hitch an eyebrow and she straightens.

A woman walks into the general store, causing the bell above the door to jingle. She heads straight for the small room with knickknacks, letting her fingers roam over the dresses.

"I have a customer. I'll see you later, okay?" Camille addresses Miles.

He leaves with a goofy smile still attached to his face, along with the hope of a date Camille clearly doesn't intend on having. I wait until he's gone to take the last sip of my drink, and then I intentionally throw it away in the small garbage next to the counter.

"Hey," I say.

"Hi." Camille meets my stare.

Her cheeks stain red. Is that for me, or the fact that I witnessed her getting asked out? Well, it's good to know she's not jumping at a chance with him.

"Date?" I fight a grin.

"Don't you have to get back to work?" she retorts, changing the subject, unwilling to discuss the topic.

I reach for the door.

"Enjoy your date with Miles," I tease, as I head back to work.

She sighs, frustrated, calling after me, "It's not a date!"

But of course, I already know that. I pretend like I don't hear her, and because all she can see is my back, I allow a grin to escape.

I wonder, if it was me asking, if it would be.

FOURTEEN

Camille

I make it a habit to take a trip to the town square once a month. It helps to get out. Plus, it's the only place where I can restock makeup, candles, and knickknacks, which is precisely why I've come today. Surprising even myself, I invited Bonnie to join me, though she politely declined. If it wasn't such short notice, she might have been able to get the day off.

I enter the clothing boutique that sits at the end of a row of shops, which are lined up like matchsticks, all crammed together. I've wanted another pair of thick jeans ever since I accidentally tore mine last year. The storeowner buys from local designers all over the state of North Carolina, and there's one in particular I admire who sews thermal linings into the jeans so they have a regular appearance on the outside, while also offering protection from the approaching cold—of which we're having a rough go of this year.

I locate the designer's rack and search until I find a pair I like. I hold them up and turn them around to see both the back and front. They're a bit faded, just the way I prefer, high-waisted, and good quality. I pluck a stray strand off the denim and throw the pair I've chosen over my arm. Just to be sure they fit, I enter the closest dressing room, locking the door behind me. I've never been in this particular changing room before. There's a framed photograph, blown up and enhanced many times from its original size, on the wall—a sandy beach I know by heart. Suddenly, a memory as sharp as a knife slices through me.

The glittering surface of the ocean shatters the sunlight, making the wave look like a living, breathing thing. It swells, as though filling its lungs with air, and then exhales, depositing a whoosh of water and whitecaps, resembling spittle on the sandy shore.

I breathe deeply, tasting the briny air on my tongue, and lick the salt from my lips. The sun's rays brush over my closed eyelids. It's bright, midday. The beach is peppered with people. I can hear their laughter, chatter, and kids playing.

I open my eyes and head straight for the sea. Watery fingers grip my ankles and threaten to pull me under with the force of the current. I take several careful steps, watching for stingrays that frequent the shallows.

My very favorite way to enjoy the ocean is late at night when the beach is pitch-black. There is not a moment that feels freer to me. But for now, I appreciate the warmth of the sun.

Most of the waves aren't big enough for the surfers who attempt to catch them, except a couple, as though the sea is only teasing them, offering glimmers of hope. A gull screeches above and I welcome its squawks like I would an old friend.

"Beautiful, isn't it?" says a voice to my right.

I look over to find a man, who appears to be in his mid-twenties, grinning at me. He has hair the color of the depths of the ocean and warm, brown skin. His eyes glitter with the reflecting sun and something close to a promise.

"Just figured you were admiring the day since you haven't moved a muscle in a few minutes."

He's right. I've stayed still long enough that my feet have sunk into the sand below. I glance into the emerald green water and notice my legs appear to stop at the ankles.

"What brought you here today?" he asks.

"I live here," I reply.

I don't have to turn around to see the mansion because it's clear in my mind, with its sweeping views, and wrap-around, distressed, hardwood deck overlooking a pool, lounge chairs, and bubbling hot tub. The halls are filled with an art deco design, meant to inspire those with fine taste. It is nothing like the foster homes I grew up in.

"Here?" he inquires, and then whistles. "As in on the beach?"

I nod.

"Impressive."

He glances at my hands, perhaps looking for a ring, although he won't find one. I don't wear jewelry into the ocean because I don't want to destroy or lose it, and it's best not to flash shiny things underwater. It could easily be mistaken for a fish. That's a good way to get accidentally bitten. If he doesn't know that, then I assume he's not from here.

"Good for you. These homes are almost as nice as the ocean itself," he remarks.

Maybe he wonders how I can afford such a property. None go for less than tens of millions, and I'm sure it's hard to tell from the outside how a young woman in a plain white bikini could swing such a prize, seeing as how money isn't the only problem. The houses themselves are highly coveted and are hardly put on the market in the first place.

Or maybe he simply means to admire the beach and its homes.

"Wanna go for a swim?" he asks.

If I wasn't already involved, I might have considered his invitation. I take note of his sinewy form, his board shorts slung low on his hips. His muscles are lean, more subtle than bulky. There's something beautiful about the way his body moves with the water that laps against him, like a buoy swaying to-and-fro. He manages to keep his balance, to not get swept away by the current that washes ashore, and then drags itself back out, somehow not taking this man with it. It means he has experience in the water and its tides. I wonder if, maybe, my first assumption is wrong and he is from here, or simply a frequent visitor.

"*Not this time,*" *I tell him with a smile that, hopefully, lets him down easily.*

He nods and gives me a playful shrug. "Had to try."

"*Enjoy the water,*" *I call.*

He wades away, allowing me an hour of peaceful swimming. It's my usual daily workout, rain or shine, the only time off being when there's an intense rip current or hurricane warning.

I walk into the water until the ocean shelf drops off and I can't walk anymore. Here, I swim the line of buoys that guide my path. My arms cut through the surface with precision. I let the sea envelop me until my muscles turn to rubber, my skin wrinkles, and my lungs burn as though they've been set on fire. This is the part of the ocean where I swim with its creatures. The deeper waters, where I've seen everything from manta rays to sharks to jelly fish in groups. I swim with marine life that, on every occasion so far, leaves me alone, perfectly content to share the water.

Today, the ocean is bare of everything but the occasional passing fish and one lone sea star. I push myself further, expanding my lungs and holding my breath as I dive down. I repeat my routine in reps until the ocean absorbs my energy, and then it's time to swim back to shore.

When I finish, I collapse onto the sand, letting it stick to me while I catch my breath. Instead of feeling tired, I feel invigorated. When my breathing evens out, I stand and make my way home, which is hardly thirty steps. The surrounding beach is public, but the fenced properties are private.

The moment I open the gate and step onto the deck, I wash

my feet and body in the outside shower, watching the sand puddle beneath me. It's therapeutic, the water mixing with bits of the ocean I've brought back.

I glance longingly at the sea. It's the place I feel the safest. Even when I'm not in it, I wish to be. The beach has always been my most favorite place.

There was a time when I used the beach as an escape from foster home life. I spent many long moments sitting in the scorching sand until it burned my skin, followed by a jump into the ocean to stanch the heat. That's how I discovered this strip of shore in the first place. It's close to the final home I stayed in, with a nice family who decided to do a good deed and allow a seventeen-year-old to spend her last year at their house before aging out of the system. It was a tax write-off for them and a decent break from bad homes for me. Too bad an emotional connection never forged. We went our separate ways, but the beach remained. I always returned, year after year, until I met Roberto and moved here for good.

The memory brings a smile to my face as I walk into the house. Roberto is waiting for me.

"Hi, love," I say, cutting a path to him.

He stands stock-still, his hands at his side, his brown eyes holding no note of what's to come, which is why I'm caught off guard.

I go to my tiptoes to press a kiss to his lips.

His fist, fast as a snake, strikes my cheek with a blow that spins me around.

I fall to the ground, shell-shocked. Out of the corner of my eye, I see Roberto's guard assessing the situation. The same one who follows Roberto everywhere since his job—owning one of the most successful nightclubs in Miami—requires him to. At only thirty-three, eleven years my senior, he's also one of the youngest successful businessmen in the city. But I wouldn't know too much about that. I prefer the beach to the bar.

"What are you—" I begin, but Roberto cuts me off with a kick to the stomach.

The air is knocked out of my lungs and I nearly wretch. My gaze falls on the guard again.

"Help me," I wheeze, reaching out to him. There's blood in my mouth. It drips steadily onto the pearl white floor.

The guard does nothing.

"Want to explain why you were talking with another man?" Roberto questions so deadly calm, that I wonder if I'm dreaming, if I'm imagining the entire damned thing.

His slight Spanish accent leaks through his words like the blood that trickles down my chin and chest, seeping into my bathing suit. I gingerly touch my lip and realize it's split.

I can't reconcile the man I've been with over a year with the monster who just hit me. I wonder if he's been drinking, but when he bends, only inches from my face, it's not alcohol I smell, but the sharp bite of his aftershave, burning my nostrils.

"Answer me," he demands.

I'm too shocked to answer. Twelve months of dating followed by three months of marriage, and I've never seen this side of him. Not for one moment would I have thought him capable of hurting me.

I push away from him, scrambling backwards like a crab on the floor. I glance around the house for something to defend myself with. I make a run for the kitchen. It's my best bet with an assortment of sharp cutlery fit for a king.

Roberto catches me by the hair and drags me backward, kicking and screaming. If only the windows weren't soundproof, maybe someone would hear my cries. Or maybe the roaring ocean would drown them out anyhow.

I am on my own with a man I thought I knew, and a guard I believe is paid enough to keep quiet. I reach for anything I can and manage to grab a drawer handle. I pull it open as Roberto continues to drag me backward. It's too far for me to reach my other hand into, to grab anything that might help me, and only a moment later, Roberto yanks me hard enough that I lose my grip on the drawer altogether.

I attempt to stand and run, but that's futile, too. Big hands close around my forearms, squeezing tightly, and they don't let up.

"You aren't going anywhere," Roberto hisses. "You belong to me."

"Please," I beg. "Roberto, how could you?"

I've never known him to be the threatening type. Not with me, at least, and I try not to pay attention to what he does with other people. To the tense phone calls he occasionally gets. I've heard of his cunningness with business associates. A business he hardly discusses with me. Work is work and has nothing to do with our personal lives. To me, he has always been kind. Shown me the type of life most women dream of. Showered me with flowers and gifts and indulged whatever whim I happened to have. Just last month when I thought I'd be good at paddle boarding, he bought me a top-

of-the-line, highest rated board. I quickly learned I'm much better with no barriers between the sea and me, which is why I ended up giving it to a teen boy when I overheard him telling his mother he wished he had one. Roberto didn't bat an eye. When I wanted a popcorn machine for the media room, he made sure I had one. I used to pretend to be a girl in a castle with my own horse that I rode through the meadow. It helped me escape the nightmare of my real-life childhood, where some of the temporary housing conditions were unfathomable. When I mentioned the dream to Roberto, he booked a week getaway to a ranch where I got to do just that—ride a horse into the sunset.

I don't know the man in front of me.

He stops at our bedroom, drags me in, and shuts the door. I have no place to hide. The resounding click of the lock sounds like a death knell. I wonder if it might actually be.

"You will tell me why you've given your affection to another man right in front of my eyes."

"I d-didn't," I stammer. "We were only talking, and I declined a swim with him."

"Only talking? Is that what those smiles were about?" he challenges, his voice steadily rising. "Do not lie to me!"

"I'm not. I s-swear."

My teeth chatter and I have to hold onto my stomach to keep from getting sick. The taste of blood brings about a fit of nausea I can't seem to squelch.

My words have no effect on Roberto.

"Did you think I wouldn't see you? You must be more careful if *you ever want to hide from me."*

Panting, I turn away from the beach painting and rush back out of the dressing room door with the force of the memory that just burst from the deep folds of my mind.

I wish I'd known then that moment was only the first incident in the violent tornado that became my life. I would soon learn that there were worse things to come.

A store employee starts toward me, concern etched into the wrinkles of her face.

"Are you okay?" she asks.

I don't bother with an answer or with the jeans, which I throw on the nearest counter. I'll get a pair later. I leave the store in a rush of nerves. But somehow, no matter how fast I go, no matter where I run, the past always finds me.

FIFTEEN

Dawson

'm partially surprised anyone bothers to visit the store at all today. The ground is covered in churned mud from the trucks that roll over it, looking like whipped brownie frosting. Most of the locals wear appropriate boots, knowing what it's like to endure the rain that mists from the sky. I immediately differentiate between the locals and the visitors simply by their footwear. I look down at my own feet, knowing the boots I now wear were only bought because I made the mistake of thinking sandals would ever work in a place like this. Well, perhaps they do in summer. I wouldn't know.

"New boots?" Camille asks.

"Salvation Army."

"The one on NC 9?"

"Yes."

I found it myself. Sometimes I like to do that. Just drive. There's something about rows of corn and open fields of cattle and bales of hay that calms me. Occasionally, I find places along the way. Like the apple orchard I plan to visit. There's also an old place with a single, hand-painted sign out front offering free samples of pies. I stopped there once and haven't been able to get the memory of the taste out of my mind since. Maybe that will be a splurge I don't mind—an entire pie. I'm beginning to like the country more and more. No one invades my privacy, there are small places you'd never find on a map, and it's easy to go unnoticed.

Three men—out-of-towners, I realize—enter the general store and proceed to throw out insults with every step they take.

"Can you believe this podunk place?" one asks.

"They sell ammunition right next to food. Who does that?" sneers another.

"Some of the roads don't even have signs. I told you we should have spent the extra money and stayed in town," the third grouses.

They've come from the city. Their polo shirts, gleaming watches, and Dockers give them away.

"My shoes are ruined," one complains.

"Can I help you with something?" Camille inquires, a hint of severity in her tone.

She stands behind the register with one hand on her hip like it's taking all she has not to lay into them about how rude they're being.

Maybe she doesn't like what the men are saying, or perhaps she's annoyed by the mud they tracked in that clearly could have been avoided if they'd had the courtesy to wipe their feet on the mat by the door. It'll be Camille's duty to mop it up.

"Hey, gorgeous," one flirts.

He eyes Camille like she's an item he might want to take home. He doesn't even need the sunglasses he moves to the top of his head, since the sky is smeared with gray, the sun hidden, which means they are obviously for aesthetic reasons. Or maybe he's used to wearing sunglasses. An uneasy feeling comes over me and I watch the men more closely from my stationary spot by the chip rack.

The tanned skin. The slight accents. The entitled air about them.

They come from a bigger city, a ritzier place, one they obviously think is superior to the small mountain town they've somehow stumbled into.

"Hey, do I know you?" one questions Camille.

"No," she snaps.

"Yeah, yeah. You look super familiar. Sure I don't know you?" He grabs a bag of churros and a pack of gum, slapping them on the counter.

"You don't know me." Camille's voice is tight, her eyes

downcast.

She eyed them bravely before, but now she almost looks frightened. Hair falls into her face like a twisted curtain, but she doesn't bother to brush it back. Instead, she quickly rings up his items.

He pulls out cash and hands it over. She roughly presses the button to open the till a couple of times before it finally does, as though she's in a hurry to get them out.

"Where are you from?" he presses.

Camille hands over his change.

"Here," she replies. "Born and raised."

The lie flows perfectly from her lips. She even throws in a slight southern twang at the end to make it all the more convincing. It works.

He shrugs and grabs the bagged items she extends. On the way out of the door, his buddies a step behind him, he offers one last parting remark.

"Thought maybe you were from Miami. Could have sworn I'd seen you before. Hey, I guess the saying is right. Everyone has a twin somewhere, huh?"

He smiles and heads into the parking lot.

Camille clutches at the fabric of her blue sweater until the men pull away, their car gone from view.

"Camille," I murmur, watching her shocked reaction.

She comes to and smooths her sweater, then attaches a smile that's almost convincing. She busies herself with breaking open a new roll of pennies and dumping them into the drawer.

"What can I do for you, Dawson?"

Because I know an escape route when I see one, I leave it be.

"Do you need help with the mud?" I ask.

She finally looks at me.

"I'll get it," she replies, relief in her voice.

I watch her for a moment longer, knowing I've seen a part of her she hadn't planned on me seeing. I want to learn more, but this is not the time or place. Maybe at the property I can get her alone and bring it up. An idea forms.

"Do you play cards?" I inquire.

She stares at me as though perhaps my question is a trick.

"Sometimes," she hedges.

"How about a game of rummy? I play often." Or at least I used to with my buddies in the army. It's something to pass the time.

I don't have anything to bet, but I'm hoping playing is enough, no stakes on the table. I need to know more about Camille, and this may be the safest way.

"Sure," she agrees. "Sounds fun."

I'm not going to call her out on the lie she knows I just heard her tell. Not yet anyway, but I do know one thing for certain— she's given away the truth, plain as day, for anyone to see.

Camille is not from Darlington. She's not even from New York. She's from Miami.

SIXTEEN

Before

M r. Cruz knows his clients have eclectic taste. Not the club variety clients. The others, the ones who pay for much, much more than drinks and the price of admission. These clients take first priority. Of course, from a legal standpoint, the club is as great a cover as any. He pays his taxes and buys his expensive luxuries—like the yacht he parks at the marina, the house that has too many rooms for what he needs, and the thirty thousand dollar watch on his wrist.

"Has the shipment arrived?" Mr. Cruz asks his men.

They open the warehouse door for him. The marina, just down

the way from the warehouse, serves as an excellent method for delivering the goods that are in high demand. He checks his watch. Right on time.

To the ordinary eye, the warehouse is a large space for boat parts and engines. The perfect alibi. Since Mr. Cruz does actually sell boat parts, another side business of his, and does pay taxes like any other working individual, the business is legit.

What isn't legit, however, is the hidden underground room.

"Yes, sir," one worker confirms. "Eight bundles will be delivered tonight. Just as planned."

At two hundred and fifty thousand a bundle, he stands to make two million dollars in a matter of hours.

"I want to see the product," Mr. Cruz orders.

It's pertinent that he stays on top of the demand, that he sees the product firsthand to ensure its quality. Three of the men guide him to the trick latch on the floor that leads to a crawlspace. He has to crouch, unable to stand upright in the tight area. They hit the battery-operated lamp switch. Through a door, stairs lead down into a room. His feet hit the bottom and he can finally stand straight again.

His eyes land on the concrete ground, and then on each bundle. He takes a moment to assess the illegal weapons. Guns gleam in the artificial light, polished clean and refracting glimmers onto the floor. His eyes roam them all until he finally reaches the last one. He nods, retrieves his phone from his pocket, and makes the call.

"We're ready," he says.

He keeps the call short. A few seconds only. Untraceable.

Next, he sends an email. The money is scheduled to show up in his offshore account in an hour or less, like always, or the transaction is canceled.

"Prepare the package to ship in two hours unless you hear otherwise from me," he instructs his lead worker, who nods his understanding.

Mr. Cruz leaves the hidden crawlspace and passes a section of the warehouse equipped with a monitoring system for outside activity and intruders. His phone pings with an email confirmation that half of the money has been delivered. The other half will be there when the package arrives safely, which should be mid-week.

He walks back to his BMW as the workers lock up behind him. Reaching for the console, he blasts cool air, hoping for a reprieve from the beads of perspiration dotting his skin. The humid, south Florida heat is not the ideal match for his pants, socks, shoes, and short-sleeved shirt. He's close to heat exhaustion without the AC. He lingers a moment, allowing himself a small smile. He's done it again. This is the fourth transaction of its type. He's made eight million dollars on his side venture in the last six months alone, pocketing a large portion of it. The rest goes to buying the product, some to delivering it. He stands to make even more if business stays steady, or if it hits what it's projected to thanks to his efficient production model and the promise of triple the orders from his buyer if he continues to impress them, which he will.

He has more money than he knows what to do with. Maybe tonight he'll celebrate at the club. It's been a full week since he's brought anyone to the back. The ringing of his phone interrupts his thoughts.

"Hello?" he answers.

The caller says only one thing.

"Two weeks from tonight. Ten bundles this time."

The call ends as abruptly as it began.

SEVENTEEN

Camille

The trees are stripped bare, and the piles of leaves are long gone, replaced by a scarf of snow. In some places, inches, in others, close to a foot. Yet people still fish in various ponds, desperate for something to do in this small good-for-hiding town.

Luke sees my approach and smiles. His beard has grown slightly past his chin, and I'd be lying if I said it didn't suit him. He sets his fishing pole in a hole he's dug in the ground, deep enough that it holds steady when he lets go.

The backdrop of our meeting location, only twenty minutes

from my property, is a blue sky frosted with wisps of clouds. The pond is no bigger than an oversized pool, fed with a small stream that is too fast to ice over. The water is muddy brown, like chocolate milk topped with ice shavings. Though I'm not at all used to the cold, I've grown to like it. I pull my jacket tighter and stuff my gloved hands inside.

"Hey, you," he says, greeting me intimately with a soft hug. It's one of the only places—almost always deserted, set back in the woods and away from it all—that we can interact on more than a first-name basis.

"Hey, yourself," I reply with a smile.

I sit right there on the cold dirt next to a cup of nightcrawlers and a bucket with one caught catfish.

"So," I murmur, biting the bullet. "What's the news?"

It's why I'm here, after all. To catch up on what's happening in Miami.

"I know you've been anxious after those men stopped by the store last week, thinking they recognized you," he begins, taking a seat beside me. "But I couldn't look into it until now. I check every few months, and it was about time for me to check again. If I looked any sooner, I could blow everything."

I shiver—partly at the thought, partly because of the cold. I glance down at my double-layered leggings, a choice I'm now reconsidering. His jeans most likely protect him more than my clothing protects me. At least my coat is dense and warm, and my boots are lined with fuzz.

"I understand," I assure him. "What'd you discover?"

"The man was right. He does know you."

His words drop like a bomb, shattering my cool. I can't help the tremor that slithers through me of its own accord. The last thing I need is for someone to recognize me, and for Roberto to know where I am.

"How?"

"He worked as a pool boy for Roberto for a year before he was late one morning and fired."

The memory pricks the edges of my thoughts. I try to place his face and can't. Roberto didn't often allow me near other men, pool boys included.

Luke rubs my back encouragingly. "Don't worry. He didn't say a word to anyone. I don't think the man realized where he knew you from. You're safe."

I let out a *whoosh* of breath. I'll take small miracles when they come.

"How do you do it?" I whisper.

Suddenly, my voice is scared to make an appearance. It's what Roberto—even the memory of him—does to me.

"How do you brave checking in?" I clarify, clearing my throat. "Are you ever worried he'll dig out your connections and trace them back to us?"

"No," Luke replies. "Not usually. I'd handle the problem before it got to that."

His underlining statement reminds me that Luke was, and still is, a very dangerous man. He hides it well with his country boy charm, all learned from years in Darlington. No one would know from the outside that he used to live in the city as Roberto's hit man.

"I thought you wanted away from that life," I comment.

Of killing.

"I do," he states, locking eyes with me. "You know I do. That's why I left in the first place, to get away from him and his never-ending list of enemies who were always relegated to me to take care of."

We both know that he did not, in any way, "take care" of them, except maybe in the act of disposing of their bodies in places people would never discover them.

"I check in for you, Camille," he continues. "I needed to make sure the ex-pool boy didn't run his mouth. I needed to know, even though it's been a year now, that Roberto hasn't placed a hit on you."

I swallow hard. "Has he?"

Luke pulls at his beard and sighs. "No. And honestly? That's even scarier."

I try to find logic in his reasoning.

"If he sent a hit man, that would mean he's done with you. He wants you alive, and that's worse."

I see what he means. If Roberto wants me alive, then he has use for me yet.

"I know what you're thinking," Luke murmurs, leaning closer. "I won't let him find you, or me for that matter. Do you think he's fond of his hit men disappearing without a trace, knowing all they know about him and his crimes? No.

When he's done with an employee, he makes sure they can never speak again. I'm the only one, Camille, the *only* one who has ever escaped him. I promised you when I learned he was abusing you that I'd make sure you disappeared, too. Remember the note I left?"

I could never forget it. I didn't know Luke when he worked for Roberto. That was shorty before I met Roberto. All I knew of Luke was from a note that appeared one day on my pillow at the hospital with a picture of me, bloody on the kitchen floor. Roberto had hit me again.

"I was close, so close, to leaving him when your note and picture arrived," I tell him, recalling the memory. "All I had to do was save a little more money and I'd be gone. Maybe I shouldn't have told him I wanted to leave. But I suppose him hitting me hard enough to cause a cracked rib and a cracked eye socket, all the while blaming it on a *car accident* when authorities asked what had happened, was actually a good thing. It allowed you to reach me. Something you never would have been able to do in his house."

Luke nods. "His home is too well protected."

"But you got the picture of me, bloody on the kitchen floor."

He tugs at the fishing line in small, jerky movements, pulling the lure along and gaining nibbles from the fish below— something I've grown accustomed to him doing.

"That was thanks to a high-powered scope. Do you know how hard it is to get a shot through those tinted windows of his? He went through the trouble of making sure most couldn't see in."

Of course, Roberto did. That way he could continue to do what he wanted, when he wanted, illegal or not, without repercussions. Maybe if I wasn't so scared he'd kill me, I might have told the hospital staff that he faked the accident, and had one of his men drive the car into the tree and place my unconscious form there for them to find. When I'd awoken in the hospital later that night, with a nurse by my side telling me I'd been in an auto accident, I attempted to tell her the truth, but I only got so far as a few words of denial when Roberto was suddenly there, stepping from the shadows of the room, claiming that I must have a concussion, and giving me a look that spoke of unimaginable pain if I uttered one more word.

"You managed to get the photo to me in one of the few moments when Roberto wasn't by my hospital bedside," I rasp, laying a hand over Luke's in appreciation. His face softens. "I'm forever grateful."

Luke pulls his hand from mine and grabs the pole quickly as the line zooms out. I watch—half stuck in memories, half in reality—as he reels in an even larger catfish than the first one, adding it to the bucket, but not before putting it out of its misery.

"I couldn't leave you there with him," Luke says. "I had to bring you here. I knew you wanted out. And, well, if you decided not to leave, I hadn't really given you any incriminating evidence, had I? Just a note to meet me at a date and time. I made sure Roberto would be distracted and if you didn't show, then at least I could sleep knowing I'd tried to help."

I remember the questions I'd asked him when he first helped me escape.

"Why me, Luke? What were you doing there in the first place? You got the photo of me bloody and beaten, but why come back when you'd already escaped? You had your life here in Darlington. You didn't need Miami anymore."

Luke risked blowing his cover, risked being caught smuggling me away from Roberto. It was a hefty thing to do, to put his life on the line for a stranger. I remember his answer clearly.

"I had heard about his new venture, the illegal weapons, and needed proof. Should he ever come for me, on the off chance he found me, I wanted leverage. But instead of proof, I got you. I might have been an asshole, and I might have eliminated criminals on Roberto's list, but I have never condoned abusing innocents. Not once. You didn't deserve what he did to you, Camille. I wanted to see your face when it wasn't bloody or broken or bruised. So, I stepped in."

"I don't know if you would have—" Luke casts the fishing line again and clears his throat, while looking pained at the words he tries to push out. "What I mean is that I'm not sure you'd still be here if I didn't get you out of there."

"Of course, I wouldn't be." I nudge him playfully. "I'd never even heard of Darlington before you brought me. You're the reason my escape was successful."

Luke leans in closer still. "No, I mean I'm not sure you'd be *alive*."

It pains him to say it. A line creases between his brows and he grimaces.

"I can't stand the thought sometimes."

His admission is a comforting balm to the jagged memories of my past.

Luke is the best friend I've ever had. Mrs. JoAnne is nice, and I appreciate her company, and Mr. Hill is lovely, too, not to mention Will and Bonnie, but Luke is the only one who knows my whole story and not only sticks around, but also *understands* what it's like to be under the thumb of a monster. More than anything, he is completely right. If he hadn't left the note, if I hadn't risked meeting him at the specified place where he had a false new identity waiting for me, I might have been deep in the ground the very same worms sitting next to me were plucked from.

"Thank you." I pause to squeeze his hand once. "I know I've said it before, but I have to tell you again. I may never stop telling you."

A look comes over Luke's features. It's one I haven't seen before, and it causes me to assess him closer. His stare drops to my lips. It's brief, but it's there. Then suddenly, he stands and offers me a hand.

"We better get back," he mutters, as though he didn't look at me with a gaze full of the very swiftest heat.

I wonder for a moment if I imagined it.

"Sure," I murmur, a bit confused.

Luke has never shown an interest in me before.

"Maybe we can meet again soon, and you can tell me more about the new renter and what you've been up to."

A lot has happened since I last informed Luke that a man wanted to rent the camper, and since Luke ran a thorough background check that Dawson passed with flying colors.

"Sounds good," I reply.

Luke doesn't offer to walk me to my truck, like usual. He busies himself with skinning and filleting the fish, which tells me all I need to know. I didn't imagine the heat in his eyes. Perhaps it was a momentary lapse in judgment, and he's embarrassed by it. I'm inclined to believe it. Any other thought would have me facing the prospect of Luke taking interest in me. He definitely didn't at first, when he brought me here, but maybe now, over time, something's changed.

I don't like the possibility. It could ruin everything. Just the thought that Luke would chance it...what if things went wrong, if we gave it a shot and it didn't work out? He's the only true friend I have. We can't lose our friendship.

"I need to go," I blurt.

Luke offers a wave and nothing more.

"Damn it."

Dawson's timbre is as smooth and warm as the liquor I no longer drink. It seeps into my body, breaching my defenses. He only has to look at me in a certain way, and somehow, he disables the wall I've put up for so long. Thankfully, though, he's talking to the pile of wood in front of him, not me. He pulls what I suspect is a splinter from his thumb.

I make my way toward the camper, stepping on leaves that crunch softly underfoot, watching a bird fly from one tree to another. I share the property with too many animals to count, but right now I try to focus on as many as I can to distract myself. My foot hits a particularly dry branch and the resulting crack is loud to my ears, although I'm far enough away that Dawson shouldn't have heard it.

He stills.

Of course, he heard. His military instincts seem to be ever-present.

Dawson pivots to gaze at me, the muscles working under his fitted shirt as he lifts another piece of wood onto the raised tree stump, the ax beside it. Wizard stretches dramatically next to Dawson's feet and meanders under the camper, turns three times in a circle, and collapses into a pile of dried moss, falling asleep. It seems like now that the cat knows he has a home, he doesn't mind spending half his time outside.

"What can I do for you?" Dawson asks.

"There's a problem with my bathroom sink," I say. "Thought maybe you could help fix it?"

Ordinarily, Mr. Hill calls someone to assist me. Just as ordinarily, the service mysteriously costs nothing, though I suspect Mr. Hill fronts the bill. I'd like to save him the trouble this time, if possible.

"Do you know what's wrong with it?" he questions.

I try not to cringe at the mistake that is entirely my fault.

"Yes. I didn't leave the faucet dripping last night. It froze."

I try not to look into his sharp eyes, choosing instead to focus on a tree to the right of him. I begin counting the branches, waiting for his response.

"Didn't you hear about the freeze warning?" he inquires, something close to suspicion in his tone.

"I fell asleep early," I tell him, silently adding, *thanks to a sleeping pill.*

I seldom take them, only when nightmares are too intense to bear or when my brain won't stop the searing flashbacks. Thankfully, Luke has a supply of them and he's willing to share. I could never tell a doctor about my past, of what causes the terror in the first place. Luke alone knows why.

Dawson watches me closely. "Do you have tools and a replacement pipe?"

"I always keep a replacement and tools," I reply.

It's a habit I picked up when going practically off grid. It's come in handy several times over.

Dawson motions for me to lead the way. I purposely wore thick leggings so bending and stretching underneath the sink wouldn't be a problem, paired with a long-sleeved shirt that I'll probably be rolling the sleeves up on once the manual labor begins.

"What do you normally do if a pipe freezes? Before I moved here, I mean."

I have a general idea of how to fix the pipe from watching repair men fix others at the house, but the problem is I'm not strong enough to pry the broken end off by myself.

Dawson begins walking toward my house, his way of letting me know he intends to help.

"Mr. Hill sends someone."

Nearly all of the grass beneath my feet has turned from a lush green to a mottled brown. Ice patches spot the ground in random patterns, and even a couple of small icicles hang from the thorns and briar bushes.

"So, you didn't want to bother him?" he presses.

I stop at the door and squint at Dawson. "Am I bothering you?"

I turn the knob, and Dawson walks in. The house is much warmer than the outside, and he visibly relaxes when the heat hits him, his shoulders slouching as he exhales. I close the front door and follow him to the back of the house.

"No," he responds, taking the liberty to find the bathroom, open the vanity, and assess the damage. "It's no bother."

I have tools and the replacement L-shaped bend on the floor. Dawson takes a seat and looks through the bag for the right wrench and glue.

"Think you could shut off the water valve?" he requests.

"Already done."

Up close, he smells like cedar. Maybe from all the wood he chopped for me this morning. Perhaps he thinks I won't notice when my supplies stay full without me having to do the work, but of course I do. So far, he's made sure only to put a little on the pile at a time. I've witnessed him wandering around the house, always helping in some way. Nailing down a loose board. Cleaning out the gutters. Inspecting the exterior woodwork. The other day when I returned home from work, I found him halfway underneath the porch, checking for unwanted critters. He's been the help I've needed around here. So far, it's only been outside the house and around the property. Today, that changes.

Dawson watches me, tension in his spine.

"Do I make you uncomfortable?" I ask, before I realize I've spoken.

His eyes lose their smoldering spark. "Sorry, no. I'm just wound up. Can you hand me the wrench?"

I perch on the edge of the tub and do as he requests as he lies on his side, a better angle to work with. He begins loosening the piece that froze, careful not to break the rest of the pipe. There's a crack in the elbow, the source of my problem, not to mention the pipe itself is as old as time, like many things around this ancient place, and needs replacing anyhow. Thing is, I tend not to bother until it absolutely needs it. A causality of constantly having little funds.

If I was strong enough to pry off the fused part, I wouldn't have asked Dawson, but now that he's here, I can't help but watch with rapt interest.

"Replacement pipe," he calls, setting the old one to the side.

I hand it to him. His shirt rises slightly as he fights to properly fit the piece. I catch a hint of his toned back, and two curves leading further down.

A lack of noise causes me to glance back up to see what Dawson is doing and if he requires assistance.

He watches me with the hint of a grin.

I try not to appear as embarrassed as I feel.

"Enjoying yourself?" he asks, his voice an octave deeper.

Because nothing I say can disguise the fact that I've just been caught, I opt for silence.

After a moment of staring me down, he takes pity on me and moves on.

"When you're ready, can you hand me the glue?"

I consider gluing his lips together so he'll stop smirking so gorgeously.

"Here," I mumble, extending the tube to him.

That's when I see that both of his hands are holding the pipe in place, and he means for me to glue it.

"Oh, sorry!" I chirp, and drop down to my knees, maneuvering around his large frame to bend under the cabinet. "Just here?"

I place the tip of the glue at the point where the PVC meets old rust.

"Yeah," Dawson replies huskily.

I glance to where his eyes have landed. In my haste, I practically deposited myself into his lap. I can't seem to move. The space is cramped and I'm not sure where else to go.

"Thanks for the firewood," I blurt, desperate for something to break the tension. "And all of your help around here lately."

"You saw that, did you?" he murmurs, not taking his eyes off me.

I nod. I can't be trusted to speak much more than simple replies, not when I'm so unbearably close to him. I love the curve of his lips. I wish I had a camera to capture his grin forever.

I don't have any pictures anymore.

His breath deepens. "Camille?"

"Yes?" I whisper, inching just a tad closer.

"The glue."

"Oh, right!"

I turn back around, and the quick movement bumps my backside right up against Dawson, eliciting a groan from him.

I hastily apply the glue, going as quickly as I can. When the top part is done, Dawson releases one hand, the other still holding tight to the bottom of the pipe. Suddenly, I feel his warm palm on my hip, his breath in my ear.

"Camille," he growls, and I nearly melt into the floor. "Hurry."

I glue the bottom half, and Dawson holds it still for a moment to allow it time to set. His fingers begin to stroke my hip in a slow, seductive pattern.

I drop the glue and risk a glance over my shoulder. Dawson watches me through eyes thick with want.

He allows his hand to travel over my shirt and up my spine. I shiver with need, my body betraying the indifference I try so hard to portray. Settling his fingers in my mass of curls, he tugs lightly.

"God, I've been dying to do that," he whispers, and then locks up as though he didn't mean to speak.

He lets go of the pipe, and me, and stands abruptly.

"It's done. Should last you a while. If you pay mind to future freeze warnings," he comments.

Without another thought but the desire to have his hands in my hair once more, I stand, too, pressing right up against him in the cramped space.

His chest rises and falls roughly, and his fists bunch, as though he's trying hard not to touch me.

"You smell like lemon pie," he murmurs.

But he doesn't say it as though it's a bad thing. In fact, it sounds as though he wants nothing more in the world than to taste a slice of lemon pie this very moment.

I lay a hand against his chest. "Dawson."

My head tilts up toward his scruffy chin. I have the urge to bite him gently. To feel just how hard his muscles are underneath that shirt of his.

"I have to go," he declares, wrenching away from me.

He rushes out of the bathroom and to the door quicker than I can blink. It's obvious he feels the current between us, but he's wiser about it. He remembered we are not meant to be close like this. He's a tenant, paying me monthly for a place to live. Somehow, this seems like an abuse of power. He looks once more my way before roughly shutting the door, closing me in with the mistake I almost made.

I nearly kissed Dawson.

Who lives next door.

A wash of shame pours over me and heats my cheeks. What kind of landlord am I? Is this sort of thing okay? Plus, I don't really know him that well, which is the biggest of my fears. How could I have let down my defenses so quickly after how hard I work to keep them up?

Clearly, I need to try harder.

EIGHTEEN

Dawson

The farmhouse stands to the side of the road like a mile marker. The only home for acres, it advertises an orchard experience not soon to be forgotten. My truck climbs up the steep drive and comes to a halt beside a wheelbarrow full of pumpkins and straw. There's a tractor as green as a blade of summer grass sitting stationary, like a prop, though I suspect it's used to churn the earthy fields during planting season. The wooden house is large, peaked with exposed beams, the utmost tip being that of a faded brick chimney. The entire structure looks to be original, with the type of smaller windows built a century ago. White joists crisscross the red front doors, matching the rest of the house, like an X marks the spot.

The moment my feet hit the gravel, a hound dog bays and bounds up to me, ears flapping as much as the American flag erected in the front yard. The sound acts as a siren, alerting the man inside. He opens the front door to greet Kenny and me.

"Well, howdy." His drawl is heavy, and his pants are worn to the point of needing patches. His flannel shirt is nearly as threadbare. "Here for the orchard experience?"

"Yes, sir," Kenny says.

He insisted I go with him, stating that I couldn't move to the country and not experience a proper apple picking.

I cast a look around. A field stretches out in hilly waves, met by a maze of corn that's already been shucked. Extra ears dot the ground for the wild animals to forage, as well as whatever is left over from the parts not harvested. To the other side of the house is a herd of cows, grazing on bales of dried hay scattered about. Fenced off and further back are three riding horses and a donkey. The rearmost section of the property is what we're interested in, where apple trees spring from the ground.

"You can pay by the bushel," the man states. "Name's Charlie. Holler if you need me. Moose here'll show you to it."

He motions to the dog slobbering on my boots.

"'Course he'll want belly rubs and an apple when you're done."

He chuckles and pats Moose on the head.

"Don't mind old Danny Boy either, if you see him. He's a male horse of mine. Likes to jump the fence to get himself a snack from time to time. He's friendly as a mutt and won't bother you none. He'll go back in the pen when he's good and ready and not a minute sooner."

I don't know what to make of the possibility of coming face-to-face with a horse. I've never ridden or seen one up close.

"I'll take a bushel please," Kenny says.

"Me, too," I add.

I pull money from my wallet, handing it to him.

The man spots the military ID I keep pressed between clear films. It's not the fake ID I showed the old man. This one is real.

I cover it, knowing I shouldn't let anyone see my full name. Now that I have what seems to be a solid place to stay, I should hide it somewhere in the camper. No need to carry it close anymore. As it is, I didn't really mean to bring it with me, but it usually sits in my wallet.

"You a soldier, son?" he asks, suddenly more alert than he was a moment ago.

Kenny perks up, eyeing me sideways. It's not something I've shared with him, and from his look, it seems he wants to know.

"Was," I reply.

The man stiffens his spine and salutes me. I'm not used to salutes in civilian life, and it instantly transports me back to the dry, desolate wastelands of a war-torn country where people actually did salute one another. I can almost hear the *pop* of bullets and the screams of the wounded. I look down at my hands, expecting them to be covered in blood, as they usually were when I patched humans, and the occasional soldier dog, back together.

I blink. Charlie's face swims into view.

"Thank you for your service, young man," he says.

"Yeah, thanks, man," Kenny adds, as though seeing me through a new lens.

The orchard owner hands the money back to me and drops his salute.

"This one is on me," he explains. "And every one after that is half off from now on."

Noticing my silence, Kenny steps in. "Thank you. We'll be back around shortly."

I hesitate to return the bills to my wallet.

"Go on now," Charlie encourages, nodding to the wicker baskets lined up by the side of the house. "Grab one and get started. You don't mind Moose going with, do ya?"

"No," I respond.

He sees the money not yet deposited in my wallet.

"Listen, son," he begins. "I don't know where you're from, but 'round these parts we take our armed services seriously and we honor the people who dedicate their lives. Now, I'm not here to argue what's right and what's wrong with the world and its fights, but I sure will thank those who serve. So put that money away and go have yourself a good time. It's the least I can do."

I stuff the bills away and nod.

Kenny makes his way to the baskets, and I follow. They all appear the same to me, so I pick one without really looking at it.

"You served in the military?" Kenny questions, even though

he already now knows.

Moose the hound dog licks my pants and bounds up ahead as though concentrating on his job of guiding us down the clear path to the orchard. Nose to the ground, he follows a scent until he comes to a halt at the opening of the trees.

"I did," I admit.

"Why didn't you tell me?"

I shrug. "Never came up."

"What branch?" he inquires tentatively.

We make our way to the edge of the orchard. I don't know how many acres the man owns, but it seems to be even more than Camille does. The line of trees sucks us in, and suddenly, we're under the cover of a million branches. Many of them are bare, with only a few apples remaining.

"Army." I pluck one down. It comes off with two browning leaves attached.

Moose barks once, sniffing the ground in earnest, before twisting through trees until he comes to a stop at a rabbit hole. He sits next to it and looks to me for praise. I give him a scratch behind the ear, and he seems to take that to mean he's done well.

The trees are planted in a pattern, leaving just enough room to amble between trunks and under dwindling leaves. I hate to think how much effort it takes for them to be covered when the snow falls. Preserving the fruit must be difficult. Thankfully, we've caught the very end of the season, according to Kenny's explanation of all things apple picking on the drive over.

"And you don't love to talk about it?" Kenny presses.

He doesn't ask in a nosy way, which is maybe why I don't mind answering.

"I got out a few years ago. Moved on. That's all."

This must be what serious looks like on Kenny.

"Well, I appreciate you all the same." And then because he's Kenny, he adds, "Even if you do drink like a wuss."

I chuckle. Everything is back to normal. Good. I prefer it that way.

We go deeper into the orchard, the scent of apple growing stronger. Shafts of light peek through branches, but the sky is mostly mottled with clouds. Occasionally, I see squirrels dart to-and-fro, Moose barking at them.

"So, what's up with you, man?" Kenny asks. "Is the army the reason you're holed up, not wanting to talk much? I mean, I know I can talk enough for the both of us, but..."

I attempt a smile at his weak joke and decide to feed him a little of my story, if for nothing else than to pass the time and get it over with so he doesn't have to ask again.

"The army is part of it, yes. Hours, sometimes days, spent in bunkers, not talking. I've gone a long, long time without chitchat, and I guess I've grown accustomed to it."

That's really only a tiny sliver of my truth, but it's the only bit I'll give him.

"Then there was a house fire back home. Some of my family didn't make it. So, I'm here. Away from there. That's pretty much my story. I'm starting over."

It takes a moment for Kenny to speak, but when he does, it's loaded with sincerity, and I almost feel bad for lying.

"I'm really sorry to hear it, man."

One good thing that comes out of this is that Kenny drops the subject.

"I could tell you about my family." He grins. "They're crazier than shit. My sister is a skydiving instructor in Florida. Can you believe that? She gets paid to jump out of planes. You couldn't give me money to jump from that high. My brother is a farmer with a pet pig named Bacon. I swear to God. Then there's my mom..."

I listen as Kenny drones on about his family. Truth be told, they don't seem half bad. A little on the weird side, but nothing too far gone.

My thoughts go to my own family. My real story. No siblings. Mom dead. Dad living in Key West, where the sun constantly shines and waves lure him to the ocean to fish and live his life as a beach bum. Occasionally, he picks up a guitar and strums a tune, singing along with it. A few local bars pay him a couple nights a week. It's enough for him to survive out of the tiny truck RV he stays in. I don't know how we share genes when I'm so disciplined and he's...not.

"So, anyway, enough about me," Kenny says. "Tell me about the new place. You liking it? And what about Camille?"

At her name, my head swivels in his direction.

He laughs. "I knew it. You're not immune to her, are you? You're so quiet most of the time, but I see it."

I sincerely hope he doesn't see how much Camille gets under my skin.

I can't help but think of her intoxicating grin, her curls falling down her bare back, and what it'd be like to feel her skin against mine. Those are all thoughts I shouldn't be having, so I try to remember something else to snap me out of it. Like the men who visited the store. They don't live here. But they knew her. She acted like she had no idea what they were talking about when they said she looked familiar. There was even a tic in her left eye, the way she fidgeted and squirmed. She was lying.

"She's great," I comment, settling on something bland.

Kenny barks out a laugh. "I'll sell my right arm if all you think about her is that 'she's great.'"

Damn him. He knows I'm interested in her. He just doesn't know anything past that.

We collect the last of the apples, throwing one to Moose who gobbles it up, juice dripping down his neck and matting his fur. He barks his appreciation, then licks my boot with a sticky tongue. Kenny offers him a belly rub and he rolls over, snorting and panting.

When Moose is satisfied with the amount of affection he's received, he lopes back up to the farmhouse, leaving us to follow. As we depart from the orchard and approach the truck, baskets full of apples, Charlie exits the front door of the house.

"Come back anytime," he calls. "You're always welcome here. Half off. Enjoy the apples."

He catches up to Kenny and hands him a paper flier. "My

wife's printed recipes for pies and bread and sauce and jelly and pretty much anything you can think of putting apples in. Thanks for your business."

I shake his outstretched hand and accept the goodbye salute he offers before setting the basket of apples in the back cab and driving off. Gravel crunches under the tires and dirt kicks up. Moose chases us the length of the driveway, tongue lolling out of the side of his mouth. He gives one howl that sees us down the road until we're too far off to hear him anymore.

And for a moment, everything feels okay. But then I remember I am not the small-town Dawson I pretend to be, the one who has a funny redheaded friend and an attractive landlord. I'm a guy on the run. As nice as this all is, it's temporary.

NINETEEN

Camille

Clear mason jars sit on the dinette tables next to ketchup, salt, pepper, and barbeque sauce, and mouthwatering scents permeate the air—honey, fried chicken, and brown sugar beans. I'd eat at Rose's diner every day if I didn't feel like it was asking too much, considering how she never accepts my payment.

"Nice to see you, Camille. What are you havin'?" Bonnie asks.

She pops her gum and smiles, pencil and pad in hand. There are no computers. Everything is done manually, with ticket stubs and verbal orders given by the servers to the cooks when orders are modified or a customer requests something different.

I, like the locals, enjoy the comfort and originality of a less modern approach. There's a clear shot to the kitchen where cooks shuffle around and large pots heat hefty quantities of everyone's favorites. Three canisters are brewed on the spot and hold tea—two hold sweet, and one holds unsweet. Two coffee makers brew the natural way, water over ground bean. They seem to always be full, thanks to the servers who know to continually make more for customers who drink it like water. Packets of sugars and creams, tossed together in a bowl, are given to each customer who requests a cup. It's a simple method, but it works well. All recipes are Rose's, and she's decided today that the menu is a choice between gumbo, fried chicken and brown sugar beans, or my favorite. I read the label, my mouth nearly salivating—country fried steak, hush puppies, and slaw.

"I'll take the country fried steak," I order.

Bonnie laughs. "Should have known. You want your usual sweet tea?"

"Of course," I respond, just as Miles walks into the diner, spots me, and makes a beeline to my booth.

"Miles, you eating, too?" she inquires.

"Yes, ma'am," he replies, flashing a smile that has Bonnie blushing.

She's too young to be called "ma'am," in my opinion, but around Darlington, that's just the way manners are shown.

"Your regular?"

"You know it," he answers.

"How can you have a regular when the menu is always changing?" I question.

"He orders here often enough that I know which dishes are his favorite out of the bunch," Bonnie explains.

She walks off to stick our ticket in the window, keeping up with the rest of the busy rush. Just like that, I seem to be having lunch with Miles, who stretches out his long legs under the table. He's not wearing his usual loose flannel shirt, instead donning a form-fitting Henley that exposes what I can't help but notice are muscles he normally keeps hidden.

"Hi, Camille," he greets. "How are you today?"

"I'm good, Miles."

"You mind if I eat with you?"

I'm not sure if it's a good idea, but I can't kick him out without seeming rude. It'll be fine. Food will arrive swiftly and then I'll be gone. Easy. People grab a quick bite with folks they know in town all the time. I don't want to make something out of nothing. He's a general store employee, and I suppose, in a way, a friend. Even if he is a flirtatious one.

"I don't mind," I reply. "As friends."

I put extra emphasis on the word "friends" just so he won't go getting the wrong idea.

"Great, 'cause I'm starved." He, thankfully, doesn't seem to mind that I turn down his actual date offers.

Today, Miles is clean-shaven. His constant few days old scruff is gone, and it suits him.

"You look different," I observe.

He laughs. "Yeah, well, I do sometimes clean up."

He winks as I take a sip of the tea Bonnie sets on our table. Just then, awareness tingles up my spine. I turn to look at the new customer entering the diner.

Dawson.

He eyes me, and then Miles, pausing briefly before passing without a word. He grins at Bonnie, and she instantly becomes fidgety and nervous, a blush seeping through her cheeks.

"Can I have a cup of sweet tea to go?" he requests.

Miles sees me watching and follows my stare.

"How is the new renter working out?" he asks.

"Good," I answer.

Dawson clears his throat, and I look up in time to see Bonnie fumble with his change. He stares right at me, not at her, and I'm reminded of my almost mistake the other day.

"Order up!" the cook calls, and Bonnie rushes to get our food before setting it clumsily on our table, still flustered by Dawson, who seems to have that effect on women.

"Y'all need anything else?" she inquires.

"I'm good," I say, just as Miles replies, "No, thanks."

I eye the food longingly while Bonnie tops off our teas.

Dawson strolls by on his way out of the diner. I try with all my might not to look up, but at the last moment, I get trapped in his stare. He doesn't say a word. He doesn't have to. His silent frustration speaks loudly enough.

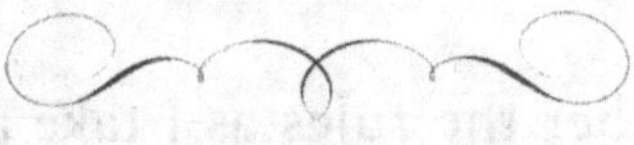

After lunch at the diner, a full day of work, and a quick dinner of leftover lasagna, a knock sounds at the door. By now I don't startle as much, maybe because I've become accustomed to having Dawson close, plus, I recognize the knock.

I unlatch the lock and come face-to-face with him.

"So, how about that card game you promised me? Still up for it?"

A single deck sits in his clutched hand.

"Of course." I welcome him in. "I don't break promises."

It's true.

He smirks, his eyes on me.

"What?" I wonder what he's thinking.

"A promise is a promise," he murmurs. "Reminds me of home. It's something my mom taught me. Promises were sacred in our family, never broken."

That's sweet.

I nod to the deck. "I haven't played in years."

Except for solitaire, which helped me pass the time as the system tossed me from home to home, never really leaving me anywhere long enough to make friends.

"Rummy?" he suggests, stepping deeper inside.

A tight, long-sleeved shirt clings to his sculpted torso, and sweatpants hang low on his hips. It's the sweatpants that get to me. He looks as though he belongs sprawled out comfortably on the couch, completely at home.

"Sure," I agree.

I try to remember the rules as I take a moment to clear

the table of a basket of vegetables, a candle, and an unpaid electric bill.

My eyes sneak across the small room to find Dawson watching me. I can just barely see him between a break in the curls that frame my face. They're freshly washed and more spiral than ever. I glance down at myself, realizing I may not be donning the most appropriate outfit, but then again, I didn't know he was cashing in on our card game today. My plum thermal pants fit like a second skin, droplets fall from my wet hair and land on my thin black shirt, and there's nothing I can do to hide the patchwork fuzzy socks I wear. I act as though it doesn't bother me that Dawson is seeing me in less layers than usual.

"Nice socks," he comments.

His frustration from earlier at the diner seems to have dissipated.

"You like my socks?" I ask dubiously.

I highly suspect he's hiding a grin by the way he doesn't answer and suddenly seems interested in a teapot on my counter, for which he needs to turn his head just far enough away that I can't catch sight of his mouth.

I make work of pulling the chair out and slowly depositing myself into it to buy time before I meet Dawson's gaze again. When I finally do, his eyes roam my body for a moment, then he blinks fast and it's gone, but I caught it.

I switch directions, changing my view from that of a man I can't seem to rid my mind of, to a far corner of the room where a fire blazes, keeping out the icy—nearly single digit—

temperatures. Beyond the window, flurries skydive in lazy patterns, not quite sticking to the ground.

With ease, Dawson slides into one of the two remaining chairs and deals the cards, drawing my gaze back to him. He pulls a small bottle from the pocket of his sweatpants and sets fire whiskey on the table.

"I don't usually drink," I disclose automatically.

"No problem." He uncaps the bottle, places his mouth at the rim, and pauses. "Do you mind if I do?"

When I have no objection, he downs a gulp. His tongue whips out quickly to lick a stray drop stuck to his lush bottom lip.

I watch with fascination.

"It's your turn," Dawson tells me.

That's when I realize I'm staring at his lips. I slowly get myself together, search my hand for a card to play, and lay it down absentmindedly.

Meow.

I look up. "Hey, Wizard."

I smile. The cat has been the perfect companion lately. He waits, roar purring, for me to scratch his head, so I oblige.

"You named him," Dawson remarks, as though my choice of moniker amuses him.

The cat is growing on me. Much like Dawson.

"Yeah," I admit. "I took him to the vet, only to learn his owner let him out on purpose and doesn't want him back."

Dawson frowns.

"He's mine now."

Wizard knows his spot is waiting for him by the flames. He saunters over and takes his time curling up just right.

Backlit and framed by the kitchen light, Dawson plays his hand. In no time, he's winning. He shoots me a look that tells me nothing, but I know there must be something going on in that brain of his.

"So, Camille," he begins, "where did you live before you came to Darlington?"

"New York."

"Oh, yeah? I've been a few times. Nice place. Which part?"

"North."

His quizzical expression is borderline accusatory. "You mean upstate?"

Yes. That's what most people call it. A simple slipup on my part.

"Right," I say.

I'm losing my hand, and I'm overthinking the night. I try to loosen up by reaching for the whiskey.

If I'm going to socialize, I need to do it without feeling like I've been chained tight. I uncap the bottle and take a sip, staring directly at Dawson in challenge. He says nothing and follows my sip with another of his own, offering the bottle up to the empty air like a cheers.

"Why do you read so much?" he inquires.

I love getting lost between the pages. I like having something to do when the seasons slow down.

"I didn't have a lot of belongings when I was a kid, but I owned a couple of books. I reread them over and over, and I swore to myself that, one day, I'd buy shelves and fill them with novels so I never had to reread one unless I really wanted to, but certainly never because I *had* to for lack of other novels."

I've just admitted a big piece of truth to him. I remember the books from my childhood clearly, could recite lines this moment if I wanted to.

"What about you, Dawson?" I question, liquid courage flowing through me. "You read, too?"

He watches me for a moment before answering.

"Maps," is all he says.

"You read maps?"

"I like them. They contain the entire world on paper. I can hold the world in my hands, let my fingers bump over mountain ridges, and calculate the distances between each ocean. Maps are easy to study. You can memorize nations and provinces and rivers. You can know a place according to its coordinates even if you've never been there."

I see his point, though I've never thought of it that way before.

"Some places aren't mapped out," I comment.

"Those are the best."

I take another sip of whiskey. It burns almost worse than the first time.

"Are you seeing him, Camille?" Dawson asks.

"Who?" The change of topic is jarring, and it takes me a moment to catch on. "You mean Miles?"

He waits.

"I'm not seeing Miles. He's a coworker. He happened to be in the diner at the same time and we had a friendly lunch."

I still blush, because it seems like Dawson cares if I'm dating Miles. Otherwise, why would he ask?

"You're sure?" He keeps his eyes on me, throwing a card onto the pile.

"I'm sure."

"He's into you."

I let a bit of truth slither free. "I don't want him."

"Hmm," Dawson replies.

"What about you?" I question. "Seeing anyone?"

A second passes before I realize I've voiced the thought aloud.

"No." Dawson smiles.

I trip on his look, forget it's my turn. I stare and stare, wondering how he does it. I can't even remember how to breathe. One minute he holds everything close to his chest, and the next he smiles, and his face opens completely. I don't ordinarily get caught up, I have my own guard to maintain, after all, but Dawson leaves me defenseless.

"Whenever you're ready," he prompts.

To play the game, he doesn't say, but I know that's what he means.

I set down a card, not paying attention to which one.

"Camille," Dawson murmurs.

"Yeah?" I look at the pile and frown.

The card isn't even facing the right way. I flip it over, but I'm not playing well. I need to pay better attention. I vow that to do this, I must not look at the man.

"What do most people do for the whole winter?" he inquires conversationally.

It'll be here in three days' time and the weather proves it.

"Hunker down," I answer. "The roads ice, so the stores close early, if they bother to open at all. In summer, most places welcome customers seven days a week. It's the busiest time for shops, and since it's when kids are off school, many families travel here for vacation, but in the cold months, the stores hardly unlock their doors for half that time. The hotels down the way close completely, the exception being the main inn that welcomes weekenders. Mr. Hill keeps the general store going year-round, though—one of the few that do. Everyone needs gas. Sometimes the roads are too bad to get all the way to the big grocery store, so he keeps the shelves well stocked. Winter months are our best months."

"Good to know," Dawson drawls. "At least I'll have work, then."

"There's always something to be fixed where Mr. Hill is concerned."

I play a card that helps me, but not enough to win.

"Another round?" he suggests.

I shuffle and deal the cards in response, careful not to touch Dawson's hand that snakes out to catch each card I slide his way.

"What do locals do when hunkering down?" Dawson asks.

I think about his question. The truth is, I keep to myself enough not to have a proper response.

"I don't know," I admit. "Maybe play cards like us? They

never stop fishing, that's for sure. We have customers buying bait even though they have to sometimes cut chunks of ice from the lakes and rivers before getting to the softer, fluid underbelly where water flows and fish wait."

This time, I play a particularly good hand. A crease appears between Dawson's brows. He seems to be surprised that I've taken the lead so quickly. There's a competitive edge to the way he sets his shoulders and lays his turn on the table.

"What do *you* do in the winter, Camille?"

"I've only spent one winter here, but I suppose I read, chop firewood, work at the general store, and grow peppers." I motion to the pots I have on the counter, freshly watered.

"Does your family visit?"

Dawson's chair scrapes slightly, as though he's moved closer to hear my response.

"I don't have family."

The silence that follows sounds like the way ice feels against my fingertips—cold and numbing. I set down my cards and fold my hands together under the table. Pinch the fleshy inside of my palm to keep myself from speaking to fill the void.

"None?" he presses. "No parents or siblings or anyone out there?"

"No one."

I try not to notice Dawson, but then I realize that if I do allow myself to look at him, it helps ease the urge to fidget. His eyes are, for once, not guarded. Not laughing. Just vast and observing.

"I grew up in foster homes," I confess. "No family and no real place to call mine."

Christ, I ought to sew my lips shut. I shouldn't be telling him this.

Dawson loses the grip he has on his cards, and one floats to the table, face up. The game seems to have paused entirely.

Determined to quiet myself from spilling any more secrets, I bite the inside of my cheek until it tastes coppery, as though I've placed a penny beneath my tongue. Right about now, I'd be jumping into the ocean for a stress reliever, but there is no ocean nearby. The itch to swim, to unload the gravity of my words, is nearly unbearable. The internal pulse and heave—breathe in and hold, dive underwater and paddle—builds up, expanding into pressure that presses on the walls of my ribcage.

"Where did your family go, Camille?" Dawson whispers.

Perhaps they didn't want the burden of a child, so they gave me away, and in doing so, they became so light that they were able to catch the nearest gust of wind and fly.

Perhaps they were young and thought they were doing the right thing, a selfless act. Or maybe they couldn't care for me and didn't want to burden me with whatever lifestyle they were living.

I've shaped the possibilities in my mind a hundred, thousand, million times. I have gone over it with a fine-toothed comb. In some stories, my mother simply gave me away to provide a better life for me. In others, there was abuse or something dark she meant to keep me from. In others still, both of my parents passed away and there was no one to take me in, so I had to go to foster care. I won't ever know the truth, however, because my case is sealed. Closed.

I answer with a shrug. Silence stretches.

There is so much truth in that one motion.

"I get what it's like to lose family," Dawson murmurs.

Our gazes collide.

I pretend not to see the thread of kinship he extends to me, instead laying down my next hand. I can't remember if it's even my turn, but I pick my cards back up and go anyhow, as though there is nothing to see here, as though the conversation hasn't happened.

Wizard slowly stretches by the fire and makes his way to me, placing his paws on my tights. Then his claws dig in. I yelp and bend under the table to disentangle him from my leg at the same time Dawson does, one hand running up my ankle and part of my calf to unhook the cat's still stuck claws.

My entire body bursts into flame. Dawson's touch ignites me through the fabric. I feel a slight tear in my tights and look down to see Dawson's face there, so close.

"Almost done," he informs me gruffly.

One last claw and he pulls Wizard into his lap, claiming his chair again.

"Do you think we could do dinner together sometime?" he requests, surprising me.

I can't afford a repeat of tonight, or else my loose lips will sink me. Then again, it's just dinner. I wonder if anything is "just" anything with Dawson. Everything seems to be done with such intensity.

Just dinner.

Dawson lays down the final hand, winning the game yet again.

"Okay." The word leaves my mouth of its own accord.

"Later this week?" he asks.

I nod, afraid to open my mouth. Dawson sets the cat on the floor, then stands, stretching to reveal a strip of skin above his sweatpants. I make every effort to look away.

"I better get back," he says, pocketing the deck. "It was great seeing you."

Dawson is out of the door and into the night before I can blink, just like last time when we almost got too close.

I can't afford to allow my mind to wander, to rearrange all the words I spoke, to somehow fit them where they belong, which is nowhere near the ears of the tenant who lives next door. Instead, I wash my face and collapse into bed, cocooning myself in a comforter that keeps me warm against the cold night. My dreams come swiftly in a blur of color.

A sprawling cityscape rolls down the streets. The nightlife pulses with energy, a beacon to those up late enough to witness it. My feet drag me toward the action, even though I want, more than anything, not to be here. I war with myself to turn around, to take a different route home. But the other roads are much less safe. Backstreets are a good place to be robbed. Or worse.

I arrive at the curb of a lavish club where entrance is said to be exclusive. Everyone tries to get in, but only some are granted access.

Even at that, there is a fee, and the drinks are more expensive than I could ever afford on my measly waitressing pay. I need to keep going. I still have several blocks until I make it home. Or, more accurately, to the place I'm staying now, paying cash to crash on someone's couch. A forever transient, but not by choice. It's the cards life dealt me. I'm only a few years out of the foster system, and this is the best I can do with no money in the bank and no family to speak of. It'll take me many more years to save enough to get my own place.

I stare at the club door, which is nearly blocked by three large men who resemble boulders. I notice one in particular because of the way his gaze sticks to me like the clingy dress I'm wearing. My feet ache. What was I thinking getting a job that requires me to wear heels all night?

"You," the guard calls. "Want entrance?"

I glance behind me, thinking he must mean someone else. He couldn't possibly be talking to me. My hair is a mess, my lipstick needs another coat, and I have a stain on the hem of my dress where a customer spilled ketchup only an hour ago. Though, come to think of it, the man most likely can't see the ketchup stain because it blends in.

"Me?" I ask.

Just then an expensive car pulls up to the curb, nearly clipping me. I squeal and jump out of the way, looking down to where my heel has caught in a crack in the ground. When I glance back up, a man in an impeccable suit is exiting the car, wearing a small grin on his face.

"You okay?" he inquires.

The scruff on his face is perfectly tailored, and I find myself wondering if he has it cut that way or if it just grows flawlessly. He's handsome. Too handsome. The suit accentuates his every muscle.

"Yes, thanks," I reply.

He appears older than me, but not by too much. He reaches out, bends, and wiggles my shoe loose. His warm fingers rest on my ankle, circling the thin silver chain there.

"Pretty," he comments in a Spanish accent, coming back to his full height, towering over me.

I don't know if he means me or the anklet.

The guards nod to him and open the door for his entrance. He's someone important, that much I gather. I wonder what it takes to get to that kind of status in society. Did he go to school for business and now he's part of one of the most successful clubs on the strip? Was he born into royalty? Maybe he inherited money, a bank account set up so he never has to worry about a thing in life. How nice that would be.

"Would you like to come in for a drink?" he offers.

His voice is honey smooth, and a grin plays at the corners of his mouth.

"I have to get going," I say. "Thanks anyway."

I bite my tongue to keep from asking him what it takes to know the kind of money he does. Usually, I'm not even close to people who have this much. I've never bypassed people who've been waiting in line for hours, hoping for entrance. Part of me is curious, wanting to accept his offer if not for anything other than to see what it would be like for one night, a single evening, on the opposite side of poverty.

"Anytime," he responds, and disappears into the club.

I don't think he actually means "anytime." Chances are, we'll never see each other again. I might have missed my only opening to experience VIP access. Still, I can't bring myself to accept the offer of a perfect stranger. And besides, it's too late now. No room for regrets. He's gone.

I walk away. Maybe one day I'll own expensive clothes and demand attention just by walking into a room, *I think to myself. A laugh bubbles up my throat. Even dreams are too far-fetched for a woman like me.*

I awake with a start, clutching my chest as tears burn my eyes. The dream was nothing compared to some of the nightmares I have, but it reminds me that I did, in fact, become a woman who demanded attention when she entered a room. All because of a certain man I met one day on the beach not long after that dream—or more correctly, memory—took place. The very same one from that night—Roberto. A man who became my destruction.

TWENTY

Dawson

Camille is getting to me. I like her. But I shouldn't. I've never allowed someone who's at such a distance to burrow so deep under my skin.

I almost kissed Camille while fixing her bathroom.

I almost walked right up to her in the diner when she sat with another man and asked her to follow me to the bait shop so I could kiss her like I wanted to.

Perhaps I need to work out my frustrations with Camille for one night. It's been several months since I last touched a woman the way I wish to touch Camille. Maybe that's the problem.

I tell myself that it's primal need that drives me ever closer to Camille, and not her laughter and smiles and the way she lights me up inside when she enters a room.

I'm nearly lost in the thought of her until instinct draws me to my surroundings.

I'm not the only one outside the camper.

I can sense it. Straining my ears, I reach for sounds on the breeze that gently threads through the air. There is nothing. And then...

"Are you sure?"

The voice is so faint, barely a whisper, that I can't decipher if it's male or female. The night is too dark, not even shadows can be seen aside from the ones close to the light that pours out from the camper's window, illuminating Camille's front door. I edge closer to the source of the noise, cautious of every footfall, of each slow and steady breath I take. If I'm careful, I can keep an eye on the camper and move closer to Camille's house at the same time. I reach into my back pocket for the jackknife kept there. It scissors open with a soft *swoosh*.

A faint glow of embers from Camille's fireplace, just slightly visible through her blinds, casts a miniscule shaft of light onto her driveway. I spot her truck and nothing more. I run a finger softly over the notched back of the blade, killing time. Holding my stance, I wait for the sound of voices once more. When I don't hear them, I edge around the side of Camille's house. That's when I catch the glow from the interior light of a truck parked on the opposite side. The engine is off, and I see why. No one is behind the wheel. Military training tells me to hold my guard, to not rush into an unknown situation.

Camille's voice drifts out from the darkness.

"Thanks," she murmurs.

I catch sight of her by the tailgate.

She looks at a man, motioning something with her hands, not appearing at all in danger. The man's back is turned to me, and Camille doesn't spot me. She wouldn't anyhow. I blend smoothly into the tree trunk beside me, into the darkness that envelops me.

"I'll see you again soon," the man whispers.

He takes a step toward Camille and her arms open for him. It hits me like a sucker punch to the gut. I finally understand what I'm seeing.

A man.

A truck.

A late night embrace.

Camille has obviously just had this man over. I actually believed for a moment that she might be in trouble. I flip the knife shut and pocket it once more.

"You can always call me, okay? Always," the man says.

I can't see Camille around the man's bulk. Her response is lost in his hold. Not once do I see the man's face. Not even when he hops in the truck, his ball cap low over his eyes. He shuts the door, and the interior light disappears. He doesn't bother with his headlights until he's nearly to the road, as though he knows her land by heart. I wonder just how many times this man has visited in the dark.

Or perhaps he saves the headlights for the road, so I won't see them from the camper. But why would they need to hide from me?

Camille takes quick strides to her front door, while I make it to her log pile in ten bounds. As she reaches the door, I step out of hiding.

Camille gasps and clutches her chest.

"Dawson, you scared me," she exclaims.

She looks beautiful under the brightness of the motion detector porch light. Her hair is somewhat tamed, twisted into a knot at the top of her head. But ever true to its unruly nature, stray strands still burst loose at her nape and temple. Her jeans are skintight, and her sweater looks to be about three times too big. She has no makeup on, fresh faced. I take note of her smattering of freckles.

Maybe she thinks I didn't see the man and the truck. But this is one thing, I decide, I won't gloss over. She's lied again. I never saw his face, but I know who the truck belongs to. I've seen it before.

"So," I say casually, "you don't know Luke well, huh?"

Camille is a deer caught in the headlights. She stares straight at me, mouth agape.

"Why lie, Camille?" I ask. "It's obvious that..." I struggle for the right words. "That you're seeing him."

It takes a moment, but Camille's expression changes. She laughs, actually laughs, her dimples caving in.

"Is that what you think? That I'm with Luke?"

"Aren't you?"

I can't quite hide the confusion in my voice.

"Go home, Dawson. This isn't your fight."

"I didn't realize it's anyone's fight."

Camille looks longingly at the fire, her arms wrapping around her now shivering body.

"It's cold," she notes absently. "And what I do is of no concern to you."

"I thought you were in trouble," I say. "I heard voices, and I came to check on you."

Her face softens. "Thank you, but I'm fine. Really."

"And Luke?" I press.

"He's just—" She pauses, and I can see the web of lies she's currently spinning like strands of silk above her mind. "A friend."

"Right," I drawl, not at all convinced.

For the very briefest of seconds, her stare slips to my lips.

"Camille." I step closer to the warmth that pours through the cracked front door. "Are you sleeping with Luke?"

I shouldn't ask. I absolutely have no right to ask.

"What does it matter?"

I don't touch her, but the urge is there all the same.

"Yes or no."

"No," she whispers.

"Never?"

She rubs her hands up and down her arms.

"Not once."

She's beautiful, and I'm not at all surprised that a man would be here. Hell, I'd jump at the chance if I thought there was any way to tell her the truth about me, or any way to not accidentally let it slip, to spend time with her without speaking about my life. And, really, she owes me no explanation, but she's chosen to tell me anyhow.

I edge just the slightest bit closer, and she leans toward me. That's all it takes for me to reach out and gently trace the galloping pulse at her neck. It hitches and throbs even more dangerously fast.

"I really can't discuss Luke," Camille whispers.

"Why not?"

"I don't know him all that well."

Her eyes shift to the right. More lies.

"You know him well enough to have him over late at night, hug him, and lie to me about how you know him in the first place," I challenge.

"Fine." She opens the door wider and slips inside. "You might be right about that. Come inside?"

She leaves the invite open for me to follow.

"How do you know him?" I question, closing the door behind me and backing Camille right into a corner, where she kicks off her shoes and pauses at my closeness.

"Can't tell you."

"Why not?"

Now that she's inside, where the fire cooks the air to a toasty temperature, she shrugs out of her sweater, revealing a skintight tank top with nothing underneath. My blood boils. I suddenly want to get her out of the tank, too.

"Because I don't want to," she states.

Desire pinwheels through her eyes. She's hiding something. I'm hiding, too. I'm not the person I presented to her, not when it comes to the facts. From Arizona. The house fire. My family dying. All lies. However, I've shown myself in other ways. My willingness to work hard. My love of southern sweet tea. My protective instincts. My longing for her.

"Camille," I murmur quietly. I wonder if she hears me at all. "I haven't told you everything either."

"Then, we're even," she whispers back.

Her eyes slip to my lips, and I can't, not even a little bit, hold back my reaction. For once, I lose control.

I pull her against me and kiss her with all the hunger that's built to a breaking point. The first taste of her is a punch of desire. Her hands weave into my hair, and she tugs roughly, attempting to get me closer. My bottom lip throbs from where she bites it. With my hands on her hips, I begin to lift her, to mold her to my body, to carry her to the bed.

I can already picture her under me, over me, claiming me. I imagine snapping that band out of her hair, her wild curls bursting free and spiraling to her breasts as she rides me. Or fanning out on the bed as I possess her. I want her now. Need her now.

She pulls away.

"You have to go," she pleads.

I watch the war in her eyes.

"I can't believe…I'm sorry. I shouldn't have kissed you. I didn't mean…I'm your landlord—"

"It's okay," I interject.

"But isn't it inappropriate?" Camille replies.

"We're both consenting, aren't we?"

"Of course," she rasps, panting when I drag kisses down her neck. "God, Dawson. Wait. I can't think when you do that."

"Does it feel good?" I ask huskily.

"Yes," she moans. "But I'm not sure if we should."

I stop immediately. I should tell her the truth of who I am now, but I'm not ready to discuss it or deal with the repercussions. It'll lead to questions I can't answer.

"What did you mean a few minutes ago when you said you haven't told me everything?" she inquires.

I won't answer that.

"Maybe we can just agree that I want you so badly I'm willing to break all the rules," I say instead.

"What rules? I don't understand," she admits.

"Maybe I can't tell you the same way you can't tell me."

She watches me silently.

I desperately want to finish where we left off, but instead I head for the door. She's right. I shouldn't have kissed her. I have to leave before I do it again. Without another word, I'm gone. I wait for regret to sink in.

It never comes.

TWENTY-ONE

Camille

The town festival is in full swing. I hardly ever attend these sorts of events, but I thought fresh air would do me good. I used to find solace on my land in the acres of sunlight and trees, the perfect place to clear my mind. But now, Dawson is everywhere, helping around the property, and even recently rebuilding the woodshed from scratch.

I unload boxes of coffee, freshly shipped and ready for the day. Luella, the cafe manager, is out front amid the town hustle and bustle, where people crowd Main Street. Mr. Hill owns the cafe, too, though he rarely visits. He would have sold it long ago if it wasn't for the fact that his wife started the café herself fifty years ago. He can't stand to see it go to someone who might make it into something else. Instead, he keeps it and allows Luella to run it. I busy myself with unpacking the new shipment to ensure the endless supply of free, refillable coffee at the outside table remains stocked, as Luella hands it out like candy to the adults. This is the only day she expects no payment from the patrons.

Somewhere past the front doors, a parade is taking place, filled with banners and townspeople and police who patrol the area, laughing freely with the locals they grew up with. Main Street is a tightly knitted blanket of family and fun, celebrating the beautiful last day of autumn before winter comes with even heavier frost and snow.

I'm already too far behind on boxes, and I have close to an hour's worth of work left before I can leave. I agreed to help when Mr. Hill asked this favor of me, which I ordinarily wouldn't do—putting myself near a crowd of people when I try my best to filter through the chaos, to stick to myself. Main Street is nothing like the general store, which is further away from the action of small-town life. However, I needed something to distract myself from the fact that Dawson has the day off and is working on trimming the bushes at the property. Mr. Hill promised I could stay in the back room of the coffee shop where no one would venture, unloading the shipment to ensure Luella has enough supplies for the day's fair and the busy week following, when people stay in town for a few days. He also promised to pay me double my usual rate. At least the café is closed for the day and locked to customers. Only Luella has the keys, using them to open the door long enough to carry the canisters to the front table where townspeople drink it up.

When I finish, I plan to slip out the back door and into an alleyway where my truck is parked.

Suddenly, there's a knock at the exit door.

I peek through the peephole to find Dawson staring back. He can't actually see me, but I bet he knows I'm inside. He always seems to know when I'm nearby.

"What are you doing here?" I ask, opening the door for him.

Pleasure slides through my veins at his ardent look.

"The old man gave me the address and insisted I help you with the boxes. Sorry I'm late. I wanted to finish the bushes I was trimming at the property first."

He's freshly showered and smells like cinnamon from the gum he chews.

"Mr. Hill told you to help?" He never mentioned that to me.

"Yes. Wherever you want me."

I grab a coffee bag to transfer to the front of the store, deposit filters and newly opened grounds into several large canister tops, and then stretch the sink hose over to fill them with water.

"What do I need to do?" Dawson questions.

He sees the tower of boxes.

"Maybe help fill the shelves with the new coffee shipment," I suggest. "It was supposed to arrive days ago but was delayed.

Which is why I'm here. As soon as the canisters are full, I'll take them outside and that should be enough."

Dawson gets right to work dismantling the tower of boxes. He takes them down methodically, opening each one as he goes. His strong muscles bunch up as he tears the tape from the cardboard.

"Thank you," I blurt.

Dawson stills. He must know what I mean.

"For the woodshed," I clarify. He's been replacing all the rotting pieces the last few days, making it look like new. "It's beautiful."

I would have had to pay way beyond my means to get something so perfect.

"You're welcome." His tone is deep and smooth, trickling over me like warm oil.

When his regard gets to be just a little too much, I look away. Get back to work.

"Why does the old man own this store if he spends all his time at the other?" Dawson asks.

"He couldn't stand letting it go to a stranger." I transfer the hose to the next canister and the next, until all six have the right amount of water. I hit the "On" switch. The smell of hot coffee begins wafting heavily through the air. "Who knows what the new buyer would do with it? They certainly couldn't run it like his wife and Luella did. Now Luella does it alone, but she hasn't changed a thing."

"Have to admire a man who holds on to family property

over the money it'd fetch," Dawson comments, arm deep in a box. "Where do these go again?"

He stands with several bags of coffee hugged to his broad chest. His method is much quicker than my one at a time. I try not to glance back as I lead him through the saloon style swinging doors to the front of the shop. Shelves line the wall behind the counter, displaying the flavor choices.

"Label forward on the shelves facing toward the lounge area," I instruct.

Dawson doesn't have to stand on the step stool like I do to reach the top, and he places them just as I've asked. He even sorts the decaffeinated to the side, and then puts them on their own shelf.

I go to the back for more. Each box has been torn open, and only a couple remain full. Before I know it, he and I have worked in tandem to stock everything. The coffee canisters are done brewing, too.

"I just have to bring these out to Luella, and we'll be finished. Do you mind breaking down the boxes until they're flat? I'll drop them by the landfill on my way home."

Dawson nods and disappears to the back. I take a second to watch him go, his pants shifting with each step. When I look up, I see Dawson has thrown a backwards glance at me, an intense expression attached. Damn it. He knows exactly where my eyes have been.

I grab one of the heavy canisters, careful not to slosh scalding coffee onto the floor or myself, and carry it to the front door where I set it down. I repeat the action until all the canisters are beside the door, and then I unlock it and take them one by one to Luella's table, which is scarcely three feet away.

She beams at me. "You're a lifesaver, doll. I am just about to run out of the ones I have. Did you finish the shipment?"

Luella's age shows in the gray streaks that thread through her chestnut hair. Her skin is mostly smooth, a fact she attributes to constant moisturizing, aside from the crinkles around her watery blue eyes.

"Sure did. You're all set. I'll get out of your hair," I tell her.

I nearly stop in my tracks. I find myself doing it more and more, using sayings like "get out of your hair," since moving to Darlington. I'm slowly letting the city fade from my veins. I like the feeling it gives me. As though I belong here.

I take a moment, just a moment, to watch the festival. A small child throws glitter into the air and it catches light and falls like rain. The man beside her laughs, even as she tells him he now sparkles like a unicorn. A woman holds an ice cream cone, smiling widely, her happiness worn for all to see. People stitch themselves into the crowd, finding a place to stand and watch it all, some drinking beverages, others diving into the bags they hold to retrieve goodies they've purchased. I take a deep breath, breathing it in—the crowd, the joy of the moment. Unfortunately for me, it is short-lived.

"I have to run," I say, knowing I've taken too long.

I'm exposed here. As beautiful as it is, I can't risk any more than these few heartbeats I've already spent. If a news crew came...if anyone from my past were here...if I ran into the wrong person who recognized me...it could all be over, this new life I've built. It's already almost happened once, with the man who visited the general store. He's seen my face before. He used to be the pool boy at the house I've tried so hard to leave in my past. He worked for the man I've run from. This world is too small, and the chances too great, not to bump into obstacles.

"Thanks, again," Luella calls, turning back to a patron who's come for a refill.

With all canisters on the table and a crowd bearing down, I reenter the shop and close and lock the door, making my way to the back where Dawson has broken down every single box and is waiting for me, arms crossed over his chest and a glint in his eyes, looking hotter than sin.

"Why do you keep looking at me like that?"

Why his words can evoke such a breathless response from me, I'll never know. He's caught me checking him out. He must understand I'm attracted to him. I'm just not sure if he minds.

"I don't know what you mean," I reply, feigning confusion.

He removes himself from the back wall and stalks over to me. The shades are drawn, so the light is soft, complimenting Dawson's features—the angle of his jaw, the curve of his chin, the dip below his bottom lip.

"I think," he whispers, stopping in front of me, his breath on my forehead, "that you know exactly what I mean. I want to hear you admit it."

He's right. I do know exactly what he means. My heart beats

rapidly in my chest. I try to control my reaction, but I don't have a choice in the matter, it seems, because my body wants him.

"Does it bother you that I'm your landlord?" I finally voice the question that's been gnawing away at me.

"Nope. Not one bit."

Huh. That's surprising.

"So, it's not an abuse of power if I try to be your—" I pause, searching for the right way to word it. "Friend?"

He chuckles like he knows I want more than that.

"You're not abusing *any* power, trust me. We can talk. We can be friends."

He says it so easily that I believe it's the truth. I exhale a sigh of relief.

He traces a finger around one of my spiraled curls, creating a pleasurable tickle on my scalp. When he tugs it gently, I bite my bottom lip to keep from groaning. Dawson's eyes are open, as clear as sunlight through stained glass, for me to see the desire churning in them.

I lean into him, beginning to tilt my head up, when suddenly he surprises me by stepping away. It really shouldn't come as a shock, though, since this is what he does every time it seems like we're getting too close—he puts space between us.

Except for the one time we kissed.

"Why don't I pile these in the bed of your truck?" He takes the liberty to open the back door and head out.

He loads my truck, using bungee cords to secure the cardboard and prevent it from flying away while driving. So many times, it seems like Dawson wants me, then at the last second, he doesn't.

"I've got to get going. See you at the property." He adds a small smile to soften the blow of his rejection, if it could be called that.

"Dawson." I reach out and settle my hand on his arm.

His eyes fall to where our skin touches, and I wonder if he feels the lure of skin-to-skin contact the way I do. It's only his arm. It's only my hand. Yet it's so much more. I want to glide my hand up to his neck, his hair. I want to press myself against him and feel the hard planes of his body.

"Are you okay?" I ask.

He opens my truck door for me. "Never better."

His voice is even. He controls himself well. I wonder how many things he saw in the army, and in life, to shape him into the measured person he is now, able to hide his emotions. His body is taut, as though I could pluck each muscle like a stringed instrument.

"I'll see you at the house," I murmur, removing my hand from his arm.

He shivers as I close the truck door between us.

TWENTY-TWO

Dawson

Camille drives off first, but accidentally leaves her purse at the back door. My vehicle is the lone truck in the lot behind the store. Three other employee cars sit down the way, behind other establishments. I can only assume their owners are on the other side of the brick building, where noise carries and people laugh, and the sound of hundreds of feet remind me of a marching platoon. There's a crack between each store, only large enough to fit my hand in, but through it I can see bodies shuffling around. I catch a glimpse of a banner, a small girl blowing a party horn, and a teenager drinking soda out of a glass bottle.

I eye the purple bag I retrieve. It's a deep color, nearly black. My finger holds up one short strap, the other hanging limp against the fake leather. It's not the outside that calls to me, though. It's what's *inside* that I'm interested in. She remembered her keys, that much I'm certain of. Otherwise, she wouldn't have been able to drive off. But somewhere in her haste, between watching me and touching my arm, she forgot her bag.

Now it's in my hand.

Inviting me to look.

Camille has so many secrets. I want to know one of them. Maybe I want to *be* one of them.

There's a charm about her—those hazel eyes and beautiful curls, that grin and elusiveness. Most people accept her smiles and non-answers. I know better. I see it in her stare, how she holds back.

Trying to ignore the impulse telling me it's wrong to snoop in her personal things, I latch onto the zipper and tug. I mean to uncover her secrets. I don't want to exploit her. Methodically, I tick through the items. A pack of gum. Hair tie. Pen. Forty-two dollars cash. No credit cards. No identification. How odd.

At the bottom, I find a cell.

I don't have to wonder if it's locked. It's an old thing, a silver flip phone with buttons instead of a touch screen. I open it and scroll through her contacts. There are only six. The old man. Mrs. JoAnne, who I learned is her neighbor. A woman, Rose—I suspect from the diner. North Carolina Electric Company. Auto insurance. The final is Luke.

I wonder if those are the sole bills she pays—electricity and auto insurance. She has a well on the property, so I already know she doesn't pay for water. And she delivers her trash to the dump, so she doesn't pay that either. She could buy prepaid cards for the phone. It's possible she doesn't have a monthly bill. She's not very rooted, aside from the house and property.

The other contacts seem to be people from town, maybe the ones she holds closest. When I press my finger to the call log, it's clear of missed and outgoing. There are no photos. No internet. No apps. It reminds me of a burner phone. Something doesn't seem right. This isn't a device that belongs to someone who normally collects life moments to look back on. It's the phone of someone who likes to keep her record clean.

Part of me grimaces with injustice. Camille will never know I've seen her personal items, though they don't say much about her anyhow. And I, of course, won't tell her. I've betrayed her trust. She's made it so easy for me to.

There's one last zippered section. I pull it open and look inside. There's a ring with a round, onyx stone encased in silver, with swirling patterns etched across the thick band. It's feminine in quality and older in design. It looks like every other natural stone mined here in the foothills of the mountains and sold at one of the stores off Main Street. I toss it back in.

Camille has left absolutely no clues for me. Smart woman.

I keep my frustration in check. If I want to know what she's hiding, I'll need to try harder.

I nearly forget about the festival until I hear a bellowing laugh that makes my head snap up and the hairs on the back of my neck stand on end. I toss the purse on the truck cab seat and grab my gun. How easily I switch modes. Now I'm alert, assessing, cunning. More so than usual.

Because I know that laugh.

Or, at least, I know one that sounds just like it.

It belongs to a man I don't want to see here, where I'm trying to blend in and go unnoticed. This is my escape. A haven in the mountains. He shouldn't be here. I catch a swath of black, the tail of a coat. Even that's familiar. There's a tiny boy on the shoulders of a man next to him, reaching out and hoping to catch a flyaway piece of confetti. If it's him, a face from my past, I can't tell clearly. The woman to his side blocks my view, hiding his features. A second more and he'll pass by completely, as soon as the crowd shifts and moves again.

I click off the gun's safety.

I don't want to shoot him. Not here. There are too many people. I don't normally make mistakes, especially not with my eye on a target, but this is risky. I don't have a clear shot. Besides, there's a little boy close by. I can't do it. But I also can't let him see me. I keep my face obscured by the ball cap low on my head.

All he has to do is shift a little more.

Look to the right.

He'll see me, but he won't know it's me.

I press my luck and stay until, finally, one boot moves in front of the other and he slips back into the crowd, nearly out of view. At the last second, he turns my way.

The face...is not familiar.

I exhale loudly. That was close. Way too close.

It was just a man on vacation with his family. No need to worry.

No one has found me. I'll try hard to make it so they can't. Unless I want them to, and I do want them to. Eventually.

But not yet.

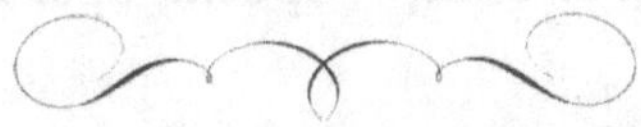

Warm fur brushes against my leg as I climb the steps to enter the camper. There's a pie waiting for me with a single note scribbled on a scrap of paper taped to the container.

Be good to our girl. —Mrs. JoAnne

It's pecan. I love pecan.

"Hey, buddy." I bend to pet Camille's cat, who comes over to sniff the pie. After a moment, Wizard walks off.

I really should pick him up and take him to Camille's place. Come nighttime, it'll be too cold for him. The weather is calling for several inches of snow. It's already begun to fall in swirling patterns.

I follow the cat outside where I nearly run into someone, and my hand whips out lightning fast in defense. I stop short. I'm still on edge from the festival the previous day.

"What the hell, Dawson?" Camille shouts, her eyes wide with surprise.

I acted on instinct. Didn't stop to think that it could be

Camille. Of course, it's Camille. No one else would be on the property. I let my defenses down, but only just a little.

I haven't seen her since yesterday when I gave the purse back, much to her relief. She was happy it'd been found and returned by me and not a stranger.

"Sorry," I apologize. "My special ops instincts are still intact."

I grab Wizard from a bush he's rubbing against.

Camille's gaze goes sharp. "Special ops? I thought you were a medic."

I scrub a hand down my face, the skin of my palm rasping over the stubble along my jaw. I do it again, a habit of mine, relishing the noise that acts like static against my racing thoughts. I've finally told her more, even though I tend to hold my cards closely.

Camille places her hands on her hips and eyes me suspiciously. Her curls are wild and springy, her clothes hidden under a long, apple red coat that meets zip-up winter boots. She tucks her hands into the coat pockets and dips her chin into the checkered scarf wrapped several times around her neck.

"What kind of special ops?"

No point in backtracking now. "Delta Force."

"You lied to me," she accuses.

"Not technically."

She cocks her head to the side. "You withheld information."

"Do you never do that?" I counter, but I already know the answer.

She huffs. "Why didn't you tell me that you were U.S. Army

Special Ops, and Delta Force, no less, Dawson?"

"Most of us don't advertise that sort of thing."

Which is the truth. The job is bloody, scary, and dangerous. The soldiers are few and far, and that is thanks to the job. Enemy forces go to extremes to eliminate us, as I know all too well. We are the select who scope out the maps and lands before other soldiers are brought in. We gather intel. Spy. Lie. Cheat.

"Why not?" she questions.

I stare at her, flummoxed. "Because, Camille. We uncover terrorist groups and uproot those interested in unconventional warfare against our country or the countries of our allies. We lead counterterrorism and foreign international defense. We gather intelligence and monitor the movements of some of the world's most dangerous organizations and people. These are the jobs I used to do. Why would I purposely parade that information around?"

Not many people find the fact that I can kill a person stealthily with my bare hands endearing. My classification put me at the heart of danger.

Camille sighs and a curl bounces into her face. Her expression changes from defensive to assessing. She watches me like she might survey a wild animal, with interest and distance.

"Okay, I understand," she concedes. "You had a dangerous job. You wanted me to think you were just a medic, but tell me this, were you ever a medic?"

"Yes."

She braves one step toward me, and her teeth begin to

chatter from the cold. Even though Wizard's fur is warm, I'm close to losing the feeling in my fingers, and I'll need a heat source soon before the effect of the bitter snow trickles into my entire body.

"Why did you switch?"

She asks too many questions, but I answer anyway.

"When on duty as a medic in the Rangers, between patching up guys, I liked to study maps. In my off time, at night, I'd read them like one would a book. Sometimes, I'd scope out the land. Watch enemies through a sharp distance lens. Recognizing patterns and movements became easier than breathing. It became natural. I predicted many instances of enemy movement, moles, and traps. Eventually, I liked it more than I liked patching people, and I told my boss. He said it was about damn time I stepped it up, and that he thought me better suited for Delta Force. It's rare for Delta Force to take someone straight from an infantry unit, but if I could make it through the assessment and training, the position was mine."

"And you made it," she murmurs. "You became Delta Force."

I don't know why I'm answering her questions. They are far too close to home, to the deep, hidden part of myself that I tend to uncover for no one.

"Yes," I reply.

"Did a mission go wrong? Is that why you don't like to talk about it?"

So, she does realize the conversation makes me uncomfortable. Yet she still presses.

"I can't talk about my missions. That's classified information."

"Will you at least tell me why you left the military?" she inquires.

"My contract was up," I divulge. "It was time to go."

She averts her gaze and glances off at the sky heavy with snow. She's infuriating, curious, and beautiful.

I don't let my truths out directly, or really at all. Yet here she is, asking for them.

She opens her mouth, and I fear it is to question more about my past, so I cut in. "Can we please move on now?"

She considers me a moment, and then turns on her heel and begins walking home.

"Okay."

"One second," I say. She pauses. "You should bring Wizard inside. It'll be too cold out here for him tonight."

Camille backtracks and grabs the cat, snuggling him to her chest. He meows as she takes him home.

Just like that, the conversation is over.

And just like that, I've given her one of my truths.

TWENTY-THREE

Before

The luxurious club isn't the type of place Mr. Cruz ordinarily meets his connections, but this one is different. This is his supplier.

"What do you need?" Mr. Cruz asks, cutting to the heart of the matter.

The man sitting across from him eyes his club with a poker face. It unnerves Mr. Cruz. He can read most people, but not this connection. The man is good. Maybe a little too good at what he does. His laid-back posture in a setting completely foreign to him tells Mr. Cruz that the man is experienced in handling himself. He's dressed well in a sharp, crisp suit that contrasts with his relaxed demeanor.

"Like I mentioned, I want to discuss our business model," he says, not touching his drink.

Smart of him. He, like Mr. Cruz, doesn't intend to be caught off guard.

"There's nothing to discuss," Mr. Cruz retorts.

The man smiles. "Oh, but there is, don't you think? See, here's the thing. You need more product from me, which means your demand has increased. Which also means that you have more money flowing toward you. It stands to be said that you now have a bigger business model to work with."

His supplier isn't wrong.

"Your point?" Mr. Cruz inquires.

There's no use denying the obvious. He does have a bigger business model. Feeling a bit on edge, he shoots his hit man a look. There may end up being a problem tonight. His hit man gets the wordless message.

"I want in," his supplier announces, pulling a flask from his own pocket and drinking from it, smile in place.

He's still just as unreadable as his stoic expression earlier. Maybe even more so now.

"You're already in," Mr. Cruz responds. "I allow you to supply me and I pay you a cut."

"Ten percent is child's play. I want thirty."

"No," Mr. Cruz argues.

"Thirty. You don't want your business information getting into the wrong hands, do you? That would be a shame. I, however, have a system in place that ensures information never gets out. Unless, of course, there's an accidental leak."

"Are you threatening me?" Mr. Cruz growls, his voice dangerously low.

He loses the smile.

"Yes," his supplier answers in an equally dangerous tone. "I'd hoped I wouldn't have to. I'd hoped you'd see reason and numbers for what they are. My business is good. And how do you repay me? You offer a shit percentage and shut me out the minute I ask for more. That ends today. You will give me thirty percent."

Mr. Cruz slams his drink down on the table.

"You do not come into my club and demand things from me."

"You have a lot more to lose than I do. What about the shipment you need in three days? Will you be able to make your connections in time if I back out? Will they give you as good a product as I do?"

Mr. Cruz grinds his teeth and swears.

"That's what I thought. You wouldn't want to disappoint the buyer, would you? We have an agreement. It's numbers, nothing personal. If you can't meet what I need, I'm done. And you will let me walk away unharmed or else your precious information, which I've secured through several channels, will leak. You should have accepted my offer without the fight."

Mr. Cruz eyes the man across from him with both disdain and admiration. He's cunning. He has what it takes to get the job done, and that's something Mr. Cruz admires.

"I'll give you twenty percent and not a penny higher," he counters.

His supplier takes another pull from his flask and thinks about it.

"Okay," he finally says. "On the condition that, in three months, you up it to twenty-five."

Mr. Cruz isn't sure the man will still be living in three months, thanks to his demands, but he nods all the same.

"Do me a favor," Mr. Cruz begins.

"What's that?"

"Don't ever come back here."

He laughs darkly. "So, phone calls and messages only?"

But Mr. Cruz isn't laughing at all. He's kept the connection because the man does provide the best product around. Until his demand of a higher cut, he couldn't have been happier with the arrangement. But if he does have a system in place to leak information to the wrong people, which he suspects is true, then Mr. Cruz has no choice but to play along.

Not that he'll ever admit it. Still, he won't go down without a fight.

"You come back here again, and I'll have my men chop your body into so many pieces that no one will find you," Mr. Cruz warns. "The bottom of the ocean is pretty deep. You'll know just how deep if you ever threaten me again."

TWENTY-FOUR

Camille

"Another winter's here," Will says, meeting me at the dividing line.

"Sure is," I reply, extending the burlap sack to him. It's full of window grown peppers, the only thing I have to offer this late into the season.

My fingers are still stained with dirt. A layer of black sticks to the underside of my nails, displaying trace evidence from the potted plants and stinging with the spice of the hot peppers.

"Smells delicious," he compliments, taking my offer and handing me a mason jar full to the brim with honey, a soft comb inside.

I notice he hasn't brought an instrument this time. He lights a cigarette and inhales deeply. Right there, on the cold earth, he takes a seat, smiling up at me as I lean against the bark of a neighboring tree.

"Tell me about the renter," he drawls.

I wonder what exactly he wants to know. Will doesn't ask about many people.

"His name is Dawson," I tell him. "He moved from Arizona where a house fire took his family."

Will's face is solemn as he pulls another drag into his lungs. A plume of smoke rises into the air between us, creating a thick, ghostly wall.

"Shame to hear," he murmurs. "Good that he got away. Sometimes it's easier to leave the past behind. Maybe he'll be good for you—allow you to have friends your age. Hard to come by when most folks who own acres and acres are older. You lucked out with that land. Hold it forever. It'll be worth a pretty penny one day, guarantee it."

I don't know if I can. It depends on if I have to run again.

"Tell me more," he requests.

"Well, he's ex-military." I notice a drop of sap oozing from the tree and scoop it up between my fingers, rubbing it over the burn of the peppers. "He's working for Mr. Hill now, and he seems to fit in just fine around the property. Even around the town."

"Sounds like you get along."

"We do."

"Maybe even enough to become friends?"

I consider it. "Maybe."

Will withdraws a pepper and bites clean into it right there, seeds and all. I don't know how he stands the heat of it without adding them to blander foods and cooking them to calm the spice.

"You're different, Camille. I see it in you. You need folks, and that's okay. I hope he stays."

"Thank you."

The fact that Will wants to see me settled and happy creates a warmth in the center of my chest.

"Better get going," he announces. With one last bite, he finishes the pepper and stands. "You take care now."

With a nod, he's gone, weaving back into the trees.

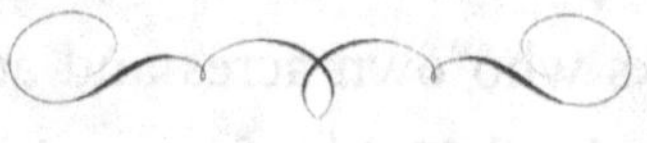

Dawson's curses reach my ears, carried on a crisp wind, a moment before I arrive back at the camper from visiting Will. The winter sun shines boldly in the sky, melting patches of snow. The paths through the trees are more pronounced, less overgrown than they used to be, in equal measures due to Dawson and his promise to clean up the place, and because of the barren season.

Another curse comes, accompanied by the sight of Dawson bent over the open hood of his truck. He's created a trail of mud leading to his bowed frame, leaving behind boot impressions.

I expect to find him layered in clothes, but he wears only jeans and a thin camo-printed shirt. He is every bit the army soldier when he hears my approach and does three things at once.

He straightens.

Turns to the noise.

Reaches into his pocket.

I'll never know what he meant to grab because, at the sight of me, he relaxes. I wonder if it's wiser for me to announce myself instead of sneaking up on him. I don't know what he intended to pull from his pocket. Maybe his keys or a phone? But come to think of it, I've never seen a cell on him. Maybe he prefers to be disconnected from the world.

"Are you okay?" I eye his vehicle.

"Truck's not running. It's the thermostat," he says. "Alternator belt, too. Snapped in half."

I peer skyward and know that the frost must have crept up from the ground and over his tires, slithering like a growing vine and attaching to the engine segments underneath the hood.

"There's a shop just past Main Street that carries parts." A small smile dares to curve my lips. In order for Dawson to get to the shop, I'll have to drive him. "I could take you."

When I allow my gaze to meet his again, I see he's moved toward me, halting a mere foot away.

"That'd be great," he replies.

While he retreats to the camper, I fetch my keys and set the jar of honey on the counter. As soon as I enter the truck, I blast the heat, waiting for him. He returns a minute later, taking the liberty to fill the passenger seat, smelling of the finest cologne.

He offers me one of two thermoses, and I'm pleased to discover that it holds coffee heavy with cream. He must have bought a coffee maker for the camper. I take a warming sip, then place it in the cup holder and begin the drive to the auto parts store, careful to mind the road, which is still speckled with ice and snow where branches hang over, blocking part of the sun's reach. Dawson adjusts the vent nearest him, so it blows heat toward his red, patchy hands. He had the audacity to work on frozen engine parts with no gloves. No wonder his fingers are angry in some parts and drained of color in others.

"You look nice," he compliments, taking me by surprise.

He's noticed that I've worn a dress over tights and boots, and my favorite wool jacket the color of pine needles, finishing the ensemble so I don't freeze. My scarf is weaved with every imaginable color, but a patch of skin below the scarf, just over my dress, leaves the tops of my breasts visible. It's an outfit I don't normally wear to work, but seeing that I have a day off, I've chosen it.

"Thank you," I say.

I want to tell him that he looks incredible, too, but I'm not bold enough.

"How far is the store?" he asks.

"Just around the next few bends, and then straight past Main Street," I tell him, taking the curves slowly.

Birds jump from limb to limb on trees growing from

the shoulder of the thin ribbon of road. It's mostly deserted, considering that the clock hasn't yet stretched its hand to the eleventh hour. The store isn't open, but it will be soon, and in any case, it's nice to be one of the first ones in before the men begin their hang outs, loitering by the side of the front door.

"Do you know how to fix it yourself?" I question, thinking of his truck. "There's a guy, Jimmy, who'll come out to the property and fix it as long as you buy the parts from him."

Dawson watches the trees go by, a steady streak of brown. His legs don't quite fit comfortably between the seat and the dashboard, on account of being too long. He shifts slightly and stretches them as much as the truck will allow.

"I know how to do it myself," he murmurs. "Just need the parts."

He's shaven recently, and I have to use a balance of willpower and focus not to stare at his smooth face. Still, I feel Dawson next to me, seeming to suck up all the air in the truck cab, creating a need to roll down the window just a crack to let fresh air in. Maybe the breeze will calm my heated blood.

"How'd you learn to fix engine parts?" I inquire.

"Taught myself. Lengthy hours as a teen spent under the hood of the very same truck parked in your drive, willing it to work long enough to get me into some sort of trouble."

He smiles and I have to remind myself to keep my eyes on the road.

"You get into trouble often?" I press.

"Yeah. Just dumb stuff."

"Like staying out past curfew?"

I take the last bend, grateful to be on a stretch of straight road from here on out. This way, I can snatch more glimpses of Dawson's profile, of his strong jaw and thick brows.

He taps his pants three times. Stops. Three times again. A repetition. I have the impression I'm making him nervous.

"Stuff like that, yeah," he responds. "Mostly, I did stupid things for attention. Whether for friends or girls, mattered none. I suppose I wanted to be seen. So, I caused trouble. Once, I plowed down someone's fence and had to work off the money it cost the homeowner to fix it. He was a mechanic. Was angry about the damage and told me to learn about cars, read up on them. I helped him around his shop. Learned some there, too, by watching others for the entire two months I had to work off my debt."

Dawson cracks his window to match mine, just enough to fit a worm, to even out the inside cab pressure building in our ears.

"Wrecked the first car I ever had by being dumb and racing a friend. No one was hurt, but it scared me into not racing anymore. That's when I got the truck, at seventeen. Did other stuff, too. Pranked teachers. Set off fire alarms to get out of classes. Accepted a dare to jump off the roof of our high school building and broke my collarbone. It still occasionally aches with the recoil of a rifle."

I think about what he'd need to use a rifle for in the army. The man next to me has most likely taken lives. The thought makes me shift in my seat, giving me an uncomfortable twinge between my shoulder blades. I'm grateful for his service, just anxious at the notion of what that must do to a person, ending another life.

Dawson turns to me, watchful.

"Who taught you to read so much?" he asks, changing the subject.

"I taught myself. I missed many days at many different schools, a whole month one time, while moving around to separate homes. Someone was almost always sick in those homes, too, with all the germs a household carried with three and four and five kids around, causing me to catch colds and viruses that meant more missed school. One home I stayed at had twelve kids. I'm not sure it was legal. They were hardly ever safe places. I didn't get the chance to learn steadily from a teacher, or progress to new grades in the case of my second and fifth years of schooling, from missing too much. So, I took the little I learned at school and figured it out."

I think back to the shabby, stiff sheets that would scratch me at night while I read past bedtime.

"I had a curfew, always a curfew, but I also had a penlight, and when everyone went to sleep, I'd steal an hour of reading. I often reread the same three books, some of the few items— along with a week's worth of clothes, a deck of cards, and a raggedy stuffed rabbit named Muffins—that fit in my traveling backpack.

We draw nearer to the auto parts store just as the clock reaches eleven. The sun shines through the gray that fades from sight. I don't tell Dawson I've taken the roads that are slower and longer, because this way I have more time with him and we are less likely to pass other cars, of which we've seen only one, making it appear as though we have the waking world to ourselves.

"My mother used to read often," Dawson shares quietly.

I don't want to know if her books burned in the fire, or if some tragedy made her stop her love of the written word. I fear Dawson will clam up if I ask. It's enough that he's told me something.

"There's an antique store in town," I tell him, thinking of the only thing Dawson likes to read. "I believe they sell maps. Maybe you could find something you like there."

It's odd that I know what Dawson likes. I remind myself that I don't intend to get too close. In the same moment, Dawson leans toward me and fiddles with the broken stereo, and I abandon all thought.

He smells even better up close. I inhale his scent as his roughened hands turn the old dial, pressing buttons as a line creases between his brows.

"I could fix this for you," he offers.

I swallow and nod, not trusting myself to speak with him so near.

"Camille," Dawson murmurs lowly.

I bite my lip and purposely avoid his stare. He brushes a curl away from my face and trails a finger down the pulse in my neck.

"Yes?" I whisper, eyes on the road.

"What are you thinking?" There's a smile in his husky voice.

Just then an image of him placing kisses where his fingertip trails comes to mind. I imagine him to be the sort of man who appreciates the curvy form of a woman, and takes his time undressing it. In my thoughts, he's a passionate lover, knowing every spot to explore and every way to please.

"Nothing," I reply breathlessly.

He chuckles. "Liar."

"We're here!" I declare with false bravado.

I quickly pull into a parking spot and relish the bite of frozen air on my face, which cools the heat from my cheeks. Dawson's eyes are on me, but I don't turn to see his expression.

The front of the store is like most of the rundown buildings in this small town—a wooden porch out front with a cat curled in a ball on old cloths, and a dog who blocks the entrance, fast asleep on the welcome mat. He opens one eye, peers at me, and decides I'm not interesting enough to get up for.

"Bear! Get outta the way and let my customers in, won't cha?" hollers a man from inside the shop.

The dog yawns and rolls over just enough to allow the door to partially open. I slip through, Dawson behind me.

"Hey, Jimmy," I greet.

"Well, hello, beautiful." He offers me a gummy smile, missing half his teeth. "What brings you out to these parts? Truck actin' up again? I might be able to fix that for free if you cook me a dinner outta those vegetables I hear you grew good this year."

"That sounds fair, but I already gave them all to Mrs. JoAnne and Will," I tell him, letting him down kindly. "Only a couple peppers left. It's not my truck that's the problem, anyhow. This is Dawson. He needs an alternator belt and a thermostat for his. I'll let him tell you about it."

Jimmy nods to Dawson. "You're new here. The name's Jimmy. What can I do you for?"

I wander off to the display beside the counter while Dawson describes the make, model, and year of his vehicle. The table holds small fairy houses and lawn gnomes, advertised on sale for a good price.

"My momma makes 'em," Jimmy says to me, momentarily breaking from his conversation with Dawson. "Swears they help rid your garden of rascals. I've told her time and time again that there's no such thing as damn fairies and that most regular folk know that and aren't keen to be buyin' houses for 'em, but she 'bout had my hide the last time I mentioned it, so they're for sale and there's no way to stop that," he explains apologetically, as though it might offend me that he's selling magical creature homes. "But wouldn't you know I've sold three of 'em already? Blows my mind. Momma's in a right state about how she told me so."

"They're nice," I reply, smiling softly.

Jimmy is dark skinned, pushing fifty, and still scared to death of his momma.

"Well, good news is I have the coolant and thermostat," Jimmy announces, returning to both his conversation with Dawson and the front counter, having slid off to a nearby shelf to retrieve the products now in his hands. "Bad news is I don't have the alternator belt. Won't get a new shipment till next month."

"I can't wait that long." Dawson takes the thermostat and coolant, laying a few bills on the counter as Jimmy finishes ringing him up.

"There's a place that'll probably have it, but it's a bit of a drive," he says. "Just off the highway in Asheville."

"That's an hour away," I say.

"Hang on," Jimmy replies. "Let me call 'em."

"So," Dawson drawls to the warm air between us. "Asheville?"

Having Dawson up close in a different environment reminds me that this landscape is foreign to him, and he needs my help.

"They have it in stock," Jimmy calls, hand over the receiver.

"I can take you, if you want," I offer.

He doesn't have another option except to wait for Jimmy's supply. Our town is too far away from the hustle and bustle, too removed from bus lines and cabs and ride companies.

"Thanks," he says.

"Tell them to hold it for us," I request of Jimmy.

"Will do," he responds.

Dawson places a hand on my arm. Our breathing falls into a rhythm. Although we're in a rundown auto parts store, I have the urge to lean into him, to stop fighting the pull of his lips, and I nearly do until a throat clears behind us.

TWENTY-FIVE

Dawson

"**W**ell, howdy, Luke!" Jimmy greets, happy as can be.

Luke looks me over, scrutinizing my nearness to Camille. His eyes are hard and assessing. It seems he has something to say, and I doubt it's in my favor.

"I got your part waitin', just like I said I would," Jimmy informs Luke.

He either hasn't heard Jimmy, or chooses to ignore him.

I reevaluate both Luke and Camille. Perhaps I missed something crucial. My knowledge only goes as far as knowing that the two of them have some sort of friendship which she mostly keeps quiet for whatever reason. She won't talk about him, and he won't come around her place when I'm there. I wonder why that is. It's like they both want to keep something quiet. But why?

Perhaps I've miscalculated. I asked her once if they were an item and she denied it. Maybe she's a better liar than I give her credit for. She refuted a relationship, but she never said if she has feelings for him.

"Camille?" I ask. Maybe she'll let me in this time.

But probably not.

She seems to be stuck in the awkward moment, not knowing what to say. Or maybe she'd hoped this occasion wouldn't come, where Luke and I meet. But it has, and there's no avoiding it.

"Dawson," I offer, being the bigger man.

I stick out a hand, wondering if he'll actually shake it.

He does. "Luke."

His voice is deep but quiet. His handshake is one of the firmest I've ever felt. There's a quiet power about him, and he doesn't look happy to see Camille and me together. I let go of the handshake.

"Luke is an old friend," Camille says, and then stiffens, as though she's misspoke, but I don't see how that's possible as she hasn't told me much yet.

Luke leans forward dand says something in her ear. I can't hear his words, though I do hear her response.

"How about later this week?" she replies quietly.

Luke nods once. Camille throws a glance my way, accentuated by a red blush seeping into her cheeks.

"So," she says to him, "picking up something, I see."

Now they've decided to talk loud enough for Jimmy and me to hear.

"A mower part," he replies.

Silence stretches. Camille fills it.

"We're here for his truck." She motions to me. "It broke down."

"Too bad." He directs this at me, and I find I'm having a hard time reading the man.

"Anyhow, nice running into you." She kisses him once on the cheek and backs away.

I follow her, though my eyes remain on Luke. Jimmy busies himself until the moment we reach the door, when he suddenly pretends he hasn't been eavesdropping.

"Y'all have a nice day," he calls. "Enjoy that drive. Perfect weather for it."

I peer out at the sky. The temperature clashes with the picturesque setting, barely hitting twenty degrees. I pull my coat closed and zip it to my chest.

Luke saunters away, down an aisle and out of sight.

"Camille," I murmur, as we exit the shop and maneuver around the potbellied dog on the entrance mat, careful not to tip the tinned plants on either side that decorate an otherwise plain, wooden porch. The dog snores loudly, barks softly in his sleep, and pays us no mind.

"Yeah?" She steps over the dog and bends to scratch behind his ear.

"I know you said you and Luke weren't an item, and I respect that, but…" I pause, wondering how to word it. "What *is* going on with you two?"

"I'd rather not talk about it."

It's the only answer she offers.

"Is there anyone in your life romantically? In any way?"

Camille takes the driver's side of her truck and waits for me to fill the passenger side. I sink into the seat next to her. When the doors close and she starts the engine, the answer I seek hangs in the air of the cab.

"There is no one, Dawson. I never planned for there to be someone here."

Never. A word with that sort of strength, swearing off the romantic companionship of another, doesn't usually belong to a woman close to thirty—so young.

"Never?" I repeat, more to myself than anything.

Then I think about my own transgressions. I never planned to leave the army. I never would have guessed I'd be where I am. Things are different now.

"You don't understand, Dawson."

Her words are whispered into the wintry day.

"Help me." I plead with my stare for her to trust me, but I already know she won't.

"I can't."

I can't. This, too, is a strange choice of words.

It's not that she doesn't want to.

More like something is prohibiting her from letting me in. Maybe…someone?

TWENTY-SIX

Camille

"This is Asheville," I tell Dawson.

Here, in the city, the wind blows cold and strong. I huddle under the thickness of my jacket and hood. The shop with Dawson's alternator belt isn't far, but since all the street parking spots are taken at the center of the busy avenue, we have two blocks to walk in the blustery weather that presses my curls into my face and makes it hard to breathe.

Suddenly, there's a warm arm around my shoulders. It mimics the best kind of heater, close and blocking the frigid wind. Dawson ducks into the nearest shop, pulling me along.

When he releases me, I smell the dregs of his cologne on my coat and smile.

"Are you a fan of art?" Dawson questions, perhaps mistaking my smile for praise, or maybe just making conversation, but it's then I realize what he means. We've happened into an art shop. Asheville is full of them, but I never stop at any for a good reason.

"No," I whisper.

I push hard at a memory that presses back at me with even more force.

"Do you see the brushstrokes?" Roberto asks. "The way they fade fluidly into one another until stopping abruptly here?"

His fingers hover over a splotch of white canvas, met by red paint. The rest of the artwork looks as though the artist carelessly splatted it with every color imaginable, no method to the chaos.

"I see it," I say.

"This is where most people think the artist purposely meant to space his art, but I know for a fact, having talked to him myself, that this is where he grew overly frustrated with the passion that consumed him, so he picked the loudest color and slammed his brush down here in anger. In the end, the painting came out better for it, for his release."

I don't quite hold the same note of fondness for art that Roberto does, but I listen all the same.

"Do you know why this painting speaks so clearly to me?" he inquires. "Do you understand why I paid the highest dollar for it?"

I give it another look, trying to see what he does, any detail that might help me understand why this painting is worth so much to him. What he paid for it could buy a house, or nice car, pay medical bills or feed the hungry. Yet Roberto spends it on this, which he claims is worth it. I want to see its worth, I truly do, but in the end, it all looks like splashed colors to me.

"I don't," I admit, and then flinch, wondering if my admission will cost me another bruise.

"Ah," he murmurs, noticing my action. "That is precisely why. What you just did there. Flinching. Afraid. You are my art, princess. Sometimes you frustrate me, and I pick the loudest color, too. So, you see, I can relate."

Red, the color of blood, I think to myself, not daring to express my thoughts aloud.

"One day, you will be better for it," he states.

Of course, Roberto made everything difficult.

I push the memory from the recesses of my mind, now that it's mostly done replaying itself. The memory isn't too horrible, but it calls my attention back to *him*, the man I wish to forget but never seem to be able to. I shudder.

"Are you okay?" Dawson asks.

Concern leaks into his tone, and I know I must have blanked again. I don't pay mind to the few customers around us, or the lady at the front desk. Instead, I focus on Dawson, all of the artwork behind him fading.

"I'm fine," I reply. "Let's get out of here."

I don't wait for his reply, if he even means to have one, before I leave the shop. I'm back to walking against the pressure of the wind, and this time it's a welcome reprieve. When Dawson grabs my hand and ducks into another shop, he makes sure it's not filled with art. His hand makes no move to release mine either.

"Okay now?" he inquires gently, as though he knows the other store upset me.

The shop is the opposite of everything I know from my past life, so directly contrary in fact, that I laugh. Hooks on the walls hold cowboy hats, and cubbyholes by the floor display spurred boots. An entire rack—the length of the whole store—showcases clothes not worn in the last century, at least. All replicas of old western days.

I look up to find Dawson giving me the oddest grin.

"I'll take that as a yes," he murmurs, tugging me toward a rack just as an employee appears from the back of the shop.

"Hi, please let me know if I can assist with anything," the employee tells us. "The posing booth is just to the side of the front window, there behind the curtain. You'll find props and two stools to sit on, if you care to do so. You'll also get a set of five pictures."

She names a price and Dawson reaches into his pocket and pays.

"We'll take the five pictures, but we want two copies of the same set," he says.

The employee accepts the money and nods us toward the rack. "Your choice of attire."

I'm startled by the fun nature of Dawson's suggestion.

"You want me to change into this?" I ask, pointing to a dress with a gaudy design and deep pockets, an apron attached.

He grimaces at the outfit, confirming that it's as bad as I thought it was.

A laugh tumbles out of me. "Fine. Then, the same goes for you."

I search the rack until I find the perfect look for him—a shirt adorned with silver buttons, a bandana around his neck, and the tightest tan pants I've ever seen for a man.

Dawson assesses the outfit with a look of concern. I thrust it at him and find the changing room easily enough. Five minutes later, I'm facing a costume-clad Dawson.

A laugh bursts from my lips as he attempts to adjust himself. He's walking funny, unused to such tight clothing. We take a seat before the camera as the timer counts down.

"What is your favorite thing in the world, Camille?" he questions, just as I smile for the flash.

There are a few seconds before the next picture.

"Swimming." I wince. "I mean, I suppose that used to be my favorite. Maybe now it's a cup of coffee and a good book."

Flash.

The camera goes off and I have no idea what expression I'm wearing, but I do know I've forgotten to smile.

"What's your least favorite thing?" he asks.

"Cockroaches." I shudder. "Gross little creatures."

He laughs just as the flash goes off a third time.

"What is your favorite thing, Dawson?"

He doesn't hesitate in his response. "Maybe you right now."

My eyes widen in surprise. *Flash.*

"And your least favorite?" I whisper.

He leans toward me and brushes a calloused finger beneath my chin to pull my mouth nearer to his.

"Every moment that I want to kiss you and have to hold back. Like right now."

I gasp as the last flash goes off. I'm left on a stool, wanting Dawson, as the boutique employee announces that our pictures are done.

Dawson removes his touch, but grins. "Ready?"

He stands first, waddling back to the dressing rooms to rid himself of the uncomfortable attire. I watch the space that once held him for a minute before I gather myself enough to change into my own clothes.

I meet Dawson at the counter, where he retrieves the photos, sticking them in his coat pocket before gently taking my hand.

"That was different," he comments, the corners of his mouth twitching.

"Sure was." I bite my lip to hide my approval.

I don't usually take photos. But these are small, developed on the spot, and now in Dawson's pocket. Not plastered anywhere for others to see.

I exit, bracing myself for the chill of the day. With hurried steps, we make it to the parts store where I stand by the door, waiting for Dawson to get what he needs. I eye the coffee shop nearby while his items are rung up and paid for. When Dawson thanks the man, I ready myself for the cold again.

"Do you want one?" comes a rumbling voice in my ear.

I close my eyes, wondering what his voice would sound like in my bed. The thought doesn't surprise me. By now, I realize Dawson simply has that effect on me. My cheeks warm.

"I would love a coffee," I reply.

Dawson opens the door for me, a bag holding the alternator belt clasped in his free hand. We wait at the crosswalk for the cars to stop and let us pass. I smell coffee before we open the door to the café, the aroma hanging in the air surrounding the brick veneered shop.

"The usual?" Dawson asks.

I nod. That he knows my usual is strange enough, but stranger still is the fact that he realizes they don't add sufficient cream. Dawson pauses at the condiment counter. He pours thick cream in the little space left in the cup, caps it, and hands it to me with a wink.

"Thank you," I say, terribly flustered.

I don't know if it's due to the fact that Dawson admitted he wants to touch me, that he's made an effort to know me in the little time we have together today, or that he's paid better attention to me since renting the camper than I have even given him credit for. But more than likely, my ruffled nerves are thanks to how close Dawson stands beside me. I pause to let people by while I take a few sips of my overfull coffee so it doesn't spill. His eyes home in on my lips around my drink's rim, and then lower to my throat, which works up and down as I swallow.

"Camille," Dawson begins as we start moving again. "Would you think less of me if I told you that my reasons for coming here with you are purely selfish?"

I'm the one who offered to bring him. "How so?"

"I could have asked Kenny or Dwayne to get the part with me, but I came with you because—" He pauses. "I can't stay away. At least not today. You have no idea how much I should. But I can't."

He pulls me into an alcove off the side of the café while setting his and my steaming coffees on a protruding ledge.

"Would you blame me if I allowed my control to slip?" he murmurs, peering down at me. "Even if it's just this once?"

Of course, with Dawson, he'd be *allowing* his control to lapse. By choice, not by accident.

I move closer to him. His lips brush over the contour of my jaw, dipping to the hollow of my throat and gliding back up again. I suddenly want to be rid of my scarf. What I need, what I want, is the warmth of Dawson's mouth, his breath against my goose fleshed skin.

My hands find their way into his jacket, to the ribbed fabric of his shirt. I want to kiss beneath the layers, where hot flesh waits. My head tilts back, angled for Dawson to reach my mouth. I can't think anymore with him this close.

"I don't blame you," I say.

He winces. "You might change your mind one day."

I highly doubt that.

"But," he whispers, his face lowering to mine, "I'm tired of fighting this pull."

A war rages in his gaze.

He finally breaks with a grumbled, "Fuck," a moment before his lips smash into mine, rough and needy.

My body unravels at the taste of him. His mouth coaxes me to surrender, to melt with each touch. The back of my head leans against the side of the building as I bask in pleasure. Dawson tugs my earlobe with his teeth, and his hand moves to cup my hip, leaving a searing imprint.

"God, I want you," he growls, as he takes my mouth again.

My fingers slip inside the fabric of his shirt to meet burning flesh, to trail over the tight ridges of his stomach. Dawson groans and I nearly forget we are in public.

His kiss dives deeper, his tongue sliding against mine, until I'm gasping and he's pulling away, and there's nothing to stop me from dragging him back to me. Except there is. The street around us, just outside of the thin alleyway, is bustling with people. None are paying attention, but it's not the most ideal place to lose myself in Dawson's touch.

He retrieves our coffees, handing one to me, and licks his lips once before sauntering into the crowd with the type of confidence I've grown to expect of him. Behind his back, I allow myself a small smile. He doesn't realize it, but he has given me the gift of a kiss not weighted by the pain of a heavy hand, not tainted with the taste of blood if I happen to speak my mind. He has presented me with desire. Raw and real and unfiltered.

He stops to buy a newspaper from a corner stand before

reaching into his pocket, pulling out our pictures, and handing me my copy. I nearly bump into someone, taking time to look at each one.

The first is of me smiling while Dawson watches me in profile. The second is of me wearing a look of deep concentration, half of Dawson's face cut off by the frame. The third shows our contrasting expressions, his sweet and mine sour. The following depicts me with a wondrous gaze while Dawson stares right back. The final showcases the both of us center frame, my lips slightly parted, eyes wide and passionate, and Dawson wearing a roguish grin.

"Do you like them?" he asks, as though my expression isn't telling enough.

"You know I do," I say.

I'm forced to set the pictures down on the truck seat and drive the hour's trip back to Darlington. But I can't erase my small grin. Dawson kissed me. Passionately. Full of want and need. I can still feel the tingle it left behind.

TWENTY-SEVEN

Dawson

"**A**re you okay?"

My words are whispered in Camille's ear. She spins around, hand to her heart. Eyes wide.

"You scared me," she exclaims with more force than necessary.

She goes back to cleaning the pizza oven, her surprise being replaced by a scowl.

"Sorry," I mutter.

What I really meant to say is that she seems distracted. I can't stop thinking about our kiss yesterday. I want more. I need to keep a level head. Both thoughts fight to gain the upper hand.

Wind batters the walls of the general store while rain pelts the windows, obscuring the outside from view. It's borderline icy. The storm is both fierce and loud, causing the inside music to be overpowered by crashes of thunder and cracks of lightning. A bolt forks through the sky, illuminating everything like a camera flash. The fluorescents overhead flicker, and I wonder for a moment if we'll need to use candles. My eyes skim the store, searching them out, until I find scented numbers lined against a far rack. I tuck their position into memory should I need to locate them in the dark. A lighter sits on the register counter.

"You've been strange today," I observe.

I don't know what, exactly, I expected. Maybe a bit of warmth from her. But not this. Not Camille furiously cleaning with a glower on her face.

Water drips from my lashes into my eyes. I blink it away and try not to shiver from the cold of my soaking wet shirt. I pinch the fabric between two fingers in an attempt to pull it away from my skin, but it only suctions right back. Camille's stare slips to my shirt and she inhales sharply. It's the first sign of an emotion I've seen besides frustration.

"I tried to make it in before the rain," I explain.

The distance between the shed and the front door is only a few yards—a sprint that would take seconds—but it was too late. The sky had already ripped wide open.

"One minute," she states, setting down the rag and removing a glove. "Wait here."

I do as she instructs. The store is empty, except for the old man sleeping in the office. I desperately try not to imagine the things I'd like to do to erase Camille's frown. Maybe we could talk to distract her from whatever it is that's upsetting her. Or perhaps something wordless would be better. Like setting her on the counter and kissing her again.

I feel myself twitch, a telltale tingle that starts low in my gut. If I'm not careful, I'll sport the evidence of where my thoughts have wandered. My mind doesn't get the message. More images of Camille slam into me. Her lips swollen from mine. Me pulling off every piece of clothing she wears before sinking deeply, deeply, deeply into her.

"Here," she offers, coming around to face me with a shirt in her hand.

It's hunter green with a small hole in the right sleeve. I shift from foot to foot, trying to adjust myself without actually adjusting myself in front of Camille. Her eyes narrow.

"It's just a shirt," she defends. "I thought you might want one since you're soaked. It has a tiny hole so we can't sell it anyhow. That's why it was in the office."

She's misunderstanding my fidgeting. It seems she thinks I'm uncomfortable with wearing the shirt. That's not it. I'm perfectly grateful for the shirt, and I prove it as soon as I manage to get myself under control.

"Thanks." I let out a sigh of relief.

Camille hands the shirt to me. I peel the waterlogged material up and over my head, tossing it on a shelf under the register. It hits with a damp smack.

"You sure you're okay?" I inquire.

When Camille's eyes find mine, I notice she's definitely not frowning any longer. Her stare drops to my chest, and then lower to my stomach.

Her tongue darts out to wet her lips, and her eyes trace my body with hunger. It's much better than the frustration I just witnessed.

I loop the dry shirt over my arms and head and pull it down.

"Why were you angry?" I press, now that I have her attention.

"I wasn't—" She begins to lie, sees my face, and changes course. "Fine. I suppose I'm a little stressed. Nothing too bad."

She gets a faraway look. The very same one that overcomes her every time her past is mentioned.

"Camille," I murmur, placing a hand on her soft arm. The old man's snore saws the air in half, nearly as loud as the following rumble of thunder. "You can talk to me."

"Oh?" she says, and I'm cautious of the challenging glint in her stare. Maybe I shouldn't push her to talk. "Are we sharing secrets now, Dawson? Is that it?"

She takes a step toward me. Her words are out of character, and that's how I know something has set her off. Was it our kiss?

"Why don't you tell me why you really left the army? Or why you're so tight-lipped, often serious, and strangely enough, not afraid of fire?"

Her words are an arrow to the gut. I have a kneejerk reaction to step away from Camille. Maybe that's what she wants—me to back off. There's a chance we got too close yesterday and now she's scared.

"What a funny thing that is," she muses, stalking closer. "You'd think you'd fear fire after what your family went through, but you don't. Not even a little. I see the way you're happy to restock the fire in my home, how you easily lean toward the flames. You don't flinch or keep your distance. So, Dawson. You tell me why you're not afraid of fire, and I'll tell you why I'm upset."

Another of the old man's snores rents the air. Rain falls even harder, lashing like liquid whips. I see what she's doing here. She doesn't want to talk about it, so she's gone in for the kill, knowing I'll back down.

"Whatever you think you know," I whisper, "you're wrong."

"So, your family perished in a fire, then? Forgive me for being crass. I wouldn't be if I wasn't certain you were lying. Can you truly stand here and tell me I'm wrong in suspecting you're being dishonest, that maybe something bad happened back home and you needed to get away, but that whatever the horrible thing is that still haunts you has nothing to do with a flame? Don't lie again. Please."

She is right, on every count. I begin feeling the itch to run, or at the very least, to cover my tracks. I mull it over. Would she tell if I did happen to mention the truth? I don't want to lie. But I can't possibly admit everything.

"Listen, Dawson, I believe you're good," she soothes. "Whatever happened, you are not one of the bad guys. I know the difference."

Seems like she's admitting she's dealt with bad men.

"You're welcome at the camper. I told you it's yours, and I meant it. I really like that you're there. I'm just trying to say that we all have buried secrets. I don't want to talk about mine, and you obviously don't want to discuss yours. Let's keep it that way, okay?"

So, she doesn't mean to utter a word about catching me in a lie. Still, white-hot suspicion races through me. If Camille knows I lied, why let me stay?

And, also, she doesn't know me well enough to say whether I'm one of the good guys or not. She needs to be careful to remember that.

"I don't know what you mean," I retort, but my tone lacks the usual conviction.

"Should I look closer into why you're really here, then?" she challenges. "If you want to press me on what's wrong when I don't want to talk about it, maybe I will press back."

I inhale sharply. Is she threatening me? My hackles rise and my defenses go up. The next words from my mouth are over the top, and I know it as soon as they slip out.

"Maybe you have a past you're running from, and you know things you shouldn't so you're hiding." I put emphasis on the word "hiding." My insinuation is clear. She's not living a full life here. She's living a protected one. "But I've been truthful with you."

She grits her teeth. It looks as though she means to say more. I brace for the impact, but instead, she huffs and storms to the other side of the store, away from me. For the first time,

I realize I can no longer hear the old man's snores. I turn to the office and find the door open, the man himself standing there.

"You're a fool, you know," he comments.

I wonder how much he heard. Is he the reason Camille stormed off? Does she not want to discuss it in front of him? That makes two of us.

"Don't you realize when a woman wants you, boy? And when she needs a little space to clear her head of demons? Why you'd go and ruin somethin' like that, I have no idea. Damn stupid of you. I thought you were smarter than that. What a shame."

"What's a shame?" comes another voice. It's the diner owner, Rose—the old lady who sometimes offers me a free meal under the pretenses that she made too much that day, or that she accidentally burned it. The food never tastes even the slightest bit burnt.

"Dawson just ruined his chances with Camille. She's angry as a bull. Might steer clear of her for a few."

God, they're nosy. I clench my jaw and wait for them to drop it. Camille returns with a large tea in her hand, acting as though I'm not standing right in her path. She sidesteps around me and continues on.

"If you know what's good for you," the old man warns, "you'll give her space to calm down, and then you'll chase her until your legs fall off if you have to, but don't, whatever you do, let her get away."

The problem with that is, she was never meant to be mine in the first place.

TWENTY-EIGHT

Camille

I silently ponder how far I will go and what cost I will pay to rid my mind of Dawson. Especially after our blowout. I goaded him. He only wanted to know if I was all right when the rain cornered us both in the store. I could have just told him I'd been having a hard day.

Thoughts of Roberto and his men, wondering if they're still looking for me, consumed me the night before. My nightmares were so real I could almost smell the cologne and taste the blood of a heavy hand. I hadn't gotten a peaceful wink of sleep.

As much as I don't want to admit it, I worry that seeing

Dawson—kissing him and wanting him—will somehow put him in danger, too. I came to Darlington as an escape, Dawson was right about that, but I'd always hoped it'd be a peaceful one. I was content being alone. There was a beauty in that.

But then, Dawson came along, and now I don't know what I want.

He seems to be everywhere—at the property, the store, in my thoughts. Then there are the little surprises he leaves like breadcrumbs. Extra wood in the shed. A pile of apples at the deer bedding. Just this morning, I awoke to find my truck radio fixed, the volume up high enough to startle me as the engine roared to life.

Today, while I think of him, I sit next to Bonnie. I normally only see her at work, but when she breezed through the hallway that connects the general store and the restaurant, asking if I wanted to get out of the house and watch a boat show with her, I found a "yes" rolling off my lips.

We sit at the edge of the lake in a spot secured by Bonnie, where trees reach finger-like branches toward our heads. It's similar to a cove, cut perfectly out of the woods. The slate-gray boulder beneath my coat is smooth to the touch.

"I'm glad you came," she says, and she sounds so sincere that I smile. "I never see you anywhere but the store, and word has it you don't talk to many people outside of it."

This town and its rumors. Let them think I'm a recluse. They're not wrong. So far, it's worked enough to keep people at arm's length.

"I talk to neighbors and customers," I counter. "And you."

Bonnie brushes back a strand of her dark brown hair. Her eyes are watchful, a shade similar to warm honey.

"It's not that I blame you. I understand your situation."

She does?

"I've been in Darlington for two years. It's hard to make friends," she continues. "Used to live a few counties south, just at the Carolina borders, before coming here. Had a nasty divorce. Needed to get away. Once I arrived, I couldn't seem to leave."

I never realized she'd been married. A stab of remorse hits me. I haven't opened up enough to ask.

"Was it hard to leave home?" I inquire.

I wish I could tell her my real story. How difficult it is to know I'll never step foot in the ocean again. How I left a bad marriage, too.

"Technically, no. It was surprisingly easy to split. We didn't share any pets or kids, and we rented the home we stayed in." She sighs. "But emotionally? Yeah. It's all I'd ever known."

I can definitely relate.

"Darlington isn't bad, though," she adds. "Pretty peaceful, actually. So at least there's that."

A bird swoops low over the lake as I eye the boats bobbing on the surface. It's not the most exciting outing, but the water calms me. It's the closest to the ocean I'll ever get. Maybe this summer, I'll swim in it.

"I know what you mean." I pause, knowing I have to lie

a little. "New York had been home before here. It's hard to transition. I also left something difficult behind."

What I love about Bonnie is that she doesn't ask questions or press for more.

A speaker booms across the lake. "Welcome, everyone, to the tenth annual Watercraft Show."

The boats line up, one after the other like ants in procession, for the rich display. Lake Lure has its share of wealthy inhabitants who take pride in their toys. There's nothing more to the show than the *oohing* and *ahhing* of the crowd. The collective sounds drift across the water like whispers and bounce off the rocky outcroppings like roars.

"Which is your favorite?" Bonnie asks.

I search the lot and pick one, though there's no real conviction to my choice. "The teal."

Perhaps because it's the smallest. If ever I could see myself on a boat, it'd be that one.

She laughs. "Boats aren't really your thing, I can tell. But I think the water is. You keep smiling when you gaze at it."

I wince at my transparency. Boats have never been a favorite of mine. My preference was the ocean without barriers, but Bonnie's right...the lake is the next best thing.

The show ends an hour later, and Bonnie and I decide on a dive bar for quick food and service. Bonnie orders a beer. The pub we choose offers less of a chance of running into the wealthy boat owners than there would be at the upscale town inn they frequent.

Here, there's the heady scent of beer waring with the balsam candle burning at the end of the lone bar. I take in the décor I've seen only once before when I happened upon the place. Distressed pine walls meet tiled floors, and there's a polished, butcher block bar in the middle. Newspapers about famous movies that were filmed at the lake hang in aged frames. A telephone booth bathroom in the back serves its purpose, decorated with nothing but an iron carved mirror.

"So, tell me more," Bonnie requests.

"More" could mean anything, so I settle on, "No siblings. Rough childhood. Happy to be gone."

She raises her mug. "Cheers to that."

It's an offer of comradery. My guess is Bonnie didn't have it that great either. As she eases into talk about the diner, I lean back in my seat and relax.

Bonnie has a way of chatting about mindless things that relieve my tension. When the pizza we ordered arrives, she sprinkles crushed red pepper on top and I tease her for it.

"This is nice," she comments.

"It really is."

Maybe I have a real shot here of being happy. It's been over a year already. Perhaps I can start, little by little, to let my guard down. The likelihood of my old life finding me is slim to none.

So, finally, in a dingy bar with good company, I forget Miami.

TWENTY-NINE

Dawson

I stand in the bait shop, marveling over how the old man expects me to clean it. I'm not sure where to start. It might be better to tear the whole thing down and start anew. The room hasn't seen a good scrubbing in far too long. I turn in circles, wondering what the best route is, as my shoes leave tracks in the gritty floor. Dust motes cower in the corners, and I've already spotted numerous spiders. They don't bother me much, though they'll still have to go. I'm now convinced that the limited supplies the old man provided won't be sufficient enough. I eye the mop leaning against the wall, its end soaking in a bucket of equal parts bleach and water. I pull off my work gloves and retrieve my burner phone.

A quick press of buttons and a voice answers.

"Hello?"

"Kenny, it's Dawson."

My gloves land next to the container of Clorox wipes that will do nothing besides maybe take off the first layer of grime, if that. I have no idea what will be waiting underneath. More dirt? Old fish guts? Worm trails? All are possibilities.

"Hey, man! So, this is your number?"

I shrug, even though he can't see the action. Sure, why not let him think this is my regular cell instead of a temporary way to get in touch. One that will quickly drown in the deepest lake or river I can find along the way home when I finally leave this mountain town.

"Yeah, this is it," I reply.

"Great. What are you up to?"

Kenny seems chipper as ever. I wonder how many cups of coffee he drinks in the morning to sound so happy at—I check my watch—10:00 am.

"Working." I frown at the space I have to somehow clean by the end of the day. "Do you think you could help me out?"

He hollers garbled words into the background to a chorus of laughter. "I'm on a job site about ten minutes north of you, been here for four hours already. I could maybe take a quick break. Why? What's up?"

I need something stronger than Clorox.

"Do you have paint thinner? Or a chemical that might get what appears to be fifty years' worth of fish slime and age off of a bait shop?"

Kenny laughs good and deep. "He finally wrangled someone into cleaning it, I see. Mr. Hill has been asking me for years to give it a go. Camille won't do it, and Miles claims he's not paid enough. I'm a roof man, through and through. I don't do bait stuff. Unless I'm out fishing. Speaking of, we should go sometime."

"Sounds good," I say, though I'm not normally one for fishing.

"I have a few products that'll peel just about any stubborn glue off of shingles and such," he offers. "That might work for you. Give me twenty minutes. Let me dig up a couple options and I'll swing by."

"Thanks." I disconnect and heave a sigh of relief.

Kenny has saved me from useless scrubbing. It's not that I don't want the hours of pay, it's just that I'm sure they'll be better spent repairing the loose floorboards and counter corners that are warping with age. As well as reorganizing the bait products and reconstructing the mesh wire cricket pen. Then there's the small fish—I don't know enough about fishing to tell which kind—that swim in the tub of murky water that the old man requested I clean out. He's given me the water purifier and instructed me on how to install it.

While I wait for Kenny, I prop the door open and shuffle through the toolbox to find nails. By the time he arrives, which ends up being an hour later, I've already secured the loose floorboards and started working on the counter corners, pulling out old, rusted nails the color of dirty pennies in favor of new ones that'll last another fifty years.

"Hey, Dawson!" Kenny walks in with a container in each hand. "One of these ought to work for you."

He sets them on the counter and takes a look around.

"Just as disgusting as ever in here." He chuckles.

I see what he means. Truthfully, the place wouldn't be so bad if all that needed to be done was a quick cleaning and a bit of organizing. But clearing the grime and repairing what's broken will eat the majority of my time.

"I really appreciate it," I tell him.

"Can't stay for long," Kenny explains. "Left the boys at the job. They all wanted a break, too, but we can't leave the site unattended, so I promised I'd buy them some of Mrs. Rose's food. That shut them up."

I grin. Mrs. Rose's cuisine is growing on me. Though, I still don't know how people eat it every day. Cornbread and fried food and everything covered in gravy. I'm used to lean meats and vegetables. I'd worry about putting on weight if it wasn't for the fact that I work enough around the store and Camille's place to burn the calories.

"You want anything while I'm over there?" he asks.

"I'm good." I decline his offer only because it's too early for one of Rose's heavy meals, and because I need to continue with the bait shop.

Kenny nods and slaps a hand to my shoulder.

"Nice to see you again. Don't worry about getting the

supplies back to me. If you don't use it all, just keep 'em here. I'm sure they'll help again sometime."

"Thanks." I pull my gloves back on and pop open the containers. The scent instantly burns my nostrils.

"I'm serious about the fishing," he reminds me with a smile. "Soon, okay?"

I agree with a nod. Kenny offers a wave and then he's gone.

I get to work right away, generously pouring the chemicals on the counters and floors. While I wait for them to soak through the grime, I assess the cabinets under the countertops. Opening each one, I see that they're mostly empty, except for a few receipts and slips of paper, one even dating back to 1999, the letters nearly faded, looking almost sun bleached though I know time is to blame—not the sun—since I find it in a dark corner. I toss everything that's no longer needed into the large garbage container next to the door. An enticing breeze wafts in, cold, but welcome. It helps air out the burn of the chemicals.

I get lost in mindless work. An hour goes by, eating years of filth. I dig out the hose and wash away the chemicals before using a cleaning brush to wipe away soot. The counters are a nice cherry mahogany underneath, and the floors are an ash-colored wood. I rewash everything until the surfaces shine, and then do the same to the insides of the cabinets. All the bait supplies are stacked in one corner, but I make sure to reorganize them and move onto cleaning and purifying the fish water. The light inside the bait room is still dim, but with the door open, sunshine illuminates enough of the room for me to see clearly.

By the middle of the day, dirt covers me from head to foot, and I can't stand the strong chemical stench. This time, I decide to take my break away from the store, using the thirty minutes I have to drive to the camper, quickly shower, and return.

I pop my head into the store to alert the old man that I'll be gone a few. "Be back in thirty."

Camille works the register, and her nose crinkles as I come near.

"It's the cleaning chemicals," I explain.

Another reason I need a shower before I continue with the lighter work in the bait shop—people can smell me when I enter a room. It doesn't help that the strong stench causes a dull pain to begin behind my eyes.

"How's the bait shop coming along?" the old man inquires.

"Probably would be going better if you actually cleaned the place sometime between when you were my age and now," I retort.

He laughs. "You might be right."

"Or better yet," I add, "just burn it down."

He laughs louder. Camille watches our exchange with quirked lips painted a soft peach, reminding me of the color of a seashell.

"Tell you what," he says. "When you come back, why don't you get a meal at Rose's on me. Will that make up for it?"

"No," I grumble, ready to get out of there and scrub the filth off my body.

The old man waves me away with a smile. "Your next check

will reflect your raise. A dollar more, okay? That ought to help some, I reckon."

At that, my eyebrows shoot up.

"Go on. You're stinking up the place."

There's a twinkle in his eyes that tells me he's still laughing at me. Even Camille can't help herself. She cracks a smile.

I wink once at her and leave.

Never thought a shower could feel so good or be taken so hot. I nearly burned my skin, but it was needed to extract the strong odor.

I arrive back at the store in a change of ratty clothes, since I'm sure I'll still get a little dirty. The only thing left to do is replace a few items and take the old man up on his offer to buy me a meal. All I've had so far is a piece of beef jerky and a small pack of crackers, both bought from the general store. It's been six hours since I began this morning, and all in all, the place looks great.

I remove the cabinet knobs and affix new ones with curling handles. The light switch is easy enough to swap out. I dig through the bag the old man gave me, locating the new water filter. I replace everything he asked, one by one, until all that's left is the overhead light. Finally, something brighter than the soft glow. It doesn't matter during the day, but if the door closes, or anyone needs to see at night, the light is insufficient.

I remember the first time I set foot in the space, seeing Camille bathed in the soft glow. I happened not to mind the haze then, come to think of it.

I wish she would talk to me. She hasn't said much other than passing greetings since a few days ago when she got too close to my truths, and I didn't handle it well.

I pull the ladder that was propping open the door to the middle of the room and set the light on the top rung. The door begins to close, and just before I get a chance to climb, there's a soft knock.

Camille enters and her eyes widen at the sight of the room.

"I've never seen it look so good," she says by way of greeting.

I'm not sure if I've ever seen *her* look so good. Leggings hug her tightly, giving me a view of her toned muscles. Her shirt is a soft gray and knotted to one side. She turns in a circle, and I get a view from behind, too.

"Hey, Camille," I say, taking a step forward. "What are you doing here?"

She didn't seem too fond of the room before, though now the place *is* clean and the fish smell is gone, replaced by the scent of pine from an aspen air freshener plugged into the wall.

"I wanted to see if..."

She faces me again and pauses, biting her lip.

"The other day..."

She shakes her head. I step closer.

"What I mean to say is..."

When we're nearly close enough to touch, she peers into my

eyes. Her breath hitches.

"I'm sorry about the other day, Camille." I come right out and say it.

My mother was always big on three rules when someone was in the wrong.

They had to accept it. They had to apologize. And they had to find a solution, even if the solution was simply to ask for forgiveness. I've never forgotten her words.

"I shouldn't have handled it the way I did. Will you forgive me?" I ask.

I tuck a strand of curly hair behind her ear. Surprisingly, it stays put for all of three seconds before refusing to be anywhere but in her beautiful face.

She seems to relax. "Yes, of course. I shouldn't have pushed you. You don't have to talk about it until you're ready."

She takes a deep breath and lets it out slowly.

"What I meant to say when I came in here is that I wondered if you'd like to eat with me. I heard Mr. Hill offer you a meal, and I haven't had much today, so I thought…"

She leaves the invitation open-ended, her eyes wide with hope.

"You're asking me to dinner with you at the diner, Camille?"

By the way her hands clench and unclench, I'd guess she's nervous. It does something to me, seeing her in this small, dim space, hearing her ask me out, though casually.

"Yes," she replies.

"When?"

She looks around. "Now. If you're done."

"I can be done."

Forget about the light. It can wait. It'll only take a couple minutes to replace tomorrow instead.

A small grin tucks itself into her cheeks. "Okay. But just..."

She pauses again, then closes the gap between us.

"First..."

She doesn't complete her sentence, whatever she meant to say—or maybe this is exactly what she meant to say—because her lips suddenly press against mine. I have absolutely zero control. I've been rigidly good over the years about building it up, directing my emotions and actions until they are practiced and precise. But now none of that matters. She's caught me off guard, and I can't help the sound of pleasure that escapes my throat.

I pull her flush against me, tilting her head back, the angle just perfect for deepening the kiss. Her hands grasp my hips, her nails digging in even through the fabric.

At first, my intentions were well thought out. I would rent the camper. Be friendly. Help around the property. But then, I found myself doing extra chores that Camille never asked of me. Like replacing her firewood. Installing a new truck radio on my dime. I kissed her against a brick wall in Asheville. I've tried so hard to fight the attraction I feel toward her. I vowed after our first—and what I planned to make our last—kiss that I wouldn't find myself here again, lost in her. But this thing between us cannot be helped.

I lift Camille, her legs instantly going around me, causing friction in all the right places as I take two steps toward the shiny counter. I set her on top of it as her name slips through my lips, a moan lost in this dark, closed space. I didn't lock the door. Anyone could enter. But I don't give a damn about that. I can't pull myself away from her now if I tried.

I know my limits.

She has disabled them today.

Camille arches into me. When I pull slightly back to get a better view of her, I see blazing desire in her eyes.

Her hand slides down my shirt and stills at my belt buckle. She leans into me, kissing me again. I'm ready for anything— everything—to happen right here and now, but Camille seems to have retained some sense. She pulls away and presses two fingers to her swollen lips.

"Dinner," she whispers. By the strain in her voice, I can tell she doesn't want to leave the moment.

She's right, though. We need to go. The bait shop is hardly the best spot.

"Okay," I concede, taking several steps back.

She opens the door to a waning sun and glances back at me as she leads the way to Rose's place. She shouldn't want to get mixed up with me. It's better for her if she doesn't.

But I selfishly wish she would.

THIRTY

Camille

Chinks of bright light slip through a crack in the window dressings, almost painful to look at. The sky shines the lightest shade of blue, bringing warmer temperatures that nearly pull above freezing. Snow hasn't fallen in a full week.

Dawson's gone to work. The property is mine alone. I set down my coffee mug and open the door, automatically reaching for my coat before realizing I don't need it with the layers I chose this morning. The log pile has stayed semi-full, but even still, I grab the chainsaw and set to it, walking a worn path down the property to a tree I mean to use.

Blinking up at the beaming sky, I pick the limbs that could use trimming, smaller ones that won't take long to dismantle and cut into appropriate sizes for kindling.

After ten minutes, sweat forms on my hairline. After thirty, I've severed all the branches I need. After an hour, I've cut them down to size. As I begin loading it into the reserve, a throat clears.

"Haven't seen you in a while," Mrs. JoAnne comments, startling me.

Her face lightens with an easy smile.

"I've been working a bit," I reply. "You know how it goes. Mr. Hill needs extra hours thanks to the last push of the tourist season. My time should revert back to normal in a few days, now that the inn went to weekend only winter hours."

I shove the last of the wood into the reserve, placing the chainsaw in the new shed Dawson built. I wave her on toward the house, where we step inside.

"What are you doing here?" I ask.

"Brought you a pie." A bag hangs from her arm. "Actually, there are two."

I take the bag and set the pies on the counter, and then wash my hands of wood shavings.

"One's for the neighbor." She can't hide the grin that forms, though she tries. "Thought maybe I could meet him."

"He's at work." I wonder if my face appears as composed as I mean for it to.

"Oh, shame." She takes a seat at the table, having already

been acquainted with my home. "Guess you'll have to invite him to have pie with you sometime, then."

My eyes narrow. "Yes, a real shame."

I suspect she is not as forgetful as she sometimes pretends to be. If my intuition is right, Mrs. JoAnne is as sharp as a tack, which means her grin is something else altogether.

"What are you up to?" I question.

"Me? Oh, nothing. I'm just the neighbor, welcoming another neighbor with a pie."

"You're a bit late on the welcoming. He's been here nearly two months," I argue suspiciously. "And it's not a good idea, whatever you're planning."

"Now, how would you know that?"

She takes the liberty of opening one of the containers and shuffling around in what few drawers I have to find a knife. I retrieve two tea saucers and set them on the table. She looks at them with disdain.

"What in the world are those for? You serving tea? Because if they're for what I think you mean them to be, you have lost your mind. Child, hasn't anyone shown you how to eat a piece of southern pie? You can't do it on that tiny thing."

She opens cabinets until she finds large, round dinner plates, setting two on the table. From the bag she brought, she pulls a tub of ice cream and whipped topping.

"Pumpkin pie is meant to be served with a scoop of vanilla and whipped cream. Surely you know that," she chides, as she cuts a quarter of the large dessert.

"That's enough to fill me up for hours," I say, watching as she makes quick work of assembling the right proportions.

Pie crust crumbles litter the plate, which is full of the rich slice with a heavy dollop of whipped cream on top, and a hearty scoop of vanilla ice cream to the side, making it an entire meal in itself.

"Am I supposed to eat the whole thing?" I ask.

"Well, what else would you do with it?"

Feed it to five people, maybe. I entertain her and take the first bite with a bit of all three ingredients. She does the same with hers. I can't help the moan that escapes. I have never, not ever, tasted something so rich in my life. Other times, I have eaten her pies in small servings with no additions. I take a second bite and third and fourth until, next thing I know, I do finish the serving, leaning back in the chair with a satisfied groan.

Mrs. JoAnne smiles. "That's better. Now that you're in a sweet coma, why don't you tell me what's going on with Dawson."

"Hey!" I exclaim. "How do you know his name?"

"Honey, when something that new and delicious comes to town, all of us old folk learn real quick. We have a crochet meeting twice a month, me and the girls from the salon—mind you, we have to drive all the way to the lake town to get our nails and hair done, but that's better than nothing—oh, and the women from the book club, well, pretty much any woman retiree who likes to look at shiny new things and learn as much as possible knows you have a hot new man on your property. Thing is, he never so much as looks at any of us."

I bite back a smile.

"Seems he's only got eyes for one woman, matter of fact," she continues. "You know Mary from down the way, right? The slender one with miles of blonde hair that the guys always fawn over?" She doesn't wait for me to answer. "Did you know she stopped by the store when Dawson was fixin' one of the sheds? Good Lord almighty was he fixin' it. You better believe the women notice, taking care to stop by there all the time now when he works. Well, anyway, she dropped in and made it perfectly clear she wouldn't mind if he wanted to take her on a moonlit walk by the lake or to a backyard dinner."

I suddenly sit straighter. I hadn't thought about Dawson bringing women to the property. He's entirely welcome to do so...except I despise the thought.

Mrs. JoAnne flashes me a knowing look, waiting me out. I grit my teeth and ask the question she's anticipating.

"What'd he say?"

A smile takes up residence, stretching wide across her face, causing crinkles to deepen like cracked desert ground at the corners of her eyes.

"He turned her down flat. Kindly, mind you. But a rejection all the same. Any idea why that might be?" she teases.

"None," I deadpan.

She grabs the dishes and places them in the sink. I stand up, ready to clean, but she puts out a hand to stop me.

"Nonsense. I like picking up. Don't have anyone to pick up after anymore. So, you just sit there and relax." She soaps the sponge and begins doing dishes. "Do you know how many women would cave at a moment's notice for his smile or touch or attention? And you have it. What are you doing with it?"

"Well," I hedge, "I suppose trying not to let anything get complicated."

I have no idea why I'm telling the truth or giving her any information at all.

She finishes the dishes, dries her hands, and pats me softly on the shoulder. Her curling fingers, marked by age, move to my hair, smoothing it in calm strokes.

"I never had a child," she says so gently that all the tension melts from my body. "Would it be okay if an old woman who has seen her share of years gives you a little advice?"

"Sure," I reply, not wanting to deny her request.

"There are two types of men in life. The one that's comfortable, that you can see yourself with," she murmurs, "and then there's the one that sets you on fire, that you can't possibly live without, even if it's only for that moment. Pick the latter."

She gives my shoulder one last squeeze and heads for the door.

"Well, I'm off to a crochet club meeting. Nice visiting with you."

"You, too," I call, mostly lost in her previous words.

The one that sets you on fire...

Only one man does that.

I meet Luke just like he asked me to when we ran into one

another at Jimmy's shop, his words whispered in my ear. We tend to prefer no audience for our get-togethers. It's safer that way.

"Come in," I offer, opening the door wider for him and laying a big slice of pumpkin pie, a scoop of vanilla, and a dollop of whipped cream on a plate like Mrs. JoAnne showed me.

He sits at the table now that my neighbor is long gone. "Thanks."

"I already had a slice," I tell him. "It's good to see you."

I haven't mentioned anything about suspecting him of wanting more than a friendship, and I don't plan to. Everything seems to be back to normal, and I intend to keep it that way.

"How are things?" His amber eyes bore into me, and I instantly relax.

Luke is sincere and kind and safe. He is friendship and shelter and protection.

"Good." I warm my hands on a fresh cup of coffee. "Want any?"

I nod to the nearly full pot, and he accepts. Two sugars, a dash of cream...I make his coffee just the way he likes it.

"Any trouble?" His eyes roam my home.

"No. Not since the guys in the shop. All has been quiet."

He drinks his coffee and winces at the burn. "Where's your renter?"

"Dawson is working."

Luke finishes the pie in no time, and when he's done, he leans back in his chair with only crumbs littering his plate. His body is sculpted with muscle from hard work. If anything, the past year has been good to him, building his bulk with all the labor he does around his property. Luke doesn't need a job due to stockpiling money from working the deadly job he did in Miami. Nonetheless, he sells his crop to local stores for extra cash. Though he's offered to help me financially, I can't accept. I like working. I don't want to owe him more than I already do.

"You two seem to be getting close."

His words hit me like a sledgehammer.

"How did you know?"

There are many people I lie to, but Luke is not one of them.

"He watches you often at the store. He looks at me like I'm a threat. You like being around him."

Luke doesn't show any indication that these truths bother him.

"You're right."

He nods. "Be careful. I looked deeper into him."

I lean closer in my seat. "And?"

He shrugs. "And nothing. He had a couple things when he was younger. Sealed cases. Plowed into someone's fence once. Had to work to pay off the damages. Never hung out with the wrong crowd. Made good grades. Lost his family in a fire. Came from Arizona. Needed a move. Showed up here. Story adds up."

I don't know how he got more of Dawson's info, and I don't often ask questions. I trust him. But I do wonder about the fire story. I accused Dawson of lying about that. Maybe he didn't.

"This upsets you," I observe.

I see it in the tense set to his shoulders.

"Yes. It's too clean. Measured."

Luke has a way of speaking that is blunt and to the point.

"How so?" I run a finger over the rim of my mug, lost in thought.

"You know what I did for a living. Always looked into targets, made sure I wasn't being duped, conned into taking out someone innocent. Not that it excuses my kills. I did what I did and there's no erasing it. But I know these sorts of things. Most backgrounds aren't this clean. Not even for good guys."

"So, you're saying his story checks out *too* much?"

He stands to refill his coffee, so I wait for him to sit again. Only then does he answer.

"Bingo."

"You're suspicious of him," I conclude. "You think he's lying?"

"Maybe."

I choose to tell him the truth. "He's not scared of fire."

Luke, who was looking down in thought, snaps his gaze to mine.

"I confronted him about it, and he didn't deny it."

He exhales heavily. "Maybe he never developed an aversion to it. Or he might be good at overcoming fears."

"You think that's possible?"

"It's an option." His eyes never leave mine.

"What's another option?"

"He could be a practiced liar."

"Is there a chance his records are false?" I ask.

Luke looks thoughtful. "Yes, but...that would mean he's in deep. Somewhere, somehow, he knows people able to erase and remake a whole life story good enough to pass even my background checks."

"And that scares you."

"I think you should ask him to leave."

I inhale sharply.

"I'm sorry to say that. I want you happy more than anything. But he could be dangerous."

"He's been kind so far," I reply. "It doesn't feel like he's here to hurt me. My gut says he's not."

Luke mulls this over. "I can't see why he would wait this long to do anything if he was in any way connected to your past. But I can't shake this weird feeling."

I reach across the table and take his hand. "I'll do whatever you think is best." I hate to say it. I don't want Dawson to leave.

Luke watches me for a moment before sighing. "It could be nothing. I might be overreacting."

"What if I let him stay just a little longer? You could dig deeper on him. See what he's hiding, if anything."

Because I'm pretty sure he is hiding something. I don't think that he means me harm, though.

"It's your choice. I'll look deeper, of course. Might only find much of the same, but I'll tell you if there's anything new. Meanwhile, I want you to be careful," Luke presses. "We are nothing if not overly cautious, right?"

"Right." I squeeze his hand in response.

"I'm here for you. Always will be. First sign of trouble, you call me."

He stands, and I walk him to the door. He pauses, and I

suspect it's because has more to say.

"About the lake..." His arms go around me for a quick hug before pulling back. "I've had a rough life, you know that. Things haven't always been easy for me. But here, now, in Darlington, they seem better. I've actually thought about a future, and I want you in it."

I don't know in which sense he means, but I hope it's the friendship we already share, forged even deeper by time.

"You're beautiful, Camille," he whispers. "You're the only one who understands me for me. Forgive me for thinking of us in another sense aside from friends."

He admits what I suspected he feels. Only, I'm not upset. I'm comforted. This is the Luke I know, always coming right out with it, discussing things with me, being open and honest.

"I don't think your head is in the same place as mine, and I would never act on it unless it was. I won't push. We will always be friends. Nothing will change that."

I sigh. "Thanks, Luke."

He knows where I stand. I know where he stands, too.

"Remember, be careful. Do what you will with Dawson, but never let your guard down." He reaches for the door. "See you soon."

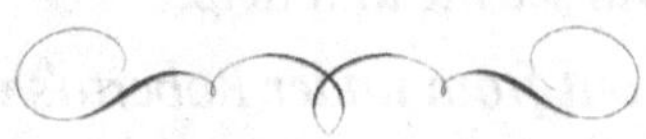

That night, I dream of Dawson. His hands slide to my hips. I beg him with my eyes to touch more, to take more of me. His lips press against mine, sure and strong and entirely him. I give myself over, my fears and desires, all that I am. He can have it.

His fingers make their way to my neck, and I moan. Something shifts, a flicker of light, and suddenly the dream is much darker. The grip tightens and I am no longer kissing Dawson. Instead, Roberto stands before me, his hands around my throat, squeezing.

You belong to me.

No matter how hard I wish to keep it at bay, the nightmare tears through me with a vengeance, reminding me that though I run, my past won't be erased.

I wake up in a cold sweat, and instantly, a memory comes.

"Where do you think you're going?" Roberto yells across a distance that's too close for my liking.

I've made it to the airport parking garage. I don't have a ticket, but there are always last-minute cancelations. Surely there's a flight out of Miami that would take me somewhere, anywhere, but here. I can't stay with Roberto another minute.

I run faster, as fast as I can, with my bag slung over one shoulder. Then in a last-ditch effort, I lose the bag, freeing weight for me to push harder, to get as far as I can. If I can make it up the stairs, surely other people will see me and help.

I hardly made it out from under Roberto's watchful gaze in the first place. His constantly revolving workforce means that, even if he is away from home, there is always someone to watch me. I was lucky to pull off an escape by pretending to be in the shower, while actually sneaking out of the window and away from Roberto's guards. But somehow, Roberto knew I left, and has caught me in time. He always does.

"Oh, princess, you really shouldn't have run from me," Roberto scolds, just as another of his men steps out of the stairwell I meant to take as an escape. He grabs me.

Though it's futile—there are already three guards on me, plus Roberto—I attempt to break free. No matter how hard I kick, scream, or claw, I'm rewarded only with curses until, finally, Roberto slams my head against the concrete ground hard enough for everything to go black.

Later, when I awake in a hospital, Roberto is there with a "went into a drug induced rage" excuse. They've found a narcotic in my system, and it is used to discredit anything I say. I'm labeled as an addict who is lucky to have people who care for her and are willing to stay long nights in the room. Roberto explains everything with a sweet smile on his face, reassuring the doctors that he has plans in motion to get me the help I need. I want to tell them he's the one who put the drug in my system. It had to have been him. I don't do drugs. I would never. It matters none. The nurses and doctors don't bother to look at me for anything more than to check my IV and vitals. They speak directly to Roberto who, with his winning smile, charms them all.

His mask is perfectly intact. I'm the only one who sees the ugly underside.

THIRTY-ONE

Dawson

I wait until I have my morning coffee, black and steaming—nearly to the point of boiling, the only way I like it—before heading out for the day. Caffeine wakes my senses and is the one routine I rely on. No matter where I move, where I was stationed, or where I ever plan to go in the future, coffee is my regular. I can wake with the sunrise and grab a cup. Scenery can change. Clothes and belongings, too. Furniture and friends. All of it. As long as I have a cup of coffee, I can normalize my situation, reacquaint myself with routine. Like now. Darlington is different than war-torn countries. I have no long-standing friends here. My home has changed for the time being. And though the coffee is much tastier here than the instant I used to pour into lukewarm water due to a lack of electricity and being in the battlefield for days on end, it's still something unchanging about my life. A quick buzz that rouses me.

I pull a thermal undershirt over my head and a long-sleeved top over that. My recently washed hair drips water onto my neck. It's cold outside again, but this time, it's not snowing. Icicles form a jagged line across the awning that protrudes from the top of the camper's front door, looking like clear, hanging knives. I stuff my hands in my jeans, both to keep them warm and to grab my keys. One look at the cloud-laden sky tells me that the sun isn't coming out for a while, even though it's already risen. Camille's truck sits in the drive, only a few yards away from my own. I hop into my old vehicle and start the engine, which coughs and sputters to life. The lights inside her house are off, and I don't know if that's because she's sleeping or due to the fact she doesn't feel like turning them on just yet. Maybe she's burning candles again. Either way, I purposely head to the general store without seeing her, knowing from the schedule in the store's office that she's not working yet.

The clock on my wrist reads seven when I pull up to the gas pump to refill. The bell above my head chimes as I enter the store, and since the diner isn't open yet, I decide to grab breakfast—a chicken biscuit and, God help me, an apple tart. Part of me wants to know why, if Miles is correct, Camille likes them so much. I've never been a fan of sweets. I hardly ever eat them. The army taught me to put only the necessary sustenance into my body. Mostly protein and vegetables. I didn't question them. I wanted to be as lethal as possible, built for the jobs they assigned. Not that I wouldn't grab the occasional pizza when I was home. But when I had a choice, when I returned stateside for short breaks, I always chose salty treats over sweet ones.

Miles is at the register.

My guess is that the old man is in the office asleep. Which is a shame, because he's the one I want to accidentally bump into.

I set the food on the counter, but Miles isn't as welcoming as usual.

"So..." He rings up my items. "You and Camille, huh?"

"What about us?"

He bags my items.

"I've heard talk around here. Guess I can't be mad that someone finally got through to her. Hell, I've been trying for a year, which you knew." He pauses to shoot me what looks like an accusatory glare. "No one has seemed to gain her interest. And, honestly, many have tried." I'm happy to have her interest, not that I'd tell Miles. It's none of his damn business.

"So, how long have you been going out?"

"We're not," I reply, my words clipped.

Miles chuckles. "Sure."

I glare at him as I grab my bag and wallet, ready to pay and get out of here.

"You're buying an apple tart," Miles comments.

He obviously remembers what he told me about Camille liking them. What's he trying to say? That I got it for her? That I plan to bring it back to the property so she can enjoy it? Or maybe he realizes I'm buying it for myself, because I want to try something she likes.

Either way, it proves his point.

"How much did you have in gas?" he asks.

He peers out of the frosty window to see the numbers on the old-fashioned pump, which look more like the combo you'd enter on a lock. Not much is electronic around here. The register. The pumps. The signs above items. All outdated, traditional models from a time long ago.

"Eighty," I reply, then throw a one-hundred-dollar bill on the counter.

Miles extends my change and I grab it.

"Give us two coffees," a voice from behind says.

I turn to find the old man leaning against the doorframe of his office, obviously listening in on other people's conversations like I've seen him do many times before, which is part of the reason why I wanted to talk to him in the first place.

Miles quickly pours two drinks and pushes the cream and sugars toward me. The old man picks up both cups and hands one over. We both decline any additions, apparently having that much in common.

"On the house," he says.

I take the cup.

"Consider it a thank you for your service in the military, and a thank you for keeping my Camille happy. Walk with me?" he requests.

I follow him out of the door to where the rocking chairs rest.

"You know, I think you and Camille might be perfect for each other. She has her secrets. You have yours. She likes you, though, all the same."

He pats the seat next to him, inviting me to join. I take a sip of the scalding coffee and watch the clouds roll by.

"I don't like the idea of you leaving her to go off on missions for months at a time."

I choose my words carefully. "You don't have to worry about me being deployed ever."

He casts a sidelong glance my way. "So, you're done with the military. Or at least with deployments, then. That's good."

When I leave Camille, it will be for a completely different reason.

"She deserves only the best," he continues.

I see what he's doing. This isn't about me. It has everything to do with Camille. He's talking to me the way a father would inquire about his daughter. He wants to see her with someone good enough, though there will likely never be such a person.

"I don't have any children. No more family left after my wife died. I have a couple of stores, my home, my dog, and this town. I only care about a few people, and I don't want to see them hurt."

"Are you looking for a promise from me?" He won't get one.

His wrinkled hand grips the coffee he brings to his mouth while his chair rocks ever so slightly. "I want to know what your intentions are."

It's a fair enough question. I force the tension in my shoulders to subside. This is what I wanted, after all. A conversation with the old man.

"She's not letting me all that close, but I'd like to be."

I let the words out. Knowing they'll cost me a little of my personal space, but also understanding that I need to say them. I want to get closer to her and I think the old man might help.

He grins. "That's my girl. Always safe. Give it time."

I wish I could tell him that I don't have time. Not much anyway.

"Miles is right, though," he remarks. "There's something between you two. Don't give up on her. It'll be worth it. I promise."

"Have you ever—" I pause and deliberate my words. "Seen her with other men?"

He stops rocking. "Well, I'm not sure that's a fair question. Surely you've been with other people before. Don't see what that has to do with now."

"It's just that she seems guarded. I'm wondering if she's ever mentioned someone before. I get this impression...that someone's harmed her."

She is so careful in life. She startles easily. She blanks out. She nearly had a panic attack in the art store. Does the old man know what made her that way? Who made her that way?

"She's never said anything to me," he replies. "But I do get the same feeling. Someone in her past must not have treated her well. One time, a while back, a customer got angry and yelled about a product being out of stock. Just a jerk who is no longer welcome to shop here. But Camille flinched when he came near, and then cried afterward in the bathroom. I didn't bring it up, but I saw her red-rimmed eyes. It was obvious. She was worried he might hurt her, which is reasonable. It's the flinch that got me suspicious."

He eyes me, a tinge of anger there.

"And if I didn't already know for certain that she's crazy about you, I'd never tell you such a thing. I want you to be careful with her, that's all. You ought to see the way her face lights up when you approach the store. I've never seen her look at anyone else like that. And no, she hasn't been with men here that I've seen. I don't know about before. She doesn't talk about her past and I respect that. But I have my suspicions. And they're not good."

"Does no one from her past ever call? Visit?"

"No. Neither."

Camille is a ghost. Whoever she used to be is forgotten.

"Where did she move from?" I ask.

If anyone knows the truth about her, I suspect it's the old man. It's in the way she looks at him like he's familiar and comfortable. She speaks highly of him. She warned me not to disappoint him when I first got the job. She's protective of the old man.

He eyes me. "What did she tell you?"

"Upstate New York."

He waves to a car going by. He seems to know most everyone around here.

"She told me the same thing," he says. "I'm not convinced."

"Where do you *think* she's from?" I press.

"Not New York."

That's what I thought. Camille says one thing, but her truth is something entirely different. I already know she's from Miami, not up north. But it's good to have confirmation.

"Did she not bring anything from her past with her?" I wonder aloud.

"Hm." He rocks more. "Don't know for sure. Seems to be close friends with one person around here. That's about it."

"Luke," I surmise.

He nods, confirming my statement.

Another vehicle pulls into the lot, and I'm worried our conversation will be cut short, but it's just Rose, here to get the kitchen ready for another busy day.

"Hey, y'all!" she greets us, her tone chipper, wearing a warm smile that makes her plump, apple round cheeks stretch wide.

"Mornin', Rose," the old man calls. "Left you a fresh batch of berries. About fifty pounds. Took 'em out of the deep freezer at home. Picked 'em from my yard. Thought you might want to bake blueberry pie for dessert today. I wouldn't decline blueberry pancakes, either. Or cobbler. Whatever you think is best."

He grins hopefully and she laughs.

"Well, I suppose I can't say no to my favorite person, can I?"

Everyone favors the old man. I'm inclined to like him, too.

"You're a doll," he says.

Rose enters the diner, and a second later, another car pulls in. Bonnie, the server, jumps out and attaches her apron, even though the diner doesn't open for another couple of hours. I wonder if she helps Rose get the food ready. Bonnie nearly misses us sitting by the entrance until she looks up at the last second and lets out a small squeak.

"Well, hello," she chirps, her eyes going to the old man and then to me. She blushes. "I didn't see you."

From what I've gathered, she's a friend of Camille's. One of her only friends.

"Hey, Bonnie," I say.

She smiles. "Nice to see you, Dawson."

The old man eyes us.

"Well, I better get to work. Have to prep everything."

She waves goodbye and enters the diner, leaving the old man and I alone again.

"Does every female here like you, boy?" he questions.

"I only like one of them, if that makes it any better."

My answer seems to be the correct one, because the old man resumes rocking and takes the last sip of his coffee before tossing it in the garbage pail next to him. I'm due to work in a few minutes, so my time, what I have left of it, is short.

"I remember her asking about a job and where to buy women's clothing the first time she visited the store," he recalls. "She reminded me of a stray. So frightened. I'll never forget it. That truck of hers is all she owned, and she'd mentioned just buying it a week prior. From where, I have no idea. Then she looked at the poster board for houses for sale and rent. Same as you did when you arrived. Lucky find, that place of hers. There were five properties up for grabs. None for rent. So, she picked one, and that's where she lives to this day."

He looks around, almost as though making sure no one is listening in.

"Word has it that she bought her cabin with cash. I hired her the same day. She went to town and got new clothes. She was on the run from something, I'm sure of it. You better not ruin this for her."

I don't plan on ruining anything. I'm trying to solve the mystery of Camille.

"You know that's not my intention, or else you wouldn't have told me any of this in the first place," I respond. "Now, is there anything you can tell me that will help me get closer to her?"

"I told you what I did because it's not really much, now is it?" he counters. "She moved from somewhere that isn't New York. She started over. She's afraid and cautious. We both have the same suspicions about that. I think you already knew all of this."

Yes, but having my conclusions isn't the same as hearing it from another person.

He stands, and I do the same. It's time for work.

"She's special. Treat her like it."

Fair enough.

"Now, do you know about the nice restaurant down the way? It's called Rockies. Sits right on the lake."

He prattles on and I'm careful to take note.

THIRTY-TWO

Camille

People are saying it's an unusually cold winter. I stare at the slate gray clouds above. I only have last winter in the mountains to compare it to, but I'd say they are right. The temperature is only nine degrees.

As I drive to the general store, I truly appreciate the beautiful country, all back roads, hills, and steep mountains. Gorgeous places to rest my eyes. Animals with hooves on the ground and birds of prey soaring above. Completely unlike a linear Miami, with its gridded streets and metal buildings. Sharp edges and hard lines. Here, barely any cars pass. Whereas there, I would have had to squeeze between rows of vehicles parked on each side of the road, clogging space.

When I arrive, Mr. Hill is toasting a bagel for lunch, preparing to slather it in blueberry cream cheese. He doesn't seem to care about bagels typically being a breakfast food.

"Howdy," he says, refilling his coffee.

He offers me the pot so I can pour a cup, too. I inhale and savor the scent of roasted beans and fresh cream in the air. The whir of the oven is the only sound to be heard aside from our voices.

"Afternoon." I pour a heaping helping of half and half, turning my drink nearly white.

I take over the shift as Miles clocks out. A couple of customers walk in. Husband and wife, retirement age, who, from time to time, like to get coffee and stay for hours on the front rocking chairs, watching the goings-on at the only store that gets much traction around these parts.

"Camille, hello. It's lovely to see you," the woman greets, wearing a warm smile to back up her gently spoken words. "Our usual."

Which means two large cups, several creamers, and four packets of sugar. How I remember such things, I don't know. The country has taken up root, making me recognize regulars and learn special orders.

"Sure thing." I grab the items, ring them up, and glance back at Mr. Hill, who is polishing off the first half of his bagel.

He waves at the customers. "Half off hot chocolate today, so come back for a cup when you finish those."

He's always upselling something to the ones who sit and stay a while. It's only fair, since they hang around like they do.

"Might bring the granddaughter up later, then. Course she'll ask for an ice cream. You opening it up?" the man inquires.

"I will if you want me to," Mr. Hill replies.

I don't see how anyone can eat ice cream when it's cold enough to snow outside. Good thing Mr. Hill keeps a portable heater by the rocking chairs, lest some of his customers freeze to death out there. They don't seem to mind either way. Routine doesn't care about things like weather. It's just the way things are. Slow, steady, and memorable.

"How do you do it?" I ask Mr. Hill when the customers take their usual spots at the entrance. "Day in and day out, year after year—the same thing over and over. Does it ever get boring?"

Lackluster as it may be, I'm thinking of staying. Darlington seems like the perfect place to sit a while. I bought the property in hopes of camping out for at least a few years and not having to answer questions from landlords or pay rent every month, wasting money. The thing is, I'm starting to see past a few years, wondering what it'd be like to stay forever.

"Why? You getting antsy? Thinkin' of leaving?" Mr. Hill frowns.

"Just the opposite, actually." I place the lunch sandwiches in the oven and prepare the foil to wrap them. They'll sit under the heat light for an hour, tops, before customers arrive and buy them all. "Thinking of staying."

"How long?"

"Depends on how you answer the question." While the

sandwiches cook, I brew hot chocolate, since Mr. Hill has it in mind to run a special today.

He finishes his bagel as a few more shoppers enter. They stop in every other aisle to chat about some dinner down by the lake, a family gathering. I tune them out and listen closely to my boss's reply.

"Camille, if you're askin' whether I think you should stay, the answer is *hell, yes*. You fit here. This is your town now, too. I'm not gonna say it never gets boring. It does. But that's exactly the point, isn't it? To not be caught up in the stress of the city life. To have places to wander without ever reaching anything but thick trees or endless fields?"

I nod. "I think you might be right."

He reaches under the counter and pulls out a round container. "Here, brought this for you. Eat it before it goes bad."

He walks off, leaving me to stare at a freshly baked cherry cobbler that is nowhere near going bad. I smile and open it up right there, not bothering to cut it into neat slices. What's the point? I don't plan to share.

Occasionally, Mr. Hill gets a wild hair to bake. I don't know why, or where his talent comes from, but since he quickly walked away the one and only time I ever asked about it, I have a feeling it has something to do with his wife, whom he can't talk about without getting emotional. I like to think they used to stand in the kitchen together, baking pies and cookies and pastries. Or maybe he just has a gift all on his own. He won't tell me, so I'll never know.

Spoon deep in cobbler, I begin eating the dessert, even though I ought to have something healthier for lunch.

More customers enter and quickly grab items, setting several drinks and snacks on the counter. I put the pie aside to ring them up.

"We're going fishin'," one says. "Heard the lake just got restocked."

The town restocks the lake with fish a couple times a year, brought in from outside sources since no natural bodies of water feed the lake. Whenever fish are caught, they have no way of replenishing, except for the few who spawn there. They drain the lake nearly a foot in rainy season and refill the same amount when it's dry. It helps to regulate the waters and aquatic life, making sure the lake doesn't flood the homes that sit practically on it.

"Should be great fishing, then," I reply, ringing them up.

It's odd to think of how the lake came to be. There used to be a town down there at the gorge of the mountains, until the people evacuated to higher grounds after deciding they needed a major landmark. To do so, they purposely flooded the underlying town. They created a lake. Now people float in boats over a sunken city while fish make homes of the places where people used to reside.

"Have a good day."

The customers leave me to my cobbler, which I begin eating again as soon as they're gone. I'm too busy enjoying the dessert to realize Dawson has taken a short break from working on the sheds. He's nearly done with all of them. Soon, Mr. Hill will give him another job, I'm sure.

By the time I do spot him, just outside the door, he's already seen me, and a smile pulls at the corners of his mouth.

"Pie for lunch?" he asks, as the hanging bell jangles above him.

"It's cobbler," I say, licking the spoon clean.

Dawson's eyes follow the path of my tongue. "Looks delicious."

"Want some?" I'm teasing him now, taking a big scoop.

He surprises me by leaning in and placing his mouth over the spoon, eating the bite I meant as a joke.

"Mmm," he hums.

My insides squirm as the sound of his pleasure reverberates through me.

"Delicious." He licks his lips.

I'm rendered speechless.

Dawson pulls back. "Hey, what do you think about dinner tonight?"

I hadn't made plans. My short shift ends in a few hours, but I suspect he already knows that since he sees the same schedule all the workers do.

Under a knot of nerves, I find my voice. "Dinner sounds nice."

"We could go out to eat," he suggests. "Maybe at Rockies?"

I nod my confirmation. A smile tucks itself into his cheeks, and I have to work to keep my excitement from showing.

"So, I'll see you at the property in a couple hours? I'll drive us, if that's okay with you."

"Sure," I reply, a bit surprised by his boldness.

"Perfect. I have to get back to work. See you soon."

He disappears outside. I wait a full thirty seconds for my erratically beating heart to calm down.

"Good Lord, the heat between you two is hot enough to sizzle an egg."

I pivot to find Mrs. JoAnne standing behind me with a full-blown smile.

"Where did you come from?" I ask.

"Rose's diner entrance." She sets her purse on the counter and leans up against it like she means to get comfortable. "Now, tell the truth, did I just hear you agree to a date with him?"

"Who's going on a date?" Mr. Hill questions, exiting his office where he managed to slip off to earlier. Funny how he always reemerges at the most inopportune times—when there is gossip to be had.

"Well, the story as I know it is—" Mrs. JoAnne begins, but I cut her off.

"Both of you stop, or I swear I won't speak to either one of you for the foreseeable future."

"Think she's serious?" Mr. Hill wonders in a low voice as though I can't hear him, even though he's only three feet away.

"Hard to tell," Mrs. JoAnne mutters. "Better not risk it."

I take the broom and head outside to sweep the grounds. Or at least that's the excuse I tell Mr. Hill. Anything is better than hearing them gossip about me in hushed tones. It doesn't hurt that I'll get to catch another glimpse of Dawson working. Preferably with his shirt off, but at this point, I'll take anything. What I get, as I begin sweeping dirt into the road, is a sideways glance from him.

I want to walk right up and kiss the grin off his face, but instead I mind my own business, sweeping briskly and trying not to get caught staring at Dawson through a thick wall of curls. After about the sixth time of getting caught anyway, and when I have no more sidewalk to sweep, I reluctantly head back toward the entrance.

Dawson picks that exact moment to stop working.

"Rockies is your favorite restaurant, right?" he inquires. "Because we can go anywhere."

He reaches for the door and opens it for me.

"Thank you," I say, wondering how he knows I like Rockies. "And yes, it's my favorite."

Only a few people know this about me, which means either he asked, or they willingly told him. My cheeks heat and something warm zaps through my body. Dawson leans in, and for a moment, I wonder if he'll kiss me right here in the doorway, but then he seems to stop himself, noticing Mr. Hill and Mrs. JoAnne with their eyes glued to us.

He doesn't kiss me, but he doesn't back away either.

"We have an audience," he whispers, humor in his tone.

I try not to care about them.

"I'll see you later, okay?" I murmur.

I trail a finger down his palm and then squeeze his hand. At this, I get a full smile. It's dazzling. Breathtaking.

I'm a goner. Not only do Mr. Hill and Mrs. JoAnne know it, but I have a feeling Dawson does, too.

THIRTY-THREE

Dawson

"Do you like the place?" Camille asks.

I glance around Rockies. The top floor view is a wall of large windows looking out over the glittering lake. The sun is setting, spilling across the sky.

"I do," I reply.

The back walls are covered in old license plates and neon signs. A bar wraps around the corner, and nearly every stool is occupied with lively people. Music plays loudly enough to drown out the other conversations around us.

Camille picks a table by the window, the last one remaining.

I can't tell whether the restaurant feels more upscale or relaxed. The atmosphere says relaxed, but the food doesn't. Everything from porterhouse steaks to blue crab legs to fresh fish decorates the pages of the menus in front of us. Standing like a table centerpiece is another menu with aged wines and imported beers, with specialty drinks and extravagant desserts. The cuisine is so different from Rose's country diner, where I've grown accustomed to eating when I decide to splurge on food not bought and cooked myself.

"Best of both worlds, huh?" Camille remarks, just barely hiding a smile behind the menu she holds in front of her.

"Looks like it."

Just then a plate is delivered to the table beside us with a steaming steak, veggies, and a loaded baked potato. I decide right away I want the same.

When the waitress approaches, Camille orders sweet tea and a chicken dinner. I order the largest steak they have.

The waitress leaves and Camille looks at me with a mix of longing and curiosity. I think we both know something has changed. I never meant to grow close to anyone in this town, and Camille didn't either. I could claim curiosity, but it's more than that now. The date has been a long time coming. Even if I can't tell her the full truth about who I am, why I'm here, or what this really means for both of us, I can still be with her now, grinning like I am, enjoying the fact that Camille turns down every guy in this town—except me.

"Want to know something?" she asks.

I want to know anything she's willing to tell me. "Sure."

The waitress brings our drinks and Camille makes me wait while she takes a sip.

"You crept up on me. At first, I thought you'd rent the camper. I'd make a little extra money. It made the most sense to stay away from you, but somehow, I couldn't."

My thoughts exactly. "What changed?"

"You. Maybe me." She glances out at the calm lake. "Or perhaps I don't feel like being as reclusive as I've been anymore. It's hard to say."

"Maybe I understand exactly what you mean." I watch a duck swoop low and land on the water. A dock extends from the restaurant, perfect for boats. One is tied up by a fraying rope, gently knocking against the piling.

"Sometimes," Camille murmurs, "I get the feeling you're running."

I pause, my gaze slowly going back to her. How could she possibly know? Somehow, she does. No one from my time before Darlington knows that I settled into this slip of a town, barricaded by mountains.

"I think we're all trying to leave parts of ourselves behind," I reply vaguely.

It's the truth, after all, and the weird thing is, saying it feels liberating. Even though we're mostly talking in code, Camille's speaking in a way I understand. Not outright stating, but revealing pieces all the same. She's good at this, telling me things without actually saying much.

"You didn't mention that Rockies has an arcade," I say.

There are five games tucked into a nook in the back wall.

She grins, a challenging glint in her eyes. "Want to play?"

I'm already standing and making my way to the change machine, which seems to be answer enough for her.

"Which one first?" she inquires.

I didn't peg Camille for the competitive type, but I like it. I take a seat at the racing one, feeling like a teenager again, carefree and alive.

"Just a fair warning" —she smiles— "I am a master at this game."

I insert the coins and learn soon enough that Camille is a lot of things, but one thing she's not is a liar about her gaming skills. She takes first place instantly and never lets it go.

"Best two out of three," I offer.

The course unravels, buildings swooshing past, bright lights flashing, illuminating Camille's face. She's beautiful, biting her lip in concentration, spinning the wheel sharply at each turn. I realize when I hear a crashing sound that I've forgotten to pay attention, and my car has careened into a wall.

"You're really not very good at this," she teases, pressing her lips together to hold back a laugh. She comes in first again. "I've already beaten you two times. You still up for a third?"

I agree with a nod. This time I do pay attention. I still don't win, but it doesn't matter because energy zaps my blood, and I can't remember when I've ever felt this free. Probably since before my mother died. Or maybe since before I entered the army to make a decent enough living.

"I give up," I declare, standing and stretching my legs. The next game isn't nearly as cramped. "What about this one?"

We stand by a target range. I grin, knowing there's no way Camille will beat me. She sees my choice and rests a hip against the wall, crossing her arms.

"Not a very fair choice, now is it?" she asks.

I step close to her, breathing in the scent that is distinctly Camille, fresh and flowery.

"When," I ask lowly, my mouth close to her ear, "have I ever claimed to play fair?"

She shivers, her eyes hooded. I want to pull her bottom lip, sensual and full, into my mouth. That's all it takes, one look from Camille, and the rest fades. But little do I know, Camille can play unfairly, too. She steps into me, her body against mine, making me ache, as she slips two coins into the slot, grabs the gun, and begins the timed challenge without me.

"Already losing, soldier." She laughs and I snap out of it.

"Cheater," I retort, but I'm smiling, too.

I use my right hand to aim and shoot, resting my left on her lower back. It distracts Camille enough for her to miss three targets. I rub slow circles on her skin, just under her shirt. She forgets to shoot altogether.

The game ends with my victory. Camille looks at me as though I have something she wants. There's no one here, in this back nook, so I place a kiss on her cheek, then her neck, and lastly, her ear.

"Food's ready whenever you are." The waitress appears

quickly and then leaves us be.

"Are we ready for food, Camille?" I murmur, hoping she'll stay a minute more.

I have every urge to press her tightly against me and forget dinner altogether, but then Camille steps back, smiles gently, and heads to the table with me right behind her.

We sit again, a candle now lit as the sun disappears. I take the first bite of my steak and know there is no going back. Not from food this delicious, and certainly not from the gorgeous woman across from me.

"What do you think?" she asks.

"I think you're more beautiful than this incredible view, and that's saying something."

Red stains her cheeks. "I meant about the food."

"It's amazing. Yours?"

She slices her chicken into thin pieces, dipping them in the extra BBQ sauce that's spilled off the top of the meat.

"Mine is incredible."

I reach a fork across the small table, waiting for her approval. When she nods, I help myself to a bite of her meal. She grins and does the same with mine. I like sharing with her. Case in point, when the waitress comes by and asks if everything is all right, I order the biggest chocolate dessert on the menu, so big that Camille will have no choice but to split it with me.

"When was the last time you were here?"

"A couple months ago," she replies. "When Mr. Hill decided to take the employees out as a show of appreciation for our hard work. Bonnie came, and so did Mrs. Rose. Of course, she wanted to be the one to cook for us, but she agreed anyway. Mr. Hill thought that as wonderful as her food is, and according to him, there's really no comparison, it'd do us all good to get out of the store environment. You should have seen Mrs. Rose, checking all of our plates, commenting on how they could have presented things better and how she would have done it had she been given the chance to cook, but in the end, her plate was completely clean."

I smile. "She liked the food after all?"

"You have to understand that it's just her way. Mrs. Rose is known for her cuisine. It's as much a part of her identity as her eye color, something that can't be helped."

Camille finishes both of her sides and nearly all of her chicken.

"We had a good time. Even convinced Mr. Hill to race me in the car game. He wasn't happy about losing. And while we're on the subject, how did you know I liked it here? Which one of them told you?"

I pause at her intuitiveness.

"The old man," I answer honestly.

The waitress arrives with dessert and sets in front of us, center of the table. It's an oversized martini glass filled with a chocolate brownie, dripping melted fudge, three scoops of ice cream—strawberry, vanilla, and chocolate—whipped cream, crumbled waffle cone, and hot caramel sauce.

"Wow." Camille eyes the decadent masterpiece.

"After you." I push it toward her for the first bite.

She moans the moment the fork hits her mouth.

"So, it's safe to say you like chocolate?"

Camille licks a stray drop from her lip. "It's probably safe to assume that."

She takes a deep breath, then a second bite. Another deep breath, more bites, as though trying to make room, but it's no use. She's done. She sets the fork down and leans her head back with smile on her face. I eat half of the dessert.

"This might have been the best meal I've ever tasted," she admits. "But don't ever tell Rose I said that."

I open the check and insert cash, along with a tip, before taking Camille's hand and helping her from the table. With our food long gone, we descend the stairs to the outside dock. Water laps against the wood, slow and dragging. I sit at the edge, dangling my feet. A turtle swims underfoot, making its way to the surface. Beneath the soft glow of the dock light, I spot various fish. They gather, waiting. I wonder if people feed them scraps. As though summoning an answer, another couple sits down the way, breaking off pieces of bread and tossing the remains into the lake. The fish leave us.

Though we drove up, I can't help but wish we could have rented a boat and come by water. It seems like the better route. Out on the lake, I spot a solitary bird. It calls, swiftly and lonely, and then again, another time. The sound lingers, bouncing off mountain rock walls.

"It's a loon," she says. "That bird has one of the most

haunting calls. The odd thing is it's not supposed to stay here. Somehow, while the rest of its kind migrated over our town, this one decided it was too pretty a place to leave."

"Is that what you did, too, Camille?" I give her hand a soft squeeze. "Did you decide you liked this place better than the one you used to belong to, and now you plan to stay?"

"That's exactly what I did," she whispers.

The loon cries again.

"It's calling for a mate that will probably never come."

It's a sad notion.

"What about you? Have you decided to stay?" she inquires.

I consider her question and what it implies. Camille doesn't seem like she's in a hurry to have me leave. But there's no possibility of me staying.

"Maybe."

I hate the lie for what it is.

I will leave.

I have to.

THIRTY-FOUR

Before

Mr. Cruz returns home in the wee hours of the morning after a night out at the club in the same suit he donned the previous evening. Making as little noise as possible, he walks quietly past the guard to the foyer. He veers left, heading to the downstairs bathroom where he can shower the perfume off. The woman he spent the night with wore too much of it, and the scent lingers on his skin. With none of the night spent actually sleeping, his feet drag a little. He's tired, and alcohol still courses slightly through his veins.

He opens the door of the bedroom where the bathroom is

adjoined, expecting it to be empty.

Only to find his wife waiting for him.

"Where have you been?" she asks.

There's no reason to lie. "The club."

He doesn't add on the rest.

In the sheets.

With another woman.

Who isn't you.

They don't have an open relationship. She wouldn't approve. Not that he blames her. He'd kill any man who touched her.

"The club," she parrots.

He expected her to be asleep in their upstairs main bedroom, where she usually is when he returns at all hours of the night. He's not sure why she's awake now.

"Why are you heading into this room?" she questions.

"Why are you in this room?" he fires back.

Unease fists his stomach. How did she know he usually comes here before he makes it upstairs to slip under the covers with her? As far as he knew, she was none the wiser about his night prowls. But maybe...

"Answer me," he demands.

She nods to the window. "Couldn't sleep. Wanted a view of the garden for a moment."

The garden—full of exotic, tropical flowers—has never been her favorite. She prefers the beach and the water, the wide wall of windows in their room that overlooks the sea.

"Noticed you were gone," she mentions.

"*Just work stuff.*" *His delivery of the lie is firm.* "*Thought I'd shower in here so as to not wake you.*"

Her head tilts to the side and he spots a healing bruise on the underside of her chin.

"*Are you lying?*" *Her voice comes out choked, as though asking has cost her something.*

And it has.

He moves quickly, fisting her thick blonde curls roughly, positioning her mouth a breath from his own. She flinches.

"*What are you insinuating?*"

He wonders what her mind is thinking and what her lips will spill.

She says nothing. He waits. Tugs harder.

"*You smell like perfume.*" *The words are an accusation.*

"*Many women wear it in the club. I mingle with them. Just friendly greetings. You know that.*" *He lets go of her, then caresses her cheek.* "*I would never hurt you in that way.*"

A simple lie. What he really means is that he'd never hurt her by admitting infidelity to her face. Why cause trouble? She's better off believing he's a loyal man. Truthfully, he is in many ways. She's the only one on his arm. She wears his wedding ring. She lives with him. The sole woman he claims. He chose her. She should be proud.

She seems to consider his lie in earnest.

"*Honest,*" *he reassures her.*

She takes a step toward him. "*If you ever—*"

He cuts her off. "*I won't.*"

Her resolve wavers. "*I couldn't be with you if you did that to me.*"

Oh, look at her, matching his lie with her own. He's done many things since they married she never thought him possible of. Yet here she still is.

"It's only you," he whispers.

He sees the moment she believes the lie.

"Come here." He tugs her close and begins unlooping the tie around the silk robe draped over her shoulders, pulling her toward the shower.

She goes with him like he knew she would.

THIRTY-FIVE

Camille

When the last inside log begins to sizzle out in the fire, I take a few sips of warm coffee, trying to wake all the way up, and throw on my coat. A blast of freezing wind tears through the house the moment I open the front door. Even with layers of clothes, the creeping cold slithers up my sleeves. I huddle into the hood of my coat and walk to the side of the house, filling my arms with wood from the outside supply while trying to keep my teeth from chattering.

I crave the heat, the sea I used to love. But, like usual, when

I think of the beach, I can't help but think of him.

Stars explode behind my eyes as Roberto's fist crunches into my cheek. I can't feel my ear, but something tickles my jaw. I reach up to brush it away and realize I'm bleeding. He's busted my eardrum.

I've burned his dinner and spent too much time ignoring him for the ocean. I press my tongue to the side of my molar and wince. It's loose. Again. It'll take weeks to heal. Like last time. That means days plugged away inside the master bedroom with the television on—I'm beyond sick of the television, my only distraction—healing from bruises, not being able to make it to swim lessons.

I've begun giving lessons to women—only women, as that's all Roberto will approve of. He thinks I do it free of charge, teaching others how to prepare for triathlons and helping some learn how to brave the currents and fickle moods of the ocean. To Roberto, swim lessons that help me stay in his sight while keeping my body in shape are acceptable.

I wonder what he'd do to me if he realized I have the women deposit money in an account he knows nothing about to make sure I'm financially set for the plan I have to leave him.

My clientele consists of rich women who think nothing of paying ridiculous prices for my services. Still, I charge less than any other trainer in our county, so I don't feel bad about their payments.

Only a couple months more, and I'll have enough.

"I expect you to talk to me when I'm home, not ignore my questions about your day," he growls.

"I didn't feel like speaking to you," I reply.

I'm pushing my luck. I'm already down on the floor, my vision slowly leaking back to me. It's hard to speak, but I've become accustomed to pressing past the pain.

"Watch it," he warns. "You do not refuse me."

That's what I've been doing nearly every day since the first moment he laid his hands harmfully on me—paying for the choice I made. If I had known what type of man Roberto truly was, I never would have fallen for him.

"Remember what could happen to you," he threatens close to my good ear.

As though all he's done to me so far has been child's play.

"You can make this easy or hard on yourself," he cautions. "Your choice."

Wrong. I have never had a choice with him. He is always the one in control.

"They're calling for a blizzard."

I turn at the sound of Dawson's voice, the memory breaking.

He stands a few feet away in a thick winter coat the color of blackberries.

"I don't know what to do in a blizzard," he continues.

"That makes two of us," I reply. "Where did you hear about it?"

"Television. Do you have a radio?"

"Inside." I head in with the wood, and then trudge back out for another bundle. "I'll have to give it a listen. All I can think to do is to keep the wood stocked and the fire roaring."

It's too frigid and late in the season to plant any more crops, but I make a note to remember to move the peppers I've grown in inside pots away from the windowsill and onto the living room table to keep their stems from freezing.

"Listen," he says. "I have a bit of a problem."

I wonder what he thinks of the impending blizzard, considering he despises the regular cold.

"What is it?"

He glances at the camper. "The heater coil. It's broken."

I immediately move toward his home, knowing there's no way he can survive a blizzard with no heat.

I open the camper door and shrink back from the icy temperature.

"I don't have the parts to fix it," Dawson tells me. "Do you?"

"No," I admit. "And you can't stay in a metal camper in these temps. You'll freeze. It's great with the heat, cocooning it in, but that's also the problem. It traps the cold."

"Then, I need to get to the hardware store," he says.

"It's not open this late."

It's 9:00 pm on a Wednesday. According to him, the blizzard will be here tomorrow.

"What about the inn?" he asks.

"It shut down for winter, except on weekends."

"I could stay in the truck. I have enough gas to run it until the hardware store opens in the morning. I'll stay awake and crack the windows."

That's not a good idea.

"I don't think Jimmy will open in a blizzard."

Dawson seems to be at an impasse. He can't leave and he can't stay in the camper, either.

"For now, I think the best thing would be to stock the wood inside the house," I suggest. "I have food and a fire. We can figure the rest out."

I walk to the woodshed to load up. Dawson helps. We bring it into the cabin. My living room is small enough already, but I move a chair to the farthest corner to make whatever space I can for extra kindling. I'd rather not brave a blizzard to collect more, even if it's only several yards from the front door.

I set the wood down and grab the radio out of one of the cabinets. Once on, it immediately streams blizzard warnings. I listen as the announcer blares cautions, recommending hunkering down and staying indoors. He mentions keeping a fire lit and having extra batteries and candles, along with foods that won't spoil easily and bottled water. It reminds me of the hurricane and tropical storm warnings I was accustomed to in Miami, only minus the snow and need for heat. The announcer goes on to mention less than favorable road conditions, with the trucks prepared to work all hours to clear as much as possible. The feet of overnight snow they're anticipating won't make it an easy task to get anywhere.

After the third round of wood gathering, I wipe the snow from my boots on the doormat and set the logs in the space I've cleared. I think about the camper and how cold it'll be tonight.

I shuffle through Dawson's options. I could call Mr. Hill. His place is twenty minutes from mine. He'd probably let Dawson stay. Even Mrs. JoAnne likely wouldn't object to his presence for a couple of days, though she'd talk him to death. Maybe Kenny has an extra room. Or…

"Listen, why don't you stay with me?" I offer. "You're welcome to the spare bedroom."

What I'm proposing might be dangerous for all the wrong reasons. Inviting Dawson so close to the comfort of my bed is tempting trouble, but worse still is him freezing when there's a perfectly warm house next door.

"You're serious?" he asks.

"Completely."

His look guarantees unnamed things and I nearly melt right there from the heat his stare holds. "You're sure that's a good idea?"

I wish I could promise that my resolve was strong, and that nothing would happen between us, but lately, it seems like I can't stay away from him. Plus, I remember how seriously he takes such things.

A promise is a promise.

I laugh. "No, I'm not sure at all. But I can't let you freeze."

My stomach flips and I realize how much I want him here.

"So, what do you think?"

He moves closer, running the pad of his thumb across my jaw.

"I think," he murmurs, "that staying with you sounds perfect."

I lean into his touch. "Get a bag. Come over when you're ready."

Five minutes later, he's back, shrugging out of his jacket and collapsing by the fire. I'm grateful for a property that supplies more than enough kindling, and for the small house that keeps me warm.

"I'm glad you're staying," I say.

Dawson gives me a small, rueful smile. "Me, too."

THIRTY-SIX

Dawson

Camille's cabin smells like pumpkin spice. A fire pops behind the grate, its warmth enveloping me. Wizard meows contentedly and drops down into a ball just beside the blaze, purring loudly. I place the overnight bag on the couch.

"You're welcome to use the bathroom and anything you need," she informs me. "The spare room is small, but adequate, I hope. If you prefer the couch, I can set up a sleeping pallet."

She appears almost shy, glancing anywhere but at my face.

"I'll take the room," I reply.

Camille leads the way to the door that opens into a quaint space—large enough for a twin bed and a nightstand. A sliding closet door reveals, upon closer inspection, several shelves. Facing the bed is a distressed wooden accent wall, decorated with hanging clear lightbulbs and several pictures—a map, a painting of a lone deer in winter, a cedar plaque embossed with the word "Home", a "Bear Crossing" sign, and a framed piece of flannel fabric with stenciled white evergreen trees front and center—all placed just so. The room has Camille's flair. I see her here in the decorations, sparse as they are. My eyes land on the bed, a red and green quilt on top.

I remove my smaller case from the overnight bag.

"There's pasta if you're hungry."

"Thanks. That'd be nice."

I set my bag on the floor, reaching in it for sweats. Camille returns from the hall closet with another comforter that she drapes over the bed.

"I'm not sure how cold you'll be. Here's an extra blanket. Do you need anything else?" she inquires. "The fire should burn through the night. It gets a little chilly by morning, but you can restock the wood if you get too cold."

Maybe in sweats, tucked under a comforter, I'll avoid chilly temperatures.

"I'm going to change," I say.

"Okay. Me, too."

Her stare quickly slips down my body and lingers, even as I turn my back and enter the bathroom with my bag. I check my reflection in the mirror. I could use a shave, but seeing as how I left my razor at the camper, I give up that notion. The pants I slip on are threadbare and much more comfortable than the jeans I stuff into the bag. I finish pulling a cotton sweatshirt over my head, the whole outfit a light gray, and return to the living room.

"The blizzard should hit tonight," she warns. "I think I need to pay better attention to the weather from now on. I don't like having almost no notice. Mr. Hill mentioned a storm coming our way a day or so ago, but I didn't realize it was this bad."

To her credit, neither did the weather forecasters. The storm shifted to the right, directly over us, and it's getting stronger by the minute.

There's a windup radio on the table. I barely hear the staticky words, a low-pitched warning to buckle down and wait it out. Already, fat flakes spiral from the sky, bare tree branches becoming laden with snowy pillows.

The sun hangs heavy, threatening darkness in an hour or two. Wind thrashes against the outside of the house, letting us know the storm is intensifying and nearing. So, we settle in. Camille with a book in the armchair, seemingly completely at ease with me here. And me on the couch, head tilted back against the cushions, waiting for night to come.

When Camille leaves her spot to enter her room, I wonder what she's doing. She returns a minute later with a magazine that she tosses into my lap.

"Enjoy." She's wearing a small smile.

I read the title and grin. She remembered.

I open the pages to find maps. Topical landscapes with mountainous terrains, deserts, and oceans. My fingers bump over volcanic peaks that launch themselves into the sky. The first half contains close aerial photos. The second half holds images from farther away, some even viewed from space.

Camille abandons her spot and takes a seat next to me.

"Where were you stationed?" she asks.

I debate telling her. I suppose it doesn't hurt, as long as I keep the details at bay.

I take her hand and lay a finger over the general area. Her eyes settle on where we're touching.

"A small town," I divulge. "There was no running water. No bathrooms. No official home infrastructure. Occasionally, there were huts made from mismatching supplies, barely bigger than a closet. Everything was war-torn and desolate. The army gave us provisions, but they didn't always hold over until the next shipment. We improvised."

She watches me with a blank stare. I can't help but wonder what she thinks.

"What did you eat?"

I stopped cringing a long time ago at some of the things I consumed to get by.

"Anything we could," I reply. "Mostly rationed packs of dried food. Sometimes wild animals. Whatever it took."

The same blank stare greets me.

"We stayed in caves or tents or even just in small packs

hidden away behind a sand dune. The weather was a beast. Everything was a challenge. We were constantly on the go. Never in one place for long. The risk of being discovered was too great, so even if we remained in one general area for a month, we switched up our location. Our sleeping quarters were often less than good, but we didn't fail missions. So, at least there was that."

I move her finger to another spot.

"This was the worst I ever stayed. I made a mistake. Took a bullet to the leg."

She gasps and I pause, letting my words sink in.

"Sometimes, we were injured. It's part of the job. I was lucky. It missed all major arteries. It doesn't even hurt much anymore. A little scar tissue. Nothing more. I've seen worse."

I close my eyes for a brief moment. I can't help the memories that haunt me. A brother in arms covered in blood. A stopped heart.

"Dawson." Camille's voice is in my ear. My eyes snap open.

I think for a moment she'll want to know more, but instead she smiles and requests, "Show me a place you've always wanted to visit but never have."

I relax and move her hand to another page, relishing the feel of her skin against mine. I stop her finger over Oregon.

"The redwood forest," she murmurs. "I wouldn't have guessed that."

"What about you?" I ask. "Where have you always dreamed of visiting?"

She guides my touch to a tiny island.

"Sandy beaches and coconuts, huh?" It doesn't surprise me. "A piece of land dropped right into the middle of an ocean."

Camille eyes the island. "Yes."

I wonder if she misses Miami and its sandy beaches. She told me she loves swimming. I imagine she'd have a blast in the deep, tropical waters.

"What do you think the sea life is like there?" she muses, her face set to wonder, her mind lost somewhere in the thought of the ocean and its inhabitants.

"I think it's full of fish and saltwater that you could swim in for hours," I reply.

She gives me a full-blown, heart-stopping smile.

"I think, Dawson" —I love the sound of my name on her lips— "that you might be right."

A couple of hours later, the sun is gone, replaced by a darkness so thick I can almost reach out and touch it, a sheet of black against the pale ground. I place another log on the fire.

Camille has gone to bed. It's peaceful here in the small home she's made for herself. The electricity flickers, as though it means to give itself over to the storm. The fire rages, its shimmers swaying along the walls.

I add two more logs to the pile to hopefully hold us over until morning. From the lack of noise in her room, I can only guess that she made good on her word of going to sleep. I, however, am wide-awake. Which is why I hear the small tap at the door.

I'm instantly alert, peering through the blinds. Luke stands on the other side. When he sees me looking, he shakes his head as though he's disappointed.

"Get Camille," he orders through the glass. "She's not answering her phone."

I don't want to answer the door without Camille knowing. I'm still not altogether sure who he is to her, but I definitely don't like the idea of him showing up in the middle of the night as a blizzard's hitting.

I enter her room and gently shake Camille awake. "Hey."

She rolls over and eyes me wearily. "Everything okay?"

"Luke is at the door." I try to keep the disdain from my tone. What the hell is he doing here?

She sits up and rubs her eyes. "Did you let him in?"

"No." I cross my arms. "I wasn't sure if you wanted him here."

"I always want him here," she replies automatically.

I have to work at not flinching.

"Okay, maybe I should go. I can call Kenny. Ask to stay with him."

She untangles herself from the sheets and sets a hand on my arm. "Stay."

At what cost? I don't want to be under the same roof as her and Luke as they hide whatever weird relationship they have from me. It seems personal, the way they keep it to themselves. But then I remember that I'm here for Camille only. I can't lose sight of that.

"Okay," I agree.

She opens the door and steps outside. I hear them through the crack.

"Wanted to make sure you're okay," he says softly, intimately.

"Dawson's here. The heater went out in the camper," she tells him. "I'm fine. Was just sleeping."

"The storm should hit fully in an hour," he grumbles gently. "Do you need anything? You can stay with me if you want."

I try not to lose it. Brave of him to ask her to leave when she's already here with me.

"I'm good, but thank you so much. Do you want to stay here?"

I'm up off the couch with that. I open the door.

"I'll go."

I head out of the house.

"We're just friends," Luke calls into the night.

I stop in my tracks.

"I know what this looks like, but trust me, you're wrong." He levels me with a withering glare.

"She offered to let you stay," he continues. "You should stay. Blizzards are a bitch. You don't want to be caught in one."

He turns to Camille, and she disappears into his hug.

"I'm heading out. Call me if there's an emergency. I'll take the snow mobile over if I have to get here."

I almost miss his next whispered words.

"Be safe."

And then he's gone, heading to his truck and backing down

the driveway.

"Dawson."

My name from her lips has me coming back to her.

"I'm not with him. Last time I'll say it. Accept it or not. Choose now."

Wind whips at me with an arctic sting.

"Accept," I decide, because something tells me that man would not have left her here with me if he did have something going on with her.

I'm wrong about them. But also, I'm right about part of it. They share a bond that creates a deep friendship, at the very least. But how is that possible if she's only been here a year?

"Let's go inside. It's freezing."

THIRTY-SEVEN

Camille

When Luke arrived, Dawson woke me from a nightmare that had my heart knocking against my sternum. The familiar panic that used to visit me at night like a lover, waking me with a cold sweat, is back again. I was never safe for long while I lived with Roberto. It's hard to forget.

But Dawson isn't Roberto. He means me no harm.

I don't mention how, when he first woke me, it took a moment to calm my erratic breaths, my eyes scanning the room, assessing the nonexistent threat. Just a phantom feeling, a memory already passed, wafting through the air like invisible smoke, nowhere to be seen.

I don't have to be afraid here. This is Darlington. Not Miami.

I hadn't expected Luke's visit, but of course he'd check on me with the storm on the way. It was kind of him to do so.

Even still, nerves wriggle behind my navel like a worm on a hook, reeling me toward the ocean, which was the one remedy that wore me out enough to lull me into sleep—a night swim, under the light of the moon. But there's no ocean here, much to my displeasure. Would anyone mind if I swam in the lake at night once the weather heats up in spring and summer? I don't know the protocol, but perhaps I should look into it. Then again, there are wild animals here. Bobcats, rattlesnakes, cottonmouths, deer, and the occasional bear. I'm not sure if I'm up for running into any of those in the dead of night.

After Luke leaves, I walk back inside with Dawson on my heels.

I used to love the sea when darkness cloaked it, thick and endless. I didn't mind the creatures of the deep, odd as that sounds. They didn't frighten me. I could never tell where the waves met the horizon, and I suppose that's what I liked most. I could dive into the depths, release everything I felt. The water was boundless and infinite, and one of the only places Roberto would not seek me. He hated the ocean and the idea of what lurked beneath.

The only thing that frightened me was him.

The ocean was my safe place.

Sometimes, I'd wait for the sun to descend just to walk into the water as far as I could go, until it dropped off into nothingness. Those were the nights Roberto wasn't home. Nights he spent at the club, staying until the early hours of morning. Probably with other women keeping him company, as I learned he was fond of doing.

Suddenly, I'm there again, the past slamming into me harder than a crashing wave.

The doorbell chimes, the ding ringing off the high ceilings, making its way into the bedroom where I'm changing into a bathing suit for a swim. I can't wait to feel the sun on my skin and salt in my hair. I pull a romper up my legs to just under my arms, where it stops like a halter top. With one hand on the banister, I take the steps down two at a time. When I come to a stop at the door, the bell rings again, accompanied by the fuzzy shape of a delivery man through the glass of the front entrance. I unlock it and swing the door open, smiling.

"Hi," I say.

I don't recognize the man. He's not the normal package guy, though he wears the same uniform.

"Delivery," he declares pleasantly, and hands me a padded envelope. My name is scrawled across the manila front in bold, cursive writing.

"Thanks. Do I need to sign?"

He's holding another package, but it must not be for me because he doesn't hand it over.

"Nope. You're all covered." He turns back to the large, brown truck and hops in, immediately driving off.

I shut the door and open the packet. It's thick in my hands, and I soon discover why. A picture falls out into my palm. Then several more. I'm too shocked to understand what I'm witnessing at first.

A man and a woman are embracing. It's dark, but their images are crisp, brought into focus though the background is blurry. The next is of the same woman, long brown hair like spilled chocolate falling down her back, matching her eyes, with a beauty mark above her left eyebrow. The details of her face are front and center, and I know I'd be able to pick her out of a crowd, though I've never seen her before the photograph landed on my doorstep.

The following photo is of the two of them again, this time kissing. My mouth hangs open, shocked by the passion captured on film. His hand is fisted in her hair, and she's pressed against him as closely as humanly possible, her little red dress flush with his black shirt. There's more. Each time, the couple is caught in some sort of embrace, aside from the single photo of only her face. They're in different clothing, too, meaning the camera obviously caught them on several different occasions. I swallow a million times, trying not to let the bile rise and find release.

I forget I'm in my home. That someone upstairs is calling my name. I can see only them—the beautiful couple.

It's the last photo that shocks me the most. It's recent, I know, because the watch the man wears—the only thing he dons—is the newest model, just released this month. It has a hefty price tag. The man and woman lie in bed, unclothed, the sheet dangerously low on their hips. She's pinned beneath him, one breast out, but its covered entirely by his hand.

I realize the delivery guy was sent here on purpose. Someone intended for me to see the photos. But who? And why? They didn't leave a note. There is no signature or return address. I double and triple check, and then I stare at the final photo until tears blur the image.

"Didn't you hear me calling you?"

The voice causes me to look up.

"What was delivered?"

His eyes land on my face, and he realizes what I'm holding. I try to speak, but I can't. Not to him, the man in front of me. The same one in the photo.

My husband.

I wasn't the type of woman to share her husband. I wouldn't stand for it. I would leave him. For good.

I shake my head to rid my mind of the memories. I need a glass of water. I fill one for Dawson, too.

We drink without comment. There's something about Dawson in the firelight that calls to me. I know if I don't return to bed now, force myself back into the sheets and into dreams, I'll likely want him closer. I wonder if that's such a bad thing.

"I better try to sleep," he says.

"Right," I agree.

He reaches for me and tugs one of my rebellious curls.

"See you in the morning."

His delicious voice wraps around me until I'm shutting the door to my room and slipping into a cold bed, wishing I had offered him a spot next to me.

I snuggle into the sheets, needing the onslaught of memories to leave me be.

I've done it. I've escaped Roberto.

A bag with just enough clothes to be easily carried rests in the passenger seat of the SUV I've stolen from Roberto. It's small enough even to be considered a carry-on. I can bring it with no effort and haul it around should I have to run. I know enough about Roberto to understand that the car I've taken is likely traceable, which is why I stop at a family-owned dealership and buy a piece of junk, with rust eating at the sides and interior. I don't bother with paperwork, except to sign a fake name to the title. An extra handful of hundred-dollar bills ensures that the salesperson asks me no questions. I am in and out in less than thirty minutes, leaving behind Roberto's vehicle, which I tell the salesperson I'll return for in the morning. I think he realizes my lie for what it is, but he doesn't rebuke it.

I can't erase the photographs from my mind, as though they're branded to the backs of my eyelids. I want them to leave me be, stop chasing me, even this far from the place I once called home.

No more.

I won't stand for another minute of him cheating. My loyalty means nothing to him. I had been looking for a way out anyhow. He's handed it to me on a golden platter.

I make it a whole hour on the road before I notice the three matching black Escalades behind me. I'm too far from the highway, which is maybe what's bought me the time I've had. Roberto would have tracked the SUV to the dealership, questioned the salesperson, and secured a description of the vehicle I bought, but I had hoped he wouldn't find me in time.

Taking back roads seemed safer. The highway is the first place Roberto would look, knowing I'd want the easiest, straightest, and quickest route away from him. The downside is that it has slowed me considerably. I have to stop at all the lights, avoid busy roads, and adhere to slower speed limits.

I take another side street, hoping I'm only being paranoid. The Escalades take the turn after me. Maybe, just this once, it isn't a bad idea to ignore the speed limits. It's the only way I'll know if they're here for me or simply a coincidence. As far-fetched as it may be, I hope for the coincidence.

I press the gas harder. The Escalades follow suit, and that's when I know.

Roberto's men have found me. Possibly Roberto, too. Maybe he's taken it upon himself to see to my capture. It wouldn't be the first time.

He must know the photos sent me running.

The streets narrow. I've made it to a back service road with hardly anyone around. One car passes, but it pays us no mind. Large warehouses stand on either side of the lane, and I wonder if anyone is inside. Maybe I can make a run for it, bang on the door, and have someone take me in, and protect me from the monsters that give chase. But even if I do find shelter, what are the chances of Roberto's men not finding a way in?

I press the pedal as hard as it will go, but Roberto's men have no trouble catching up. The first rams into me with such force the car careens off the road and into a ditch. My head slams into the steering wheel and my body explodes with pain. Hands force their way into the car, grabbing me roughly and pulling me onto the grass.

Roberto is there. His fist drives toward my temple. That is the last thing I remember before waking up in a hospital.

Light blinks like stars in the night sky, my vision swimming. A sea of nothingness promises my safekeeping. I'm about to go willingly, anything to escape the last tendrils of a memory, of what landed me in the hospital in the first place.

"They always find me," I whisper into the nothingness.

A nurse emerges from the corner of the room. An IV twists like a tie beside my head. Something cold flows into my veins. A machine beeps, attached to me. The parts of the room I can see through my blurry gaze are covered in ethereal sweeps of gray, looking like shadows on the snow after the sun has set. I'm strapped to a gurney, unable to move, not that I could, anyway, under the heaviness of the drugs.

A doctor speaks in a hushed voice just outside the door. "Dr. Martinez. Yes, I'm in charge of the patient. She's claims threatening people are looking for her."

I take a deep breath and wince at the ache in my side. Someone intentionally caused me pain.

The nurse adjusts buttons on a machine.

"...begging to leave before she's found," he continues.

I do need to leave, but how? The sheets tangle around me and I can't move enough to escape the restraints.

"...doesn't remember the accident."

Accident? That's not right. I search my mind, attempting to swat away the lingering grogginess. Exactly how long have I been out of it? How long have I been here?

"...combative."

A memory comes. Agonizing pain. Being rushed into the emergency room. Medical technicians surrounding me, cutting my clothes open to determine the extent of my injuries. They wheeled me into surgery. What happened next?

"...delusions," *the doctor suggests.*

No. They're wrong. I didn't imagine anything. I was attacked. There were men. Screams. Too much blood. I need to get out of the hospital before they find me again.

I can never...

I won't ever...

Go back there.

There's no time to form a plan. The nurse plunges a needle into the tube attached to my vein. My eyelids grow heavy, dragged down by an invisible weight. I can no longer make out the doctor's words. It feels like biting snow is falling on me. I'm cold, frigid, unable to breathe under the solidity of it.

Help, I try to say.

No words escape.

When I'd awoken in an inpatient wing, with a nurse by my side telling me I'd been in a wreck, I attempted to tell her the truth, but only got so far as a few words of denial when suddenly Roberto was there. He always seemed to get me admitted to different hospitals so the authorities wouldn't notice too many "accidents" and look closer into the situation. Maybe if I had been stronger, I wouldn't have closed my mouth. Maybe I would have spoken up more. Yelled about his abuse over and over again until someone listened. But fear had me by the tongue. Roberto made sure my story matched his. When they released me, he tried to atone for his deceitfulness with apologies, roses, and chocolates, as though such trivial gifts could erase my memories or the torture I felt every day being near him.

Fighting back didn't help. Calling the police didn't help, as I learned when I dared to defy him by using a stranger's phone on the beach to call the police and report a history of domestic violence. An officer arrived at the house to take my statement. He spoke in a placating tone, promising me he'd file a report and look into it. Nothing ever came of it. The report was deemed unfounded. I imagine my husband's deep pockets had something to do with it.

Roberto assigned guards to me—one during the day, and one at night. He began staying out at night again. It didn't matter anymore. I had become numb. My thoughts weren't dedicated to shock and hurt. They transformed into something calculating. Manipulative. Cunning. He said I couldn't leave him. He warned me it'd cost me my life.

But he didn't know about the mysterious letter sent to me at the hospital. He didn't know about Luke. As far as he was concerned, Luke had quit being his assassin, run out on him, the only one to ever escape Roberto's clutches. He didn't know I was now linked to his former employee, and that he had a plan to help me.

I healed just in time for the party Roberto threw, as though he hadn't attempted to murder me.

The cocktail event, an annual affair of Roberto's, begins without a hitch. The house, bejeweled from the many dazzling lights, twinkles like stardust. Cameras flash. Doormen wait. Guests arrive decked out in their finest attire. They filter in until the bottom floor of the house is full, and when there's not enough room, they spill out onto the deck, too.

The night air is warm, sticky to the touch. Humidity threatens to frizz the curls I've tried hard to tame. I stand against the railing, overlooking the glittering ocean. It's a view I see daily, but it's now interrupted by my husband's guests. This is my home, too. I'd rather not entertain people. But he doesn't care. His money bought the home. His friends and business associates fill it.

Tonight, I look like a queen.

A teal dress encases my curves, flaring at the ankles like a mermaid's tail. It sparkles with crushed diamonds. Maybe I could dive into the water with it on. I accept a glass of champagne as a server makes his rounds, swallowing the laugh that threatens to burst free from my lips. I imagine it, me diving into the water like a fish, disappearing beneath the depths. I wish I could live there instead of here.

I'm feeling reckless. Full of brazen strength. Soon, I'll be free of this place.

One of Roberto's guests approaches me. He looks young. Late twenties, perhaps. His hair is the perfect shade of brown and just a little on the messy side. His tie is loose, and the sleeves of his button-down shirt are rolled up to the elbow. It's a good look for him.

"Hi," he greets.

I haven't seen him around before.

"Hello," I reply.

My eyes immediately scan the crowd for Roberto, wondering what he thinks of another man talking to me. These parties are the only instance in which I've witnessed his restraint.

I feel him before I see him.

"Ah," he says. "I see you've met my wife."

The man's eyes widen just a fraction before his face falls back into a bemused expression. He didn't realize I'm married to Roberto.

"Not officially," he replies. "I was just about to introduce myself."

"Don't bother," Roberto warns, pulling me in the opposite direction.

I go without argument.

"Do not embarrass me tonight," he warns.

"I won't," I agree.

I will be a good puppet until the time comes. Until Luke arrives for me. A thief in the night.

And then I'll be gone.

My mind never drifted from my plan. I was going to leave Roberto. In my secret thoughts, I dreamed of a small town tucked away in the mountains to disappear to.

He said I couldn't find any place that would hide me from him.

But clearly, I did.

THIRTY-EIGHT

Dawson

The next day, the blizzard rages, sending fat flakes down in parachuting patterns. Trees shudder under the weight of the powder that accumulates on their branches. There is not a creature in sight, aside from Wizard curled by the fire.

I finally get my answer as to what people do when snowed in during the coldest season in Darlington. So far, Camille and I have drunk too much coffee, read, played cards, eaten food, and restocked the fire.

It isn't until darkness falls again, the second night of the blizzard, that my restraint wears thin, a bow drawn too tightly, ready to snap. I've been careful not to let this thing between us go too far. She doesn't make it easy on me, though. Not when she keeps glancing my way, her eyes passing over my body. A radio on the table softly broadcasts weather in the background. If it's correct, the storm will end by morning, and I'll be back to the camper tomorrow.

A timer goes off and Camille pulls a tray of cinnamon rolls out of the oven. The dough sizzles with sticky sweetness. She sets them on the stovetop and expertly spreads icing, which promptly drips down the sides of the rolls. A half hour ago, I didn't understand why she insisted on making so many, ten to be exact, but now I'm grateful. From the smell alone, I know I won't be able to stop myself at just one.

"They're better when they're hot," she says, turning to me.

I join her in the cramped kitchen, reaching for the closest roll.

"If you say so," I reply.

I wouldn't know. My life didn't provide many chances for me to have homemade desserts. My mother wasn't much of a cook. She mostly bought takeout, or frozen meals she could easily pop in the microwave, but I never minded.

Camille likes to grow and make food herself. I saw it when I first arrived and found her grilling outside, even in freezing temperatures. And I've witnessed it many times since. I don't know the first thing about homemade, homegrown meals.

"Have as many as you want," she offers.

Her hair is extra crazy today, and I find that I like it best this way. She hasn't bothered with makeup, leaving her freckles on full display. The sexy dimples I've seen drop into her cheeks nearly every day since moving here make an appearance again. I wonder if they'll ever lose power over me.

"I can make more if we need," she continues.

The first bite burns my tongue. I watch Camille lick white icing off of the side of her cinnamon roll before it drips on the floor. Even though I don't usually like sweets, I scarf down the rest of mine and grab another.

"So good," she murmurs.

I'm not sure if Camille is aware of how sexy she looks, licking and biting and moaning the way she is. I'd give just about anything to be the source of her pleasure.

"What do you think of the rolls?" she asks, meeting my stare.

Whatever she finds there makes her eyes heat. Does she know what she's doing to me? I watch her tongue dart out again.

"I think they're delicious," I compliment, finishing my second one.

Sugar coats my mouth, and icing sticks to my fingers. I want to grab Camille, tug her to me, and see if she tastes just as sweet.

Her cheeks are rosy with a blush as she reaches for another roll. I blatantly stare, wondering how her mouth would work over other things, namely my skin.

"Do you want more?" she inquires, her tone becoming softer.

Does she mean of the cinnamon rolls, or her? I step closer.

I either need to get the hell out of this house right now, or I need to sink into her. I don't think there's a middle ground anymore. Where did the space I normally keep go? My focus has homed in on her. Camille is so beautiful in the light of the fire, with flames brightening her hair and exposed skin. She wears a tank top, sweatpants, fuzzy socks, and nothing else. I grab another roll. She watches me finish it in three bites.

Camille reaches up and drags her finger across my lower lip. It comes away with a drop of icing. The second she pops that finger into her own mouth, heat floods my veins. Dark night presses against the glass windowpanes. The world is quiet. There is only snow outside of the walls around us, trapping Camille and me together.

"Camille," I growl. "How am I supposed to resist you when you touch me like that?"

"Maybe I don't want you to resist," she whispers.

Her mouth tilts toward mine, and the last thread of my restraint snaps.

"Don't say I didn't warn you."

My lips crash into hers hungrily.

Fireworks explode under my skin. I'm not gentle, nor slow. There's desperation in my movements. I can't get the intoxicating scent of her out of my mind—a field of never-ending wildflowers. Her head tilts to the side, giving me access to her neck, where her pulse shudders.

"Camille," I groan, nipping the spot above her collarbone.

This is it, what everything has built up to—months of wanting her but holding back. Maybe that's why I have lost total control. Perhaps that's why I feel as though I might burst if I don't take every inch of her right now.

She fans her fingers through my hair, forcing my mouth back to hers. My hands travel to her sides, gripping them tightly as I press as closely as I can. For a beat, Camille pulls back and searches my gaze. I hope she finds whatever she's looking for, because words elude me as I bite the skin just under her jaw, and then the shell of her ear.

It's not enough. I'm not nearly close enough.

"More," she demands.

Her lips sear mine. An arrow of sensation lances my insides when she traces a thumb down the column of my throat. She offers me a hand that feels smooth against my calloused one, before tugging me toward her bedroom. She's a vision, eyes hooded with lust. I must look rough next to her with two days' worth of stubble covering my jaw and hunger in my stare. When we stop next to her bed, Camille arches, her soft curves pressing into me. She tugs at my hair, her hand rasping against my cheek.

"Dawson," she pants.

Her curls bunch up around her face and dive down her back. I want to know what they look like against her bare, creamy skin.

I lift her into my arms, her legs wrapping around my waist, and reposition her on the ivory comforter. Camille pulls at my shirt, wishing it gone. The heat from the thick fire reaches fingers into the room, warming us both. Something pulls low in my gut, a desperate need.

My shirt makes its way to the corner of the bed, and then Camille pauses to take in my features. My chest rises and falls rapidly. Her touch heats my skin, scorching like a shot of whiskey as she trails a finger down my stomach where she sucks in a breath, and then finally to the tie on my sweatpants where I strain to be set free.

Her fingers fumble. I reach for the hem of her shirt, ripping it over her head. I nearly lose all resolve at the sight of her. She's not wearing a bra.

"So fucking beautiful," I whisper, lowering my head to her chest.

Her nipples harden. I take one into my mouth, and then the other, before nipping the underside of her breasts, eliciting a plea.

"Please, Dawson," she implores, tugging at my sweatpants.

They slide down with my boxers close behind. I hiss at the feel of Camille's hand wrapped around me.

Eagerly, I peel off the rest of her clothes, and then look at her bared for me. I kiss her hips, down her thighs, and up the softer, delicate inside of her legs until I'm at her center.

"Yes," she pleads.

I want to devour her.

Camille's fists close on the comforter, bunching it in her grip. I lower my head and follow the commands of her body, licking straight up her center. She nearly flies off the bed with that. I press a palm to her stomach and hold her down as I lick again and find the sensitive bundle of nerves that coaxes several moans from her lips. My tongue discovers the rhythm Camille likes, slow at first, and then faster. I repeat it over and over again. She runs a hand through my hair and whispers my name while I get lost in the feel of her.

"More," Camille begs.

I slip two fingers into her. She gasps.

"You taste fucking incredible." I work my fingers, watching the way her legs open even wider for me.

I could stay like this forever, tasting Camille.

She arches, her body on full display, a hand flying to her mouth to quiet her moans as I increase the pace.

"Don't," I say. "I want to hear you."

She lets her hand fall back to the bed. I smile against her warmth and give her what she wants until Camille is moaning and moving against me, too. As soon as my fingers curl inside her, hitting that special spot, I feel her begin to tremble and clench.

With a need so strong I can barely stand it, I watch her orgasm hit, feeling what I've done to her, how wet she is for me.

"God, Dawson!" She shakes and whimpers, and it isn't until she pushes at my head, saying, "too sensitive" that I finally stop.

When I wring out every bit of her pleasure, she collapses deep into the sheets. I rise above her, licking the remains of her from my lips.

"Jesus, Camille," I groan.

She is every fantasy come to life. She's a dream made real, beckoning me closer. I marvel at the way the pulse in her throat spikes as I lay a kiss on it, as though it's about to burst free from her skin. My gaze crawls over her. All of her. From her puckered breasts down to the legs she's not shy about letting me fit between. I bury my hands in her wild curls while my mouth moves over her soft skin.

"I knew it'd be like this between us," I admit. "Fucking explosive."

I don't stop anywhere, laying kisses like a trail to follow later. I want to memorize Camille, but I can't stand the strain of needing her so badly.

"You're perfect," she murmurs. Then, as though just remembering something, her eyes go big. "I don't have protection."

Her confession makes me grin. She wasn't expecting to hook up with men in Darlington.

"My wallet," I tell her a moment before removing myself from the bed. I return seconds later, and tear open the foil, rolling the condom on.

Camille watches with rapt attention, her mouth slightly parted. The mattress dips as I place myself above her again, the entirety of my body covering hers. Then finally, I do what I've been dying to for far too long.

I sink deeply into Camille.

The sensation makes curses fly from my mouth as she releases a low, guttural moan. Camille softly begs things of me in a throaty tone. My need builds, sending us into an immediate deep, hungry pace.

"You feel amazing," I say on a raspy breath, repositioning to lift her hips and gain deeper leverage. I glance down to where we're connected and feel my whole body react to the sight. "Look at you."

It's been a while for me. Maybe that's why Camille feels so

damn good. Or maybe it's because I've wanted her for a long time. I can see just enough creamy skin in the dim firelight that bounces off the hall walls to tell me she's more beautiful now than ever, lost in passion. There's a scar that spans her side. I don't know what hurt her, but I'll do all I can to bring her only pleasure.

I let my defenses down so she can witness everything in my eyes. How she drives me absolutely wild. The fathomless longing I feel. The way I wish for nothing else but to be here, in this moment.

I can hear the slippery noises we make as I slide in and out of her. She's utterly drenched. I move my thumb over her mouth, tracing her lips, tugging on the bottom one until it pops free.

She is almost there. I sense it in her trembling body and quickened breaths. I promise her release with my hands, my mouth, my movements. She moans, and then a violent orgasm hits.

"Dawson!" My name flies from her lips.

I bite out a curse, grab her hips, and slam into her with everything I have. I had a feeling this would happen eventually, didn't I? It was inevitable, her and I, even though it goes against every rule and restraint I've erected.

Camille was going to end up in my bed. Or me in hers.

It was only a matter of time.

I want to take all the time in the world—minutes and hours—in her, tasting her, pleasing her. I want days and nights with Camille. But right now, I don't think I could slow down even if my life depended on it. I can't help our hungry pace. This is what being inside of Camille does to me.

I sink impossibly deeper, ravaging her, knowing my own orgasm is close. Camille has only just stopped trembling, but I feel her tighten around me again.

Yes.

I can't control a single, coherent thought anymore. She is my undoing. Warmth coils inside me, drawing me up tight until I'm there, too, lost in the bliss of both of our releases.

THIRTY-NINE

Camille

I wake the next morning—still riding the rush of knowing I brought Dawson fierce pleasure—to find I'm in his arms after spending the night together for the first time. Also, for the first time, I'm late to work.

"Shit!" I exclaim, clumsily getting out of bed.

It's not the most graceful exit. Dawson smiles in my direction.

"Mmm," he mumbles. "Morning."

His thick, sleepy voice is the sexiest thing I've ever heard. Flashbacks of us together last night come to mind and my cheeks heat. Well, maybe *second* sexiest thing.

"Where're you going?"

"Work," I reply, running to the bathroom.

Mr. Hill messaged last night asking if I could come in since the blizzard passed.

There's only enough time to brush my teeth and splash water on my makeup free face. One glance out of the window confirms that the blizzard has moved on and the world beyond is as pale as ivory. I return to the room.

"Don't go," he mutters into the pillow.

His eyes open and his breath catches. I look down at myself, bathed in the morning light that filters through the blinds. I haven't dressed.

In one quick movement, he pulls me back into bed and kisses me so thoroughly that I wonder why anyone invented work in the first place and how hard it would be on Mr. Hill if I called out. But then reality reminds me that Mr. Hill has done so much for me, and it would be terrible to leave him without an employee the day after a blizzard. Everyone will be out and about, shoveling the roads and trying to escape their houses. I saw it last winter—not with a blizzard, but with a storm that downed several trees on either side of NC 9 forcing everyone to stay indoors for days while they cleared debris. The people of Darlington love getting out and about after being cooped up. Today will likely be no different. I can't bail on him.

When Dawson's hands move to my hips, I very nearly lose all train of thought. The scruff on his face rubs against my neck, making me shiver.

"I have to help at work," I insist. "At least for a few hours. Will you be here when I get back?"

I know from the schedule that he's off today.

"Possibly."

He nips my ear. My neck. My shoulder. I moan.

"God, Camille," he murmurs against my lips. "If you don't leave now, I'm going to keep you here."

I grin and kiss him once more. "See you in a bit."

I quickly dress. Dawson watches me with hunger in his eyes. My truck is parked close to the road, providing easier access to snow plowed, travelable streets, unlike my driveway. As soon as I get to the store, there's an excuse forming on my lips, but Mr. Hill holds up a hand.

"It's no big deal," he assures me. "I'm not worried about the half hour you missed, just happy to see you're well. I'm sure the blizzard kept you. Is your place okay?"

I sigh with relief. "Yes. No issues."

I get to work brewing coffee, savoring the smell.

"How about your place?" I ask.

Mr. Hill places a bagel in the oven.

"No problems." He retrieves two Styrofoam cups for us, the logo of the general store front and center, and places sugar and cream on the side.

As I wait for our coffee, my mind wanders to Dawson. Last night, what I imagined would be a quick burst of passion, turned into an all-night exploration.

I expected something light and fun, but this, I accept, is deeper. I can only hope I'm not making another horrific decision like I did with Roberto—that Dawson isn't a liar like Roberto was.

I remember the exact moment I realized my marriage was a sham—when the photos of Roberto's infidelity arrived. Likewise, I recall the juncture when I truly understood Roberto was never truthful with me. When I learned what he *really* does for a living.

The club is hot and stuffy from the many bodies roaming the close quarters. Even though the lavish interior of the Lux Lounge— the club owned by my husband—is spacious and inviting, it also gives me a sense of claustrophobia from the many, many people who enter. Over time, I've learned that some patrons are here for business, and some are here for fun. People, men and women alike, understand this place drips money. They'd appreciate nothing more than to stand under the expanse of wealth and meet some of Miami's finest bachelors and bachelorettes. Some aren't even opposed to the ones who are married.

The Lux Lounge is the last place I want to be, but Roberto insists I show up from time to time. It looks good for him that he has a wife at home. A steady household that he maintains just as well as he does his club. It speaks of his ability to run all aspects of his life smoothly. Looks better to potential investors.

He mostly wants me at the club on the nights he meets with future business clientele. Roberto hasn't gotten where he is on his own dime. He has people who back him, making their own profit in the process. Roberto is a fan of never spending his own money if he doesn't have to. That way his assets are protected, and his bank account stays plump.

A waitress arrives with our drinks. A martini for me, even though I hardly ever finish a drink, garnished with three green olives and a twisted lemon rind. My lips pucker at the first taste. Roberto drinks his usual. Two men sit across from us. One with dark skin and eyes that easily drift to my plunging neckline. The other, a man with meaty hands and a mustache, gives me the creeps. Both are in their fifties, by my guess. Neither can stop assessing me for long. I suppose that's Roberto's plan. After all, he suggested I wear the red number that dips nearly to my navel and stops above my knees. The nude stilettos, and simple four-carat diamond wedding ring finish off the ensemble. My curls are swept to the side, pinned there, the clip digging into my scalp.

While the men talk, I catch bits of conversation, but mostly I think of what it would be like not to be in the club. The ocean calls to me. It's not that far from where we are on the strip. I imagine letting my hair down, the saltwater washing away the product that holds my controlled curls in place. My tight dress nowhere to be seen.

One of the men laughs, bringing me back to the conversation.

"And when would the shipment take place?" he asks, his Spanish accent leaking through.

I frown. What shipment?

Roberto cuts a look my way. I see the indecision in his gaze. This wasn't part of the plan. Normally, he meets with potential investors here in the lounge, introducing me and having a few drinks together, then he invites them back to his personal quarters upstairs to discuss more serious business, leaving me in the club where I usually slip out and take the family car home to promptly change and jump into the ocean.

This is different.

The man wants to discuss business here, something Roberto clearly isn't thrilled about. But I see the moment he changes his mind. He decides to let me in on whatever it is they'd planned to discuss.

I take a sip of my martini, my ears perking. Roberto sits next to me, leaning a tad closer to the men whose names I've already forgotten.

"The shipment leaves in a week," Roberto informs them. "A cargo boat full. Everything has been arranged."

I don't know why Roberto would be shipping materials when all of his product is here and is delivered to him. The club doesn't require much, just alcohol and ritzy food, mostly in the form of overpriced appetizers.

"And the buyers?" the man presses.

He seems to be doing all the talking, while the other gentleman sits mutely.

"They've paid half already. The other half is expected to be delivered to an offshore account upon arrival of the goods," Roberto explains.

I still don't understand. I know Roberto has accounts, but I don't remember hearing about ones offshore. The hairs rise on the back of my neck.

"And the weapons?"

I bite back a gasp. What weapons?

Roberto cuts another look my way. It's severe enough to warn me that not a single word should be spoken. He must know I have questions.

"Everything is being tracked by me and my guys. There's nothing to worry about." Roberto offers them a reassuring smile. One I know well. It used to fool me, too.

"The government?"

"There's no need to concern yourself with them. My product is never discovered by U.S. authorities. I have people on the inside in my pocket. I hear of everything before they can ever get to me. They are not aware of my illegal standings. At least, not on paper anyway. Anything they hear by ear gets swept away. I pay them enough for it to never be pursued. The weapons will ship, arrive, and be paid for as planned. You have my word. Your money is greatly appreciated. It will be worth it for you."

The men grin in unison. Roberto has convinced them of all they needed to know.

As they shake hands, blood rushes through my veins.

"Nice doing business," Roberto says, relaxing next to me.

How he could relax, I'll never know. I'm strung too tightly. Everything makes sense now. The secret meetings he takes at the club. Hushed phone calls. Roberto has been holding onto a lie. The club is his production, sure. But it's only a cover.

I'm married to an illegal arms dealer.

I take a sip of scalding coffee swimming with cream and sweetness, standing in the general store, while I try, hard as I might, to wash away all remnants of the life I thankfully, mercifully, left behind.

FORTY

Dawson

I don't wake again until a few hours later. With only several minutes until noon, I can't remember the last time I slept so soundly, or so late. A smile pulls at my lips, thanks to a long night spent with Camille. But then I remember that we're not supposed to be spending long nights together. The smile drops away.

Damn, what have I done?

I've fallen for her.

Somewhere along the way, my defenses crumbled. Days turned into weeks spent near her, with her, and I can no longer see the line drawn in the sand. At some point, it blurred, and then disappeared from sight completely. Maybe it was the trip to the parts store, or Asheville, or working together. Maybe it was her smile, her laugh, her kindness, or living so close by. This place has slowed me down, pressed pause on a hectic life. Maybe it's the combination of everything here with her.

Camille has broken through all the barriers I've erected.

I had a six-week deadline, and that was after I'd already been in Darlington for a while. I've run out of time. I scrub a hand down my face. My clothes are somewhere on the floor. Camille's pajamas are there, too.

I wish she was still here.

I assume she's busy at the store. She mentioned the old man needing her help. I wonder if I can forget about my timeline and fall back asleep, twist up in the sheets that smell of her while I wait for her return.

I don't regret a thing about my time with Camille, but part of me feels guilty for deceiving her. And I know for a fact she's deceiving me. Last night, while she slept, she had a nightmare. Uttered another man's name. Begged him to please stop. "No more," she said. She has nightmares about a man she knows. I reach over the side of the bed to retrieve my clothes. I find my shirt, but have to feel around for my pants. I bend slightly and reach farther.

My sweatpants are mere inches away. I throw them on and head back to the camper, determination pounding through every step I make across the thick snow. As I reach into the depths of the closet behind my clothes, my fingertips close over the envelope I brought. I yank it out and immediately go back to Camille's room.

I can't keep deceiving her. Not after all of the days and weeks here at the camper. Especially not after last night and the time we spent together. I have to come clean.

There, on the floor, I pull a folder out of the envelope and lay everything out. I pause, taking in the details, each and every paper. I grab them and read over the aged letters. They're regarding her birth parents and their choice to give up their rights.

Camille was a foster kid.

The names are blacked out, and the papers mark her case as closed. Her biological parents never wanted any ties. There's nothing certain except that they chose, for whatever reason, to give Camille away, their identities eradicated.

I pick up the printout of her ID next to the papers. The names match, but it's not the one she gave me. Her real name— the name she was given at birth—stares back at me.

Angela Craft.

I cannot see her as an Angela. I can't really see her as anyone but Camille.

But even that's wrong.

I dig out a recent driver's license copy under the papers. It tells a different story. It shows a Miami address. The name is still Angela, but the last name isn't Craft.

Angela *Cruz.*

Just beneath the license is a marriage certificate.

Camille is married.

I check the man's signature. *Roberto Cruz.* Roberto and Angela Cruz. Husband and wife. I drop the contents back into the folder like they've burned me.

Her past is entangled in mysteries and deceit. Camille has never been whom she claimed.

But, of course, I already knew that.

Beneath the papers are all of the photos snapped of Camille in Miami, back when she went by Angela. There's one of her at a club, sitting alone on a barstool. In her hand, she holds a martini with three olives and a curled lemon rind, but she's barely drinking any. Looking for everything in the world as though she'd like to be anywhere else.

There's another of her on a large deck, enjoying a lavish party at a mansion on the beach. A teal dress hugs her perfect body while a single pearl pendant dangles from her neck. In the background, a crowd of people mill about. Most of them are laughing, having the time of their lives. Her eyes, however, stay on the water.

In the next photo, she's there—in the ocean. This is the only one where she wears a real smile. Fresh faced, her freckles on display. Water droplets cling to her skin. Her hair is drenched, making her curls look like tightly wound ribbons.

I flip through more. Camille at the grocery store, the bank, the gas station. Camille reading on the sandy shore, swimming, and retrieving a ball that took off with the waves. She hands it back to a little boy who smiles at her like she saved his world.

Camille dressed up and dressed down. Eating fancy diners. Buying makeup. Having her clothes dry cleaned. Wealth at her fingertips and no reason to want for anything. Living an existence so completely, unequivocally different than the life she has in Darlington.

I flip back through each photograph. Over and over. Camille has been lying every day since the moment I met her.

But, so have I.

FORTY-ONE

Camille

Bonnie sets a container of to go food on the counter, a warm smile on her face.

"For you," she says.

The store has been open for hours, but I haven't had a second to myself until now. I was right in thinking everyone would be out today. Filling the aisles with stories of downed trees, power outages, and farm animals refusing to come out of their stalls this morning. The ground is still thick with layers of snow, nearly every inch covered in winter's touch. But not the roads. Those are plowed.

"Bonnie," I groan happily, "you're a lifesaver."

The buttery scent hits my nose, and my mouth begins to water. I open the lid to find brisket and gravy with a side of creamy mashed potatoes and collard greens. She hands me a disposable fork.

"What do I owe you?" I ask around a mouthful.

Might as well eat while I have the chance. I don't bother to take a seat. I stand right at the register while I enjoy the meal. The momentary lull in customers isn't likely to last.

"Nothin'," she replies. "Rose said no charge. I'll be back with a large sweet tea, too. You need something to wash that down with."

I won't turn away a tea.

"How about you tell Rose that I'll bring her the last of my jalapeño peppers," I offer as I scarf down the food. Every bite is heaven. I still don't understand how Rose makes the plainest foods taste richly good. "It's not much, but I'd love to give her the final harvest."

If anyone can make a meal out of the peppers, it's Rose.

She smiles. "I doubt she'd turn it down."

I make a mental note to pick the rest and bring them to work tomorrow. There should be enough to fill a large bowl.

"You get through the storm okay?" Bonnie inquires.

Funny thing about this small town—everyone cares what happens to each other's properties. Back in Miami, storms blew through often. Hurricanes were the worst, and many people were affected, but most didn't stop to ask how your property faired or how they could help.

"I did. You?"

She nods. "Power only went out once for a few minutes. Came back on soon enough."

Her gaze pours over me. I wonder if she's noticing how I didn't have time before leaving the house to put on my normal makeup and jewelry. I threw on jeans, a shirt, and a jacket without even looking at what I'd picked.

"I didn't realize you had so many freckles," she remarks.

That would be because she hardly gets to see them thanks to the foundation I usually apply. The speckles are earned by growing up underneath the Florida sunshine, my days spent surrounded by UV rays and salty sea.

I shrug off her observation. It's not like I can tell her about Miami.

"Give me a sec," she says. "I'll be right back with your tea."

But her words are muted by the memories of beach days. They were the only things that balanced out the other times I spent unbearably unhappy.

His hand crashes down with a resounding slap, reminding me of the sound a body makes when belly flopping into the water. My cheek stings worse than a sunburn.

"You will never, ever leave me," Roberto hisses. "Not with all that I've given you. This life. Your clothes and jewels. A home on the beach. A constantly stocked fridge. Cars. Toys. Manicures. Anything—everything—you could ever dream of. The world at your fingertips. You have it."

His face is only inches from my own. Beautifully warm skin I used to caress. Lips I once kissed with passion. A person I thought I knew. But that was before.

I told Roberto I want a divorce, and he's handled it about as well as I imagined he would. Which is to say not well at all.

He's right, though. I cannot depart with everything he's given me. That's why I plan to leave it all behind.

"You are mine."

His words roll off me like the underside of a wave. There are days that I dive deep beneath the ocean's surface and watch the swells spool overhead. It's like that now. His words wash over me. He can't hurt me any more than he already has. Unless he kills me. Which he will have to do in order to stop me from leaving. Nothing short of that will prohibit me this time.

It's sad that the thought of him going too far has crossed my mind. But that's what living with an abuser for the last four years has done to me. The next day isn't guaranteed. It's hell. He is power hungry. He lives for control.

I need out of here.

I've already planned my escape. Luke is waiting. All I have to do is dial the number. The rest has been arranged. Luke and I are the only ones who know the full extent of my agenda, that way no one can sell me out to my poor excuse for a husband. He may not agree to divorce me, but in my heart, I've already left him.

I wait for Roberto to finish threatening me. I haven't been listening to most of his words, but I catch the tail end of a sentence.

"...and then you can clean up."

Maybe he means my lip. I taste blood. It's likely split again. I run my tongue over the achy spot. There's a small cut. Nothing too bad. I've had worse.

"I need to make an appearance at the club. I'll be back late tonight, and I expect you to be in a better mood," he growls, as though all of this is somehow my fault.

I never asked him to lay a hand on me. I never wanted to be called the degrading names that fall from his lips. His face used to be so beautiful. His words, too.

"Our marriage is fine," he states. "You just need to learn how to listen."

I nearly laugh. He thinks our marriage is "fine."

It is a disaster.

"I still love you, Princess." His lips close over mine.

He kisses me like he can't get enough. I nearly vomit right there. If he only knew how disgusting I think he is.

He breaks away. "Wait up for me tonight," he whispers.

"Okay," I agree.

I've become an expert liar.

I will not wait up.

I will not be here.

Roberto says something in Spanish to the guard he has assigned to me. The guard nods, always following orders. Meanwhile, Roberto turns and leaves. I wait. The sound of his car fades into the distance and the clock ticks by. I pretend to read. My mind is elsewhere. After an hour, when I'm sure Roberto has made it to the club and isn't coming back anytime soon, I leave the house in a swimsuit. It's one of the few activities Roberto has approved. To the guard, it looks as though I'm enjoying an extra long dip in the ocean as the sun sets. He watches from his spot in a lounge chair on the back deck. Past the sand, where the buoys mark more dangerous currents, I tread water. It forms droplets on my skin. The guard can't possibly distinguish between them and my tears.

I'm saying goodbye to the ocean.

It's harder than I thought it would be.

I am leaving for good. The beach is just another thing Roberto has taken from me, right along with the last few years of my life, my freedom, my trust. But he hasn't taken the fight out of me.

He can never have that.

I don't plan to return from my swim. I spin in a slow circle, committing the beach I love to memory, and then I take the deepest breath I can and hold it, diving down beneath the waves. Roberto's guard is still waiting, looking down at his phone, expecting me back inside in an hour. I won't be there. Not ever again.

With my head beneath the sea, I swim.

I swim like I've never swam before, and yet exactly as I've swam before. This is what I've prepared for. Spending every single day in these currents has taught me how to handle the ocean. Only this time, I push harder than I do during my training. This time, I am swimming for my life.

I've been under for over a minute. Close to two. I need a breath. I break the surface with only my chin, just enough to pull air into my aching lungs, and then I disappear beneath the depths again. Four more times of this and I'm so far out I hardly see the shore. Here, bigger creatures lurk. I can only hope nothing sees me as food. I swim longer, miles out. The farther I get from the beach, with many bodies in the water, any one of which the guard could mistake for me, the better chance I have.

I've tried driving away.

I've run on foot.

I've booked flights.

Roberto always finds me.

This time, I leave by ocean.

In an account, money waits for me. It is minor, insignificant, yet it's everything. It's the pay I've saved from training others to compete in triathlons. I'll be able to settle down somewhere small and unassuming. Maybe even purchase a tiny home. Nothing like what I'm used to, but if it has four walls and a roof, and doesn't have Roberto, then I'll be happy.

I left my wedding bands, jewelry, and everything Roberto gave me behind—he can keep it, I don't want it—except the tiny six by eight inch fireproof box that contains my birthparents' case info and the one thing my real mother left me—a family ring. I wear the ring daily, except when I'm in the ocean. I've already mailed the container to a P.O. box Luke gave me. He'll have it.

I've made it three miles out to sea. Finally, I spot what I'm looking for.

A boat.

Luke is aboard, smiling at me.

"Camille."

At the sound of my name, I blink.

"I brought your tea," Bonnie tells me with an odd look. "Are you okay?"

I stare at the lemon wedge underneath the translucent lid.

"Are you okay?"

For the first time in a long while, I can answer the question honestly. My smile comes naturally.

"Yes," I reply.

I am, finally, after all these years, okay.

FORTY-TWO

Dawson

I'm missing something. I reevaluate the photos. Every bit of information I've gathered on Camille is laid bare before me. I always knew she was hiding. She's lied to me about *everything*.

She's from Miami. Not upstate New York. Not Darlington either. Camille isn't even her real name. She's married. I flinch at that. She's built such a nice life with her web of lies.

Everything I've built here will mean nothing soon. Becoming friends with Kenny. Working for the old man. Enjoying Rose's cuisine. Living simply.

It will disappear the moment I leave Darlington.

Camille sure knows how to vanish. One day, she lived in a giant beachside mansion. The next day, gone. And now I'm left staring at photographs, wondering what I'm missing here.

I assess the small details in the backgrounds, but all of them vary. Then I do the same with the tiny facts about her. Diverse clothes. Dissimilar shoes. Changed purses. Varying swimsuits. The same ring.

Wait.

The same ring.

She's not wearing it in any of the beach photos, which is maybe how it became an oversight on my part.

In every single picture besides those taken at the beach, she has on the same ring. Not her wedding band, which she doesn't always wear, but a silver ring with a twirling pattern that encloses a dark jewel. Onyx, maybe.

Maybe that's it.

The clue.

I drop the photos and scan her room. I need to find that ring. Haven't I seen it before? The day she left her purse behind, I think. Does she normally keep it in there? Her purse isn't here, though. It's with her at the general store.

In the time I've rented here, I've combed the entirety of her property, hoping to locate the one thing I need to go back home, I just never realized it might be the ring. I've looked inside her home, as well, when I've had stolen moments. I've found nothing. This time, I go through her place quickly, searching for the stone, and finally spot it next to the kitchen sink. I sigh with relief. I don't know what this ring means to her, but it might mean everything to me. I race to the toolbox outside, retrieving a flathead screwdriver and a pair of pliers.

I work away at the onyx, which seems to be set solidly. That gives me more hope. Sweat beads on my brow. I consider throwing the ring against the ground and shattering it, but if my hunch is right, it holds significance to Camille. So, I continue laboring over the thing, hoping to remove the jewel without damage.

Finally, there's a pop, and the stone releases. Beneath it, resting on the flat, rounded metal of the ring where the back meets the jewel, sits a tiny opening. The dark stone has concealed it all along.

But it's empty.

Yet, there are scratches on the inside.

I am almost certain she stored something there.

Where is it now?

I grab my burner phone to make another call. This time, I don't have the luxury of driving a long way away or of getting another burner phone to replace this one just in case. They are supposed to be unplottable, but I don't like to take chances. Only now, I think I'll have to.

"Hello." The voice on the other end answers the same as always with a slight Spanish accent.

"Hey, boss," I say. "I need a few more days. I've almost found it. Fucking finally."

The missing piece.

"Where are you?" he asks.

"You know I can't tell you. Someone has compromised us before. Can't let it happen again."

The line goes silent, and then, "Fine. But listen, come straight to me when you locate it. Go nowhere else. I have a feeling people are coming for you. A member of our crew—Broderick—has disappeared."

Broderick was supposed to handle a big shipment, last I'd heard.

"There's a traitor on our team, as we've long suspected. They have eyes on us. Be careful."

"I'll find a way to get it to you once I have it," I reply. "I don't trust that your lines aren't tapped."

"Good idea," he agrees. "One more thing before you go. Her location has been compromised."

I nearly drop the phone.

No.

"They don't know precisely which town, but in time, they'll find her. They're close, Dawson. If you're near her in North Carolina like I suspect you are, get what we need and get the hell out. They're gaining. You hear me? You have a day or two at most."

"I will," I agree.

The call disconnects. There's no time left to spare. I gather the folder and photographs. It's time Camille and I had a talk.

FORTY-THREE

Camille

I've never seen Dawson look so unhinged as I do the moment he bursts into the general store. Eyes determined. Jaw set. Movements hurried.

Mr. Hill stands beside the counter, looking at him like he's wondering the same thing I am.

What happened?

"Camille." He says my name with authority. A surge of power with both syllables. "You need to come with me."

He offers no other information.

"Are you okay?" I walk out from behind the register to meet

him at the door.

The store isn't empty, but the two customers who browse the aisles don't seem like they're in a hurry to decide on anything just yet. Dawson takes stock of the scene, his eyes quickly scanning.

"I'm fine." His tone is clipped, suggesting he is anything but "fine."

"What's goin' on?" Mr. Hill asks.

Dawson eyes him. "Remember our talk and my intentions toward Camille?"

I don't recall Dawson and Mr. Hill speaking about me, which means it took place when I wasn't around. Nice of them to let me know.

Mr. Hill doesn't even appear embarrassed when I shoot him a questioning look.

"'Course I remember," he replies.

"Well, this is me looking out for her." His voice sounds how I imagine shattered glass would when being trampled on—hard and grating. "You need to find someone to cover for her immediately."

My boss seems to think whatever Dawson says holds merit, because his next words aren't ones I've ever heard him say.

"Camille, you're no longer workin' this shift. Take the day off."

I've never missed work or been sent home early. I open my mouth to protest, but Dawson grabs my arm, diverting my attention.

"Please, Camille."

The desperation in his voice dispels all of my resolve. I

lean across the counter to grab my purse, fishing my keys out. Dawson promptly takes them from me.

"Hey!" I exclaim. "What do you think you're—"

He cuts me off with a kiss, and I get lost in his lips.

"Just trust me right now." His words are spoken softly against my mouth. "I'll drive."

He has to know I'd follow him anywhere when he kisses me like that. There's only a moment to say goodbye to Mr. Hill before the door closes.

"I'll see you tomorrow!" Mr. Hill waves me on.

"What the hell is this about?" I hop in my truck and turn to Dawson. "If it's because of last night—" I begin, but then stop when I see the passion that flares in Dawson's eyes.

"It's not about last night." His voice softens. "Even though it was the best evening of my life and I want to repeat it a thousand times."

My cheeks burn as bright as the sun with his compliment.

"I have something to tell you," he states.

Nerves wriggle like live worms in my belly.

"And something to ask you."

The worms grow into snakes. I make an effort to swallow down the bile that wants to rise. Something's not right.

"You're acting strange. Please tell me what's going on."

We haven't left the lot behind the store where I've parked. Dawson clicks the locks on the truck, and I think of last night. He deserves to know about me. *All* of me. But how do you tell someone you're falling for that you have a wretched, dangerous past?

Does he know something already? The way he looks at me sparks a warning.

He sighs, waits, then seems to give into an internal battle.

"When I tell you this," he starts, "I need you to remain calm."

I'm even more unnerved.

"Roberto has found you."

Each word drops like a bomb on my life and everything... Stills.

Dawson shouldn't know his name. He shouldn't know anything about my past. How can he?

I think back on everything.

How Dawson arrived. Rented the camper. Wedged his way into my life. I fell for him. Trusted him. And he made sure it worked out perfectly. He's known Roberto all along. This was a trap.

I unlock the door and clutch the handle. I need to get away. I only manage to crack it open when Dawson reaches over to pull the door closed.

"What are you doing?" He locks it again and grabs my hands.

I wonder if my eyes reflect how frantic I feel inside. Dawson knows Roberto. Oh my God, does he work for him?

"Help!" I scream, looking around wildly.

There's no one here.

"Somebody, help!"

I let loose a bloodcurdling scream. I need to get out of this truck.

I try to hit him, kick him, bite him, anything that will free me, but he's too strong.

He pulls me to him, depositing me directly on his lap, and then restrains my hands behind my back.

"Stop." There is authority like I've never heard in his tone. "I'm trying to help."

"Liar! You work for him, don't you? Did he send you to get to me, to bring me back to him? I won't let you! I'd rather die, you piece of—"

He clamps a strong palm over my mouth while the other keeps control of my wrists. I bite him hard, and he hisses out a breath.

"Listen closely," he growls. I bite harder. "I don't work for Roberto. I'm not here to hurt you or bring you back to him—the opposite, actually. I want to protect you, Camille. That's all I've *ever* wanted. We both want Roberto to suffer for everything he's done."

I want to believe him, I really do, but I don't understand how he knows any of this.

"I'm not who I've been pretending to be," he explains. "My real name is Dawson Jacobs. Just like your real name is Angela Cruz. Wife of Roberto Cruz—illegal arms dealer."

He should not know my old name. I bite down harder into the meaty part of his palm, and I'm finally rewarded with the taste of blood. Dawson's eyes are two sharp points.

"Stop biting me. I'll will let go if you do, Camille," he barters.

I bite harder. He slams me into him as far as I can go, making my back arch and my wrists ache.

"I didn't lie about being special ops. I know how to break a wrist in a single move."

His words sink in. He could hurt me, but he hasn't. He could have already made me release his palm, but he's giving me a choice.

"Please, trust me. I don't want you here alone if Roberto shows up. *When* he shows up. He has a general idea of your location. He might not know your exact address yet, but he'll figure it out. You know he will. Someone's handed him a lead that's paid off."

I've worked hard for everything, running away and building a life, all for Roberto to have tracked me down. I guess I always knew this day would come.

"Let go, Camille," Dawson warns. "I can't have an injured hand, and you're getting close to tearing too deep. I need to be ready to help you."

"No," I snap, though it comes out muffled.

"Please," he whispers.

"No."

He chuckles. "Stubborn. I guess that's part of what draws me to you."

He looks at me through wistful eyes and delivers an explosive truth.

"I am not employed by Roberto."

He's already said that, yet he still knows my husband.

"I'm a federal agent."

I do let go of him then, and he releases my wrists for me to wipe his blood from my mouth. Dawson presses his hand hard into his jeans to stop the bleeding.

"You're...FBI?" I ask incredulously.

"Yes. Do you want to know the story? Will that help you trust me?"

"Maybe."

"Two years ago, I was a Delta Force soldier. Someone in high places got wind of my ability to complete every mission without fail. They saw something they liked and recruited me. I couldn't turn down the chance to be stateside. Working for the FBI is a dream job, and I was ready for a break."

My head spins with this information.

"They came at the right time. I accepted their offer. My first case was pretty simple, open-and-close in four months. The next took two months. I guess third time's the charm because, on that assignment, I was in charge. It was a big one. I needed to infiltrate the world of an illegal arms dealer by the name of Roberto Cruz. My mission was to take him down, but he was slippery."

Dawson glances quickly at his hand, noting the bleeding has finally slowed.

"You got me good," he comments.

"You deserved it," I snap. "You could have just led with being FBI. I might have been less scared."

"That's fair."

He retrieves a napkin from the glove box and places it over

the light bleeding like a bandage.

"The more I watched Roberto, the more I watched you." His words sink in. "I conducted daily surveillance. I had the photos of him cheating delivered. I wasn't authorized to do that, but how could I not tell you? I'd hoped you'd find a way out of a bad situation. And then, one day, you disappeared. Imagine my shock when I saw you swimming in the ocean the evening before, and then you were gone by sunrise. I made it my personal mission to find you and the evidence."

He must see the surprise on my face.

"You made a mistake. A car you bought while trying to flee Roberto was signed under the name Camille. He found you and put you in the hospital. But still, it felt significant. That name. *Camille.* I searched the entire United States database for vehicles and homes bought under Camille. Thousands upon thousands came up. It's taken me a year and several failed attempts, but I pieced it together, and then switched paperwork to cover for you. I worried that if I could make the name connection, Roberto could, too. He finally has. I don't understand how, but he has."

How could I have been so stupid? I don't remember the name I signed on the papers. I've always loved *Camille* after having read it in a book. I wouldn't have used it again had I remembered I did before. I wouldn't have made it my request that my fake identity have that specific name.

"We got close to busting Roberto, but we could never catch him. Each takedown, he'd slip through my fingers, clean out evidence, and move drop-off and pick-up locations, always one step ahead of us. There had to be a mole in the FBI. How else would he have known we were coming? How else did he eventually learn about the name Camille? But I never told the FBI where the name led me. I came here secretly. I thought I could crack the case. I never thought I'd fall for you."

I try not to let his words affect me.

"We finally caught a break when we witnessed Roberto on a call, admitting proof of a FBI partnership. If the FBI discovered that one of their own betrayed them, it'd be the end of them both. For his own protection, he kept the evidence—a video chip. That way the mole wouldn't double-cross him without exposing themselves, too. This is why I came. I need proof of Roberto's illegal activities and of the agent sabotaging the case. But somewhere along the line, I got caught up in you. Intentions blurred."

His hand finally stops bleeding. I think he wants me to say something, but I can't find the words.

"I found your ring with a hidden compartment under the stone. Want to know what I think?"

I already know he's figured it out.

"I believe you discovered the evidence and took it before you left. It's a nice touch, really, a bargaining tool if Roberto ever found you. Am I right?"

He must see confirmation in my eyes, because his next words are...

"Where's the chip, Camille?"

FORTY-FOUR

Dawson

She has the evidence. I know she does.

"Scoot over," Camille orders.

"Tell me where the chip is."

"I will." She worries her lower lip, a nervous tic. "But I have to drive you there to retrieve it."

I switch places with her, wincing as my hand presses against the door.

"Where are we headed?"

"Luke's place."

I still. "That's your connection to him? He knows about

Roberto?"

"Yes. He helped me escape. He's the one who got the fake identity for me with the name Camille. He's the reason I got away."

Well, damn.

The engine grumbles to life, and Camille drives over the speed limit. The whole ride I think of our conversation between sheets, when we spent the night together with very little sleep.

We fall onto pillows, our limbs entangled.

"Tell me about your family," Camille requests. "The real one."

She knows the fire is a lie, and so I give into her entreaty.

"My mother was the only one who was truly interested in my life."

I can tell the words aren't what she's expecting, but they immediately pique her curiosity.

I grin nostalgically, staring off into a memory.

"She would sing at the top of her lungs just to make me laugh." *My smile grows. "She had the worst voice."*

Camille traces circles on my bicep.

"When I was a kid, we took biweekly grocery trips that only her and I went on since my father was always off in nature. He preferred to hike trails, not work. My mom took on the brunt of the bills. I asked her once why she stayed with him. She claimed love. I thought we did better, just her and me."

My jaw tightens for a moment, remembering how uninvolved my father chose to be.

"Each time before we visited the grocery store, my mom would

ask, 'What'll it be this time?' and I'd answer her on a whim. I'd pick a theme, and we'd go dressed that way. Pirates. Spies. Ninjas. Detectives. Superheroes. Zombies." I chuckle, the sound vibrating my insides. "You should've seen the looks we got. She made life fun. I have no idea how she ended up with my father. I personally think she saw one of the saddest souls in existence and thought she'd make him brighter. She did. God, she did."

Camille hangs onto my every word.

"What was your home like?" she asks.

I register the feeling of her snuggling closer.

"Absolutely perfect," I reply. "Old, always creaking like ancient bones during rough storms. The exterior was the lightest shade of blue. Only two bedrooms, but we didn't need more. I was an only child, so I got my own space."

I take a moment to look at her—really look. My admission lingers heavily, so different from my original house fire tale.

"The yard outside had the wildest creatures. Gators, birds, even a giant python once. My mother would let her hair loose, no makeup, no shoes, and run around the grass with me. Even as I got older, she encouraged me to be free, to chase my dreams, to climb trees and follow trails and love fiercely."

I pause, wondering if I should tell her the next part.

"You were right about the fire."

I wait for her to react. She remains calm, so I continue.

"She passed away from a heart attack. Died in her sleep. I felt her absence immediately. I didn't have a reason to stay. So, I turned eighteen a couple months later and enlisted. My dad never said goodbye."

My stomach clenches at the memory. I shouldn't be giving her real pieces of myself.

"Those are my favorite memories, Camille. Ones involving her. But I lied about the fire because it's hard to talk about her without feeling both happy and sad. And because I never intended to be vulnerable or let anyone close to me here."

She nods as though she understands.

"My favorite memories are of the ocean," she murmurs.

I wonder how many bad are interspersed.

"I can still feel the sting of salt on my skin, the water enveloping me, the pressure on my lungs. When I close my eyes, I see ripples of sunlight above my head as I sink deeper into the ocean. Even before I lived at the beach, I visited the water as much as I could. I'd run along the bottom seabed—the surface five, sometimes ten, feet above my head. I pushed my lungs to hold while I pretended to be a fish. Somehow, beneath the depths, I felt more at home than on land. I swam for miles with sharks, dolphins, sea turtles, and manatees. It's quiet under the water. No yelling. No talking. Not even my thoughts had much of a voice. It all dissipated, nothing but calm. I needed that, being a foster kid. My life was always in shambles."

I eye her wearily. She's trusting me with the most intimate parts of her life. I want to kiss her right now, but I also don't want her to stop talking.

"Sometimes, I simply entered the ocean, laid on my back, and floated wherever the current took me. I exercised by swimming *daily. I taught lessons. That's how I saved enough money to live on my own. I trained triathlon athletes in the swimming portion."*

The way she speaks fondly of it makes me want to follow her into the depths.

"Why do you love the ocean so much?" I need to know. "Under the water, I mean."

There's a difference between liking an ocean view and wanting to be in the sea. Camille is the later.

Her lips relax into a soft, raw grin, holding a secret she's about to share with me.

"Because it's a place with absolutely no air, yet it has so much room to breathe."

Just like that, I understand.

"You were happy there," I murmur. "Why relocate to a place far from the shore?"

"I had to," she says.

Her touch moves from my bicep to my stomach. I clench in anticipation. Then she kisses me long and deep.

And we talk no more.

"You deserve better, Camille," I murmur softly, breaking the strained silence in the truck cab. "Better than me. I hope you know that I would have told you about my job sooner if I could have."

Her eyes flick to mine.

"I'm sorry. I knew not to let this get romantic, but I just—" I yank off my ball cap and run a hand roughly through my hair before replacing it. "I started falling for you. But even before that, before things turned romantic, I knew you were incredibly beautiful and talented. I used to watch you in the ocean. I saw the way you sliced through the surface like the sea belonged to you. You commanded it. I respected that, and you."

I spot the wash of tears she refuses to let fall.

"I have always *seen* you, Camille. The real you. The person you've become, too."

FORTY-FIVE

Before

The moment he walks into the beach house, he looks for her, the woman he's come to expect, ready to greet him. His princess. His wife. But the house stands still.

Though the call from his guard warned of her escape, he still can't believe it.

How many times is she going to try to leave him?

He won't allow it.

His footsteps are flawless, quieter than death, as he makes it to his bedroom, and quickly pushes open the door. There is nothing to see. He runs a hand over the comforter. As he suspects, it's cold to the touch. No one has been here for at least a few hours. In the dead of night, with morning not quite approaching, she should be lying curled up on her side as she normally does.

She has finally done the impossible.

She has escaped.

His answering roar shakes the walls. He will find her. He will track her down to the ends of the earth and he will make her pay every day for the rest of her life. He does not take kindly to losing what is his.

That's not the worst part, though.

Her wedding rings sit neatly on the bathroom counter. She left them to mock him. Her box with information on her birth parents is gone from her bedside table.

What else did she take with her?

He goes to his study and rifles through paperwork. There are important documents here. She hasn't touched them. He goes to the safe. She shouldn't know the combination, but just in case, he checks the contents. It doesn't look as though she's opened it. She's taken none of the money. The gun is still there. Everything seems to be in place. He's about to close the door when he realizes his mistake.

The most important item?

Gone.

"No," he says to himself, shocked.

"Mr. Cruz?" A bodyguard turns the corner. "Everything okay here?"

He's not the same worker from a couple of hours ago, the gentleman who allowed Angela to escape, even if unknowingly. That man pled for his life. Claimed Roberto's wife was lost to the sea. His execution was quick and quiet.

His wife knew those currents. She never would have been swept away by them. Plus, her box is gone, her rings left behind. Deliberate. Premeditated.

She's succeeded.

Not for long, though.

He reaches into the safe, searching for the microchip once more, but it's nowhere to be found.

"Goddammit!" he thunders.

She stole it. The only evidence that can take him down for good.

FORTY-SIX

Camille

Dawson knows about the evidence I have against Roberto. He's discovered the only bargaining chip I possess if my ex comes for me. The information I've transferred onto a USB could save my life. That's the hope I've always held on to. That it might buy me a few seconds, maybe even minutes, to get away. I'm not sure Roberto would take the bait, but it's all I've got. I never planned to hand it over to the FBI—or any authority, for that matter. Who's to say the friends Roberto has on the inside won't destroy it? I trust none of them.

Now, Dawson is here, and I don't know what to think.

As I drive, silence stretches like a rubber band ready to snap. Luke only lives twenty minutes away, but it feels like longer. The tires bump along the uneven road, finally coming to a stop in front of a brick ranch house. I barely exit the vehicle before Luke appears outside, his eyes sliding to Dawson with a question in his gaze.

"We have trouble," I declare.

He knows I wouldn't have brought Dawson if he meant us harm, so Luke welcomes us inside, his home opening up into an expansive living room with white couches and navy-blue throw pillows. I sink down, my head dropping into my hands. I rub my temples, readying myself.

"Luke." When I look up, he stands over me, offering a can of soda. I take it but don't drink. "Sit, please."

He does without question, tossing the other can to Dawson and sliding down next to me.

"I'm sorry I brought him here," I begin. "I wouldn't have if there was any other option. I know we promised to keep people far away from us, our link."

"It's okay. Tell me everything." His gentle words are a contrast to his rigid form.

"Dawson is FBI."

Luke is, if possible, even more alert.

"He knows about my past and that you helped me escape Roberto." His name turns my stomach inside out. "Nothing else. Just that."

My look makes it clear that I didn't mention a word of Luke's time as an assassin. He relaxes some, still watchful.

"Is there more I should know?" Dawson's head cocks to the side, calculating.

"No," I reply.

I will never tell him Luke's secrets.

Luke turns to Dawson. "Explain," he orders.

"In a second," Dawson agrees. "First, I need the microchip."

"Not until I have a minute alone with Camille."

I nod and follow Luke to the next room. As soon as we're out of earshot, his eyes soften.

"What's happened?" he asks.

I want to spill it all, detail by detail, but we don't have time. "Roberto's found me. If we give the chip to Dawson, he can help. I trust him, Luke. He can put Roberto behind bars. We can finally be free."

He sighs and shakes his head, as though not believing my declaration. "I knew his record was too clean."

"Please. This is our only chance." To hand over the USB copied from the chip I hid in the ring. The evidence Luke now has.

I didn't want it easily found at my residence if Roberto ever came. I needed leverage.

"Trust me?" I ask, squeezing his hand.

He concedes, "Of course I do."

We return to find Dawson in the same spot.

"I'll show you the evidence, and then I want you to explain everything," Luke demands, addressing Dawson. "But I'm warning you, if you're planning to double-cross us, don't. I have backups on hard drives in undisclosed locations. The evidence is not the only in existence. If you destroy it, we have more."

Dawson tugs at the brim of his ball cap. "Understood."

"Follow me." Luke nods to the room he uses as an office.

He boots up a wide screen computer and clicks on an attachment. I've seen the video before, but it still causes my lungs to squeeze at the sight of Roberto on the clear monitor. His skin richly brown. His hair cut neatly and precisely.

"There are several photos and one video of a deal going down. Of an FBI informant meeting Roberto," Luke explains. "At first, you can't see the second man, but then he faces the hidden camera. He never knew Roberto was filming. It was smart of Roberto to get evidence. That way he would always have something to hold over the FBI's head. He'd always have an in."

Luke clicks through each photograph. The last is especially focused. But it's the video that seems to get to Dawson.

He controls his features, as usual, but still, I notice the clenching of his jaw, the slight widening of his eyes.

The video lasts four minutes, but by the end, it takes everything I have to tamper down the sick feeling of seeing Roberto again.

"No way. No possible way," Dawson mutters. "Play it again."

Luke does, but nothing changes about the dialogue or recording.

"This whole time, I've had it wrong," Dawson whispers.

"Do you know the FBI spy?" I inquire.

His answer is what I expected. I knew from the moment the informant turned and Dawson caught sight of his face.

He swallows thickly. "Yeah, I know him. He's my boss. Agent Hernandez."

I anticipate anger from him, but what I get instead is hurt.

"It fucking kills me." He rasps a hand down his face. "I trusted him. But I withheld my, *your*, location on instinct, which has paid off. No wonder he was so anxious to find it."

"I'm sorry you were let down." I squeeze his hand. "Believe me, I know a thing or two about trusting the wrong people."

I hate the weak tremble in my voice.

Dawson flinches. Maybe he thinks I mean him, and maybe I do just a little, though I'm beginning to understand why he felt the need to withhold information from me. I withdraw my hand.

"I'll give you a minute," Luke says, exiting the room.

Once he's gone, Dawson's head bows.

"Roberto made life unbearable," I disclose, which he likely knows. "He beat me. He brought on nightmares and flashbacks. He drove me into seclusion. I no longer get to swim in the ocean or see the shore or live my life without worry of him finding me."

"I'm sorry, Camille," Dawson whispers.

I don't like that he only told me half of his story. His involvement in the army was real, but his employment with the FBI was not made known to me. Even though I probably would have done the same thing he did, I still hate that it's come to this. The first time I find myself falling for a good guy, he is somehow tied to Roberto. I can't seem to rid my life of him.

Luke joins us again, and Dawson straightens.

"We have to leave," I tell him.

He nods to a small duffle in his grip. "Figured. I keep a bag packed just in case."

"I want to stop by my place for a few personal items and the ring," I say. "It's the only remaining piece of my parents. I can't bear to part with it."

Luke reaches in his pocket, retrieves the small black USB, and holds it out to Dawson.

"Camille may trust you, but I'm not completely convinced." There's an edge of warning in his tone. "Do not make me regret this."

Luke is fiercely devoted to me and to our friendship, our kinship. I hug him, conveying how much he means to me. "I love you," I mumble into his shirt. "Thank you."

From the corner of my eye, I see Dawson take the USB Luke offers.

Luke sighs into my hair. "Love you, too."

"Hurry," Dawson warns. "Your place first, and then we skip town. Got it?"

"Yes," I agree. "Loud and clear."

"If you don't mind, I need a favor," Dawson requests. "My phone is unplottable, but yours isn't. I have to call to the Bureau, someone other than Agent Hernandez. They need to know what's happening. They'll trace the call, and that's the point. Backup for us. So, if it's not too much to ask..."

He holds out a hand and I drop my cell into it.

"Thank you," he murmurs.

Eerie sweeps of gray-blue span over snow-splotched ground. The air is so cold it feels devoid of oxygen. My hands are gloved, trying not to catch hypothermia. It's in the single digits. Winter rushes ahead like an icy river, and nearly everything is frozen solid. The smoky cloud bottoms are heavy, bruised. This year, the season has a distinct color—ash. The sky, mountain foothills, and even the driveway as we pull up to my cabin are a tinged in the same hue.

"Make it quick, okay?" Dawson instructs. "The FBI has deployed a team. They'll be here as soon as possible."

He takes his own advice and exits the truck, heading to the camper door. He'll pack what he brought, which is barely anything at all. Same goes for me. I'll have to leave my books and more behind, but there's always the chance I'll return.

"I'll wait as a lookout," Luke offers.

Smart idea.

"I won't be long." I hurry to my door.

The key is icy against my thin gloves as I unlock the deadbolt. There's no fire going, so the inside nearly matches the outside. Wizard is nowhere to be seen, but I know I left him in the cabin. He's taken a liking to wedging himself under the spare bedroom quilt, curling up, burrowed deep enough to ward off the cold.

I'll have to drop him by Mrs. JoAnne's as we leave. Tell her we're taking a few days off to hike or fish or anything that allows her to look after Wizard, and me to escape.

I check the spare room. Wizard's exactly where I suspect.

"I have to go away for a little while," I tell him, petting his furry body. "I'll come back for you soon."

He purrs and stretches. I empty his litter and place the box by the door along with his food. He fits perfectly into a carrier. Then I go to my room for a small bag of clothes.

I can't help the feeling of déjà vu. It hasn't been that long since I escaped Roberto, and here I am again, running. I wanted more time. I needed a larger sense of security. But there's nothing to be done. He's close. I can't let him find us. He'll know Luke right away, and we'll both meet an unlucky fate. Hopefully the FBI will intercept him, and I'll never have to worry again.

My fingers reach for the duffel under the bed, the firesafe box, too. I shove it inside and open my closet, tug clothes off the hangers and haphazardly throw them into the bag. I need toiletries. I pull open the shower curtain to retrieve shampoo.

And nearly jump out of my skin.

"Hello, Princess."

A scream rips from my throat. Only, it never leaves my mouth because Roberto is too fast. He's always been too quick. His hand slaps over my mouth, cutting off all sound but my muffled attempts.

It's his eyes I notice first, murderous in their wrath. I know that look. It promises unimaginable pain. The simple brown of them has transformed into a guarantee of agony to come.

I claw at him, attempting to free myself from his iron grip. It's no use. He's too strong. He steps out of the dry tub, placing my back to his front. My foot connects with his leg, but he only grunts, his hold strengthening. He presses my lips against my teeth with a force sure to bruise.

"It's nice to see you again." His breath is hot on my ear.

I should have been more careful. I should have asked Luke to join me. Oh, God. Roberto has found me.

"It's no use fighting," he growls. "Haven't you already learned this lesson?"

How did he get in? He always travels with more guards, but we saw no one outside the property. No vehicles, either. No tracks in the snow. He must have covered them. Suddenly, I worry there are more men hidden in the trees like shadows. Would Luke see them coming? Is Dawson held up in the camper with Roberto's guys?

"Why is there a man living so close to you?" he questions, tightening his hold on me, one arm around my waist, the other clamped over my lips.

As always, his jealousy is forefront. He knows I can't answer him properly. He won't let me speak, and if he did remove his hand, I'd scream. I struggle to wedge even an inch of space between us. I pull in a deep breath through my nose and attempt to shout, then lift my foot and stomp down as hard as I can, but Roberto simply steps out of the way.

If I could slip from his grip and get to the front door, I might stand a chance. This cabin that used to feel so much like home now feels like a death trap.

"We should have this conversation face-to-face, don't you think?"

Of course, he'd want to. He gets off on watching my pain.

He turns me around with difficulty. I try to bite his hand but can't get a good hold. He's as slippery as a snake. He removes something from his pocket, a scrap of fabric I realize he means to bind my mouth with.

I shake my head back and forth, as much as his grip will allow, begging him not to.

He smiles.

It's the most horrifying thing I've ever seen.

"It's taken me a long time—an entire year of false leads and dead ends—but finally, I've found you," he says. "Now, where's the chip you stole from me?"

I attempt to shake my head again. I won't hand it over. Where are Luke and Dawson? It's been too long. They should have already come for me.

"Hold still," he demands.

As if I'd ever do such a thing.

He releases my waist to tie my mouth, and I manage to take one step away from him, his hand still clasped over my lips, before he replaces his palm with the fabric and ties it so tight that my eyes water with pain. I can't shout around it, but I still try.

The cloth muffles sound better than his skin does.

I want to tell him that I loathe him, despise him. I will all my thoughts into my look, hoping he sees how much I hate him.

We don't leave the bathroom. I don't know what he's waiting for.

I suppose he knows he has leverage. Me, as a hostage. It's unlikely Luke or Dawson would attack with my body as his shield.

"Do you understand what it was like," he snarls, his gaze piercing mine, "to know you'd left me? And with evidence, at that?"

That was his greatest fear, to come home and find me gone. To know I, for once, had power over him. He thought once I knew his secrets, that he was an illegal arms dealer and a cheater, I'd abandon him.

He was right.

He doesn't like losing.

"I warned you." There's a slight curl to his lip, an angry twitch. "I told you not to leave. I want that chip. You will lead me to it."

I relax my body just a sliver, giving him the impression that the fight has left me. A false sense of security. It's the same thing he offered when he promised me a good life together.

One, two, ten heartbeats pass, and then I kick out with all my strength into the slim space between his legs. His knees hit the floor.

I run.

I almost make it to the door when he pulls my shirt from behind with a strength that nearly strangles me. I fall back, gasping for breath, trying to crawl past him.

Roberto blocks the door.

I take off for the kitchen. If I could just reach a knife. If I could...

"You are mine," he hisses, tackling me to the floor. His hand is in my hair, ripping strands from the scalp.

I grab for something, anything.

There's a sudden pop on the side of my face, his fist making contact. All I can hear is ringing, pressure making my ear numb. I know this feeling. He's burst my eardrum again.

"You asshole!" I scream.

Nothing comes out but a garbled, muted curse. I yank at the binding to free my lips and scream.

Roberto attempts to drag me back farther from the door, my only escape. I grab for the dining table, trying to get it between the two of us, creating an obstacle. I manage to wrap my hands around it just in time for him to grab me. The table topples, its contents scattering like a deck of cards—bills, a letter opener, pen, stamps.

The candle shatters.

Someone must have heard. Luke. Dawson. Yet they don't respond to my screams or the noise.

Which can only mean one thing—Roberto's men have gotten to them.

"No!" I yell, as Roberto tugs me closer.

I lash out, scraping nails down the side of his face and drawing beads of blood like paint drops on a canvas.

Roberto smiles wickedly. "You will pay for that."

His elbow connects with my stomach and knocks the wind

out of me. His fist punches the flesh of my cheek. My mouth tastes like the metal iron of blood. My vision blurs.

This is usually when Roberto stops. A few hits. Enough to subdue. Only this time, I won't surrender quietly. His fist comes down again, hitting my shoulder. I hear something pop, and he raises it once more.

I know now that what I've dreaded has come.

He's not stopping.

He means to kill me.

"If you won't hand over the chip, I'll make sure you aren't here to use it," he growls, his fist slamming into my stomach. I heave. "If I can't have you, no one will."

It's what I've always known. The options have forever been the same.

Escape Roberto.

Or die.

With one hand, I push back at him, trying to create enough distance, but a searing pain rushes up my arm. Something is wrong with my shoulder. With my other hand, I reach around on the floor, grabbing for something, anything that will free me.

"Goodbye, princess," he says, and I know he means the deadly words.

His hand covers my mouth and nose. I don't have time to gather a deep breath. I can't breathe. He did this to me once before.

I decided to take a warm bath after an ocean swim. He decided to teach me a lesson about being late to dinner. At first, I mistook Roberto's look for one of attraction, as his stare raked my soap sudded body. When he sat on the ledge of the porcelain tub and stroked my hair back, I hardly expected what came next. He fisted the strands and shoved my head underwater. I kicked and pushed and fought. Roberto never let go. He waited until I lost the fight. Until I nearly ran out of air and drowned. Until my eyes opened under the water, begging him to let me live.

Only then, did he relent.

I surfaced coughing and gagging and spitting up water.

"Remember that your life is mine," he warned.

And then he dried his hands on a plush towel and walked out of the bathroom as though nothing had happened, knowing full well everything had happened.

Roberto still believes my life belongs to him. It doesn't. My life is mine alone.

My fingers close around what I'm looking for. I never had another option. I thought I could go to the police, but I was betrayed. Thought I could fight him off myself, but I was overpowered. Thought I could run, but even now he's found me.

The moment hangs in front of me like a still photo. Roberto above me, choking the very life from my lungs. Me, struggling on my back.

My arm streaks forward like a camera flash, blindingly fast.

I sink the metal letter opener into his neck.

Roberto pauses, shocked, mouth permanently open on a gasp.

It slips into his artery like a warm knife through butter. I yank it back out just as quickly. And finally...I let go.

His hands slacken around my face, allowing me to gulp

down air. Blood spurts from his neck, soaking into the collar of his shirt and splattering the lower cabinets. I look at my palm, the skin torn open.

Suddenly, the picture bursts. Shatters into a million pieces and everything comes rushing back full speed. Roberto topples over, face down, the letter opener now laying in a puddle of red.

The door flies open and Dawson rushes in, clutching his side as he falls into the counter in an effort to stay upright.

"Camille." His eyes are unfocused. "You're alive."

There's immense relief in his voice. I try to get to my feet, slipping in the wash of blood flooding the floor.

"Luke is hurt," Dawson pants. "There were men outside. We got them. So sorry I couldn't make it in time."

He sees Roberto on the floor, and his eyes clear just a little. "Is he?"

I don't have to look to know. I already saw.

"Yes," I confirm.

"I've called everything in," he tells me, using the counter for support.

"Dawson." I make it to his side and pull away the hand he presses against a spot just above his left hip. What I find is a wound so bloody I can't tell what made it.

"Isn't the first time I've been stabbed," he grumbles.

Knife, then. I apply pressure to his side with both hands to stop the bleeding despite his yells of protest. I can tell that it's worse than he's letting on.

"How long until backup arrives?" I ask.

His feet give out. I shoulder his weight the best I can, my own body protesting in pain, my own flesh hurting from Roberto's blows.

"Soon. Don't worry," he whispers. "I don't go down that easily, love."

But he's wrong. Because he does go down.

His eyes slide shut and his body crumples to the ground, taking me with it, the weight of his muscles like boulders.

"Dawson," I call.

No response.

"Dawson!" I shout louder.

Still, nothing.

His eyes remain shut.

And just like in the depths of the ocean, we both sink under.

FORTY-SEVEN

Dawson

After gunning for Roberto for so long, it's surreal to know he's dead.

The electronic file I sent ensured Hernandez would find a home behind bars. I hardly see how he will come off as anything but the rat he is. He'll get his day in court, life in prison, his career revoked. Everything he worked hard for, gone. And for what? Was it worth it to betray those who trusted him?

I'll never know.

With Roberto dead, some of his top guys are now in the

hands of the FBI. Many are talking. That's what the threat of forever locked away will do to a man, loyalties waver in the face of destruction.

"Try not to pull your stitches," my new boss says, "but have a seat if you can."

It's been two weeks since I took a knife to the side. Twelve days of hospital stay and a nicked spleen, followed by a couple days of waiting for this meeting.

I'm dying to see Camille, but first... "What's the verdict?"

That's the real question. Do I still have a job? What are the consequences for abandoning ship and going so dark that I couldn't be found until I wanted to? I did take down their mole and meet my target goal, stopping Roberto. That ought to count for something. Agent Foster holds my stare, his own calculating. His office is grand, and his gaze is narrow.

"What made you do it?" he asks.

I roll his question around in my mind as I sit across from his desk, wincing at the pull in my side.

"Tell me something," I counter. "If you had the chance to crack the most important case of your life, maybe even at the expense of your own aspirations because you understand that it'd save lives, would you?"

He closes a file on his desk. "Probably."

"There's your answer." I shrug.

His eyes narrow, but I know he understands.

"You broke protocol."

"I helped others."

"You went dark."

"Sometimes we have to."

"You should have alerted someone."

"Who? My old boss Hernandez? How well would that have worked out?"

Foster is backed into a corner, and he knows it.

"Fine. But you still broke protocol. If I let you get away with it, no one will take anything seriously."

I wish he'd say it already, whatever punishment he means to deliver.

"Out with it," I insist. "What's the damage?"

I hold my breath and hope he doesn't fire me on the spot, looking for any sign that what he means to say won't spell the end of my career.

"Eight weeks suspension."

He delivers the blow, but it feels lighter than expected.

I usually wouldn't show emotion, but right here, in the middle of Agent Foster's office, I smile like the sun has risen after two years of absence. Because it has. That's how long it took me to crack the case.

I haven't lost my job. Eight weeks? That's doable. I need a vacation anyway.

"See you in two months." I stand.

"Try not to look so happy about it," he grumbles.

"You're welcome," I offer.

I did the FBI a solid, even if I will have to face suspension for it. It helped save Camille's life. I could never regret that.

"For what?" he inquires.

"You already know what." I tip my ball cap at him.

He grins the slightest bit. Yeah, things will be fine around here. I might even grow to like my new boss.

"Hey," he calls, right before I open the door. "I heard you enjoyed North Carolina. That true?"

"Yes," I confirm. "Why?"

He taps the folder on his desk. "Have a case not too far from where you were. A neighboring city. Interested?"

"Yes." My answer is immediate.

"You can't go dark again."

"Got it," I agree.

"You'll report to me."

"Not a problem."

"Then, it's yours. I'll brief you later."

I turn toward the door.

"Yes, is the real response," he says.

I pause. "The real response?"

"To your earlier question. Yes, I would have done the same. But I have bosses as well. Procedure must be followed. Consequences if broken. You understand."

My boss approves, even if he can't officially say so.

"I do."

"Fine. Go. You're dismissed."

I don't hesitate. I'll be gone from Miami as soon as the FBI approves my request for an out-of-town leave. I need to see Camille.

Excitement surges in my veins. Even still, I can't shake the persistent, nettling feeling that I've lost something for good. Regardless, if that's the case, I have to say goodbye.

FORTY-EIGHT

Camille

The last time I saw Dawson, four weeks ago, he was bleeding, needing medical attention, and had a knife wound under the meat of his side. I haven't heard a word since. Today, he stands on my porch, unannounced, like a gift the frigid winter wind dropped off as it weaved through the magnolia trees.

"What are you doing here?" I ask.

The door is open just enough to not let in the frosty cold. A fire rages in the hearth, warming the backs of my knees and calves. Dressed in a woolly sweater dress, coffee in hand, I had no way of knowing Dawson would arrive at nine in the morning on my day off.

It's not an unpleasant surprise. But I'd be lying if I said I hadn't wished for a call, a message, some sort of communication from him. I worried about his injuries. Had he healed? Was he thinking about me like I was him? No one would tell me anything, not even the contact at the FBI who'd given me his number to call regarding the case. They only said Dawson would be in touch when he could, if he wanted.

I was beginning to think he didn't want to.

"Came to see you."

His deep timbre sends a shiver down my spine. His thick arms are accentuated by layers of thermal shirts, and his jeans sit just right before ending at the boots on his feet. He's wearing a ball cap, of course. He doesn't look like he was stabbed only a month ago.

I debate whether I should invite him in, but as soon as I look up and our eyes connect, the breath whooshes out of me. I step back, the wind opening the door for him. He moves inside and locks us in. Dawson stays a foot away and yet...everything calms.

It's a moment where we're hanging off a precipice of time. A miniscule blink amid seconds, frozen. The space between where the hand of a clock ticks from one mark to the next. We are locked in a stare so intense I don't know if the emotion cartwheeling through his eyes is permanent or fleeting.

He's happy to see me.

"The kitchen's different," he remarks, breaking the spell.

I glance at the space he mentions. I couldn't have possibly left it the way he saw it last, drenched in blood. I couldn't even leave it with the same décor as before, where I kept recalling Roberto's lifeless body on floor. A permanent, stained reminder. Now, the kitchen floors have been replaced with new wood, the counters are white marbled concrete, the sink is a large country thing, and the appliances are stainless steel.

Mr. Hill claims he doesn't know who paid the contractors that showed up at my home a few weeks ago, demolition ready, transforming the old, mousy area into something gorgeous, but I think he had everything to do with it.

Mr. Hill also claimed not to care one iota about my past once I told him the real story—that I ran from an abusive husband. Said outright that no person should ever look backward while flying forward. That's all the opinion he had on the subject. Mrs. JoAnne was the same. As though their acceptances rewound time, much has gone back to the normal, syrupy slow southern life, with the exception of the new kitchen design.

I don't like that it took Luke and I a few weeks to heal. Him, from the beating Roberto's men delivered, and me from Roberto himself. We only ever wanted to escape our past lives, and here it was again, trying to take us down.

Now, though, it's almost like my past, Luke's past, never existed. It feels good to breathe easy.

"I needed something new," I reply, motioning to the counter. "Want coffee?"

Dawson's hands tuck into his pockets. "Maybe later."

The moment his eyes lock on mine again, I find questions brimming on the tip of my tongue. I want to know where he's been for the last month. Is he back for good? Does he want to be?

"How much time do we have?" I set down my empty mug.

"I arrived last night and rented a cabin five miles away. Would have been here as soon as they released me from the hospital, but I needed authorization to leave the state. I grabbed the first flight. I'm on vacation for a bit."

"Your job gave you vacation for going dark?" I expected a little more of a punishment from a federal institution.

"Well, not exactly."

He makes my entire day by grinning.

"Which means?" I wait for him to clarify.

"I was suspended for eight weeks. I'm glad you're healed. I thought you'd end up going with the farm sink."

The farm sink? My eyes narrow.

"You weren't by chance aware of the kitchen remodel before you saw it, were you?"

When he doesn't deny it, I huff.

"Funny thing, a contractor showed up with several options. They let me pick and my kitchen was done shortly after. Already paid for. I thought it was Mr. Hill, but now I'm reconsidering. Did you have something to do with this?"

As always, his face is guarded, his strong jaw locked in stubbornness. "I might have."

"Dawson," I groan, exasperated. "You cannot buy me a new kitchen!"

"What if I can and you pretend you don't know? Then, you can be happy about it like you were before. No harm done."

The crazy man redid a third of my home in a kind gesture. I blow a curl out of my eyes and sigh.

"I thought..." I don't want to offend him with my next words, so I choose them carefully. "I was under the impression you didn't have many funds. You asked to work around here to pay off part of the rent."

He nods. "I didn't want my location traced. I couldn't access my bank account or credit cards here. Because if I did, they'd find me...and you. All I could do was withdraw a lump sum of money before I arrived and make it last."

"That's why you paid cash," I say, realizing.

"Yes. I needed to make the money stretch, since I didn't know how long it'd take to break the case. I have access to my account and cards again."

"This was too much," I admit.

"Well, it's already done." He shrugs.

"But—" I glance around the kitchen. "I would give it back if I could."

"You can't, though," he says. "Plus, you were going to accept it when you thought it was from the old man."

"No, I wasn't," I argue. "At least, not for free. Do you know how much work I planned to do around there for him, to pay as much of it back as I could? I was going to pick up all the odd jobs he once wanted you to do. But now, I don't know what to do. I don't know how to pay you back. Is there an address or account where I can send money?"

"No. I won't accept it."

"What am I supposed to do, then?"

"Simple," he replies. "Live the way you were before. Be happy. Nothing has to change."

But everything has already changed. Before, he was a guy I fell for, renting the camper. Now, though? He has a secretive career. He doesn't live in North Carolina. We're worlds apart.

"What did you come for, Dawson?"

He wets his lips and delivers a blow that knocks me off center.

"To say goodbye."

Goodbye?

I guess I already knew in a sense. I try not to let my reaction show. The emotion pulling me under reminds me of a snapping ocean, full of whitecaps and destruction, a surge of water threatening to take me down. But still, I will not cry. I will gather the pieces of myself and hold them together long enough to say goodbye to Dawson.

"So, do it already," I reply.

And then he does the absolutely, positively unthinkable. He pulls my body against his, lifts my chin, and speaks directly to my soul.

"I don't want to. I'm terrified that this whole situation might have cost me you."

He takes a breath, his face opening with emotion.

"I think I started falling for you when you opened up to me, smiled at me, cooked me dinner, took me to Asheville, and broke every defense I ever set up."

My shoulders lift on a surprised inhale. His words wash over me like a soothing storm.

"I hope you don't hate me," he whispers.

"I could never hate you."

Not ever.

"Undercover work is dicey, and this job means life might not always be safe with me. You deserve safety and peace. I'm not sure that I'm any good for you, but I still want you."

"Are you saying—" I struggle for the right words. I wonder what voicing them aloud will mean for us.

"I'm saying, Camille" —his gaze sears into mine— "that I'm crazy about you and have been for a while."

"You're not really here to say goodbye, are you?"

"Only if I have to? But, what if...What would happen..."

Go on.

"Can I stay instead? Can I be in your life in a permanent way? Because I don't know how to be without you, Camille."

His words are what I know truth to feel like, calming and real.

"You claim to be no good for me," I reply.

"And I mostly meant it," he confesses, his breath on my skin. "I wish I could always stay here with you, work at the general store, and live a simple life. But I can't. Not now, at least. Who knows about the future? Doesn't mean we don't belong together. I have a crazy career, but we can exist outside of that. We can be more than the job I perform, can't we?"

I feel it then, intertwining with each pounding heartbeat,

this link to him.

"You want us to be together?"

"If you can forgive me, yes."

He rests his forehead against mine, a gentle movement.

"Please, Camille, forgive me?"

He lied to me. But he also helped save my life. He warned me about Roberto coming. He called for backup. I know exactly what would have happened if I had been on this property alone without warning of Roberto's impending arrival, without Luke and Dawson fighting off Roberto's men. The outcome would have been much different.

"We're great together." His eyes plead with me to agree. "More than great. We're magic."

His words are beautiful. His tenderness, even more so. I have a feeling this softer side is reserved for me alone.

"I know. I remember," I confess. Because how could I forget? "But how would it work?"

"Just say 'yes,'" he replies. "There's a new case once I go back to work. It's located here in North Carolina. Could take a month. Could take a year."

"And then?"

I can feel his heart galloping beneath the palm I place on his chest.

"Then we'll see. Didn't you say you wanted to visit the ocean again? What if you came to see me in Miami from time to time? We'll figure out something more permanent later. Don't make me live this life without you."

His look isn't what it usually is—cloudy and unreadable. He lets me see that he wants me. Needs me.

"If we do this, no more secrets about us. The job, I understand," I request.

"There's an us?" He says it like it's both a statement and a question. Like he knows it to be true and wants to know if I feel the same.

"I think there could be," I admit.

"So, that's a 'yes'?" he says.

I'm still a bit fearful, but I don't want it to run my life anymore.

"Yes," I agree.

Our future hovers, not really tied down to anything, but I want to be with Dawson, there's no denying that.

"What if I told you that I dream of you? That this is it for me?" His words are slow and sure.

I feel a grin tug at the corner of my lips. "Then, I'd say... prove it."

He leans in, his lips a sliver away.

"My pleasure," he murmurs, right before his mouth lands on mine.

It's fireworks on a frigid day. My nerves explode with heat. When I finally give into him completely, it's the greatest reward. Like dropping something heavy when you've been carrying it for far too long.

Roberto is gone.

My past is already lived.

This, here and now, is my future, a life with Dawson. Maybe we'll stay or maybe we'll go. Maybe we'll sit lakeside or sail the ocean. The specifics are not important. What's important is us.

It's all I want. All I've ever wanted. The freedom to choose. To be. To love.

A world with no fear.

I pull away. Dawson watches me steadily. He surprises me by grinning. It's heart-stopping.

"We're going to have so much fun," he says.

It startles a laugh out of me. Yes, we are. Like many of the greatest stories, ours begins small. A ripple forms in the ocean and turns into a rogue wave a hundred feet high. An underwater volcano trembles and an island juts up out of the sea because of it. Who knows what we could become.

"Did I ever tell you that my house in Miami is a block from the beach?" he asks.

My interest piques. "No."

"If you get up early, when the sky is gray, you can catch the tip of the sun rising over the water. It's exhilarating. I used to love that moment more than anything."

"Used to?" I question.

"Used to." He nods. "Until you. Now, that's what I love the most."

I close my eyes. Picture it. The love he offers me. I imagine it's like the brilliant blue of an undisturbed sky. The sun stretching rays out over the sea's surface like bright fingers touching the water. Dawson and me, toes in the damp sand.

"Show me your beach one day?" I request.

He strokes my cheek gently. Every square inch of my body reacts in goosebumps.

"I'd love to."

Days, minutes, seconds. They're ours. All of them.

My eyes snap open. I think of the slow churn of the country and know I need that, too. Sweet tea and deep accents and open fields. Quiet and peace. Maybe we can have both.

"Thank you for giving me a chance," he tells me softly.

I know suddenly, without doubt, that I will give him all the chances. I will wake up in the morning and go to sleep at night needing the man who makes my heart beat with passion. We are a combination of winter mountains and summer beaches. I choose him.

"Dawson?" I murmur.

"Yeah?"

"If I agree to spend time with you in Miami, maybe even an entire summer, spaces in between, too, it has to consist of two things."

"I'm listening." His voice is deep, gravelly, like a country road.

"Endless days in the ocean," I barter, "and endless nights in bed with you."

"Oh, really?" A sly grin curves his lips.

Dawson edges nearer.

"Prove it." He winks.

I like a good challenge. But before I can kiss him, he requests something of me.

"Don't I get to state my demands?"

I arch a brow. "Sure."

"There's really only one."

"Which is?"

"Promise to love me back."

That won't be hard to fulfill. I already do.

"Deal."

We lean into each other. Our possibilities, infinite.

Remember, *a promise is a promise*.

ACKNOWLEDGMENTS

Thank you to everyone who made this book possible. My editor, Jenn Sommersby, who skillfully navigated the messy first draft. My editor, Jess Rousseau, whose critical eye and military expertise helped shape this novel. My editor, Ellie Folden, every book you touch is better for it. My literary agent, Stacey Donaghy, who has stuck by each version of this story, and by my side, throughout the years. My cover designer, Emily Wittig, who constantly impresses me with her talent. I knew the moment I saw this cover for the first time, that you'd created something magical. My beta readers—Amy Horn, Corina Quinn, and Amanda Kay—I'm so grateful for your insight and encouragement. Gabriel Horn, White Deer of Autumn, you were the first to truly believe in my writing. I'm where I am because you set my foot on this path. I miss you. Lexi Bissen, thank you for helping me go hybrid. I'm super grateful for my extended family, for cheering me on. And my dad, for always taking me to libraries to read in dusty corners when I was little. My two beautiful sons, you are everything to me. Noah, my calm and steady. Hudson, my wild storm. I love our family. You both make me proud every day. My husband, Rodolfo, whom I met when we were teenagers, who loves me through every day of our crazy life, is the reason I write (mostly) happy endings. In any existence, wherever we are, I will find you, and I will love you.

And for every reader who picked up this book, thank you.

ALSO BY AMBER HART

The Untamed Series:
Until You Find Me (#1)
Captured By You (#2)

The Before and After Series:
Before You (#1)
After Us (#2)
Maybe Me (#3)

Wicked Charm

ABOUT THE AUTHOR

Amber Hart is the author of several romance novels for teens and adults. She lives on the Florida coast with her husband and sons. For more, you can find her on social media, or visit her website at www.amberhartbooks.com